Jimmy Gownley's

AMELiA RULES!™

When the PAST IS A PRESENT

Atheneum Books for Young Readers
New York London Toronto Sydney

ATHENEUM BOOKS FOR YOUNG READERS
An imprint of Simon & Schuster Children's Publishing Division
1230 Avenue of the Americas, New York, New York 10020

Atheneum Books for Young Readers is a registered trademark of Simon & Schuster, In
For information about special discounts for bulk purchases, please contact Simon &
Schuster Special Sales at 1-866-506-1949 or business@simonandschuster.com.
The Simon & Schuster Speakers Bureau can bring authors to your live event. For more
information or to book an event, contact the Simon & Schuster Speakers Bureau at
1-866-248-3049 or visit our website at www.simonspeakers.com.
Book design by Sonia Chaghatzbanian
Manufactured in the United States of America
1209 WOR
First Atheneum Books for Young Readers paperback edition January 2010
2 4 6 8 10 9 7 5 3 1
CIP data for this book is available from the Library of Congress.
ISBN: 978-1-4169-8607-2
This title was originally published individually by Renaissance Press in 2008.

This book is for:

Kerensa Bartlett, Hailey Cook, Ethan Gourlay,
James Elmour, Frances Cooke, and everyone at
Small Pond Productions. And especially to
Kasey Perkins, who brought Amelia McBride
to life before my very eyes.

That's what magic is.

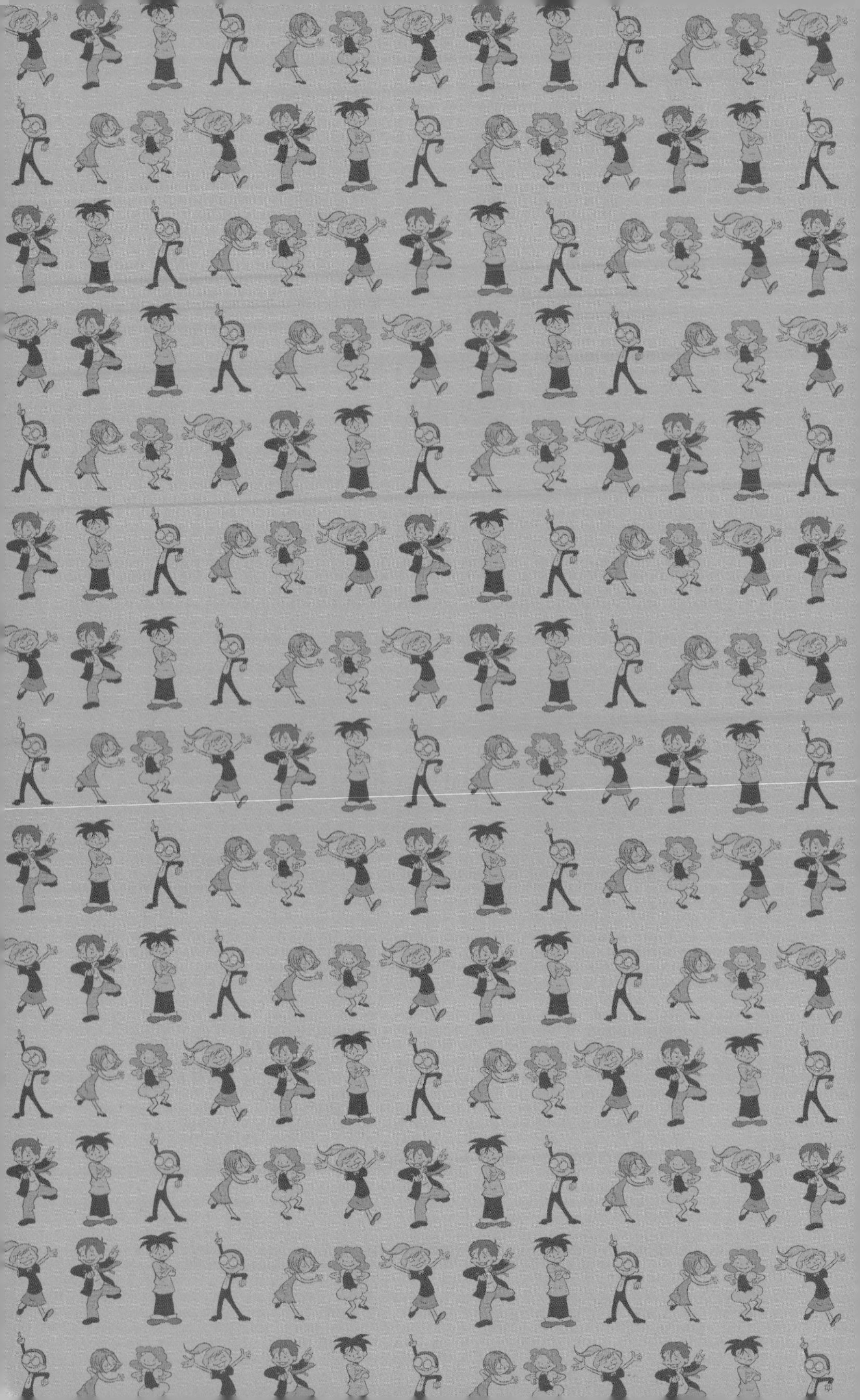

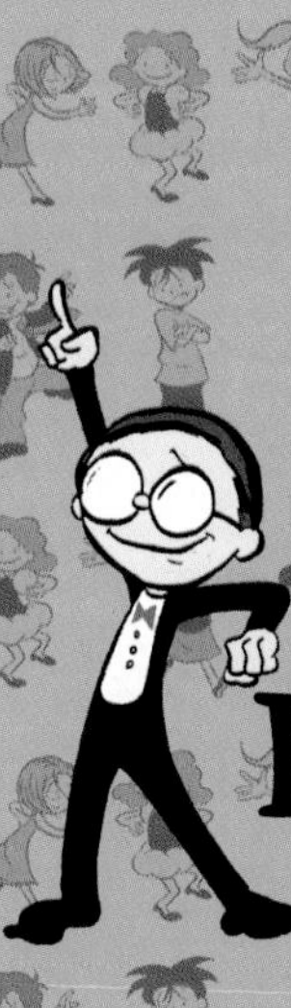

Funny Story

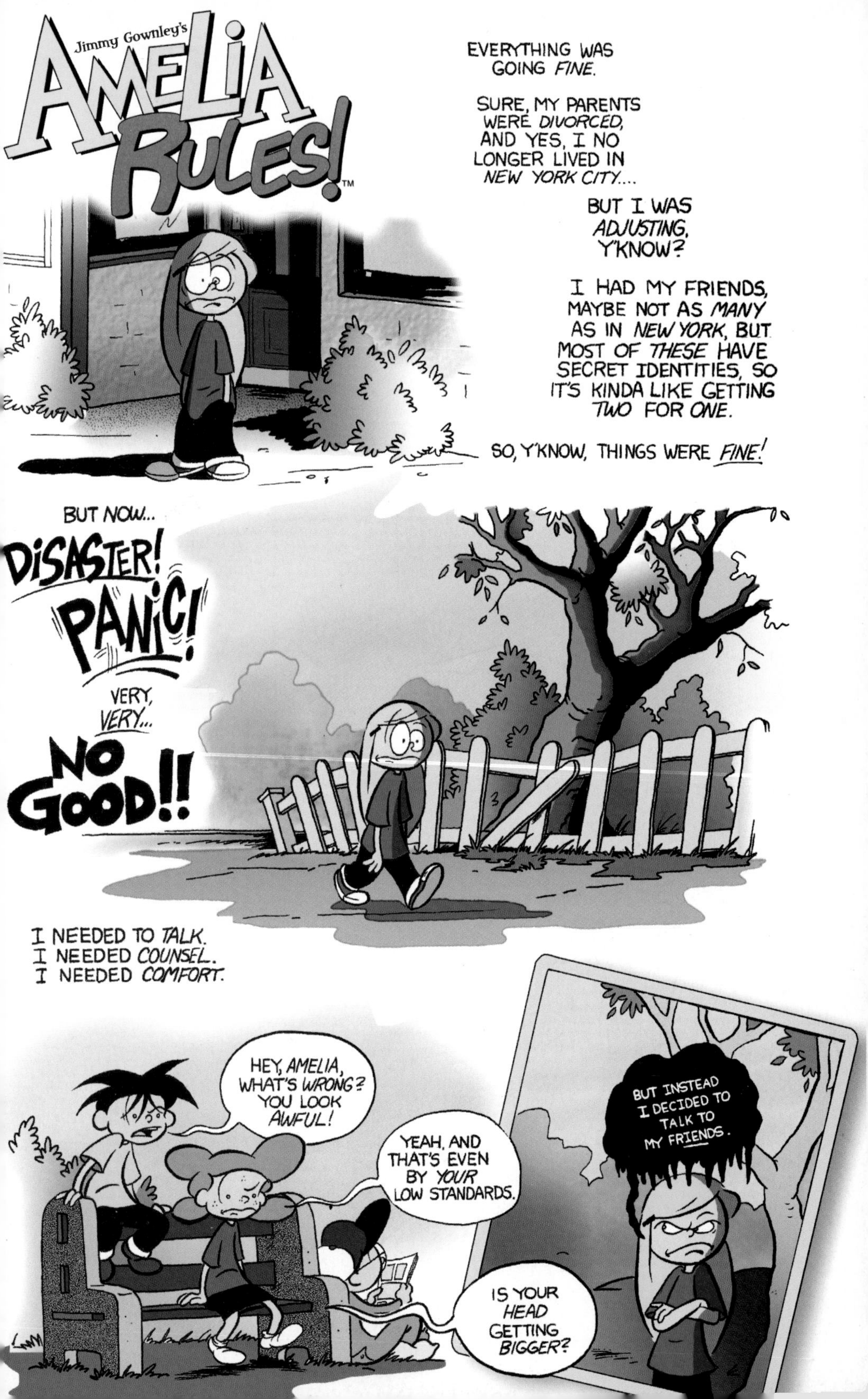

Jimmy Gownley's
AMELIA RULES!™
EVERYTHING WAS GOING FINE.
SURE, MY PARENTS WERE DIVORCED, AND YES, I NO LONGER LIVED IN NEW YORK CITY....
BUT I WAS ADJUSTING, Y'KNOW?
I HAD MY FRIENDS, MAYBE NOT AS MANY AS IN NEW YORK, BUT MOST OF THESE HAVE SECRET IDENTITIES, SO IT'S KINDA LIKE GETTING TWO FOR ONE.
SO, Y'KNOW, THINGS WERE FINE!
BUT NOW...
DISASTER!
PANIC!
VERY, VERY...
NO GOOD!!
I NEEDED TO TALK.
I NEEDED COUNSEL.
I NEEDED COMFORT.
BUT INSTEAD I DECIDED TO TALK TO MY FRIENDS.
HEY, AMELIA, WHAT'S WRONG? YOU LOOK AWFUL!
YEAH, AND THAT'S EVEN BY YOUR LOW STANDARDS.
IS YOUR HEAD GETTING BIGGER?

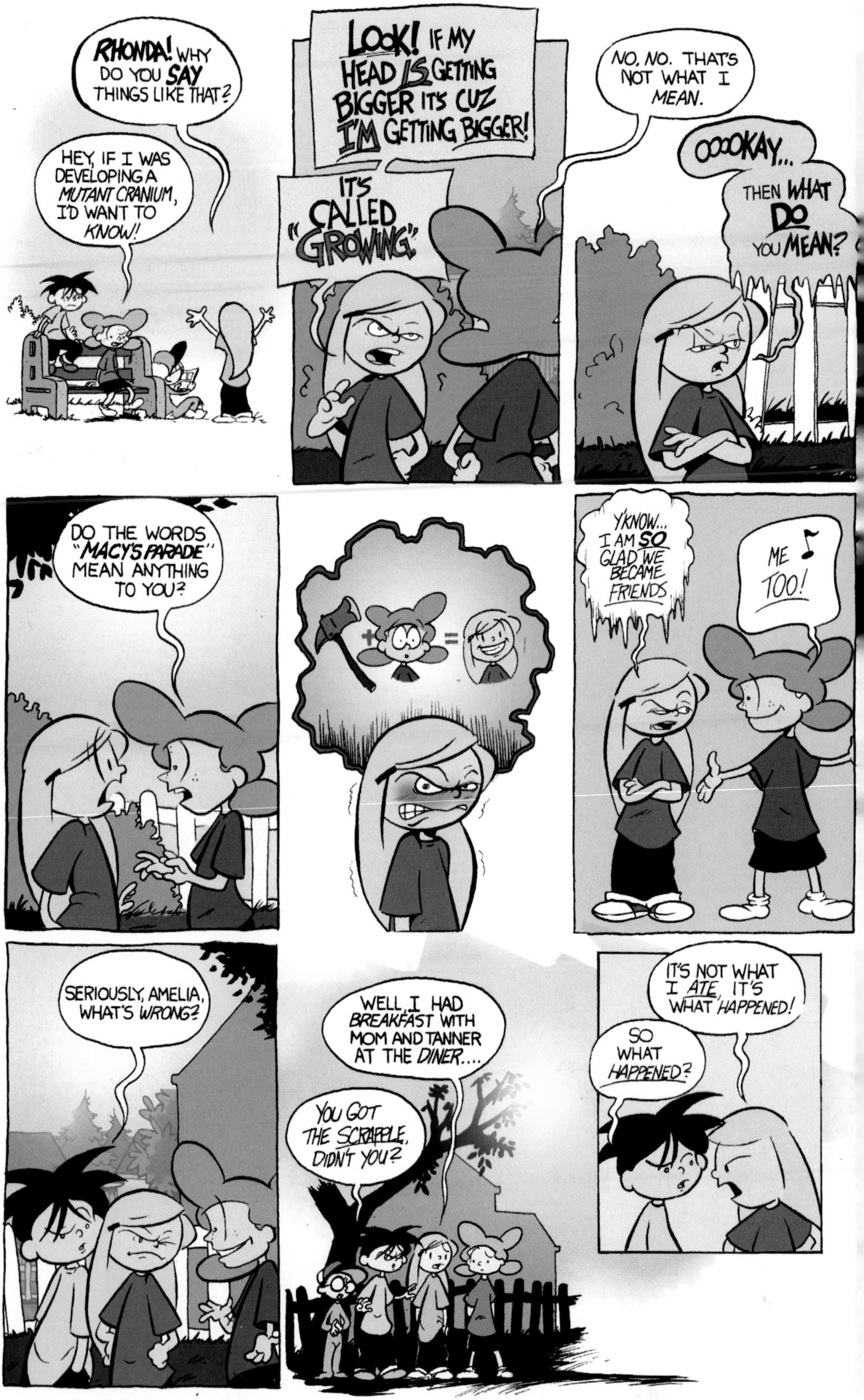
RHONDA! WHY DO YOU SAY THINGS LIKE THAT?
HEY, IF I WAS DEVELOPING A MUTANT CRANIUM, I'D WANT TO KNOW!
LOOK! IF MY HEAD IS GETTING BIGGER IT'S CUZ I'M GETTING BIGGER!
IT'S CALLED "GROWING."
NO, NO. THAT'S NOT WHAT I MEAN.
OOOOKAY... THEN WHAT DO YOU MEAN?
DO THE WORDS "MACY'S PARADE" MEAN ANYTHING TO YOU?
Y'KNOW... I AM SO GLAD WE BECAME FRIENDS
ME TOO!
SERIOUSLY, AMELIA, WHAT'S WRONG?
WELL, I HAD BREAKFAST WITH MOM AND TANNER AT THE DINER....
YOU GOT THE SCRAPPLE, DIDN'T YOU?
SO WHAT HAPPENED?
IT'S NOT WHAT I ATE, IT'S WHAT HAPPENED!

WELL, LET ME TELL YOU...

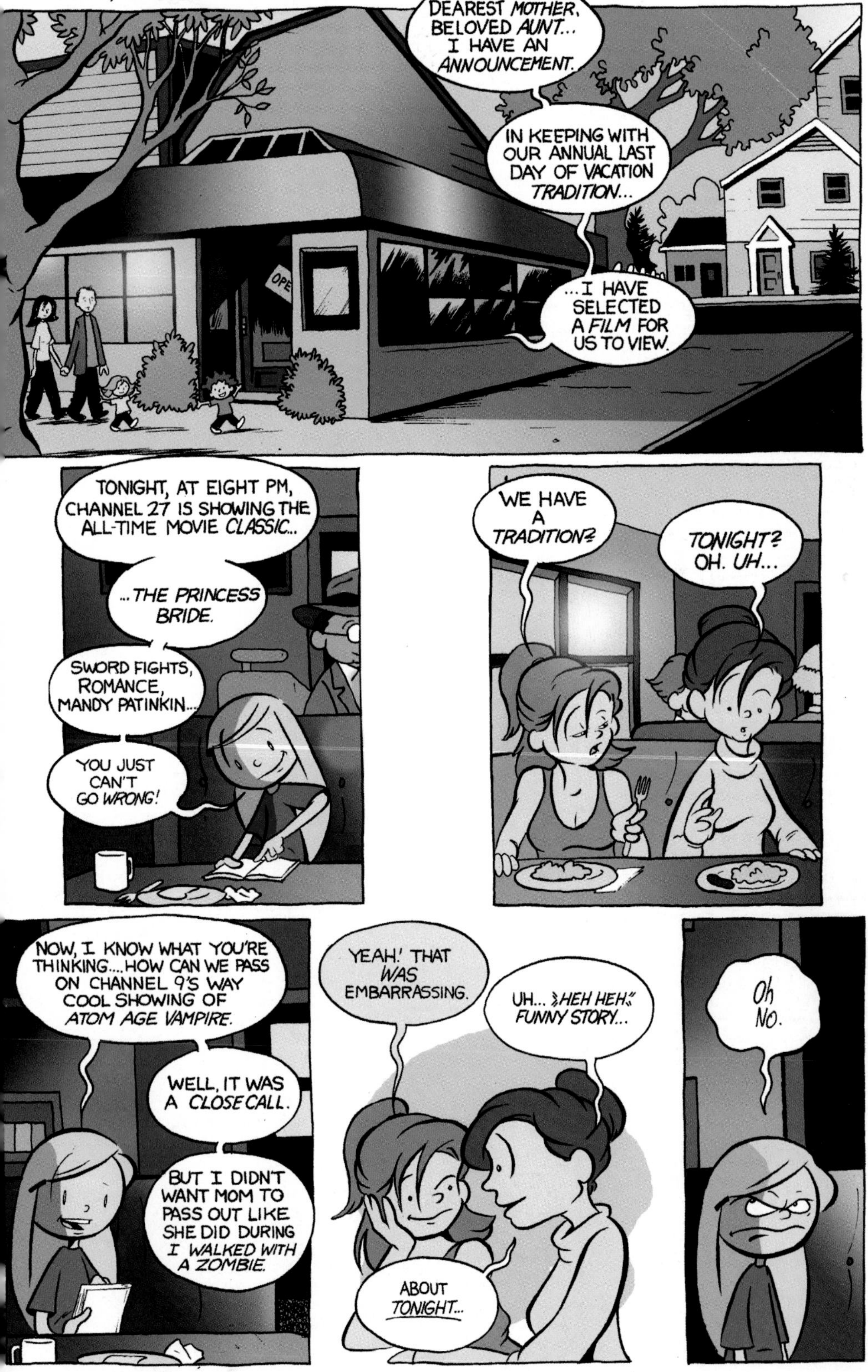
DEAREST *MOTHER*, BELOVED *AUNT*... I HAVE AN *ANNOUNCEMENT*.
IN KEEPING WITH OUR ANNUAL LAST DAY OF VACATION *TRADITION*...
...I HAVE SELECTED A *FILM* FOR US TO VIEW.
OPE
TONIGHT, AT EIGHT PM, CHANNEL 27 IS SHOWING THE ALL-TIME MOVIE *CLASSIC*...
...*THE PRINCESS BRIDE*.
SWORD FIGHTS, ROMANCE, MANDY PATINKIN...
YOU JUST CAN'T GO *WRONG*!
WE HAVE A *TRADITION*?
TONIGHT? OH. *UH*...
NOW, I KNOW WHAT YOU'RE THINKING.... HOW CAN WE PASS ON CHANNEL 9'S WAY COOL SHOWING OF *ATOM AGE VAMPIRE*.
WELL, IT WAS A *CLOSE CALL*.
BUT I DIDN'T WANT MOM TO PASS OUT LIKE SHE DID DURING *I WALKED WITH A ZOMBIE*.
YEAH! THAT *WAS* EMBARRASSING.
UH... *HEH HEH* *FUNNY STORY*...
ABOUT *TONIGHT*...
Oh No.

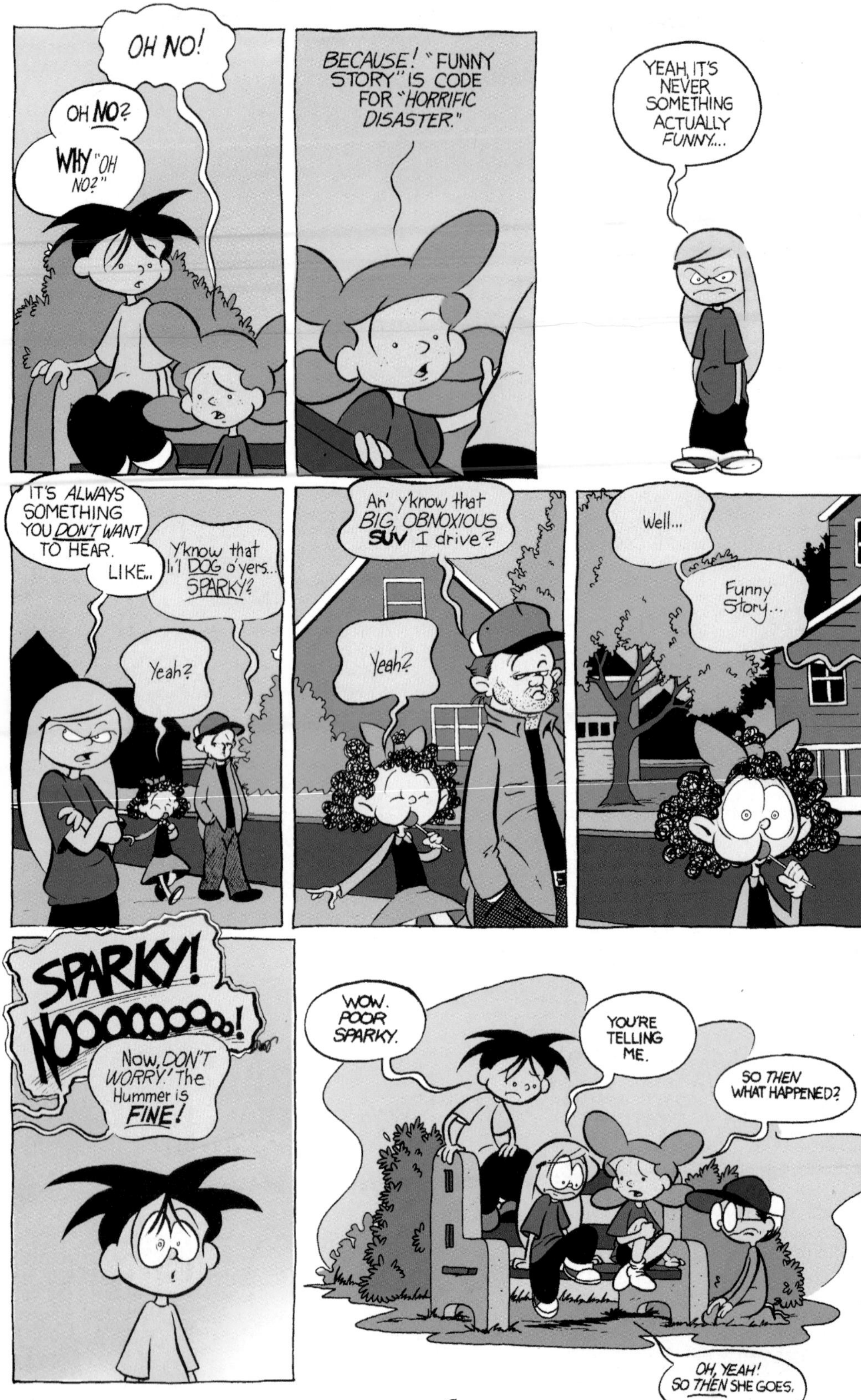
OH NO?
WHY "OH NO?"
OH NO!
BECAUSE! "FUNNY STORY" IS CODE FOR "HORRIFIC DISASTER."
YEAH, IT'S NEVER SOMETHING ACTUALLY FUNNY...
IT'S ALWAYS SOMETHING YOU DON'T WANT TO HEAR.
LIKE...
Y'know that li'l DOG o'yers... SPARKY?
Yeah?
An' y'know that BIG, OBNOXIOUS SUV I drive?
Yeah?
Well...
Funny Story...
SPARKY! NOOOOOOOOoo!
Now, DON'T WORRY! The Hummer is FINE!
WOW. POOR SPARKY.
YOU'RE TELLING ME.
SO THEN WHAT HAPPENED?
OH, YEAH! SO THEN SHE GOES,

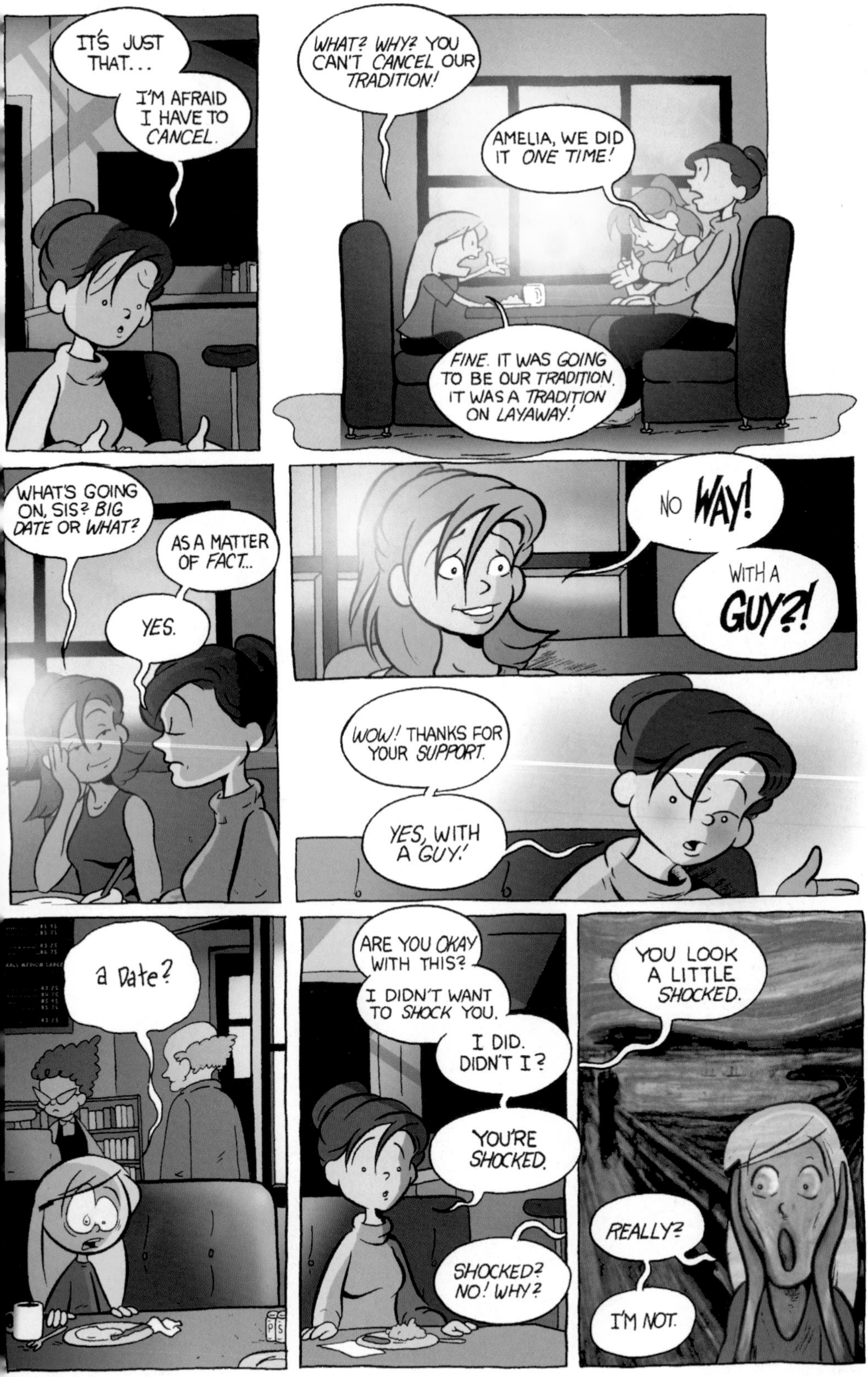
IT'S JUST THAT...
I'M AFRAID I HAVE TO CANCEL.
WHAT? WHY? YOU CAN'T CANCEL OUR TRADITION!
AMELIA, WE DID IT ONE TIME!
FINE. IT WAS GOING TO BE OUR TRADITION. IT WAS A TRADITION ON LAYAWAY!
WHAT'S GOING ON, SIS? BIG DATE OR WHAT?
AS A MATTER OF FACT...
YES.
NO WAY!
WITH A GUY?!
WOW! THANKS FOR YOUR SUPPORT.
YES, WITH A GUY!
a Date?
ARE YOU OKAY WITH THIS?
I DIDN'T WANT TO SHOCK YOU.
I DID. DIDN'T I?
YOU'RE SHOCKED.
SHOCKED? NO! WHY?
YOU LOOK A LITTLE SHOCKED.
REALLY?
I'M NOT.

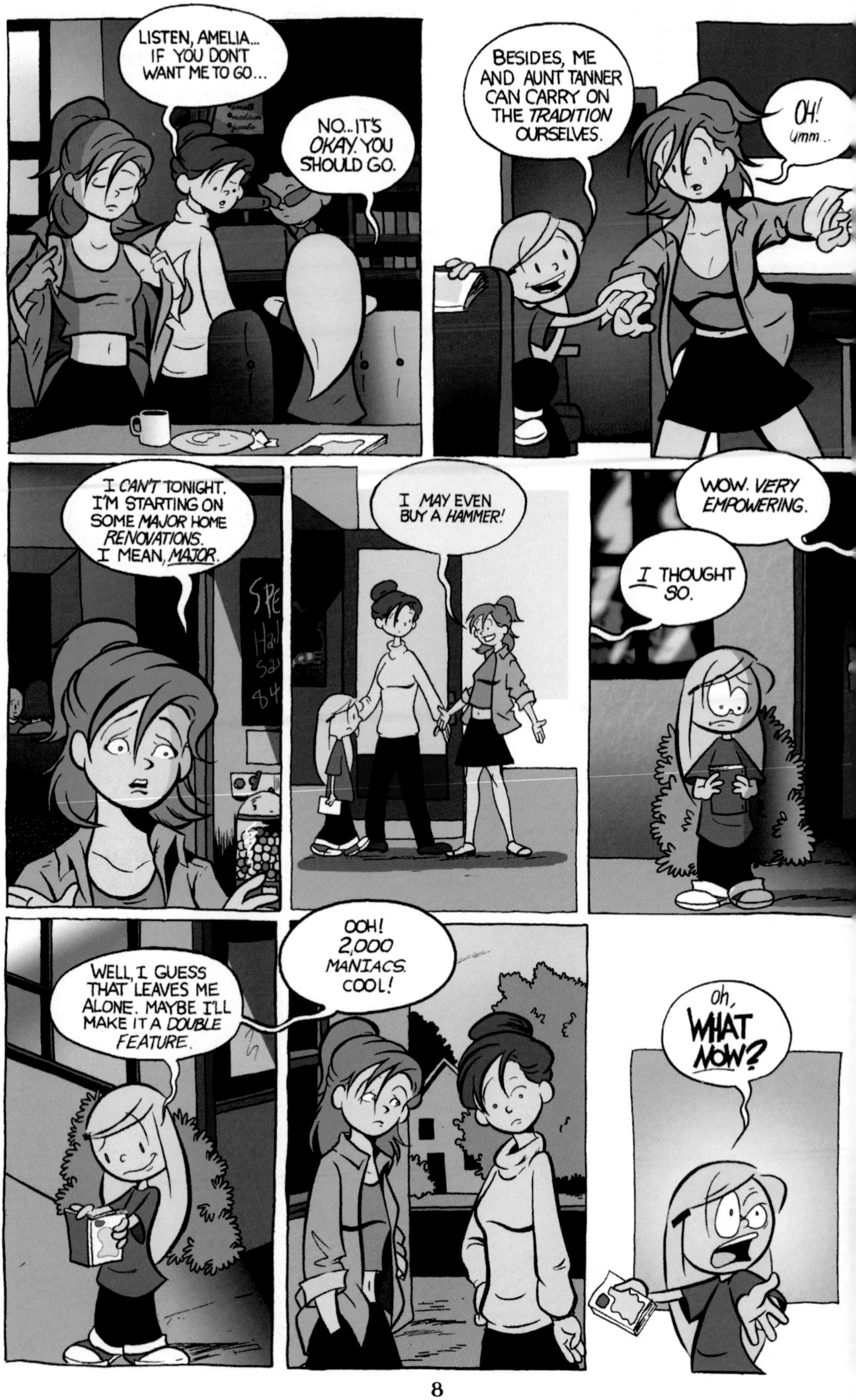
LISTEN, AMELIA... IF YOU DON'T WANT ME TO GO...
NO... IT'S *OKAY*. YOU SHOULD GO.
BESIDES, ME AND AUNT TANNER CAN CARRY ON THE *TRADITION* OURSELVES.
OH! Umm...
I *CAN'T* TONIGHT. I'M STARTING ON SOME *MAJOR* HOME *RENOVATIONS*. I MEAN, *MAJOR*.
I *MAY* EVEN BUY A *HAMMER*!
WOW. *VERY EMPOWERING*.
I THOUGHT *SO*.
WELL, I GUESS THAT LEAVES ME ALONE. MAYBE I'LL MAKE IT A *DOUBLE FEATURE*.
OOH! *2,000 MANIACS.* COOL!
Oh, WHAT NOW?

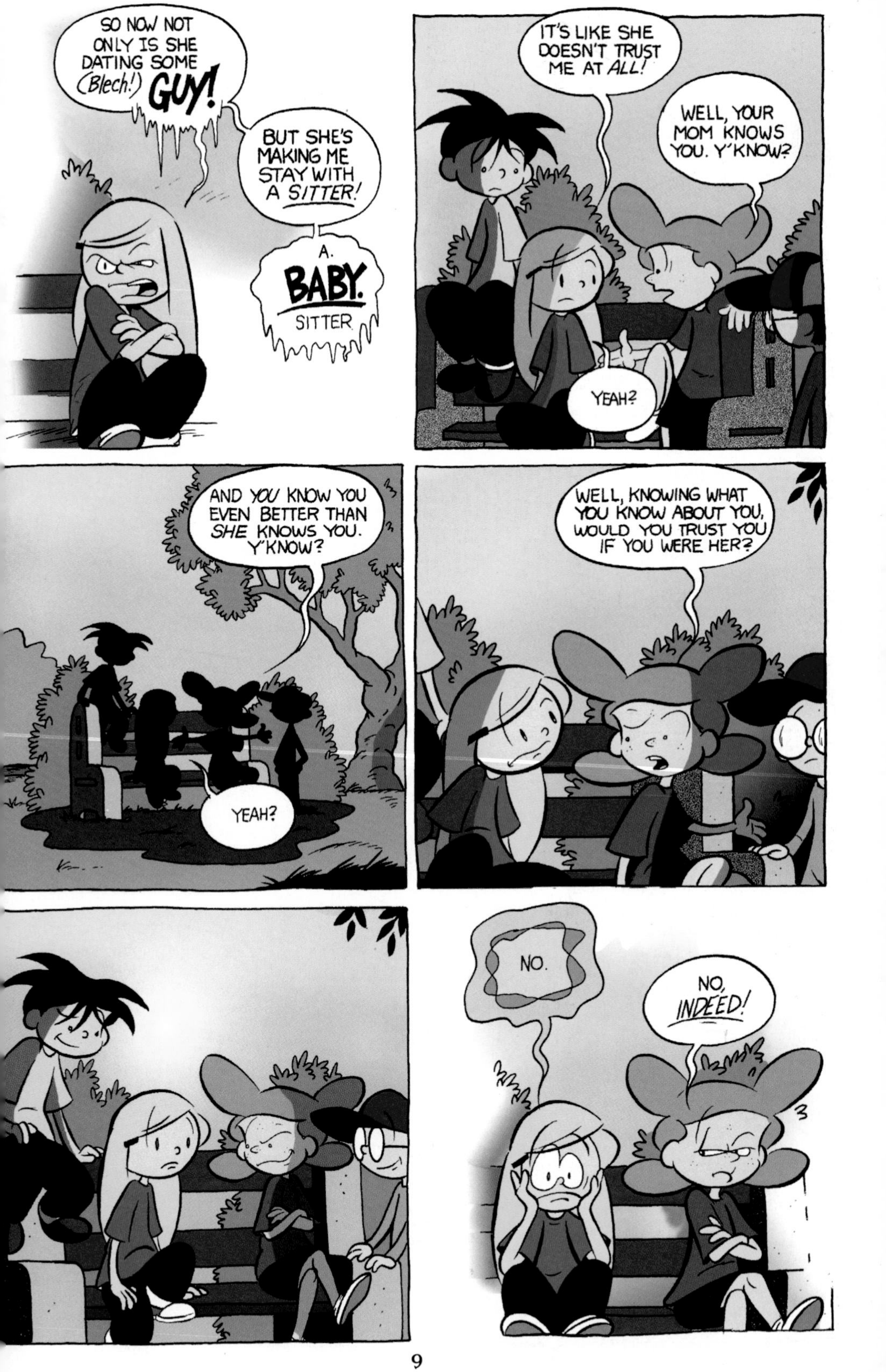
SO NOW NOT ONLY IS SHE DATING SOME (Blech!) GUY!
BUT SHE'S MAKING ME STAY WITH A SITTER!
A. BABY. SITTER
IT'S LIKE SHE DOESN'T TRUST ME AT ALL!
WELL, YOUR MOM KNOWS YOU. Y'KNOW?
YEAH?
AND YOU KNOW YOU EVEN BETTER THAN SHE KNOWS YOU. Y'KNOW?
YEAH?
WELL, KNOWING WHAT YOU KNOW ABOUT YOU, WOULD YOU TRUST YOU IF YOU WERE HER?
NO.
NO, INDEED!

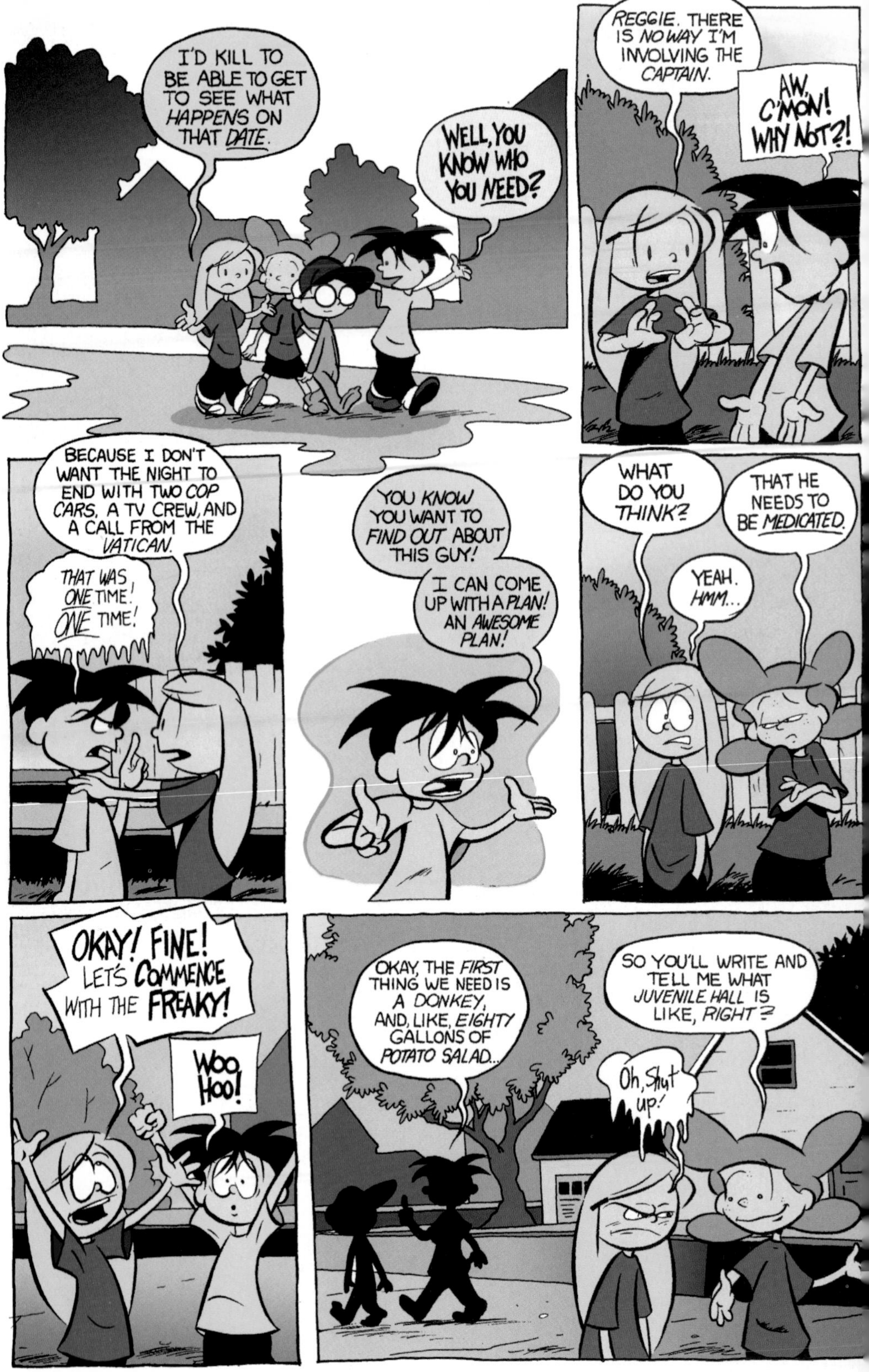

I'D KILL TO BE ABLE TO GET TO SEE WHAT HAPPENS ON THAT DATE.
WELL, YOU KNOW WHO YOU NEED?
REGGIE. THERE IS NO WAY I'M INVOLVING THE CAPTAIN.
AW, C'MON! WHY NOT?!
BECAUSE I DON'T WANT THE NIGHT TO END WITH TWO COP CARS, A TV CREW, AND A CALL FROM THE VATICAN.
THAT WAS ONE TIME! ONE TIME!
YOU KNOW YOU WANT TO FIND OUT ABOUT THIS GUY!
I CAN COME UP WITH A PLAN! AN AWESOME PLAN!
WHAT DO YOU THINK?
THAT HE NEEDS TO BE MEDICATED.
YEAH. HMM...
OKAY! FINE! LET'S COMMENCE WITH THE FREAKY!
WOO HOO!
OKAY, THE FIRST THING WE NEED IS A DONKEY, AND, LIKE, EIGHTY GALLONS OF POTATO SALAD...
SO YOU'LL WRITE AND TELL ME WHAT JUVENILE HALL IS LIKE, RIGHT?
Oh, Shut up!

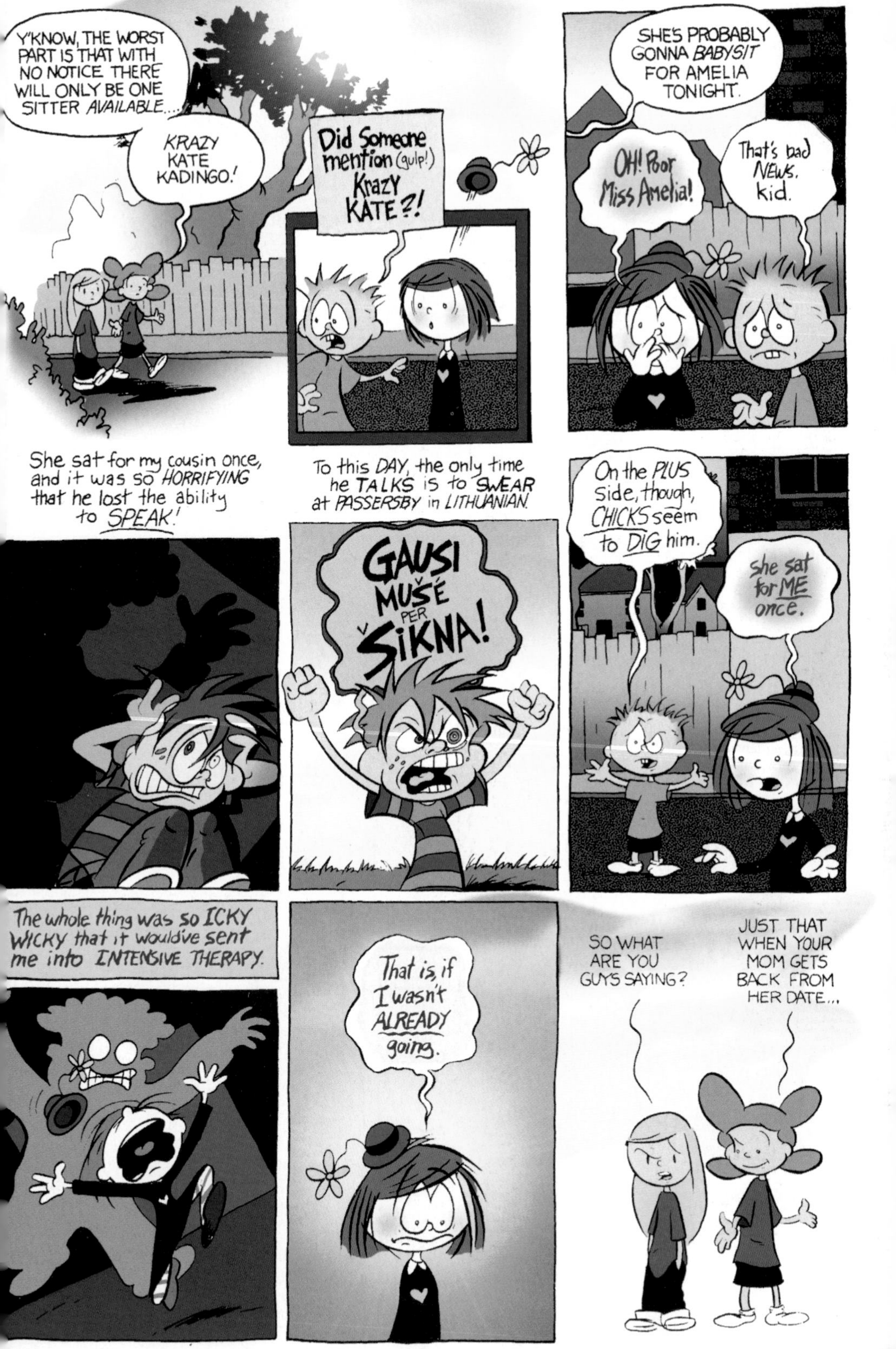

Y'KNOW, THE WORST PART IS THAT WITH NO NOTICE THERE WILL ONLY BE ONE SITTER AVAILABLE....
KRAZY KATE KADINGO!
Did Someone mention (gulp!) Krazy KATE ?!
SHE'S PROBABLY GONNA BABYSIT FOR AMELIA TONIGHT.
OH! Poor Miss Amelia!
That's bad NEWS, kid.
She sat for my cousin once, and it was so HORRIFYING that he lost the ability to SPEAK!
To this DAY, the only time he TALKS is to SWEAR at PASSERSBY in LITHUANIAN.
GAUSI MUŠĖ PER ŠIKNA!
On the PLUS side, though, CHICKS seem to DIG him.
She sat for ME once.
The whole thing was so ICKY WICKY that it would've sent me into INTENSIVE THERAPY.
That is, if I wasn't ALREADY going.
SO WHAT ARE YOU GUYS SAYING?
JUST THAT WHEN YOUR MOM GETS BACK FROM HER DATE...

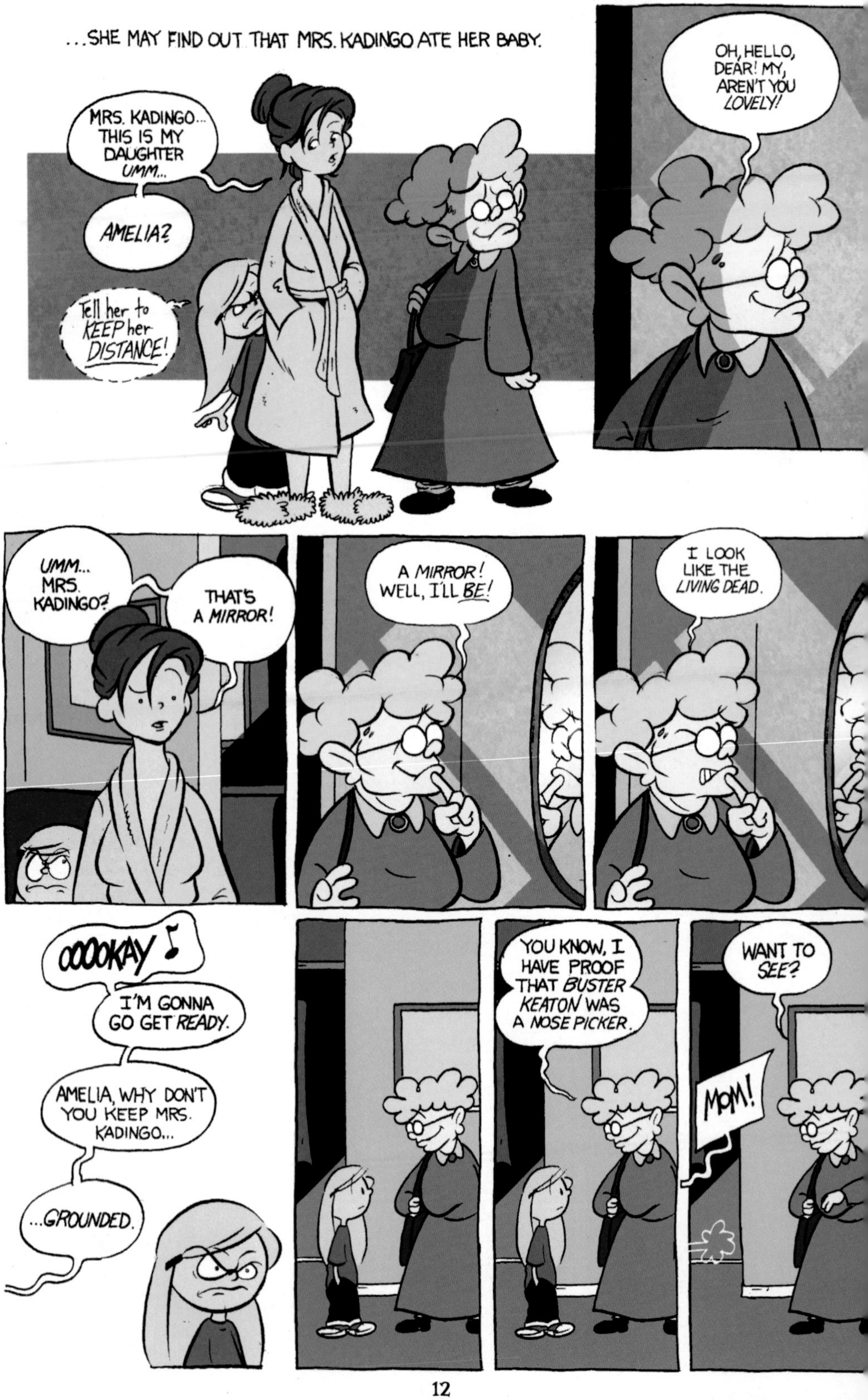

...SHE MAY FIND OUT THAT MRS. KADINGO ATE HER BABY.
MRS. KADINGO... THIS IS MY DAUGHTER UMM...
AMELIA?
Tell her to KEEP her DISTANCE!
OH, HELLO, DEAR! MY, AREN'T YOU LOVELY!
UMM... MRS. KADINGO?
THAT'S A MIRROR!
A MIRROR! WELL, I'LL BE!
I LOOK LIKE THE LIVING DEAD.
OOOOKAY
I'M GONNA GO GET READY.
AMELIA, WHY DON'T YOU KEEP MRS. KADINGO...
...GROUNDED.
YOU KNOW, I HAVE PROOF THAT BUSTER KEATON WAS A NOSE PICKER.
WANT TO SEE?
MOM!

SO, BEING TOTALLY ***GROSSED OUT***, I WENT UPSTAIRS TO WATCH MOM GET READY. LOOKING IN THE MIRROR, I DIDN'T SEE THE ***LIVING DEAD***, BUT I FELT LIKE THE ***WALKING WOUNDED***.

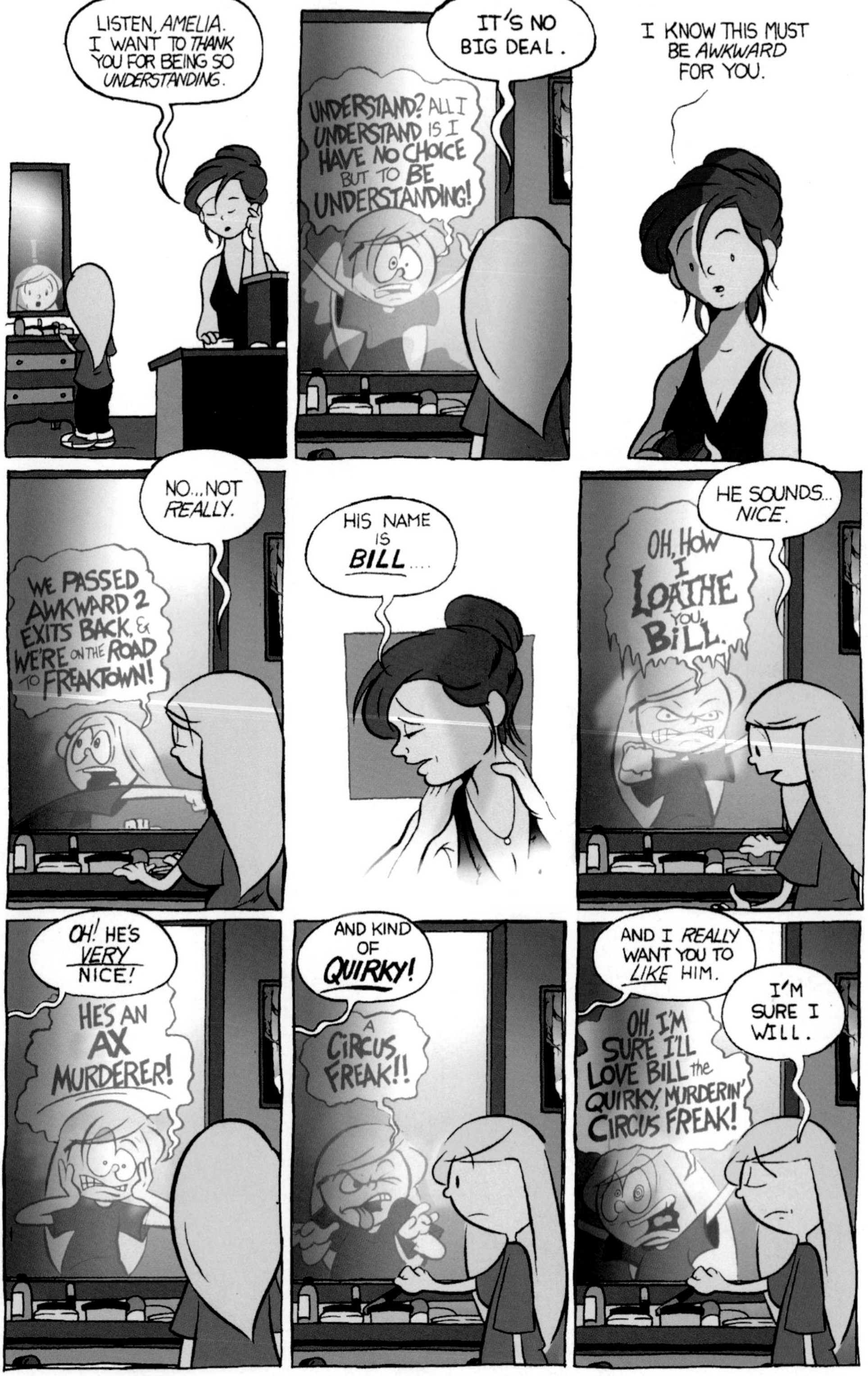
LISTEN, AMELIA. I WANT TO THANK YOU FOR BEING SO UNDERSTANDING.
IT'S NO BIG DEAL.
UNDERSTAND? ALL I UNDERSTAND IS I HAVE NO CHOICE BUT TO BE UNDERSTANDING!
I KNOW THIS MUST BE AWKWARD FOR YOU.
NO... NOT REALLY.
WE PASSED AWKWARD 2 EXITS BACK, & WE'RE ON THE ROAD TO FREAKTOWN!
HIS NAME IS BILL....
HE SOUNDS... NICE.
OH, HOW I LOATHE YOU, BILL.
OH! HE'S VERY NICE!
HE'S AN AX MURDERER!
AND KIND OF QUIRKY!
A CIRCUS FREAK!!
AND I REALLY WANT YOU TO LIKE HIM.
I'M SURE I WILL.
OH, I'M SURE I'LL LOVE BILL the QUIRKY, MURDERIN' CIRCUS FREAK!

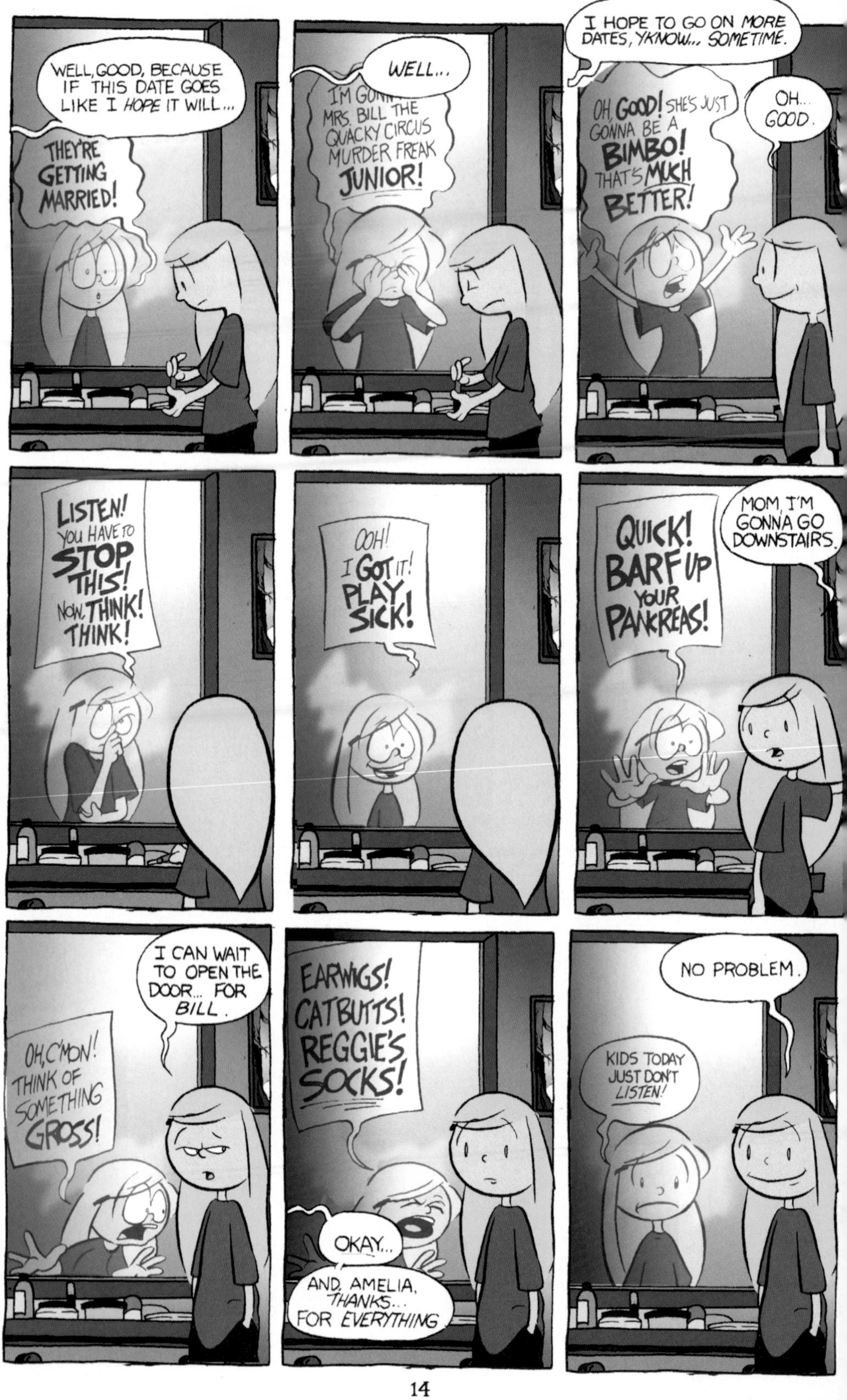
WELL, GOOD, BECAUSE IF THIS DATE GOES LIKE I HOPE IT WILL...
THEY'RE GETTING MARRIED!
WELL...
I'M GONNA ... MRS. BILL THE QUACKY CIRCUS MURDER FREAK JUNIOR!
I HOPE TO GO ON MORE DATES, Y'KNOW... SOMETIME.
OH, GOOD! SHE'S JUST GONNA BE A BIMBO! THAT'S MUCH BETTER!
OH... GOOD.
LISTEN! YOU HAVE TO STOP THIS! NOW, THINK! THINK!
OOH! I GOT IT! PLAY SICK!
QUICK! BARF UP YOUR PANKREAS!
MOM, I'M GONNA GO DOWNSTAIRS.
OH, C'MON! THINK OF SOMETHING GROSS!
I CAN WAIT TO OPEN THE DOOR... FOR BILL.
EARWIGS! CATBUTTS! REGGIE'S SOCKS!
OKAY...
AND, AMELIA, THANKS... FOR EVERYTHING.
NO PROBLEM.
KIDS TODAY JUST DON'T LISTEN!

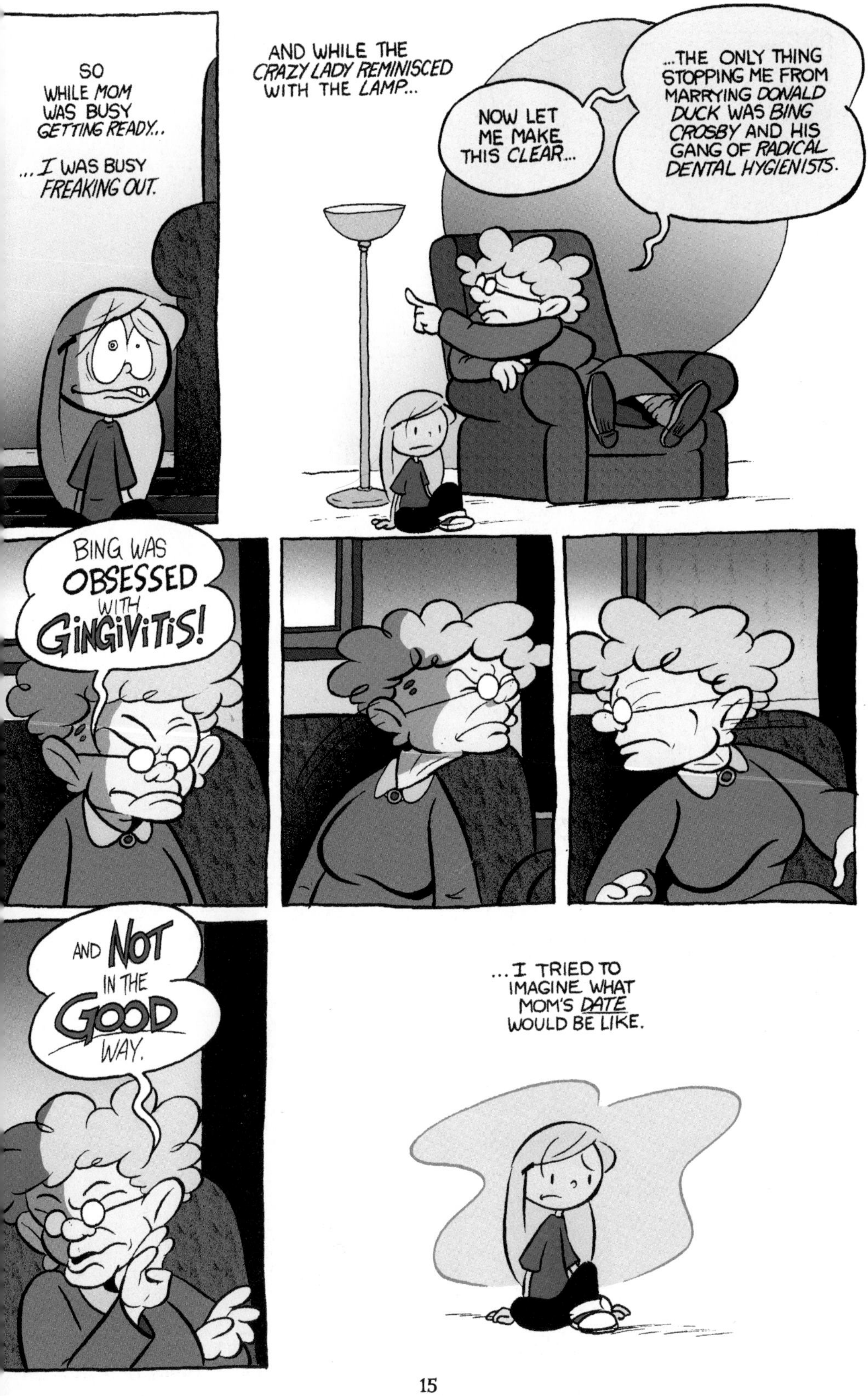
SO WHILE MOM WAS BUSY GETTING READY...
...I WAS BUSY FREAKING OUT.
AND WHILE THE CRAZY LADY REMINISCED WITH THE LAMP...
NOW LET ME MAKE THIS CLEAR...
...THE ONLY THING STOPPING ME FROM MARRYING DONALD DUCK WAS BING CROSBY AND HIS GANG OF RADICAL DENTAL HYGIENISTS.
BING WAS OBSESSED WITH GINGIVITIS!
AND NOT IN THE GOOD WAY.
...I TRIED TO IMAGINE WHAT MOM'S DATE WOULD BE LIKE.

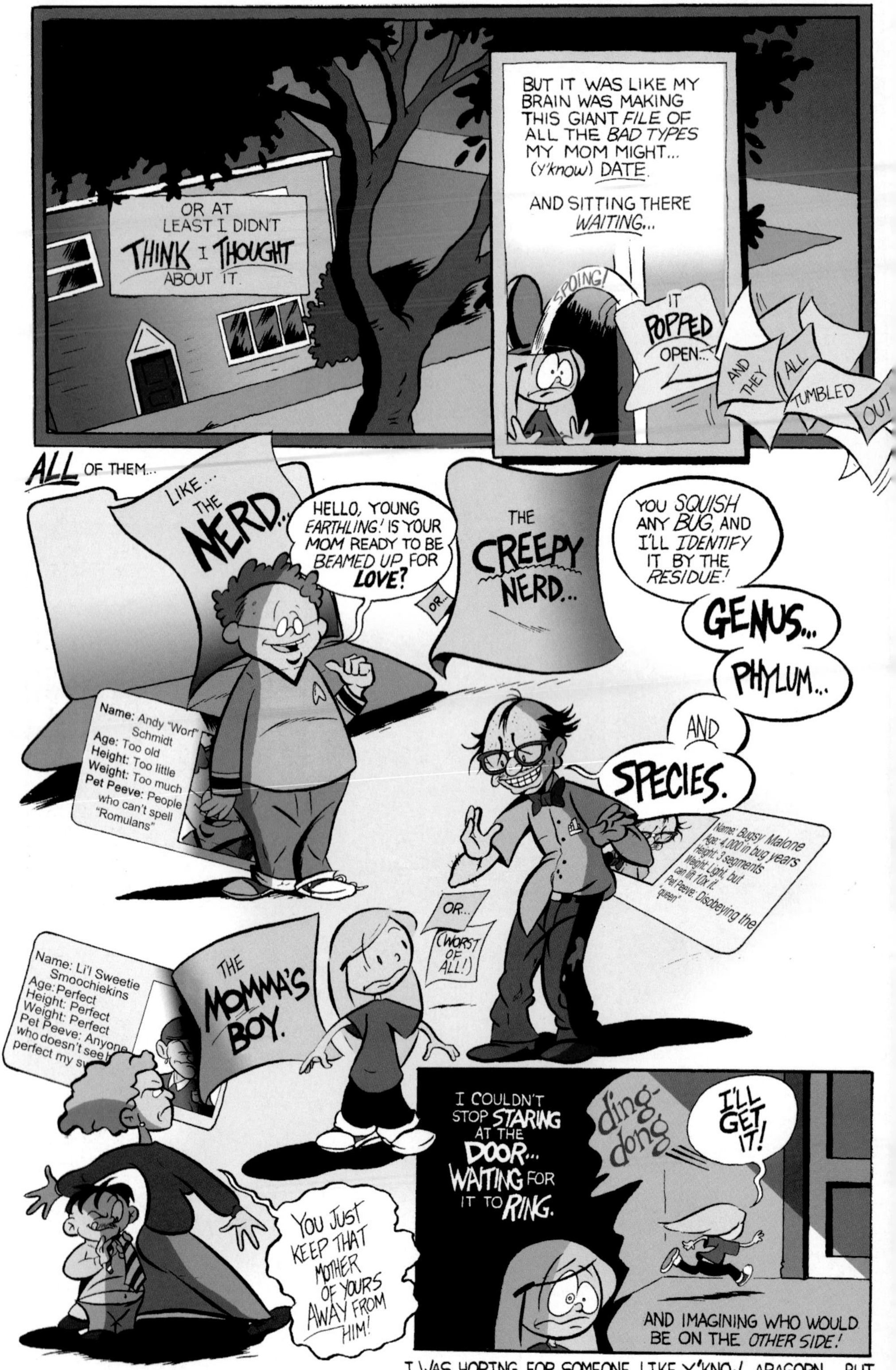
OR AT LEAST I DIDN'T THINK I THOUGHT ABOUT IT.
BUT IT WAS LIKE MY BRAIN WAS MAKING THIS GIANT FILE OF ALL THE BAD TYPES MY MOM MIGHT... (Y'know) DATE.
AND SITTING THERE WAITING...
SPOING!
IT POPPED OPEN...
AND THEY ALL TUMBLED OUT
ALL OF THEM...
LIKE... THE NERD...
HELLO, YOUNG EARTHLING! IS YOUR MOM READY TO BE BEAMED UP FOR LOVE?
Name: Andy "Worf" Schmidt
Age: Too old
Height: Too little
Weight: Too much
Pet Peeve: People who can't spell "Romulans"
OR...
THE CREEPY NERD...
YOU SQUISH ANY BUG, AND I'LL IDENTIFY IT BY THE RESIDUE!
GENUS...
PHYLUM...
AND
SPECIES.
Name: Bugsy Malone
Age: 4,000 in bug years
Height: 3 segments
Weight: Light, but can lift 10x it.
Pet Peeve: Disobeying the "queen"
OR... (WORST OF ALL!)
THE MOMMA'S BOY.
Name: Li'l Sweetie Smoochiekins
Age: Perfect
Height: Perfect
Weight: Perfect
Pet Peeve: Anyone who doesn't see
perfect my
YOU JUST KEEP THAT MOTHER OF YOURS AWAY FROM HIM!
I COULDN'T STOP STARING AT THE DOOR... WAITING FOR IT TO RING.
ding-dong
I'LL GET IT!
AND IMAGINING WHO WOULD BE ON THE OTHER SIDE!
I WAS HOPING FOR SOMEONE LIKE, Y'KNOW... ARAGORN, BUT...

the PLAN
By: ReGGIE G. Art By: PAJAMAMAN
1. Amelia + Reenie Switch Places*
2. Thus Fooling the Gullabull Babysitter
3. AMeliA ukumpaneez Captain Amazing
cookie?
thank you.
*Reenie will need $
4. They follow Guy and Mom, to Date ~~locash~~ ~~lokash~~ place.
start
5. Captain Amazing Gets Dirt on Guy
6. Mom Dumps Guy
HA HA HA HA
HEY! that's MUD!
Note: Too Literal - R.G.
HA! HA!
Boo Hoo!
7. Captain Amazing is Adored by Many Fine Ladies
8. And Amelia Agrees to be his Personal Slave.
Here's your homework Master.
9. Justus Prevails!
THE END
© Reggamaman Industries LTD.

OKAY, SO MAYBE IT WAS A DUMB PLAN, BUT SINCE I HAD NO DESIRE TO BE "SAT" BY "KRAZY KATE," I TRADED SHIRTS WITH RHONDA'S SISTER AND SENT HER INSIDE, LEAVING ME FREE TO CAVORT WITH THE INFAMOUS CAPTAIN AMAZING.

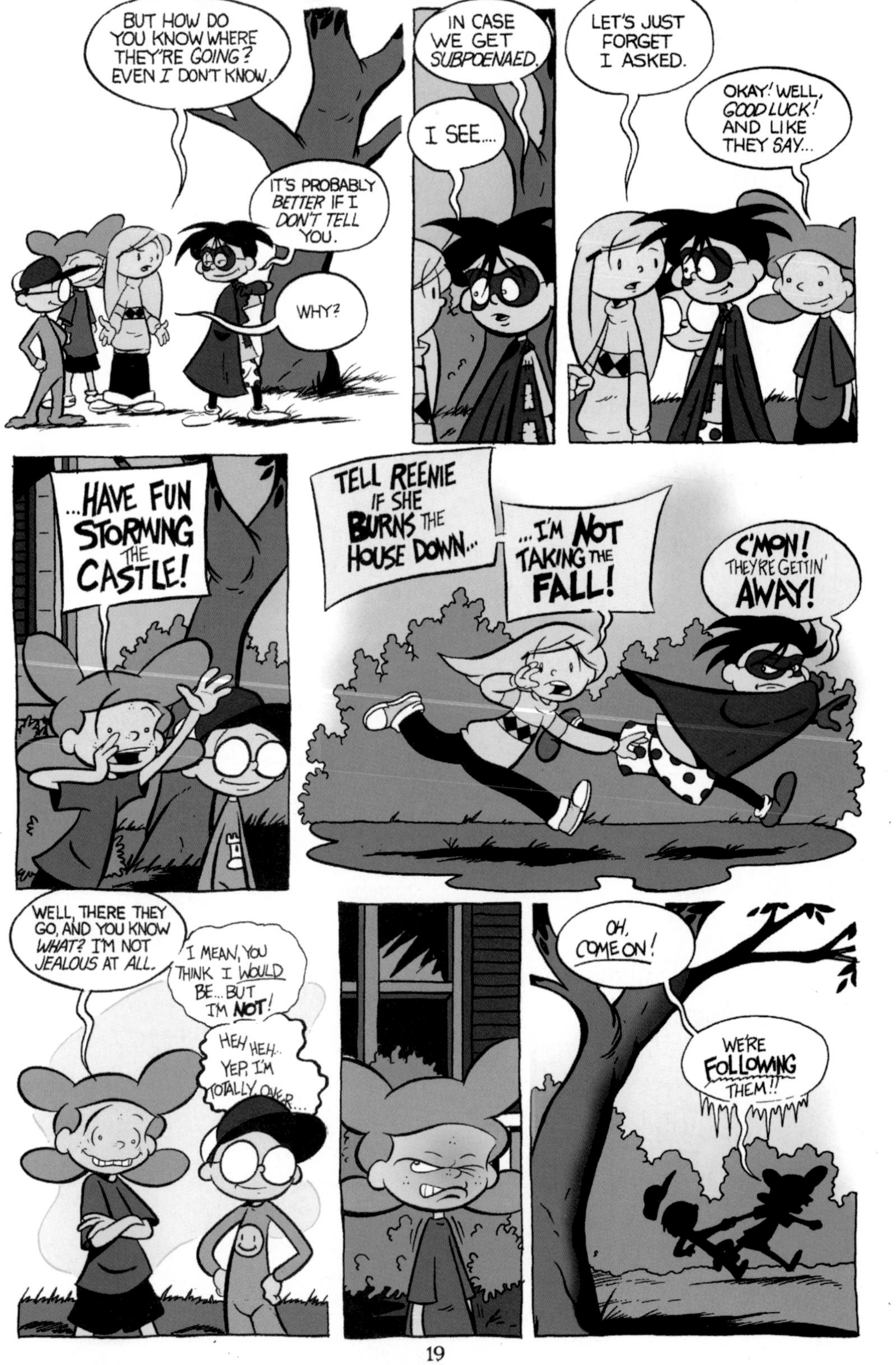

BUT HOW DO YOU KNOW WHERE THEY'RE *GOING*? EVEN *I* DON'T KNOW.
IT'S PROBABLY *BETTER* IF I *DON'T* TELL YOU.
WHY?
IN CASE WE GET *SUBPOENAED*.
I SEE....
LET'S JUST FORGET I ASKED.
OKAY! WELL, *GOOD LUCK*! AND LIKE THEY *SAY*...
...HAVE FUN STORMING THE CASTLE!
TELL REENIE IF SHE BURNS THE HOUSE DOWN...
...I'M NOT TAKING THE FALL!
C'MON! THEY'RE GETTIN' AWAY!
WELL, THERE THEY GO, AND YOU KNOW *WHAT*? I'M NOT *JEALOUS* AT *ALL*.
I MEAN, YOU THINK I WOULD BE... BUT I'M NOT!
HEH HEH.. YEP, I'M TOTALLY OVER...
OH, COME ON!
WE'RE FOLLOWING THEM!!

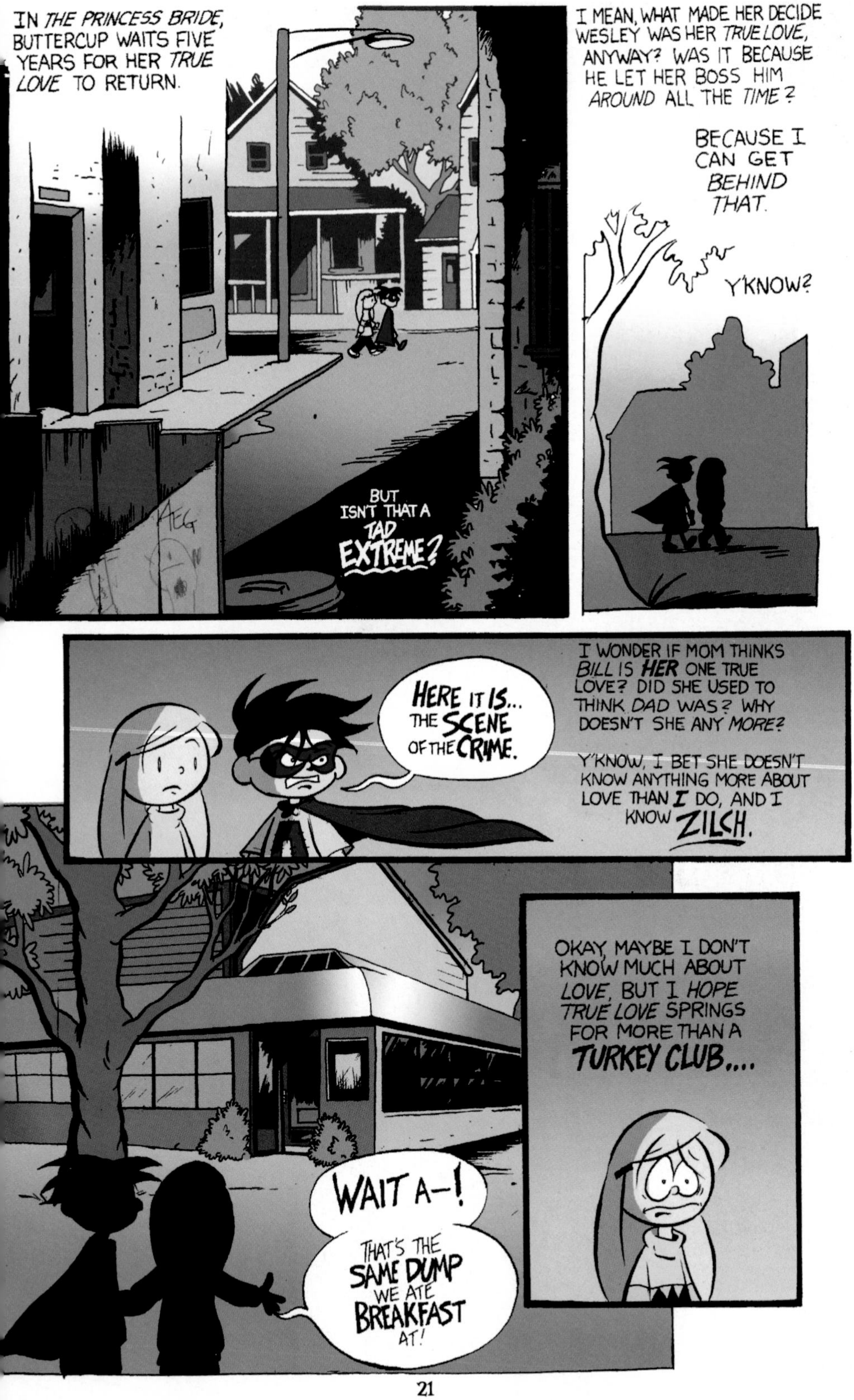
IN *THE PRINCESS BRIDE*, BUTTERCUP WAITS FIVE YEARS FOR HER *TRUE LOVE* TO RETURN.
BUT ISN'T THAT A TAD EXTREME?
I MEAN, WHAT MADE HER DECIDE WESLEY WAS HER *TRUE LOVE*, ANYWAY? WAS IT BECAUSE HE LET HER BOSS HIM *AROUND* ALL THE *TIME*?
BECAUSE I CAN GET *BEHIND* THAT.
Y'KNOW?
HERE IT IS... THE SCENE OF THE CRIME.
I WONDER IF MOM THINKS *BILL* IS **HER** ONE TRUE LOVE? DID SHE USED TO THINK *DAD* WAS? WHY DOESN'T SHE ANY *MORE*?
Y'KNOW, I BET SHE DOESN'T KNOW ANYTHING MORE ABOUT LOVE THAN **I** DO, AND I KNOW ZILCH.
WAIT A-!
THAT'S THE SAME DUMP WE ATE BREAKFAST AT!
OKAY, MAYBE I DON'T KNOW MUCH ABOUT *LOVE*, BUT I *HOPE TRUE LOVE* SPRINGS FOR MORE THAN A **TURKEY CLUB**....

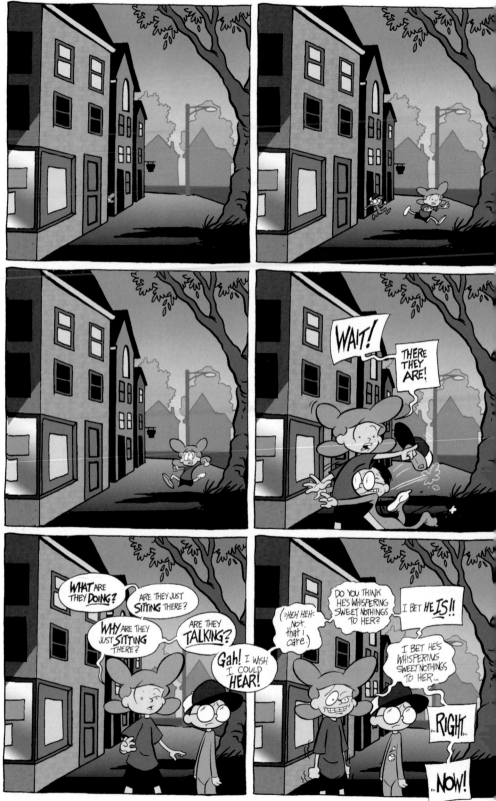

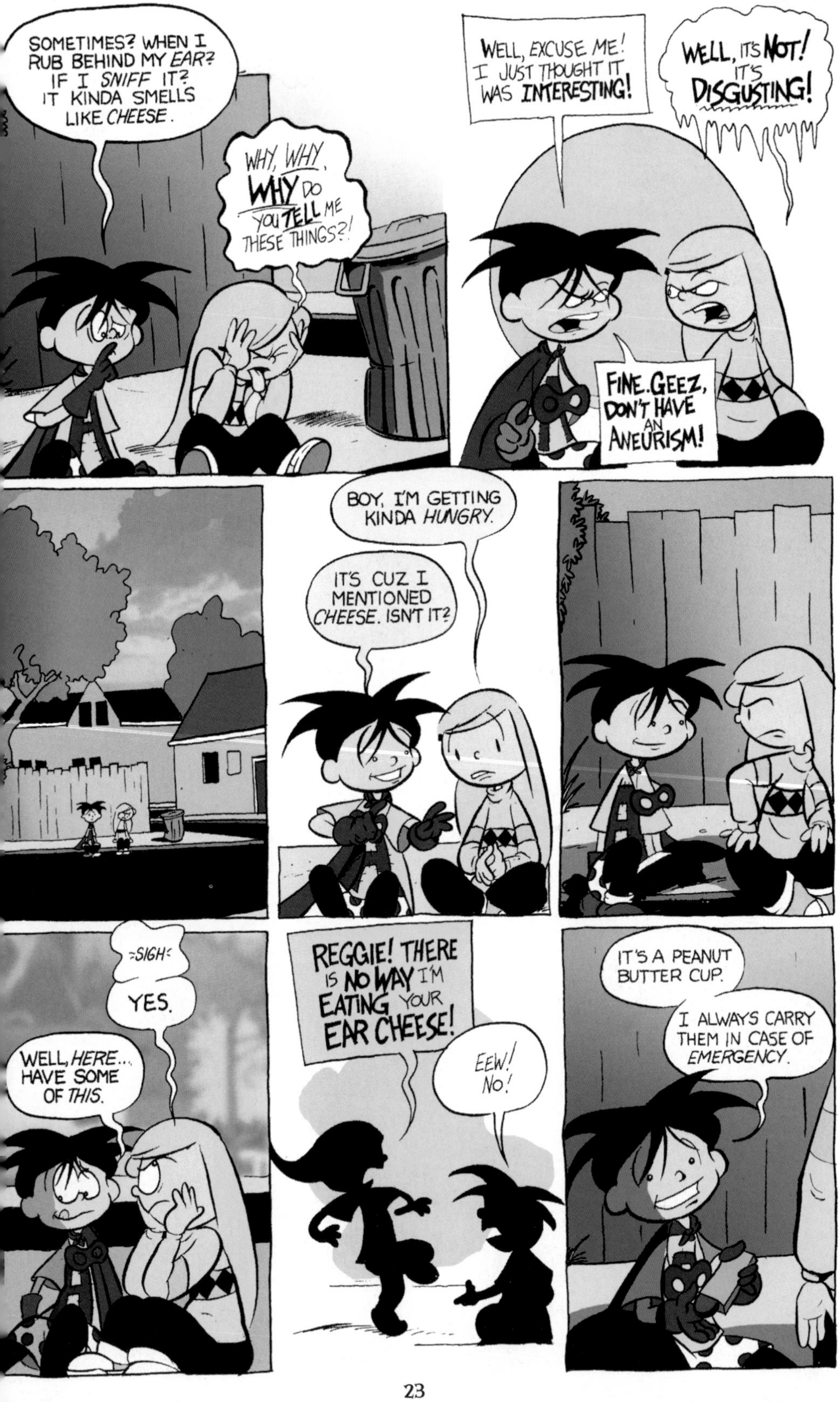
SOMETIMES? WHEN I RUB BEHIND MY EAR? IF I SNIFF IT? IT KINDA SMELLS LIKE CHEESE.
WHY, WHY, WHY DO YOU TELL ME THESE THINGS?!
WELL, EXCUSE ME! I JUST THOUGHT IT WAS INTERESTING!
WELL, IT'S NOT! IT'S DISGUSTING!
FINE. GEEZ, DON'T HAVE AN ANEURISM!
BOY, I'M GETTING KINDA HUNGRY.
IT'S CUZ I MENTIONED CHEESE. ISN'T IT?
SIGH
YES.
WELL, HERE... HAVE SOME OF THIS.
REGGIE! THERE IS NO WAY I'M EATING YOUR EAR CHEESE!
EEW! NO!
IT'S A PEANUT BUTTER CUP.
I ALWAYS CARRY THEM IN CASE OF EMERGENCY.

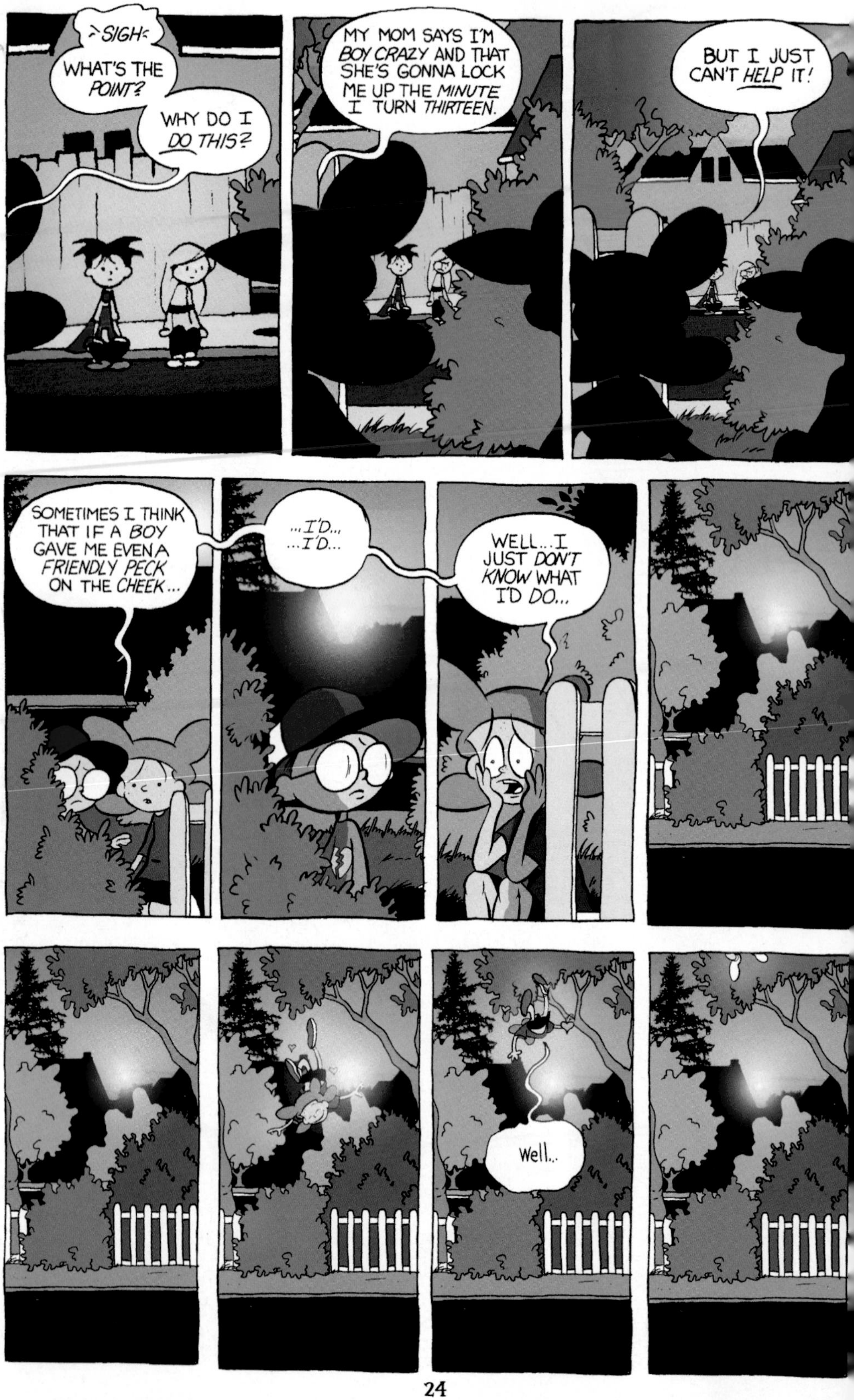
~SIGH~
WHAT'S THE POINT?
WHY DO I DO THIS?
MY MOM SAYS I'M BOY CRAZY AND THAT SHE'S GONNA LOCK ME UP THE MINUTE I TURN THIRTEEN.
BUT I JUST CAN'T HELP IT!
SOMETIMES I THINK THAT IF A BOY GAVE ME EVEN A FRIENDLY PECK ON THE CHEEK...
...I'D... ...I'D...
WELL...I JUST DON'T KNOW WHAT I'D DO...
Well..

THAT ANSWERS *THAT* QUESTION.

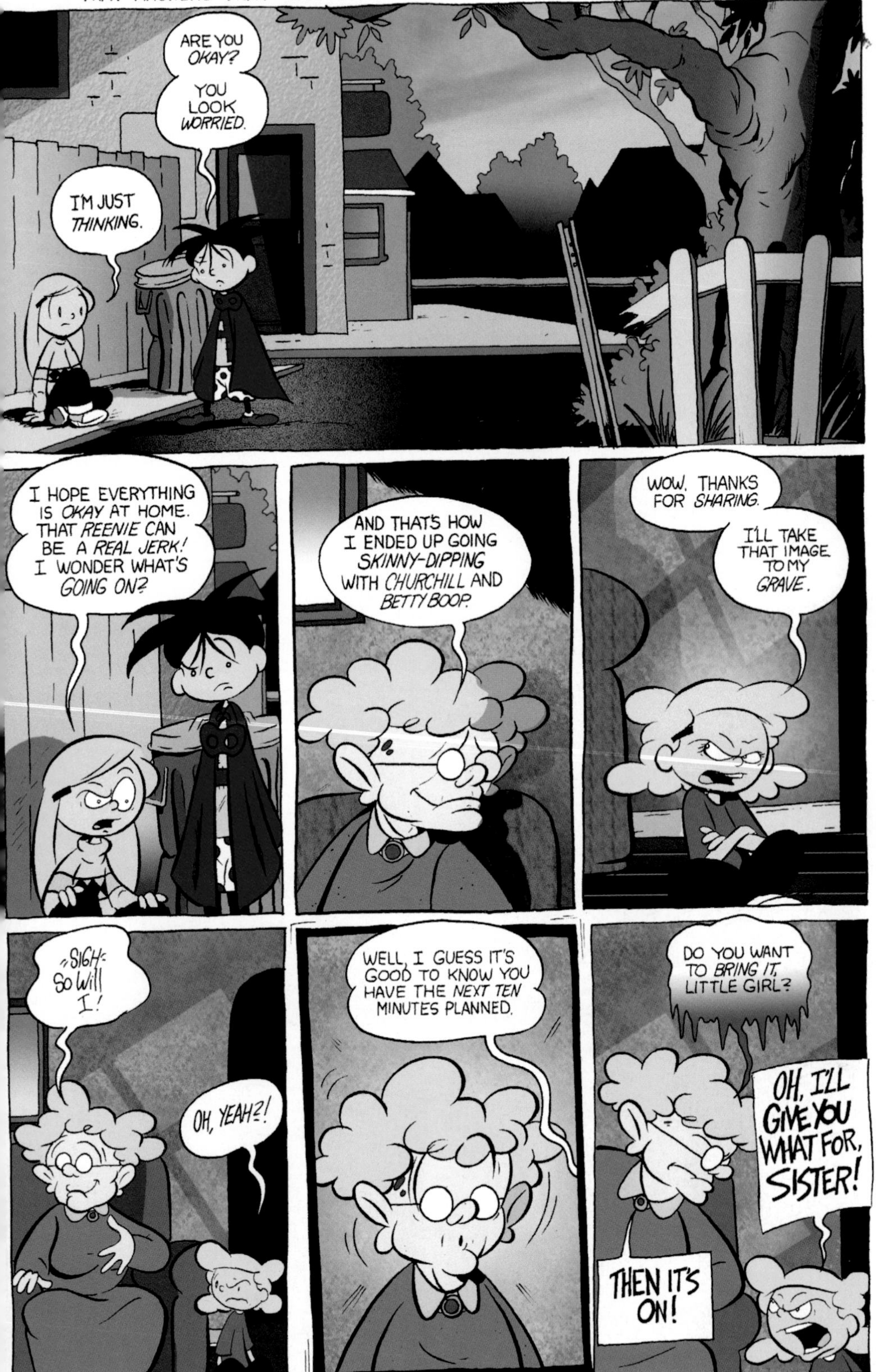
ARE YOU *OKAY?*
YOU LOOK *WORRIED.*
I'M JUST *THINKING.*
I HOPE EVERYTHING IS *OKAY* AT HOME. THAT *REENIE* CAN BE A *REAL JERK!* I WONDER WHAT'S *GOING ON?*
AND THAT'S HOW I ENDED UP GOING *SKINNY-DIPPING* WITH *CHURCHILL* AND *BETTY BOOP.*
WOW. THANKS FOR *SHARING.*
I'LL TAKE THAT IMAGE TO MY *GRAVE.*
-SIGH- So will I!
OH, YEAH?!
WELL, I GUESS IT'S GOOD TO KNOW YOU HAVE THE *NEXT TEN* MINUTES PLANNED.
DO YOU WANT TO *BRING IT,* LITTLE GIRL?
OH, I'LL GIVE YOU WHAT FOR, SISTER!
THEN IT'S ON!

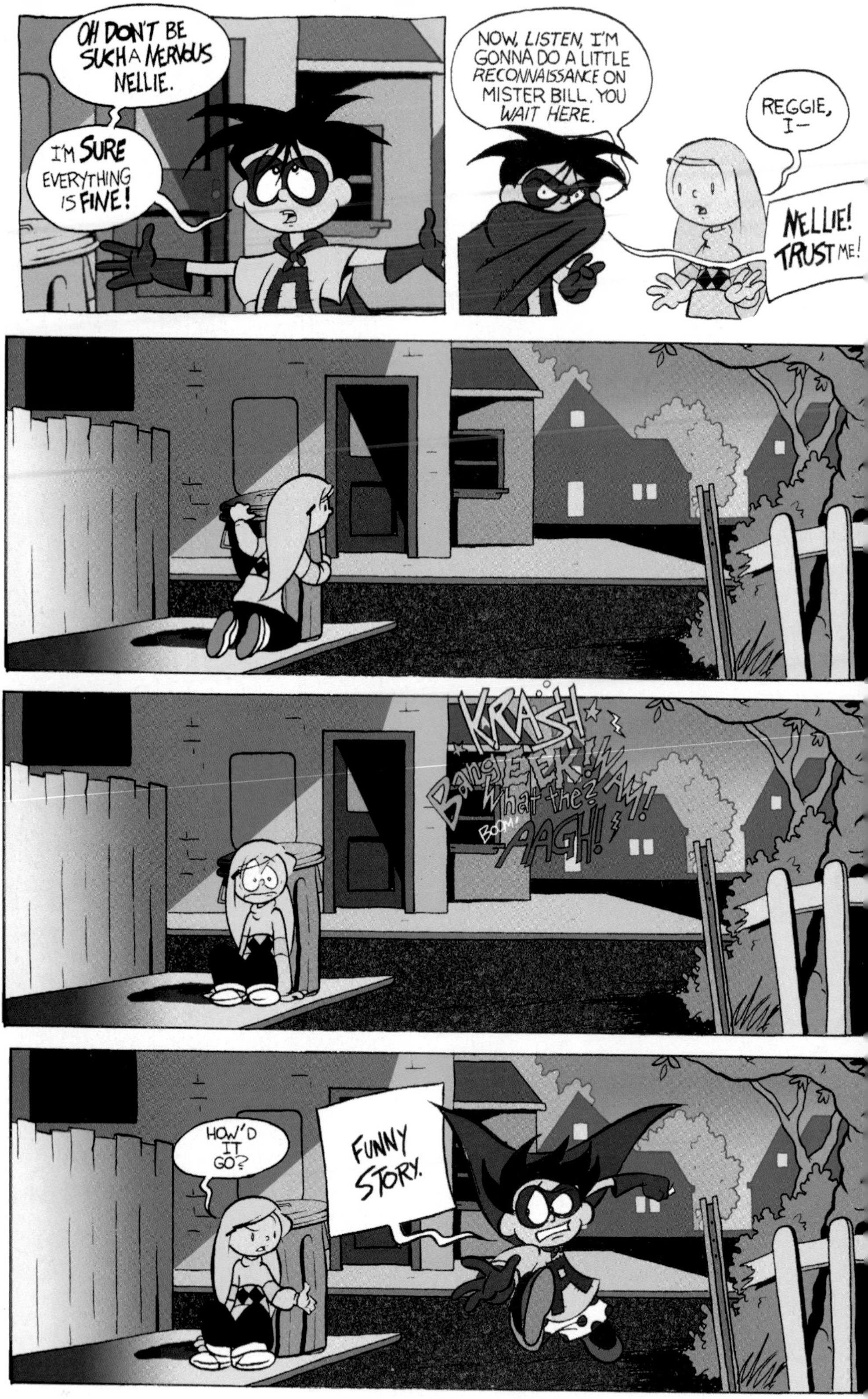
OH DON'T BE SUCH A NERVOUS NELLIE.
I'M SURE EVERYTHING IS FINE!
NOW, LISTEN, I'M GONNA DO A LITTLE RECONNAISSANCE ON MISTER BILL. YOU WAIT HERE.
REGGIE, I—
NELLIE! TRUST ME!
KRASH
Bang
EEEK!
WAM!
What the?
BOOM!
AAGH!
HOW'D IT GO?
FUNNY STORY.

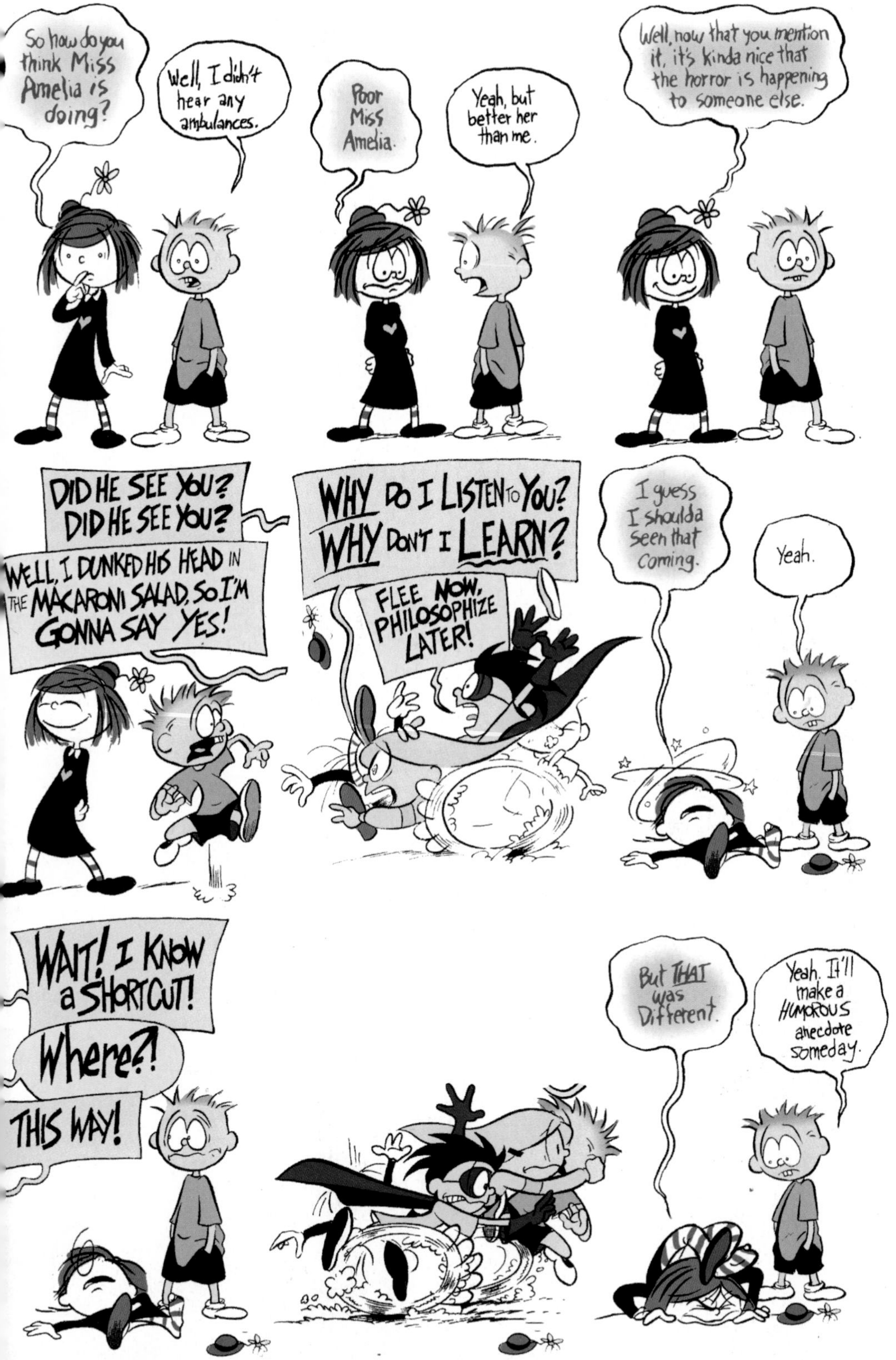
So how do you think Miss Amelia is doing?
Well, I didn't hear any ambulances.
Poor Miss Amelia.
Yeah, but better her than me.
Well, now that you mention it, it's kinda nice that the horror is happening to someone else.
DID HE SEE YOU? DID HE SEE YOU?
WELL, I DUNKED HIS HEAD IN THE MACARONI SALAD, SO I'M GONNA SAY YES!
WHY DO I LISTEN TO YOU? WHY DON'T I LEARN?
FLEE NOW, PHILOSOPHIZE LATER!
I guess I shoulda seen that coming.
Yeah.
WAIT! I KNOW a SHORTCUT!
Where?!
THIS WAY!
But THAT was Different.
Yeah. It'll make a HUMOROUS anecdote someday.

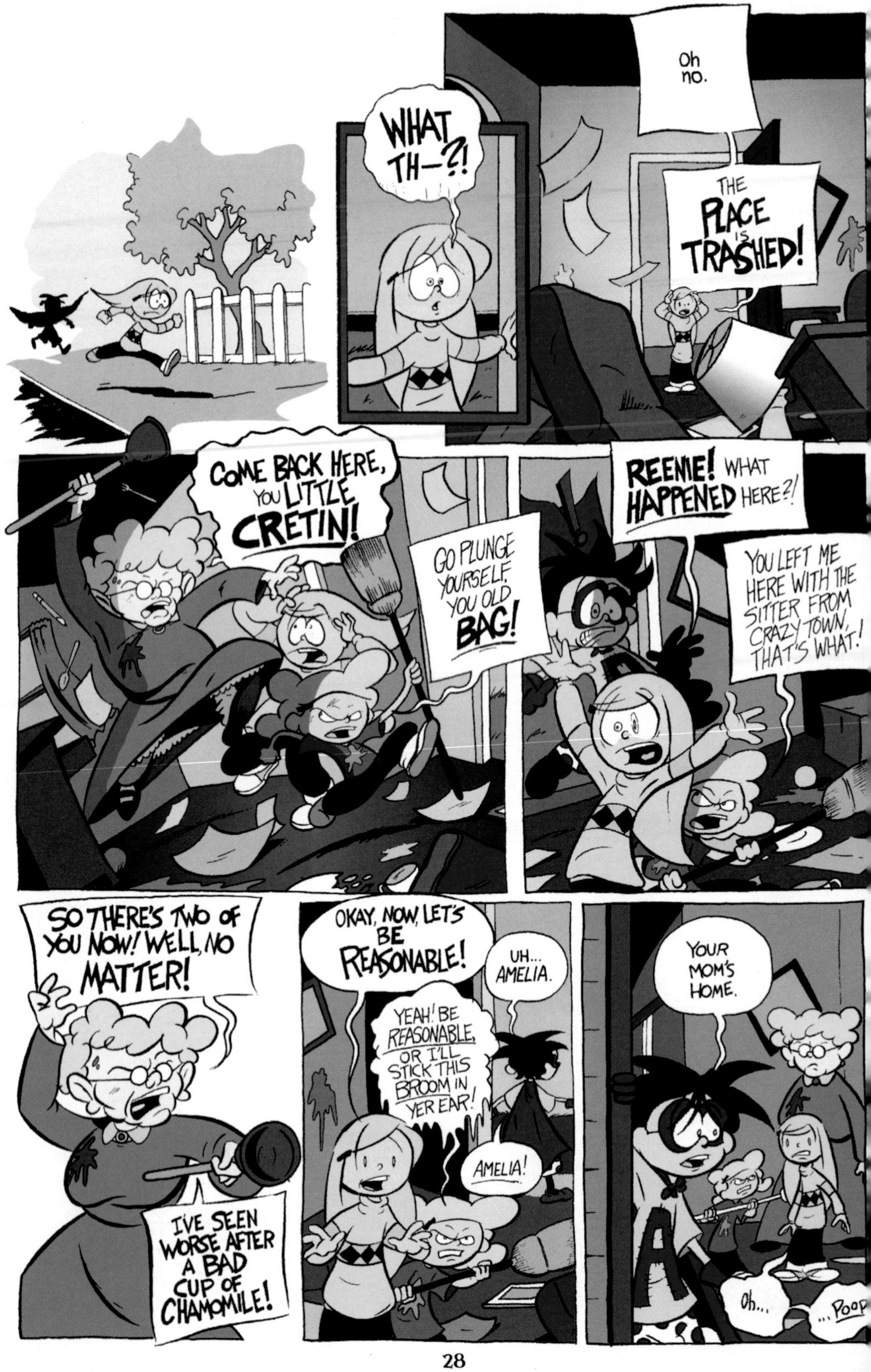

Oh no.
WHAT TH—?!
THE PLACE is TRASHED!
COME BACK HERE, YOU LITTLE CRETIN!
GO PLUNGE YOURSELF, YOU OLD BAG!
REENIE! WHAT HAPPENED HERE?!
YOU LEFT ME HERE WITH THE SITTER FROM CRAZY TOWN, THAT'S WHAT!
SO THERE'S TWO OF YOU NOW! WELL, NO MATTER!
I'VE SEEN WORSE AFTER A BAD CUP OF CHAMOMILE!
OKAY, NOW, LET'S BE REASONABLE!
YEAH! BE REASONABLE, OR I'LL STICK THIS BROOM IN YER EAR!
UH... AMELIA.
AMELIA!
YOUR MOM'S HOME.
Oh...
...Poop

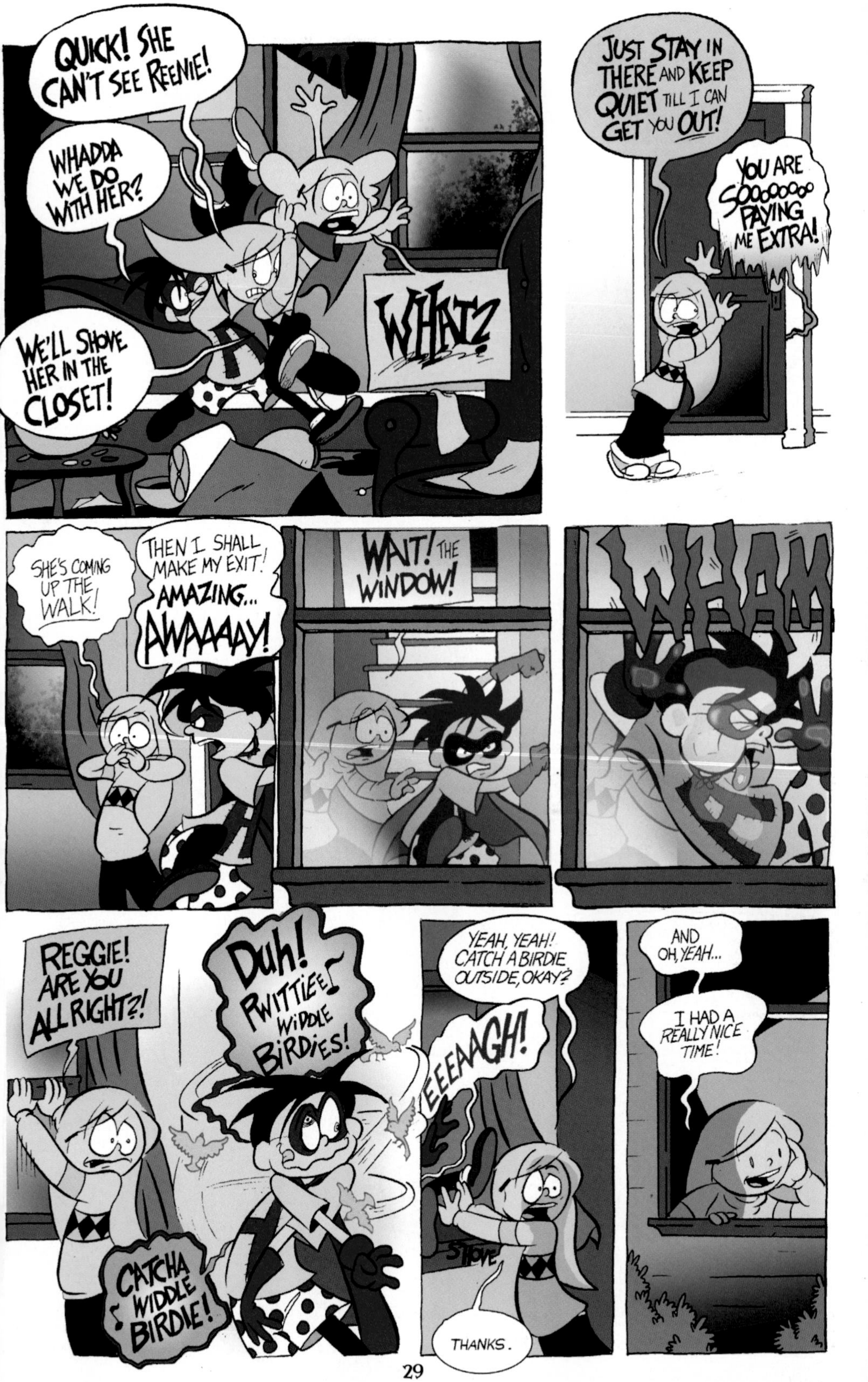
QUICK! SHE CAN'T SEE REENIE!
WHADDA WE DO WITH HER?
WE'LL SHOVE HER IN THE CLOSET!
WHAT?
JUST STAY IN THERE AND KEEP QUIET TILL I CAN GET YOU OUT!
YOU ARE SOOOOOOO PAYING ME EXTRA!
SHE'S COMING UP THE WALK!
THEN I SHALL MAKE MY EXIT! AMAZING... AWAAAAY!
WAIT! THE WINDOW!
WHAM
REGGIE! ARE YOU ALL RIGHT?!
Duh! RWITTLE! WIDDLE BIRDIES!
CATCHA WIDDLE BIRDIE!
YEAH, YEAH! CATCH A BIRDIE OUTSIDE, OKAY?
EEEAAGH!
SHOVE
THANKS.
AND OH, YEAH...
I HAD A REALLY NICE TIME!

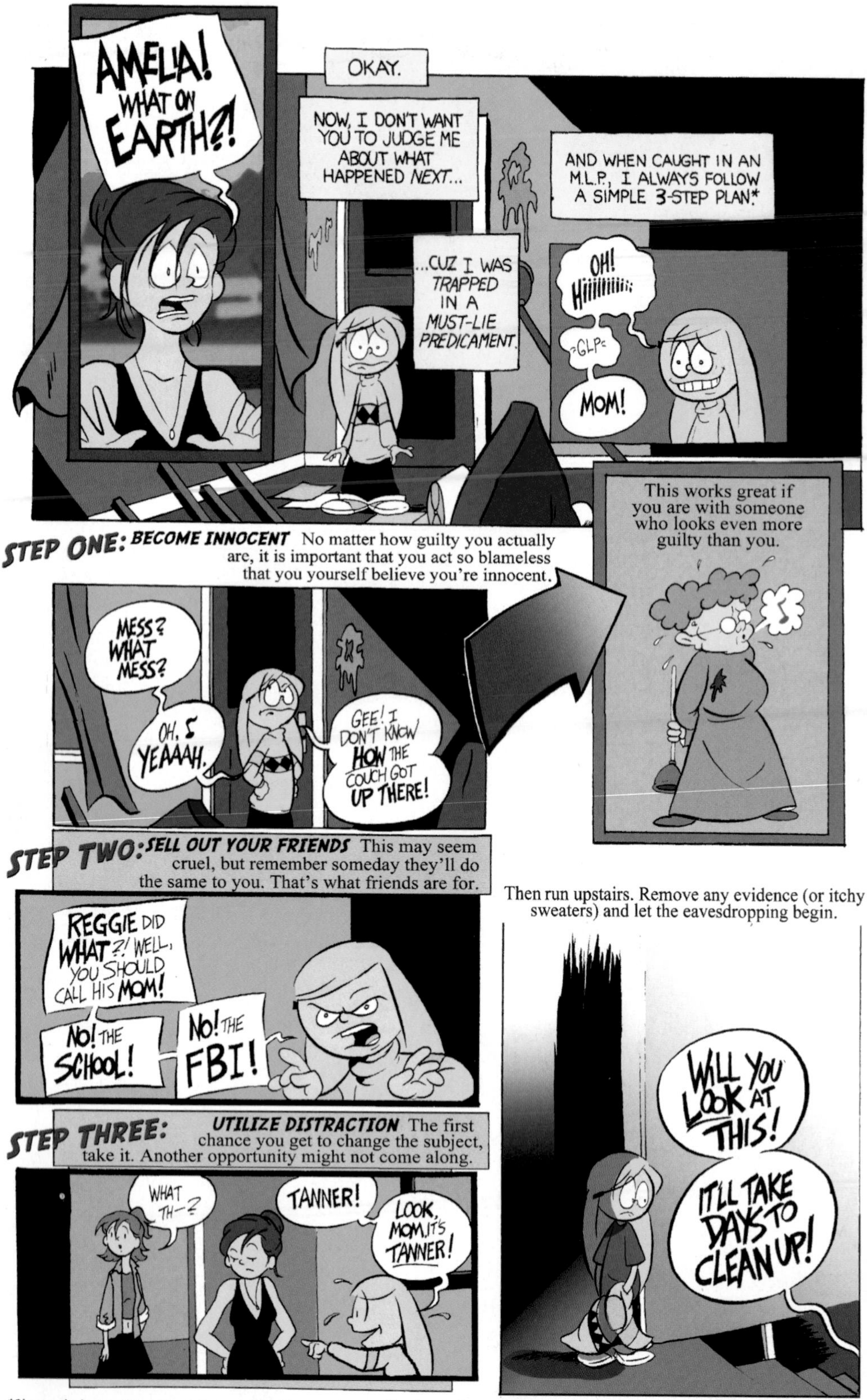
AMELIA! WHAT ON EARTH?!
OKAY.
NOW, I DON'T WANT YOU TO JUDGE ME ABOUT WHAT HAPPENED NEXT...
...CUZ I WAS TRAPPED IN A MUST-LIE PREDICAMENT.
AND WHEN CAUGHT IN AN M.L.P., I ALWAYS FOLLOW A SIMPLE 3-STEP PLAN.*
OH! Hiiiiiiii
GLP
MOM!
STEP ONE: BECOME INNOCENT No matter how guilty you actually are, it is important that you act so blameless that you yourself believe you're innocent.
MESS? WHAT MESS?
OH, YEAAAH.
GEE! I DON'T KNOW HOW THE COUCH GOT UP THERE!
This works great if you are with someone who looks even more guilty than you.
STEP TWO: SELL OUT YOUR FRIENDS This may seem cruel, but remember someday they'll do the same to you. That's what friends are for.
REGGIE DID WHAT?! WELL, YOU SHOULD CALL HIS MOM!
NO! THE SCHOOL!
NO! THE FBI!
STEP THREE: UTILIZE DISTRACTION The first chance you get to change the subject, take it. Another opportunity might not come along.
WHAT TH-?
TANNER!
LOOK, MOM, IT'S TANNER!
Then run upstairs. Remove any evidence (or itchy sweaters) and let the eavesdropping begin.
WILL YOU LOOK AT THIS!
IT'LL TAKE DAYS TO CLEAN UP!

*Please don't try this plan at home, and when you do try this plan at home, please leave my name out of it—Amelia Louise McBride

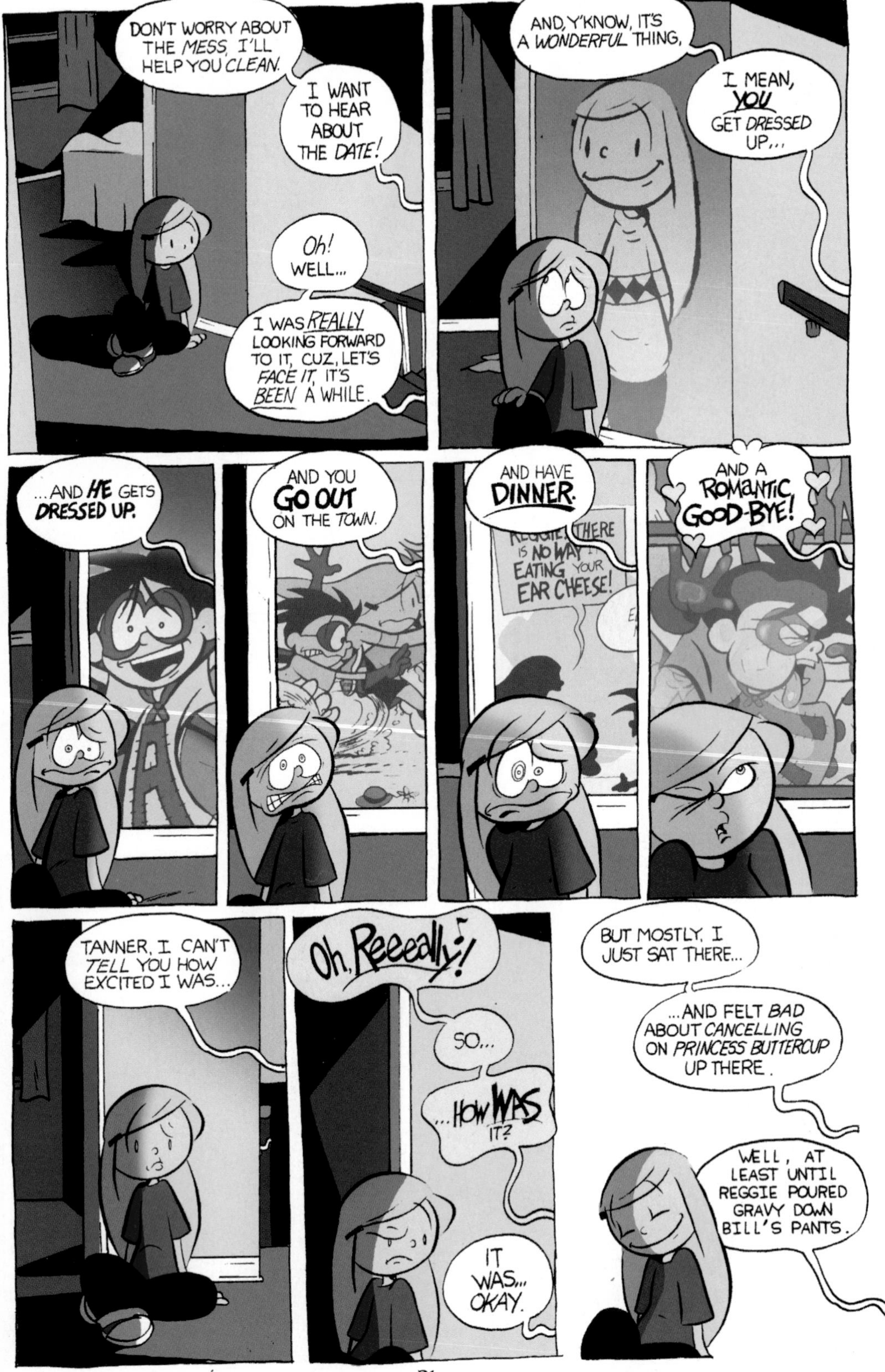
DON'T WORRY ABOUT THE MESS, I'LL HELP YOU CLEAN.
I WANT TO HEAR ABOUT THE DATE!
Oh! WELL...
I WAS REALLY LOOKING FORWARD TO IT, CUZ, LET'S FACE IT, IT'S BEEN A WHILE.
AND, Y'KNOW, IT'S A WONDERFUL THING,
I MEAN, YOU GET DRESSED UP,...
...AND HE GETS DRESSED UP.
AND YOU GO OUT ON THE TOWN.
AND HAVE DINNER.
THERE IS NO WAY EATING YOUR EAR CHEESE!
AND A ROMANTIC GOOD-BYE!
TANNER, I CAN'T TELL YOU HOW EXCITED I WAS...
Oh, Reeeally!
SO...
...HOW WAS IT?
IT WAS... OKAY.
BUT MOSTLY, I JUST SAT THERE...
...AND FELT BAD ABOUT CANCELLING ON PRINCESS BUTTERCUP UP THERE.
WELL, AT LEAST UNTIL REGGIE POURED GRAVY DOWN BILL'S PANTS.

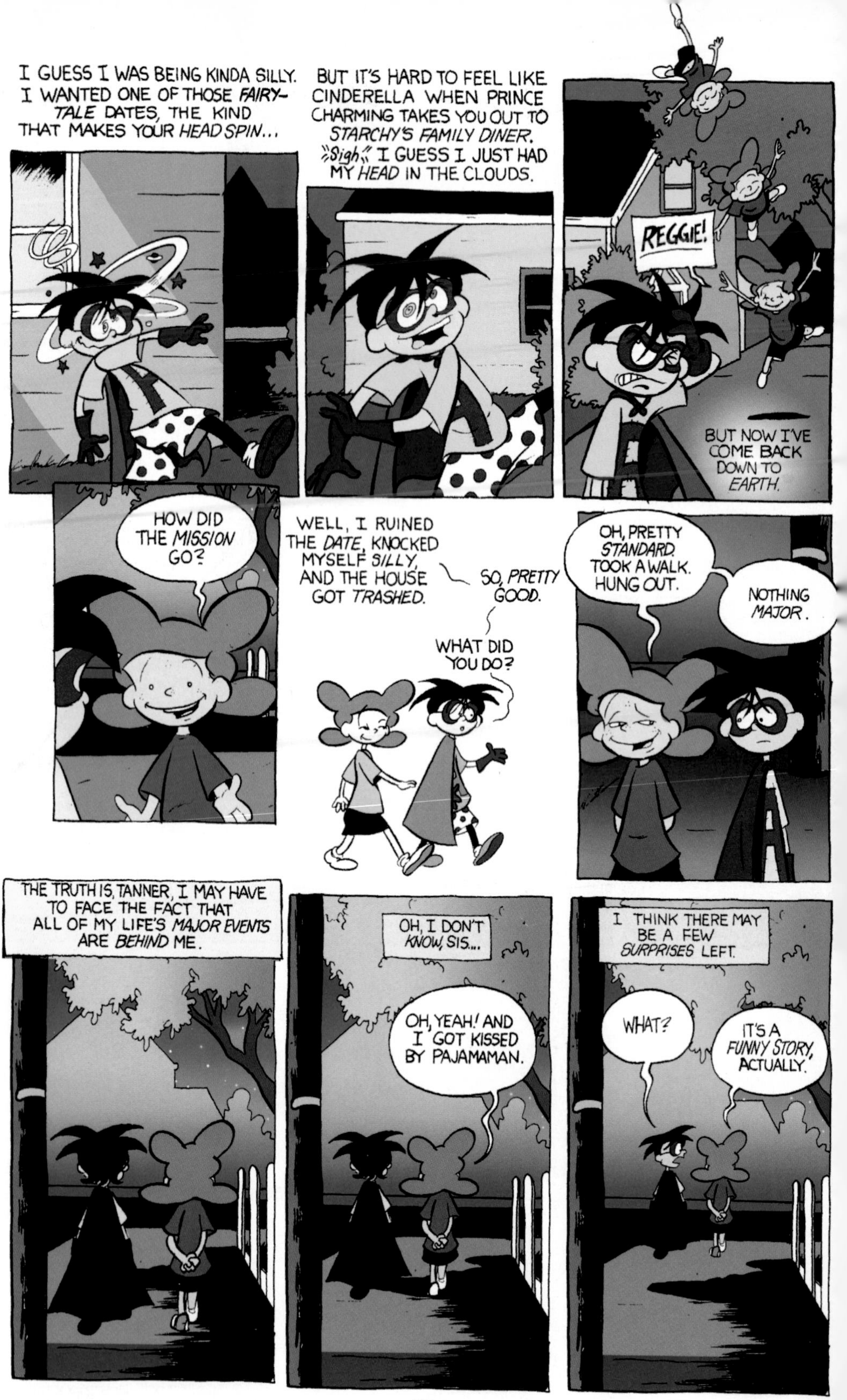
I GUESS I WAS BEING KINDA SILLY. I WANTED ONE OF THOSE *FAIRY-TALE* DATES, THE KIND THAT MAKES YOUR *HEAD SPIN*...
BUT IT'S HARD TO FEEL LIKE CINDERELLA WHEN PRINCE CHARMING TAKES YOU OUT TO *STARCHY'S FAMILY DINER.* *Sigh* I GUESS I JUST HAD MY *HEAD* IN THE CLOUDS.
REGGIE!
BUT NOW I'VE COME BACK DOWN TO *EARTH.*
HOW DID THE *MISSION* GO?
WELL, I RUINED THE *DATE*, KNOCKED MYSELF *SILLY*, AND THE HOUSE GOT *TRASHED.*
SO, *PRETTY* GOOD.
WHAT DID YOU DO?
OH, PRETTY *STANDARD.* TOOK A WALK. HUNG OUT.
NOTHING *MAJOR*.
THE TRUTH IS, TANNER, I MAY HAVE TO FACE THE FACT THAT ALL OF MY LIFE'S *MAJOR EVENTS* ARE *BEHIND* ME.
OH, I DON'T *KNOW*, SIS...
OH, YEAH! AND I GOT KISSED BY PAJAMAMAN.
I THINK THERE MAY BE A FEW *SURPRISES* LEFT.
WHAT?
IT'S A *FUNNY STORY*, ACTUALLY.

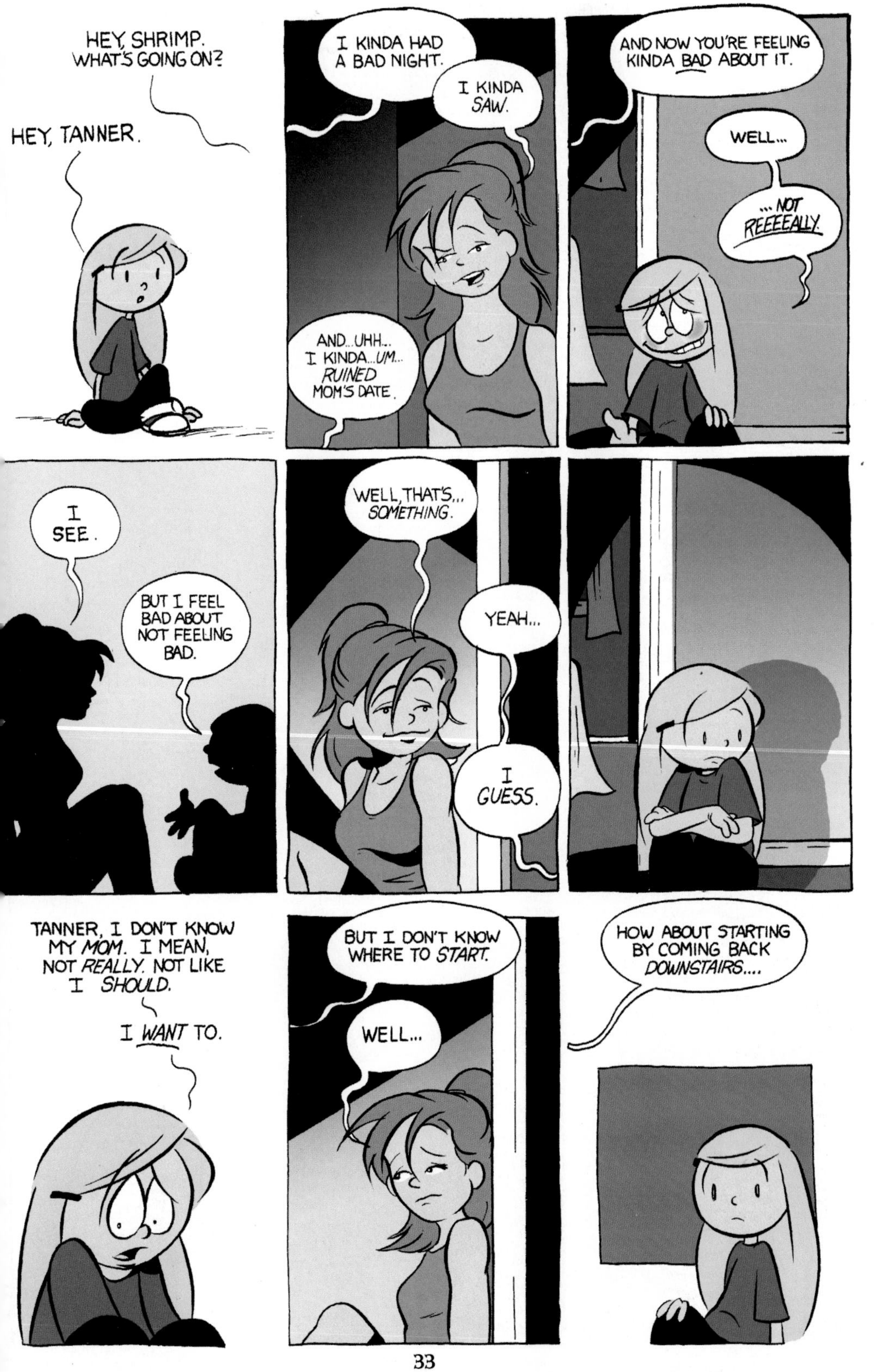
HEY, SHRIMP. WHAT'S GOING ON?
HEY, TANNER.
I KINDA HAD A BAD NIGHT.
I KINDA SAW.
AND...UHH... I KINDA...UM... RUINED MOM'S DATE.
AND NOW YOU'RE FEELING KINDA BAD ABOUT IT.
WELL...
...NOT REEEEALLY.
I SEE.
BUT I FEEL BAD ABOUT NOT FEELING BAD.
WELL, THAT'S... SOMETHING.
YEAH...
I GUESS.
TANNER, I DON'T KNOW MY MOM. I MEAN, NOT REALLY. NOT LIKE I SHOULD.
I WANT TO.
BUT I DON'T KNOW WHERE TO START.
WELL...
HOW ABOUT STARTING BY COMING BACK DOWNSTAIRS....

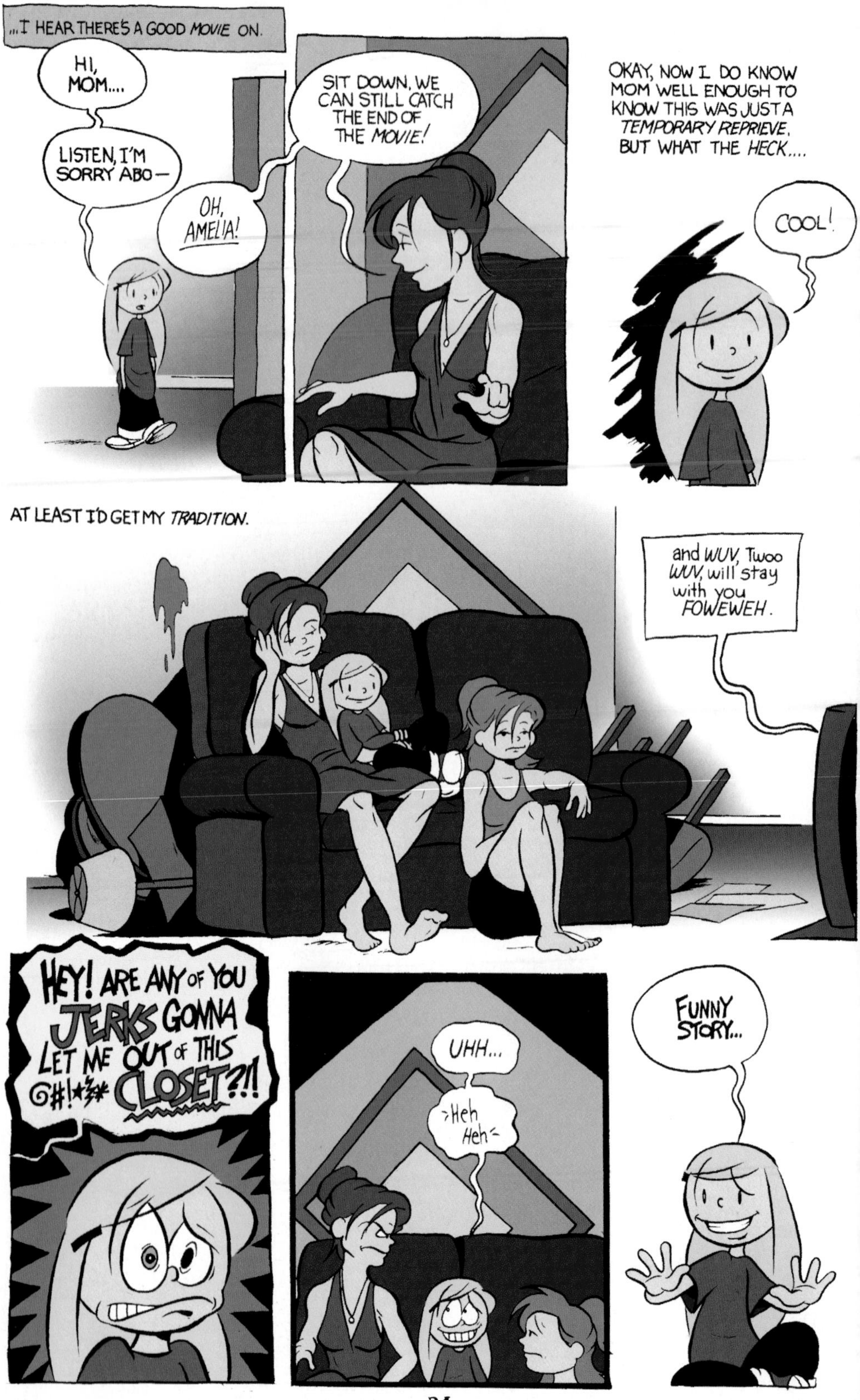
...I HEAR THERE'S A GOOD MOVIE ON.
HI, MOM....
LISTEN, I'M SORRY ABO—
OH, AMELIA!
SIT DOWN, WE CAN STILL CATCH THE END OF THE MOVIE!
OKAY, NOW I DO KNOW MOM WELL ENOUGH TO KNOW THIS WAS JUST A TEMPORARY REPRIEVE, BUT WHAT THE HECK....
COOL!
AT LEAST I'D GET MY TRADITION.
and WUV, Twoo WUV, will stay with you FOWEWEH.
HEY! ARE ANY OF YOU JERKS GONNA LET ME OUT OF THIS @#!*%* CLOSET?!!
UHH...
>Heh Heh<
FUNNY STORY...

The Runaways

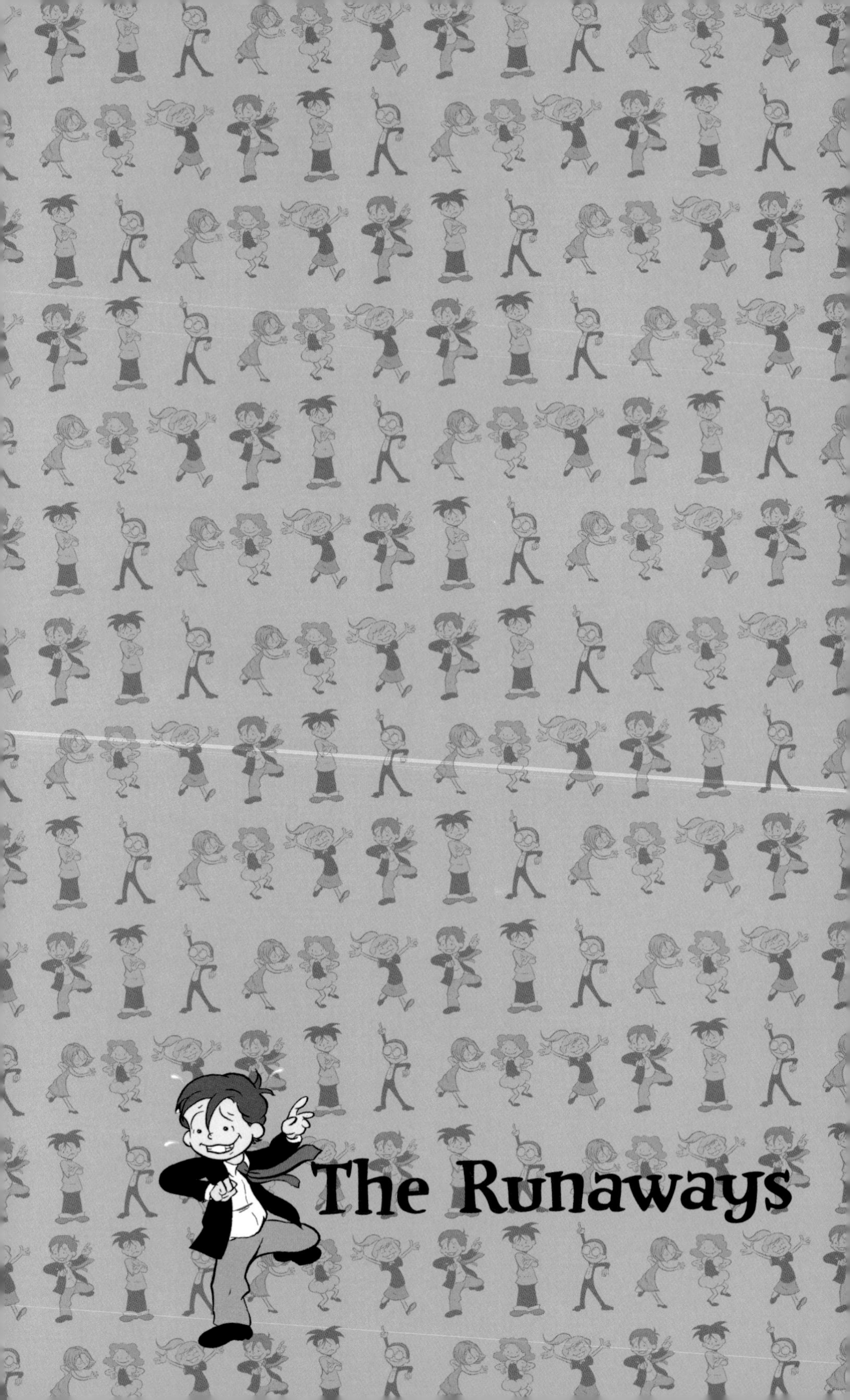

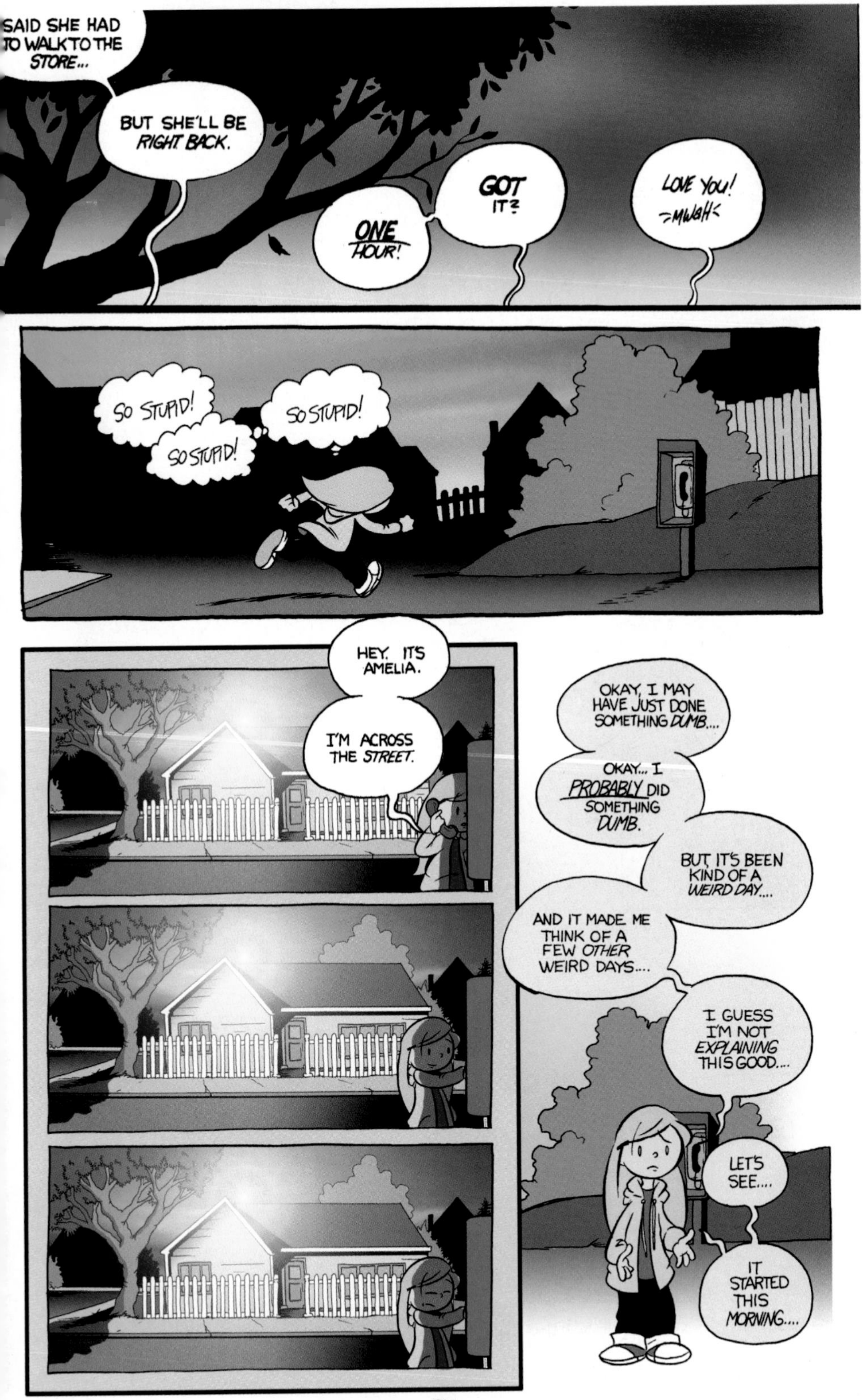
SAID SHE HAD TO WALK TO THE STORE...
BUT SHE'LL BE RIGHT BACK.
ONE HOUR!
GOT IT?
LOVE YOU! =MWAH!=
SO STUPID!
SO STUPID!
SO STUPID!
HEY. IT'S AMELIA.
I'M ACROSS THE STREET.
OKAY, I MAY HAVE JUST DONE SOMETHING DUMB....
OKAY... I PROBABLY DID SOMETHING DUMB.
BUT, IT'S BEEN KIND OF A WEIRD DAY....
AND IT MADE ME THINK OF A FEW OTHER WEIRD DAYS....
I GUESS I'M NOT EXPLAINING THIS GOOD....
LET'S SEE....
IT STARTED THIS MORNING....

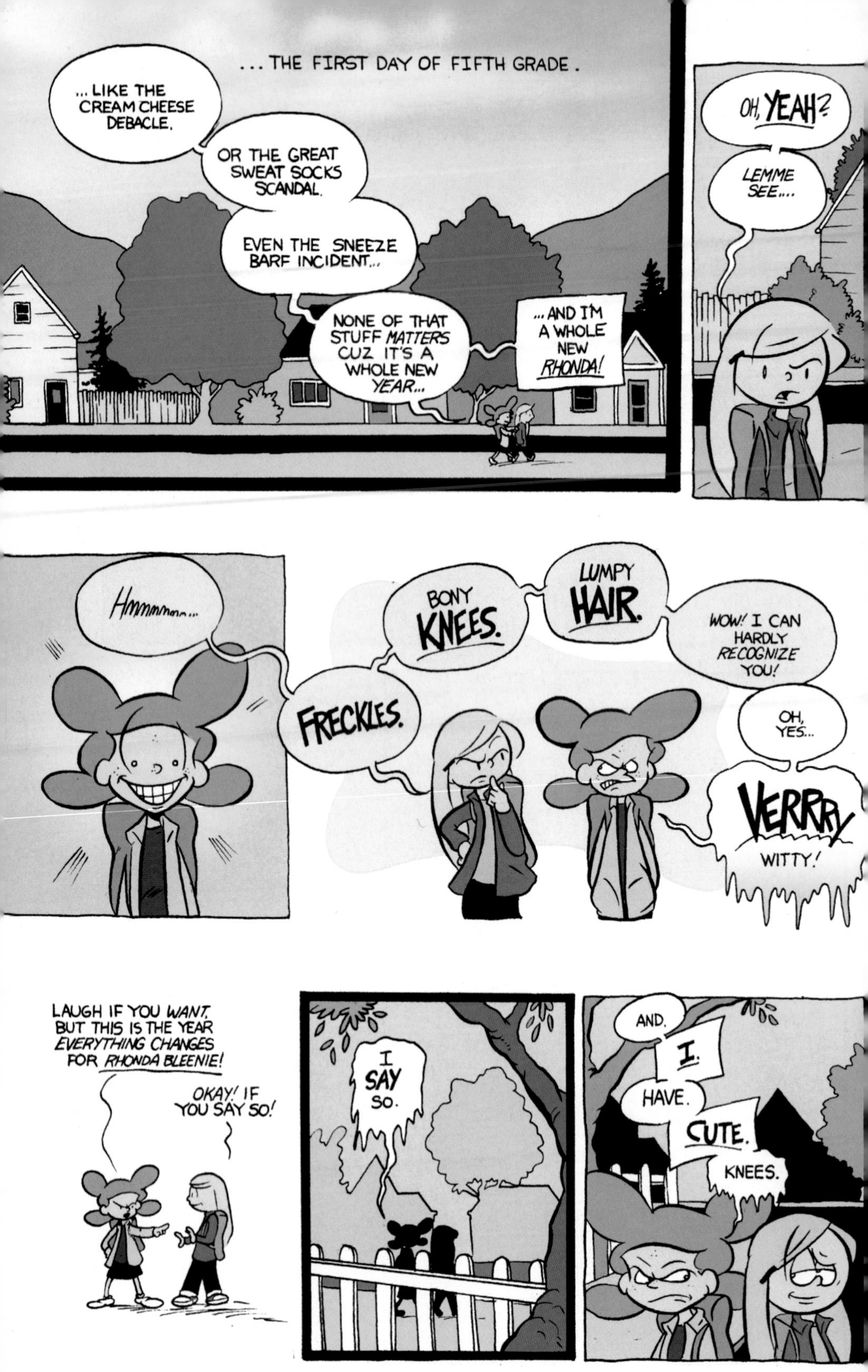
. . . THE FIRST DAY OF FIFTH GRADE .
... LIKE THE CREAM CHEESE DEBACLE.
OR THE GREAT SWEAT SOCKS SCANDAL.
EVEN THE SNEEZE BARF INCIDENT...
NONE OF THAT STUFF *MATTERS* CUZ IT'S A WHOLE NEW *YEAR*...
... AND I'M A WHOLE NEW *RHONDA!*
OH, YEAH?
LEMME SEE....
Hmmmmm....
FRECKLES.
BONY KNEES.
LUMPY HAIR.
WOW! I CAN HARDLY *RECOGNIZE* YOU!
OH, YES...
VERRRY WITTY!
LAUGH IF YOU *WANT*, BUT THIS IS THE YEAR *EVERYTHING CHANGES* FOR *RHONDA BLEENIE!*
OKAY! IF YOU SAY SO!
I SAY SO.
AND.
I.
HAVE.
CUTE.
KNEES.

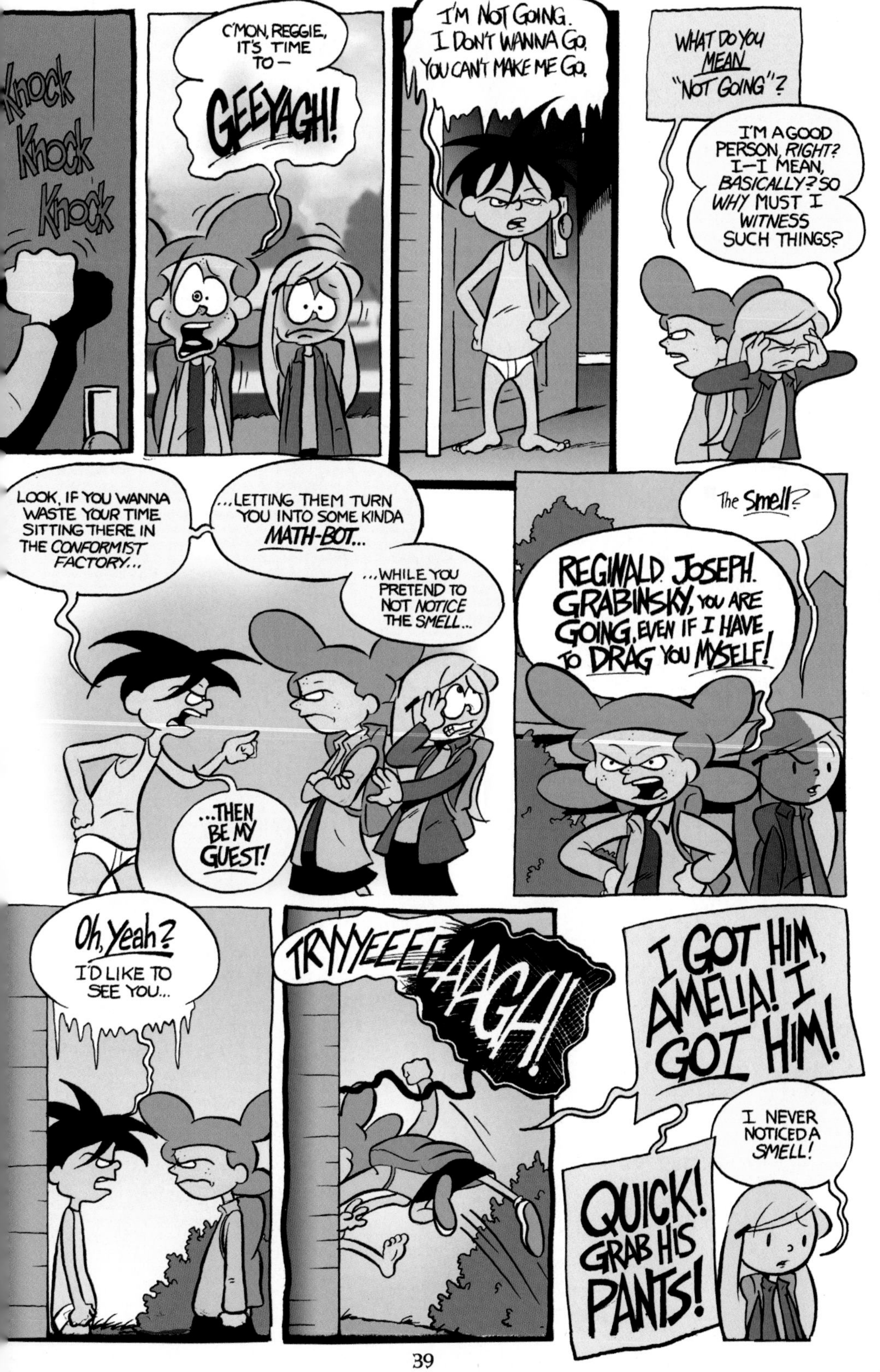
Knock Knock Knock
C'MON, REGGIE, IT'S TIME TO—
GEEYAGH!
I'M NOT GOING. I DON'T WANNA GO. YOU CAN'T MAKE ME GO.
WHAT DO YOU MEAN "NOT GOING"?
I'M A GOOD PERSON, RIGHT? I—I MEAN, BASICALLY? SO WHY MUST I WITNESS SUCH THINGS?
LOOK, IF YOU WANNA WASTE YOUR TIME SITTING THERE IN THE CONFORMIST FACTORY...
...LETTING THEM TURN YOU INTO SOME KINDA MATH-BOT...
...WHILE YOU PRETEND TO NOT NOTICE THE SMELL...
...THEN BE MY GUEST!
The Smell?
REGINALD JOSEPH GRABINSKY, YOU ARE GOING, EVEN IF I HAVE TO DRAG YOU MYSELF!
Oh, Yeah? I'D LIKE TO SEE YOU...
TRYYYEEEEAAGH!
I GOT HIM, AMELIA! I GOT HIM!
QUICK! GRAB HIS PANTS!
I NEVER NOTICED A SMELL!

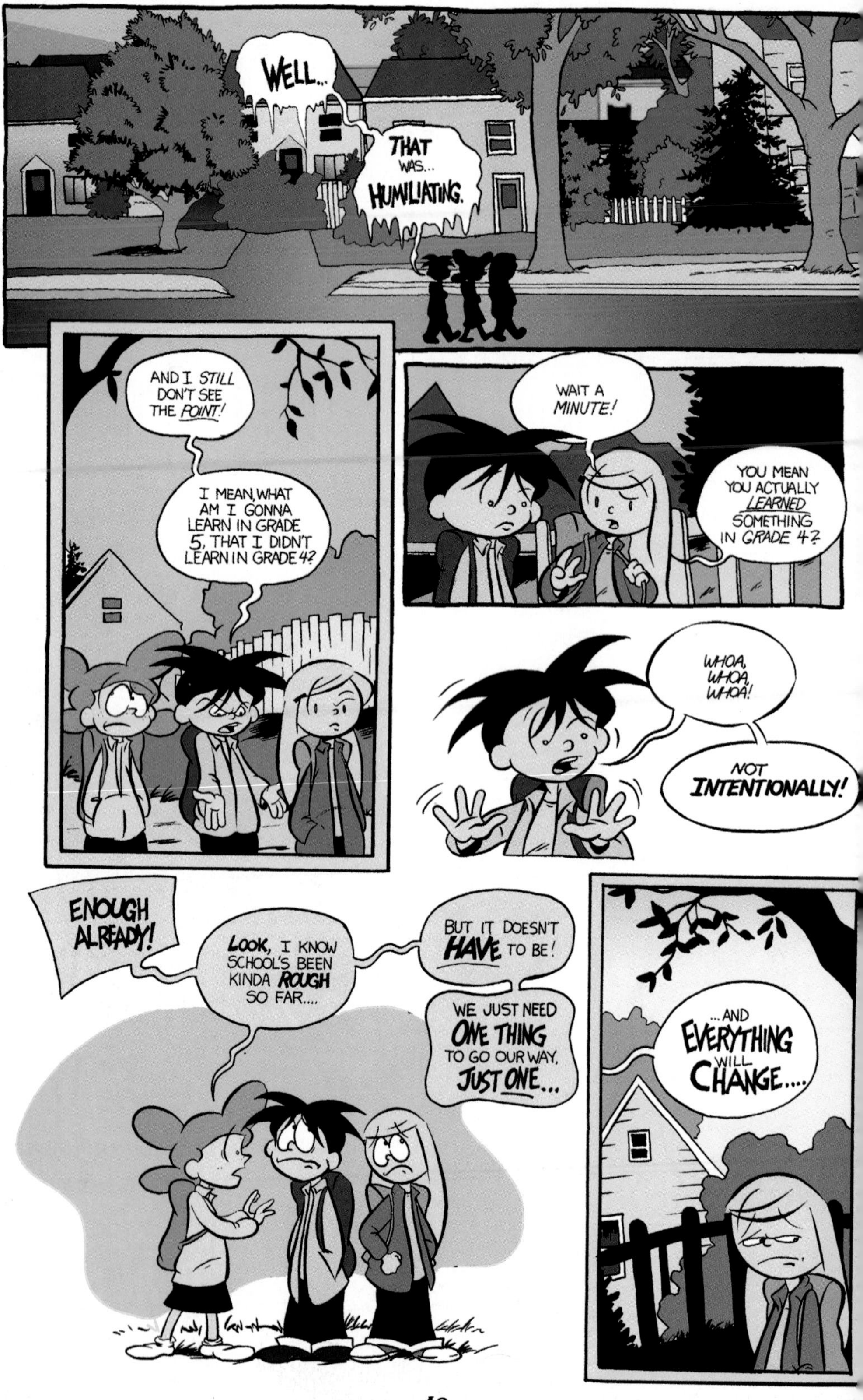
WELL...
THAT WAS... HUMILIATING.
AND I STILL DON'T SEE THE POINT!
I MEAN, WHAT AM I GONNA LEARN IN GRADE 5, THAT I DIDN'T LEARN IN GRADE 4?
WAIT A MINUTE!
YOU MEAN YOU ACTUALLY LEARNED SOMETHING IN GRADE 4?
WHOA, WHOA, WHOA!
NOT INTENTIONALLY!
ENOUGH ALREADY!
LOOK, I KNOW SCHOOL'S BEEN KINDA ROUGH SO FAR....
BUT IT DOESN'T HAVE TO BE!
WE JUST NEED ONE THING TO GO OUR WAY, JUST ONE...
...AND EVERYTHING WILL CHANGE....

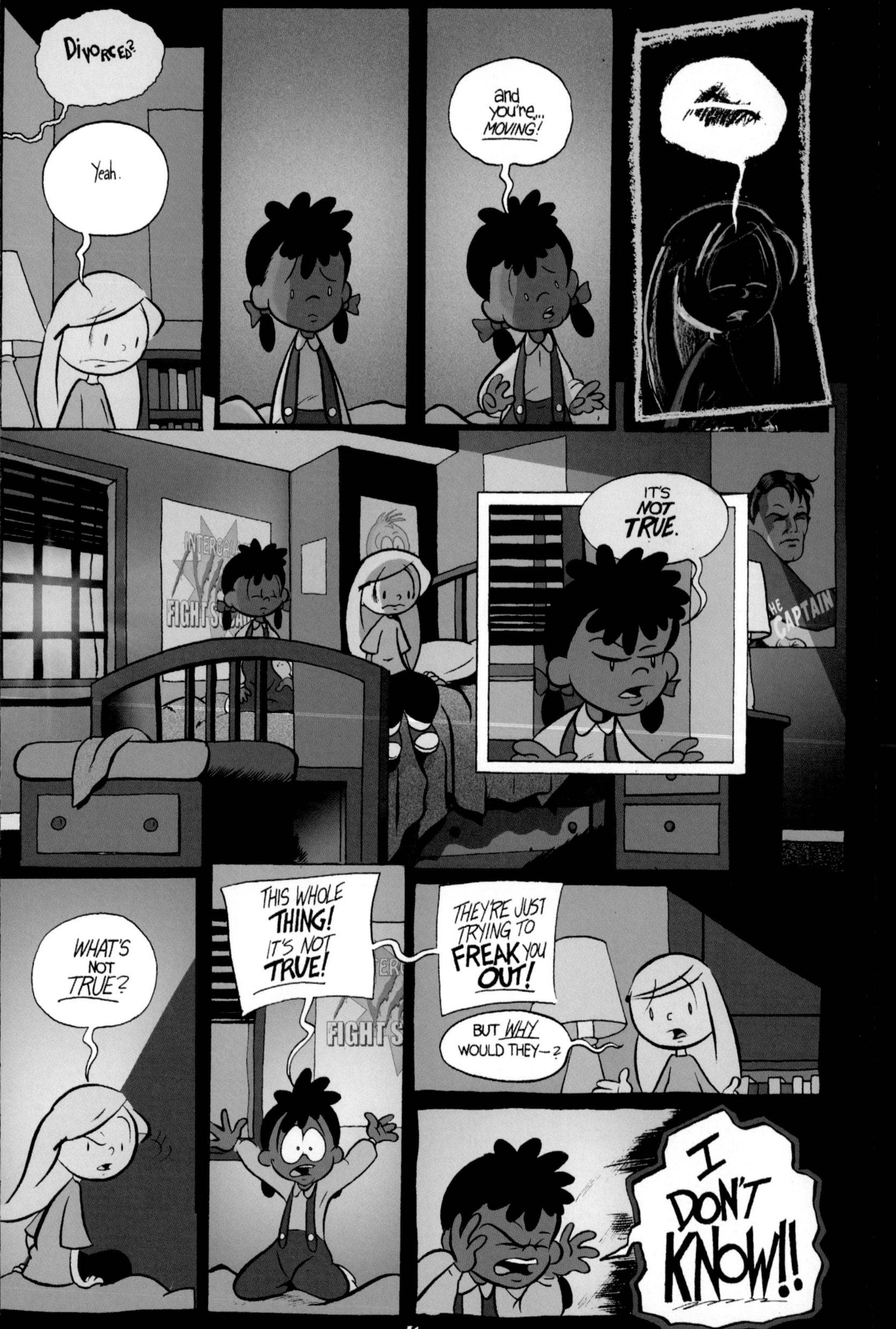
Divorced?
Yeah.
and you're... MOVING!
IT'S NOT TRUE.
WHAT'S NOT TRUE?
THIS WHOLE THING! IT'S NOT TRUE!
THEY'RE JUST TRYING TO FREAK YOU OUT!
BUT WHY WOULD THEY—?
I DON'T KNOW!!

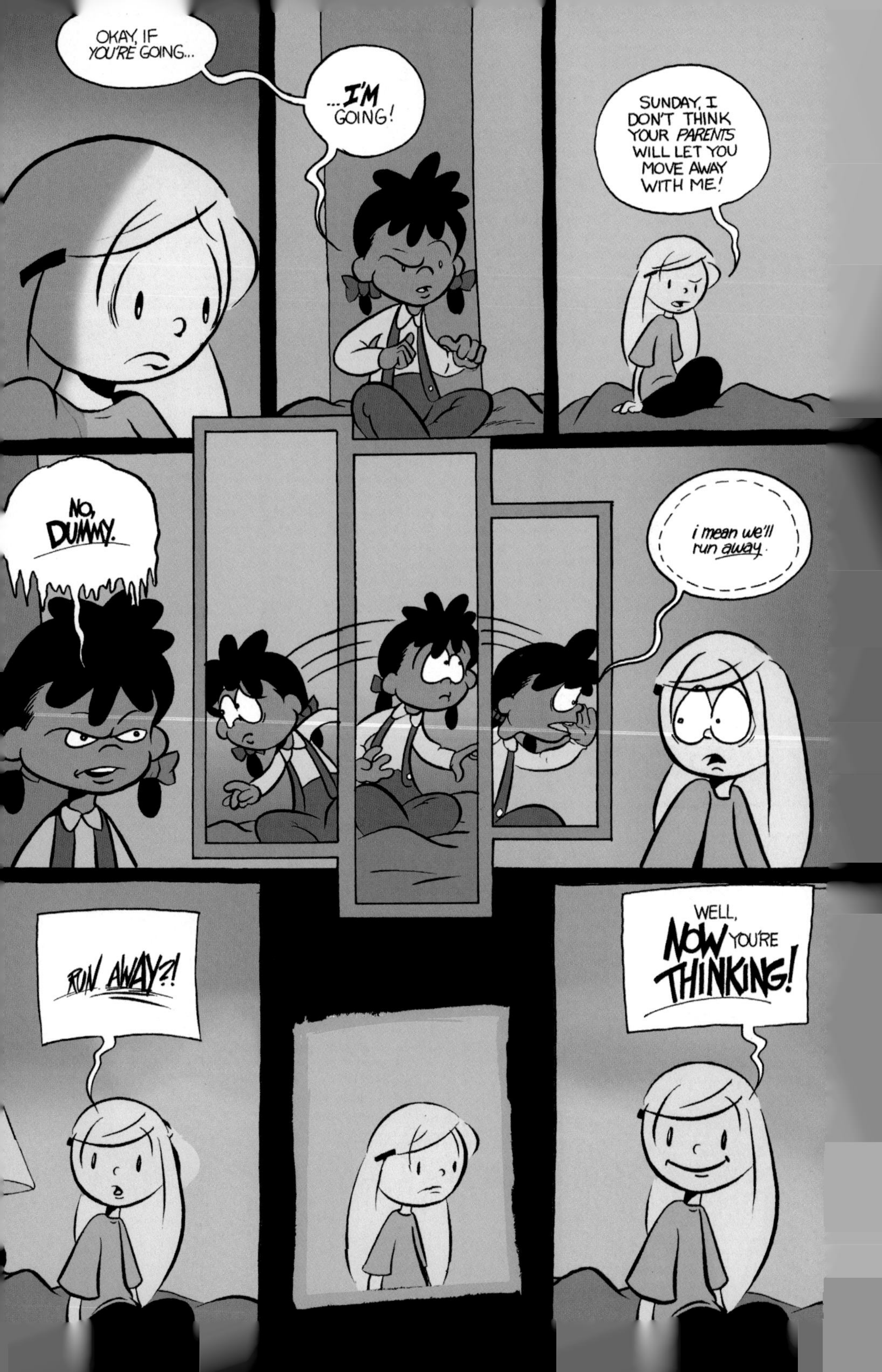
OKAY, IF YOU'RE GOING...
...I'M GOING!
SUNDAY, I DON'T THINK YOUR PARENTS WILL LET YOU MOVE AWAY WITH ME!
NO, DUMMY.
i mean we'll run away.
RUN AWAY?!
WELL, NOW YOU'RE THINKING!

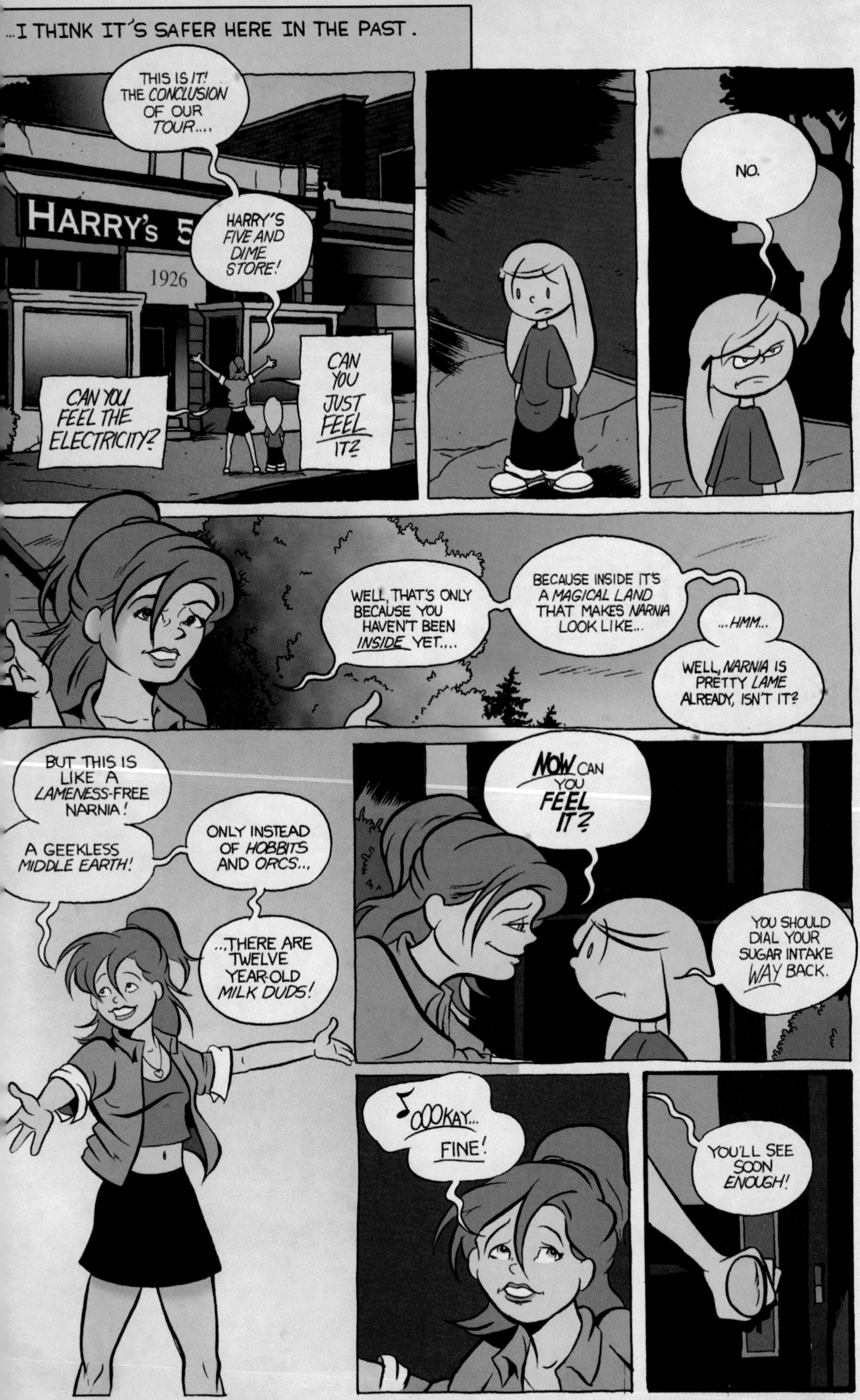
...I THINK IT'S SAFER HERE IN THE PAST.
THIS IS *IT!* THE *CONCLUSION* OF OUR *TOUR*....
HARRY'S 5
1926
HARRY'S *FIVE AND DIME STORE!*
CAN YOU FEEL THE ELECTRICITY?
CAN YOU JUST FEEL IT?
NO.
WELL, THAT'S ONLY BECAUSE YOU HAVEN'T BEEN INSIDE YET....
BECAUSE INSIDE IT'S A *MAGICAL LAND* THAT MAKES *NARNIA* LOOK LIKE...
...*HMM*...
WELL, *NARNIA* IS PRETTY *LAME* ALREADY, ISN'T IT?
BUT THIS IS LIKE A *LAMENESS-FREE* NARNIA!
A GEEKLESS *MIDDLE EARTH!*
ONLY INSTEAD OF *HOBBITS* AND *ORCS*...
...THERE ARE TWELVE YEAR-OLD *MILK DUDS!*
NOW CAN YOU *FEEL IT?*
YOU SHOULD DIAL YOUR SUGAR INTAKE WAY BACK.
OOOKAY... FINE!
YOU'LL SEE SOON *ENOUGH!*

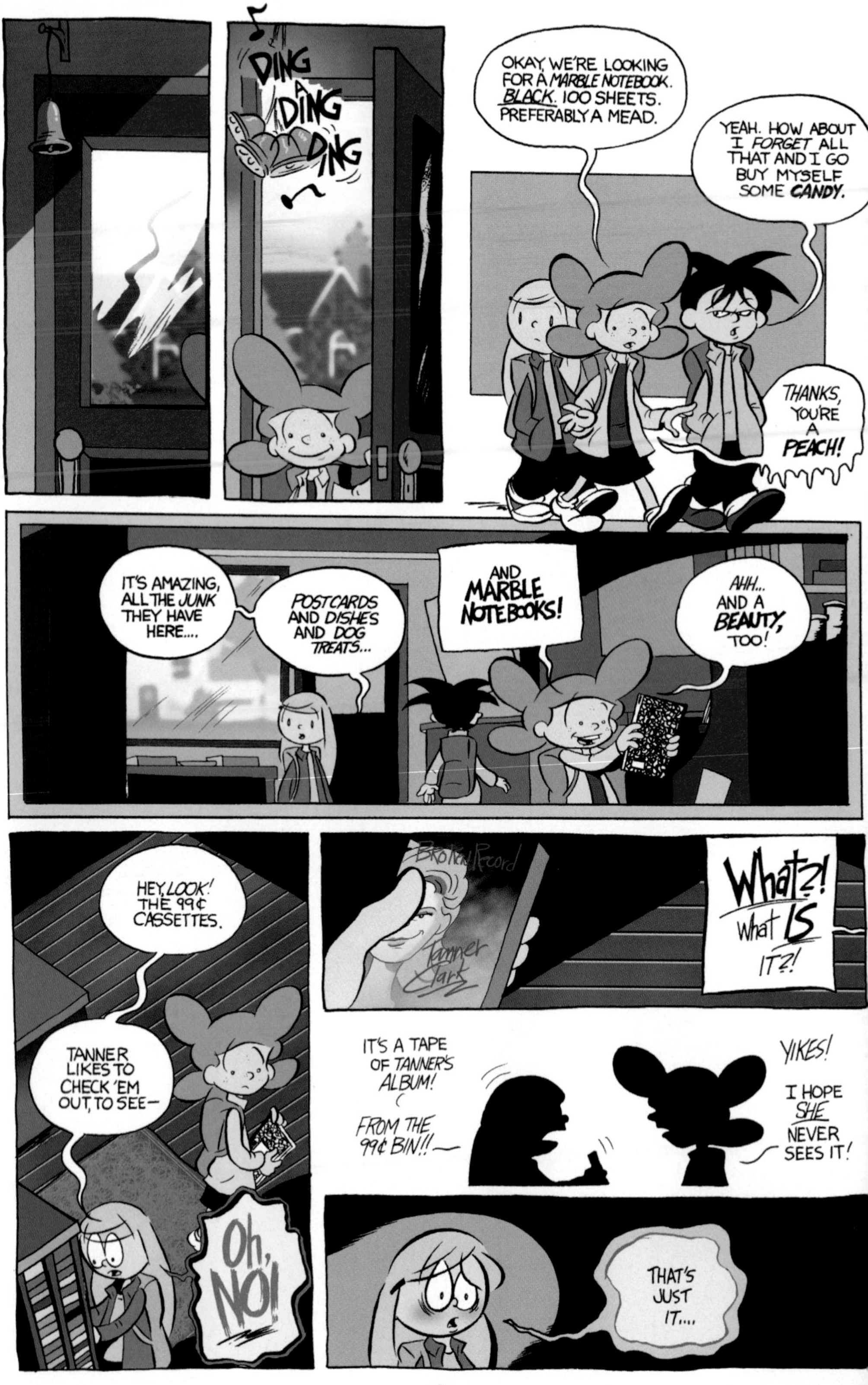
DING A DING DING
OKAY, WE'RE LOOKING FOR A MARBLE NOTEBOOK. BLACK. 100 SHEETS. PREFERABLY A MEAD.
YEAH. HOW ABOUT I FORGET ALL THAT AND I GO BUY MYSELF SOME CANDY.
THANKS, YOU'RE A PEACH!
IT'S AMAZING, ALL THE JUNK THEY HAVE HERE....
POSTCARDS AND DISHES AND DOG TREATS...
AND MARBLE NOTEBOOKS!
AHH... AND A BEAUTY, TOO!
HEY, LOOK! THE 99¢ CASSETTES.
TANNER LIKES TO CHECK 'EM OUT, TO SEE—
Oh, NO!
Broken Record
Tanner Clark
What?! What IS IT?!
IT'S A TAPE OF TANNER'S ALBUM!
FROM THE 99¢ BIN!!
YIKES!
I HOPE SHE NEVER SEES IT!
THAT'S JUST IT....

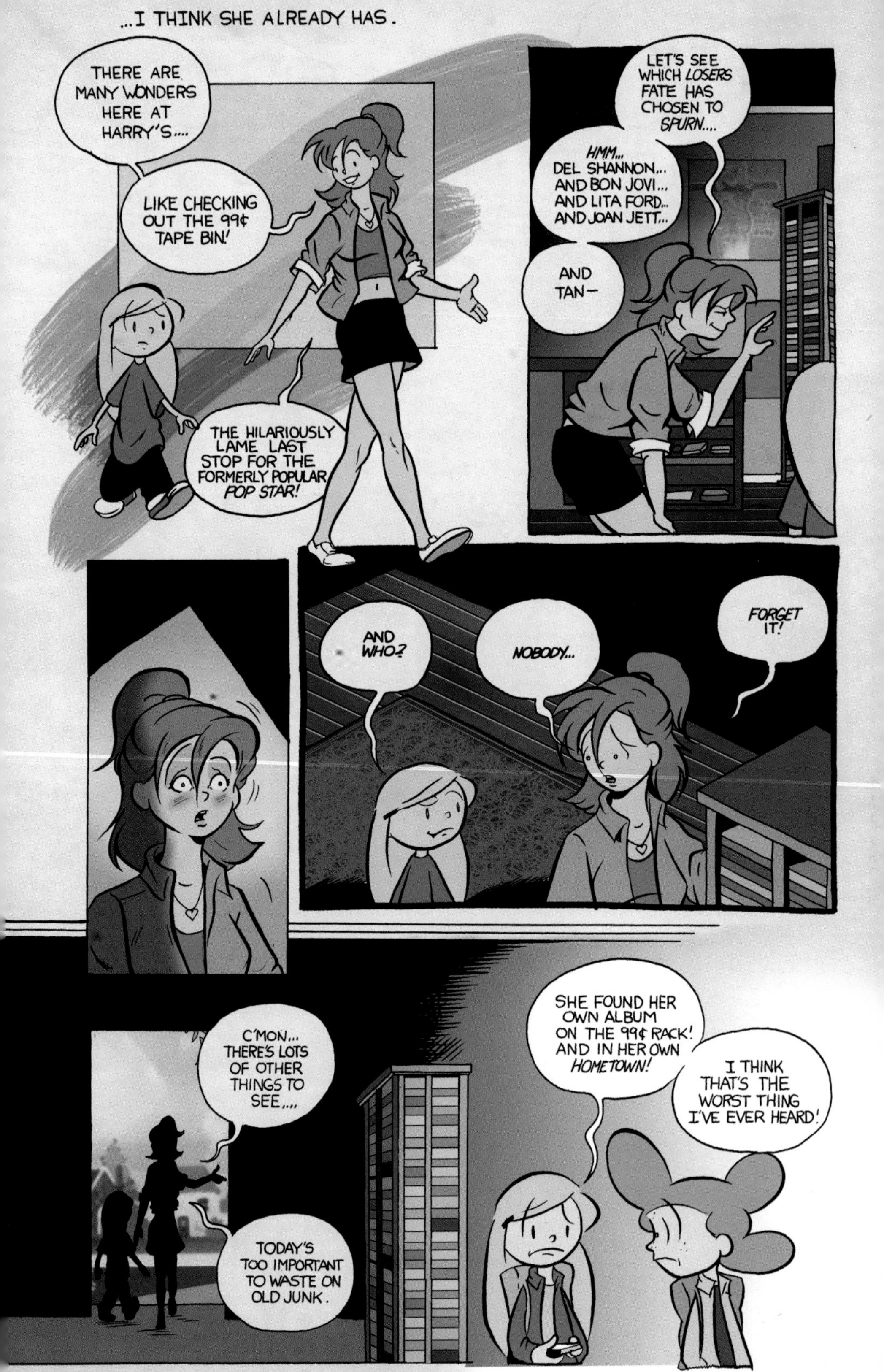

...I THINK SHE ALREADY HAS.
THERE ARE MANY WONDERS HERE AT HARRY'S....
LIKE CHECKING OUT THE 99¢ TAPE BIN!
THE HILARIOUSLY LAME LAST STOP FOR THE FORMERLY POPULAR *POP STAR!*
LET'S SEE WHICH *LOSERS* FATE HAS CHOSEN TO *SPURN*....
HMM... DEL SHANNON... AND BON JOVI... AND LITA FORD... AND JOAN JETT...
AND TAN–
AND WHO?
NOBODY...
FORGET IT!
C'MON... THERE'S LOTS OF OTHER THINGS TO SEE....
TODAY'S TOO IMPORTANT TO WASTE ON OLD JUNK.
SHE FOUND HER OWN ALBUM ON THE 99¢ RACK! AND IN HER OWN *HOMETOWN!*
I THINK THAT'S THE WORST THING I'VE EVER HEARD!

48

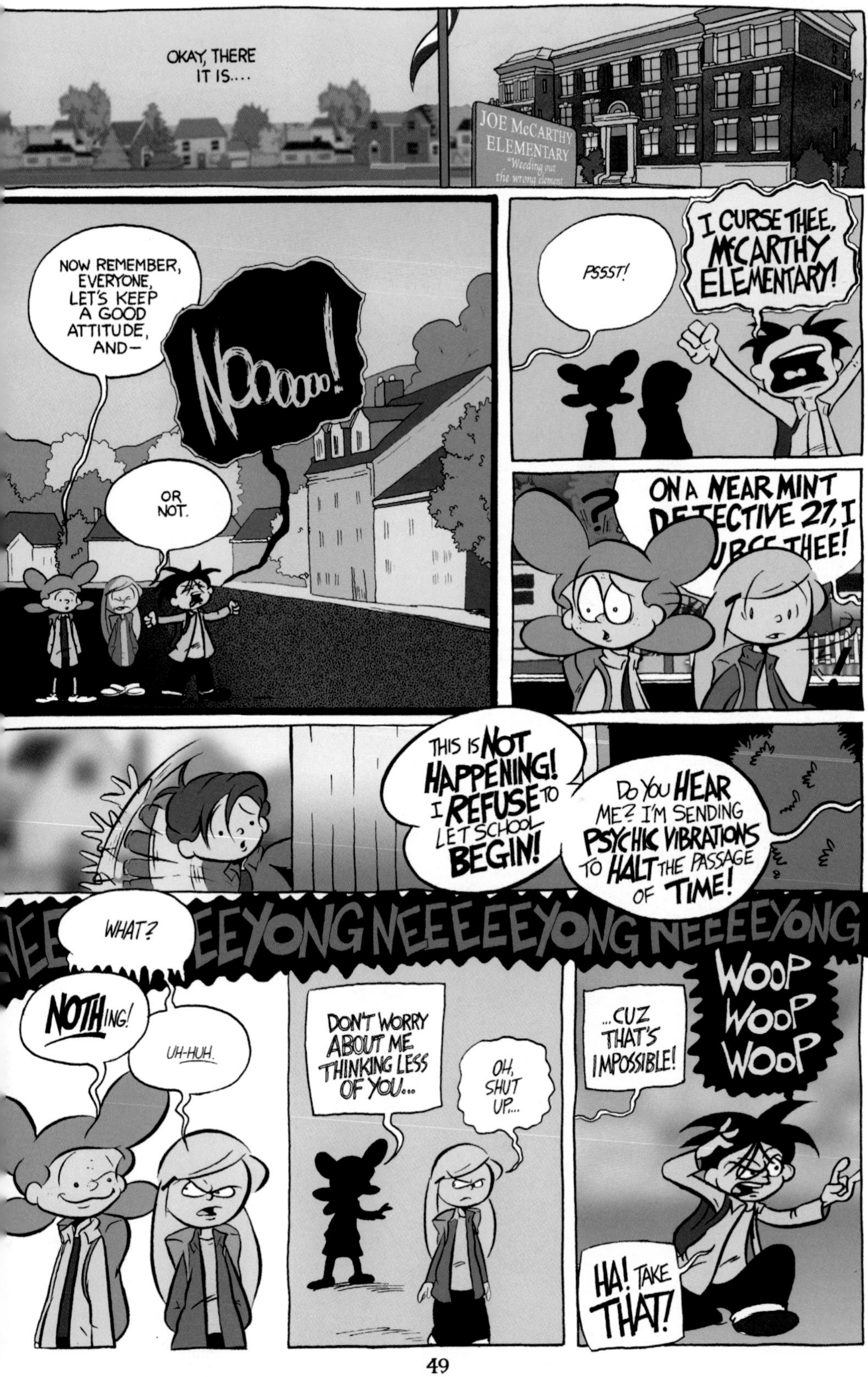
OKAY, THERE IT IS....
JOE McCARTHY ELEMENTARY "Weeding out the wrong element"
NOW REMEMBER, EVERYONE, LET'S KEEP A GOOD ATTITUDE, AND—
NOOOOOO!
OR NOT.
PSSST!
I CURSE THEE, McCARTHY ELEMENTARY!
ON A NEAR MINT DETECTIVE 27, I CURSE THEE!
THIS IS NOT HAPPENING! I REFUSE TO LET SCHOOL BEGIN!
DO YOU HEAR ME? I'M SENDING PSYCHIC VIBRATIONS TO HALT THE PASSAGE OF TIME!
NEEEEEEYONG NEEEEEEYONG NEEEEEYONG
WHAT?
NOTHING!
UH-HUH.
DON'T WORRY ABOUT ME THINKING LESS OF YOU...
OH, SHUT UP....
...CUZ THAT'S IMPOSSIBLE!
WOOP WOOP WOOP
HA! TAKE THAT!

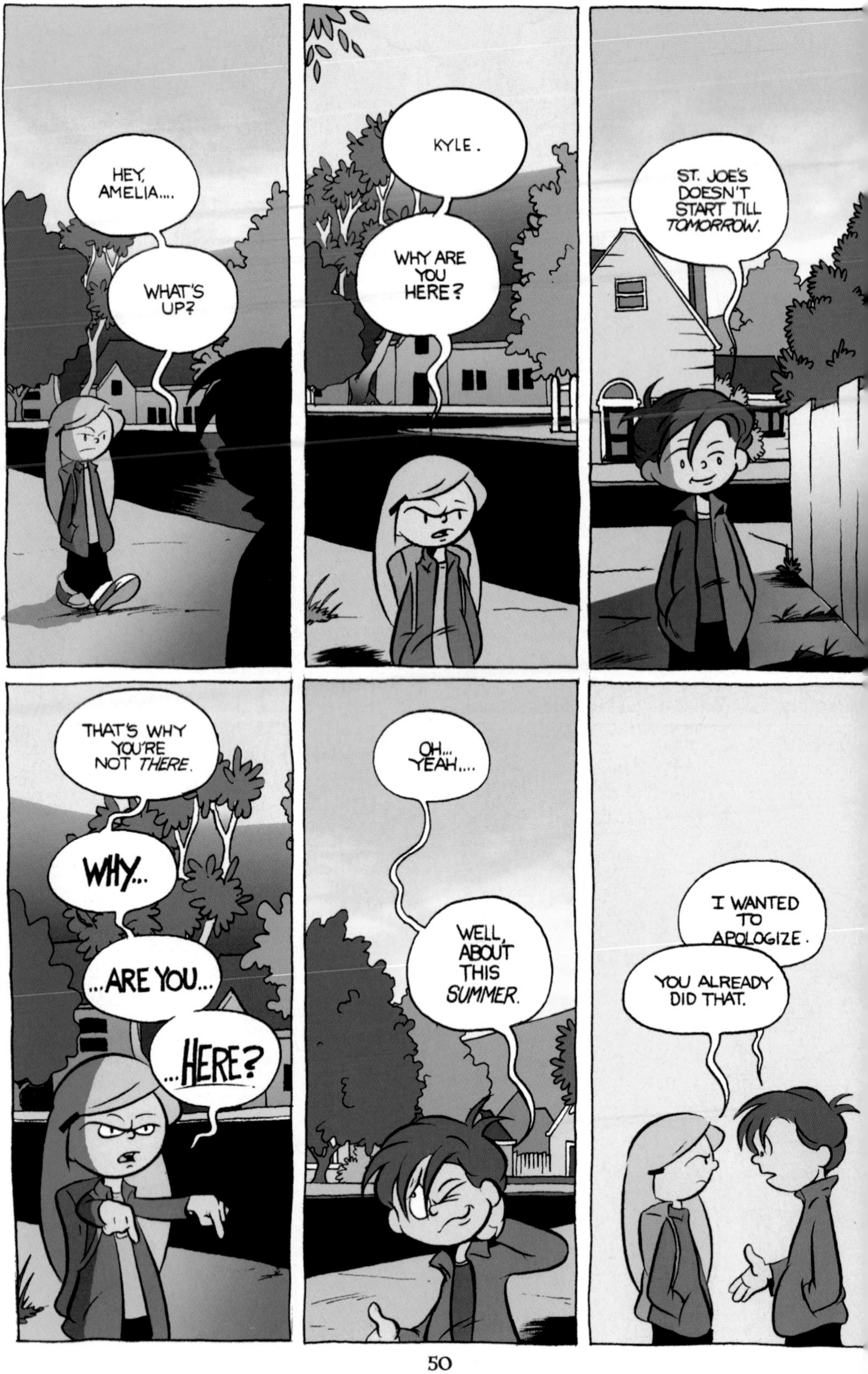
HEY, AMELIA....
WHAT'S UP?
KYLE.
WHY ARE YOU HERE?
ST. JOE'S DOESN'T START TILL *TOMORROW*.
THAT'S WHY YOU'RE NOT *THERE*.
WHY...
...ARE YOU...
...HERE?
OH... YEAH....
WELL, ABOUT THIS *SUMMER*.
I WANTED TO APOLOGIZE.
YOU ALREADY DID THAT.

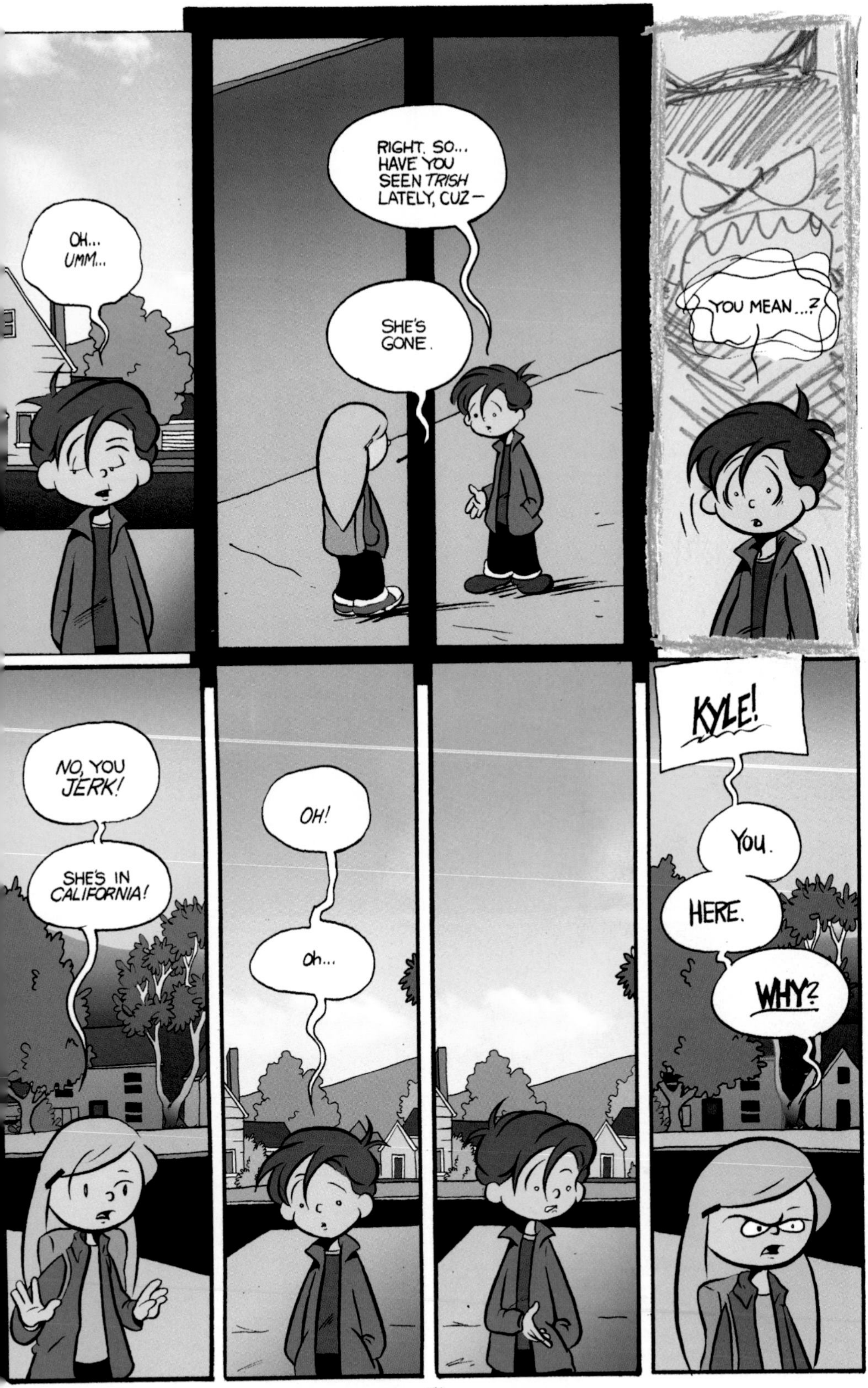
OH...
UMM...
RIGHT. SO...
HAVE YOU
SEEN TRISH
LATELY, CUZ—
SHE'S
GONE.
YOU MEAN...?
NO, YOU
JERK!
SHE'S IN
CALIFORNIA!
OH!
Oh...
KYLE!
YOU.
HERE.
WHY?

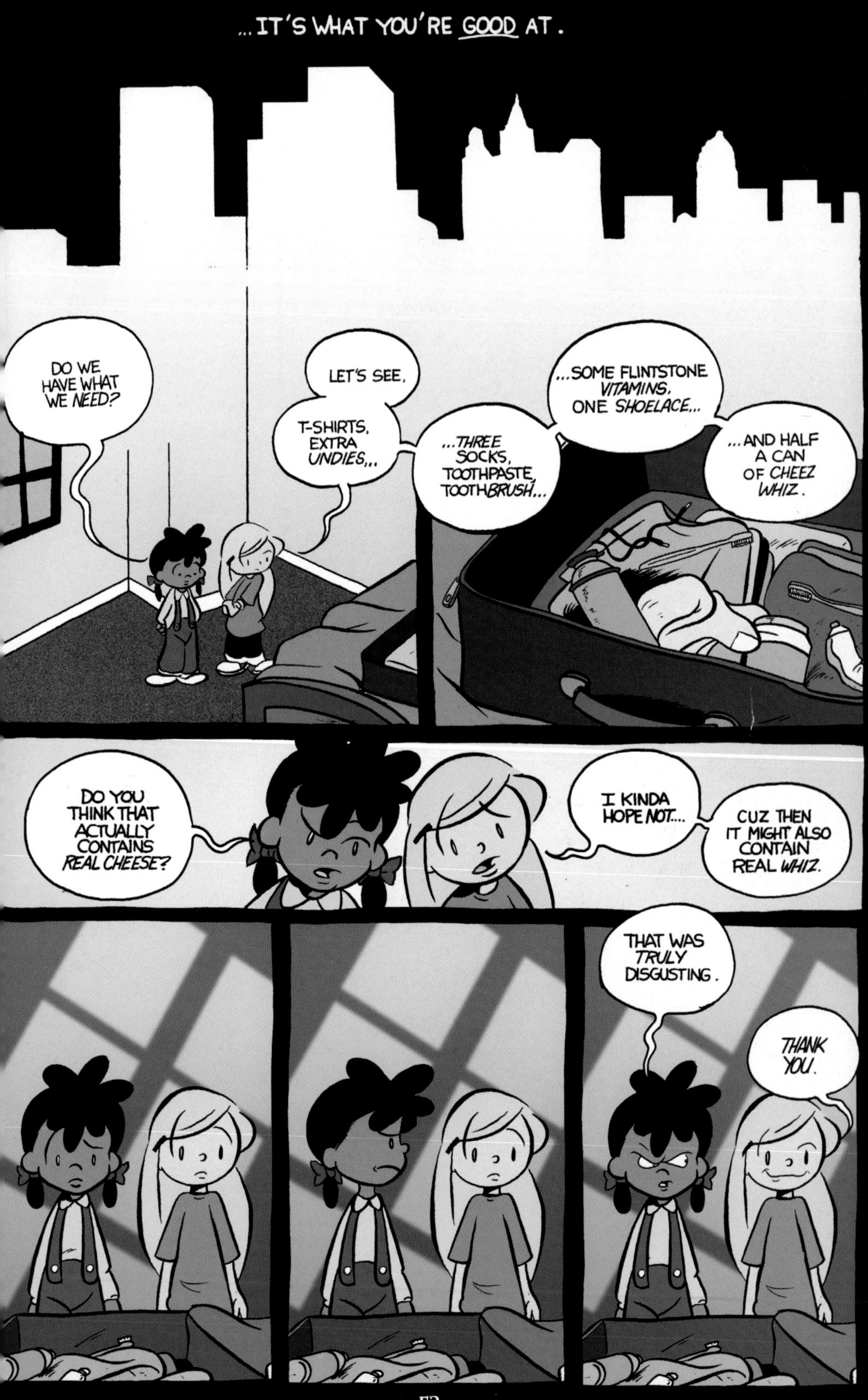

...IT'S WHAT YOU'RE GOOD AT.
DO WE HAVE WHAT WE NEED?
LET'S SEE.
T-SHIRTS, EXTRA UNDIES,...
...THREE SOCKS, TOOTHPASTE, TOOTHBRUSH...
...SOME FLINTSTONE VITAMINS, ONE SHOELACE...
...AND HALF A CAN OF CHEEZ WHIZ.
DO YOU THINK THAT ACTUALLY CONTAINS REAL CHEESE?
I KINDA HOPE NOT...
CUZ THEN IT MIGHT ALSO CONTAIN REAL WHIZ.
THAT WAS TRULY DISGUSTING.
THANK YOU.

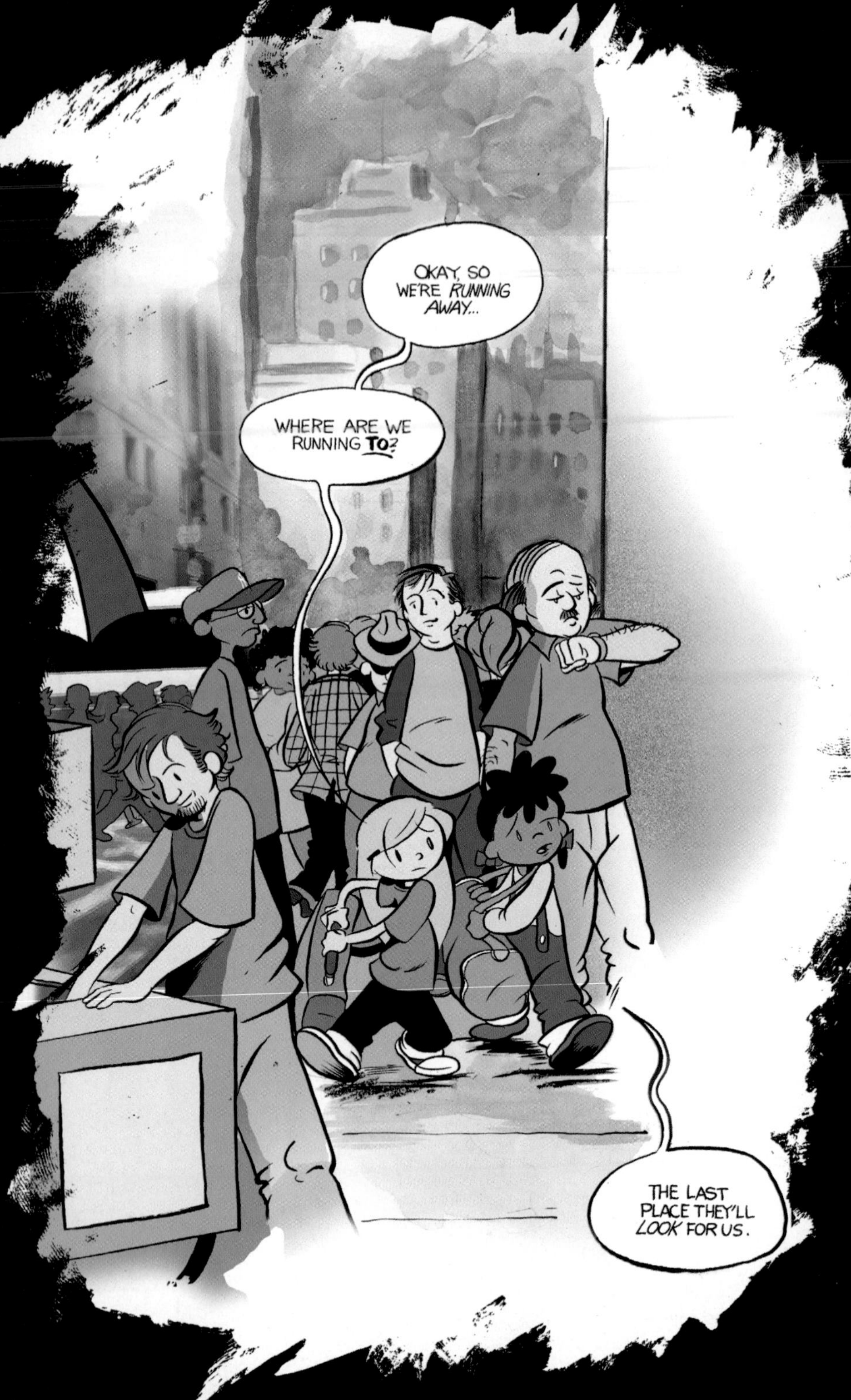
OKAY, SO WE'RE *RUNNING* AWAY...
WHERE ARE WE RUNNING **TO**?
THE LAST PLACE THEY'LL *LOOK* FOR US.

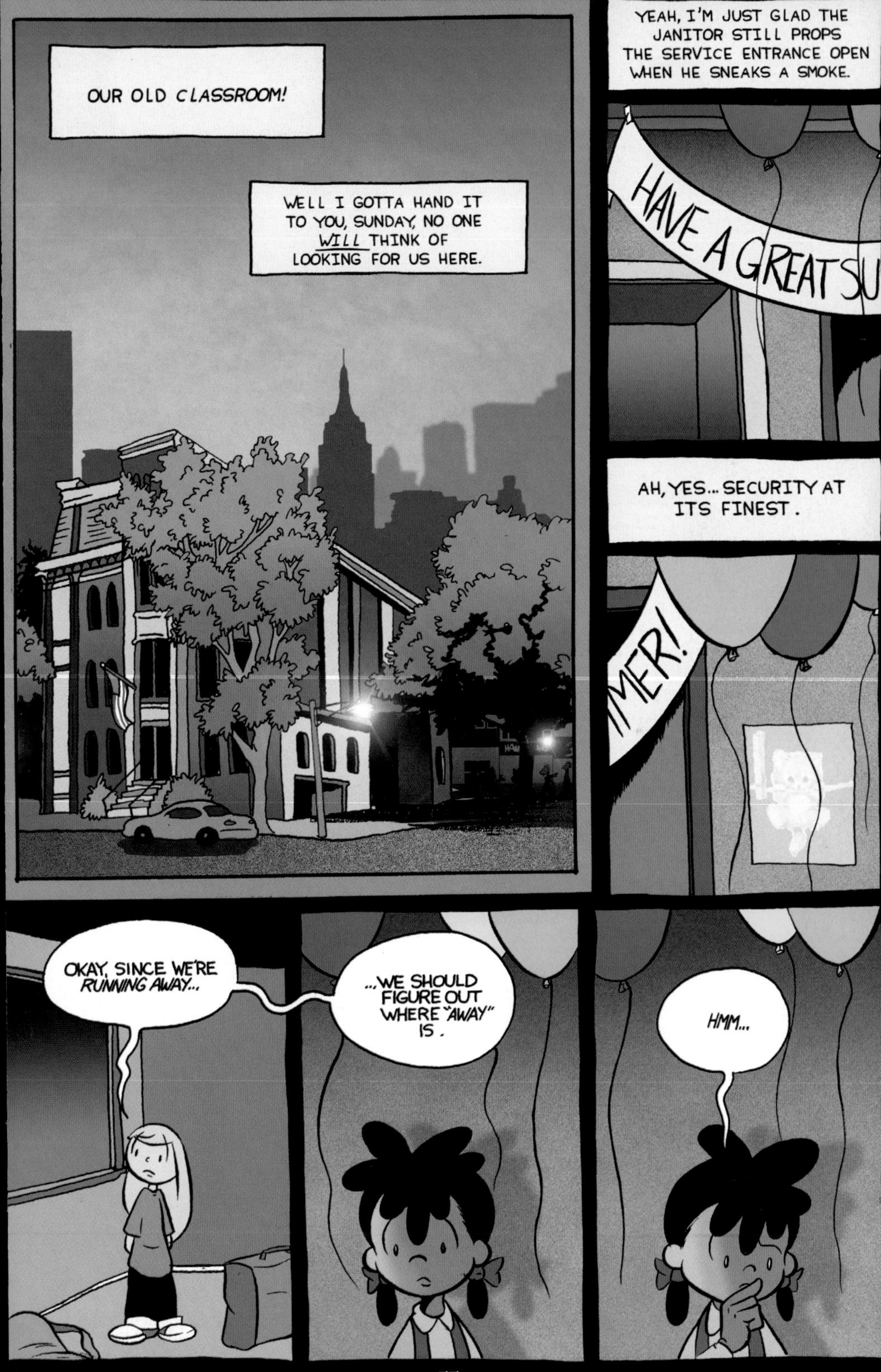
OUR OLD CLASSROOM!
WELL I GOTTA HAND IT TO YOU, SUNDAY, NO ONE WILL THINK OF LOOKING FOR US HERE.
YEAH, I'M JUST GLAD THE JANITOR STILL PROPS THE SERVICE ENTRANCE OPEN WHEN HE SNEAKS A SMOKE.
HAVE A GREAT SU
AH, YES... SECURITY AT ITS FINEST.
MER!
OKAY, SINCE WE'RE RUNNING AWAY...
...WE SHOULD FIGURE OUT WHERE "AWAY" IS.
HMM...

58

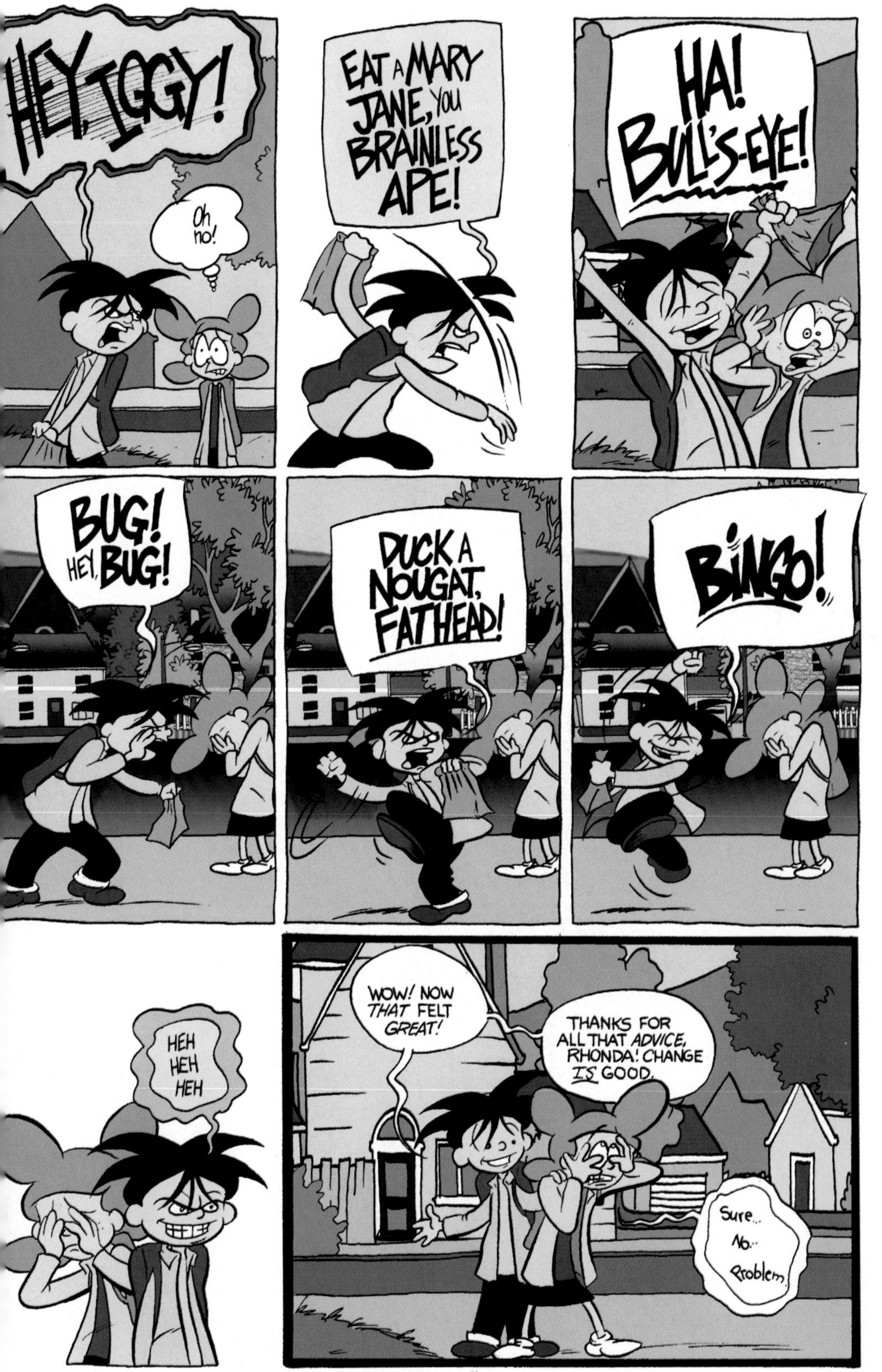
HEY, IGGY!
Oh no!
EAT A MARY JANE, YOU BRAINLESS APE!
HA! BULL'S-EYE!
BUG! HEY, BUG!
DUCK A NOUGAT, FATHEAD!
BINGO!
HEH HEH HEH
WOW! NOW THAT FELT GREAT!
THANKS FOR ALL THAT ADVICE, RHONDA! CHANGE IS GOOD.
Sure... No... Problem.

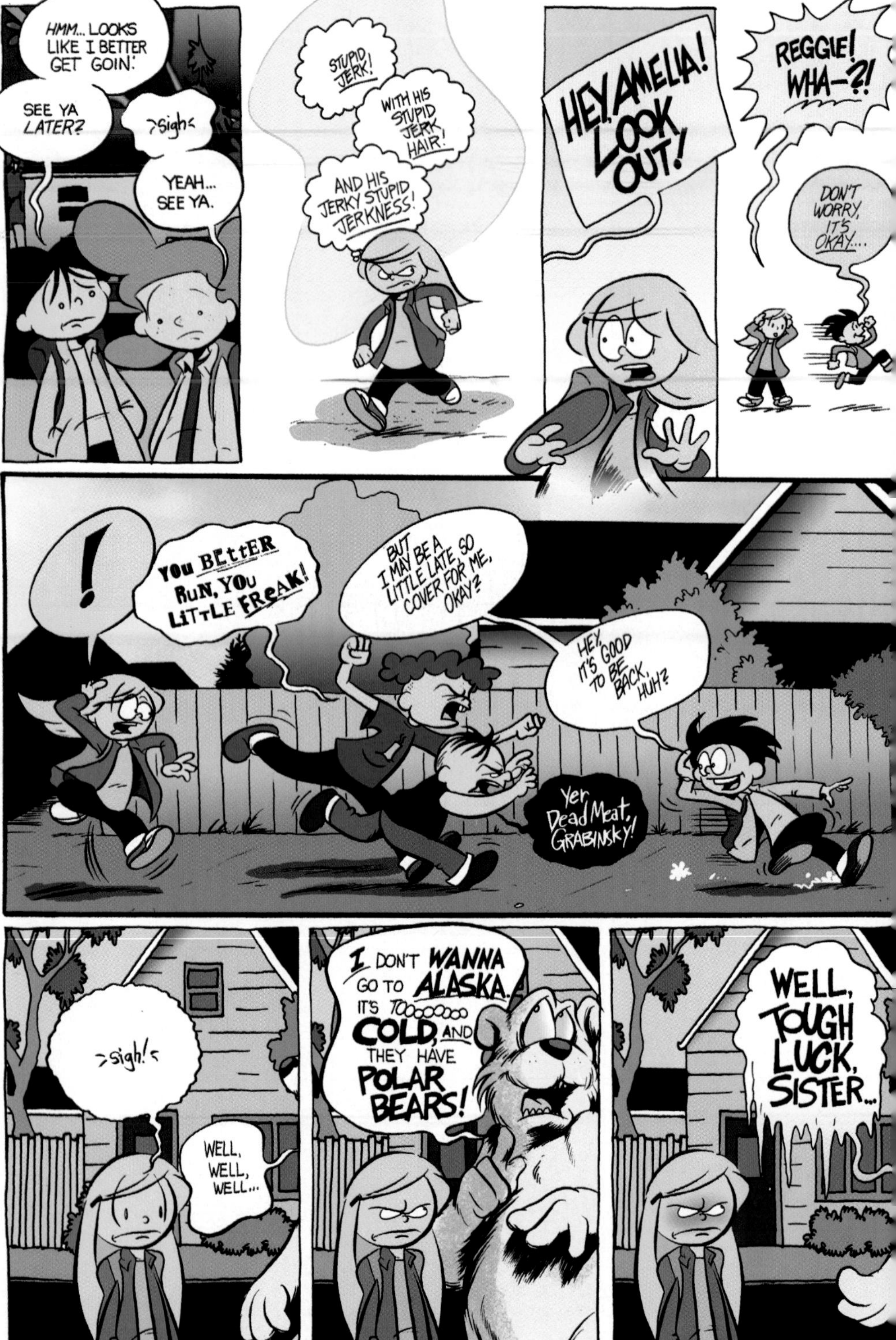
HMM... LOOKS LIKE I BETTER GET GOIN'.
SEE YA LATER?
>sigh<
YEAH... SEE YA.
STUPID JERK!
WITH HIS STUPID JERK HAIR!
AND HIS JERKY STUPID JERKNESS!
HEY, AMELIA! LOOK OUT!
REGGIE! WHA-?!
DON'T WORRY, IT'S OKAY....
!
YOU BETTER RUN, YOU LITTLE FREAK!
BUT I MAY BE A LITTLE LATE, SO COVER FOR ME, OKAY?
HEY, IT'S GOOD TO BE BACK, HUH?
Yer Dead Meat, GRABINSKY!
>sigh!<
WELL, WELL, WELL...
I DON'T WANNA GO TO ALASKA. IT'S TOOOOOOOO COLD, AND THEY HAVE POLAR BEARS!
WELL, TOUGH LUCK, SISTER...

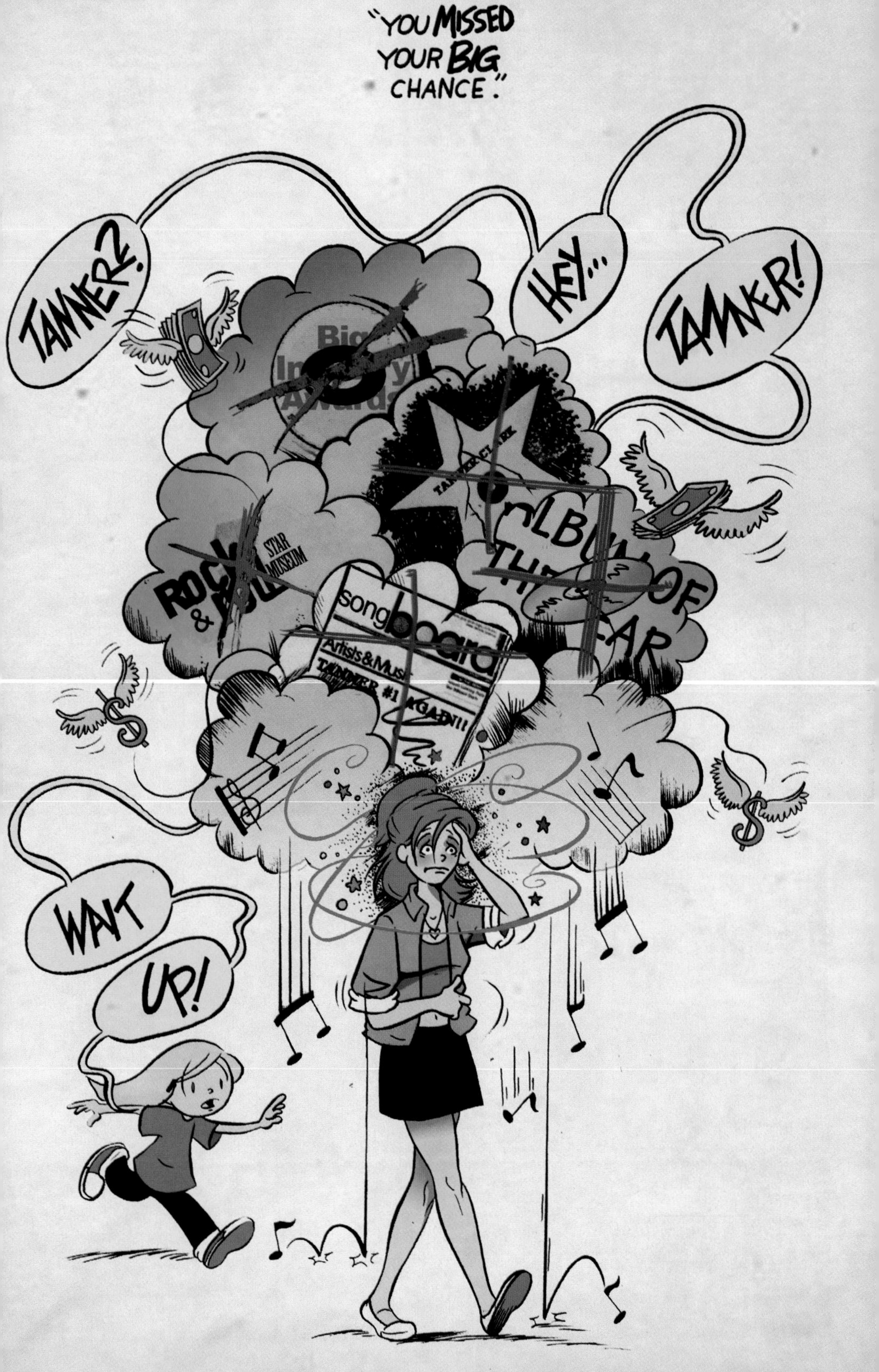
"YOU MISSED YOUR BIG CHANCE."
TANNER?
HEY...
TANNER!
STAR MUSEUM
songboard
WAIT UP!

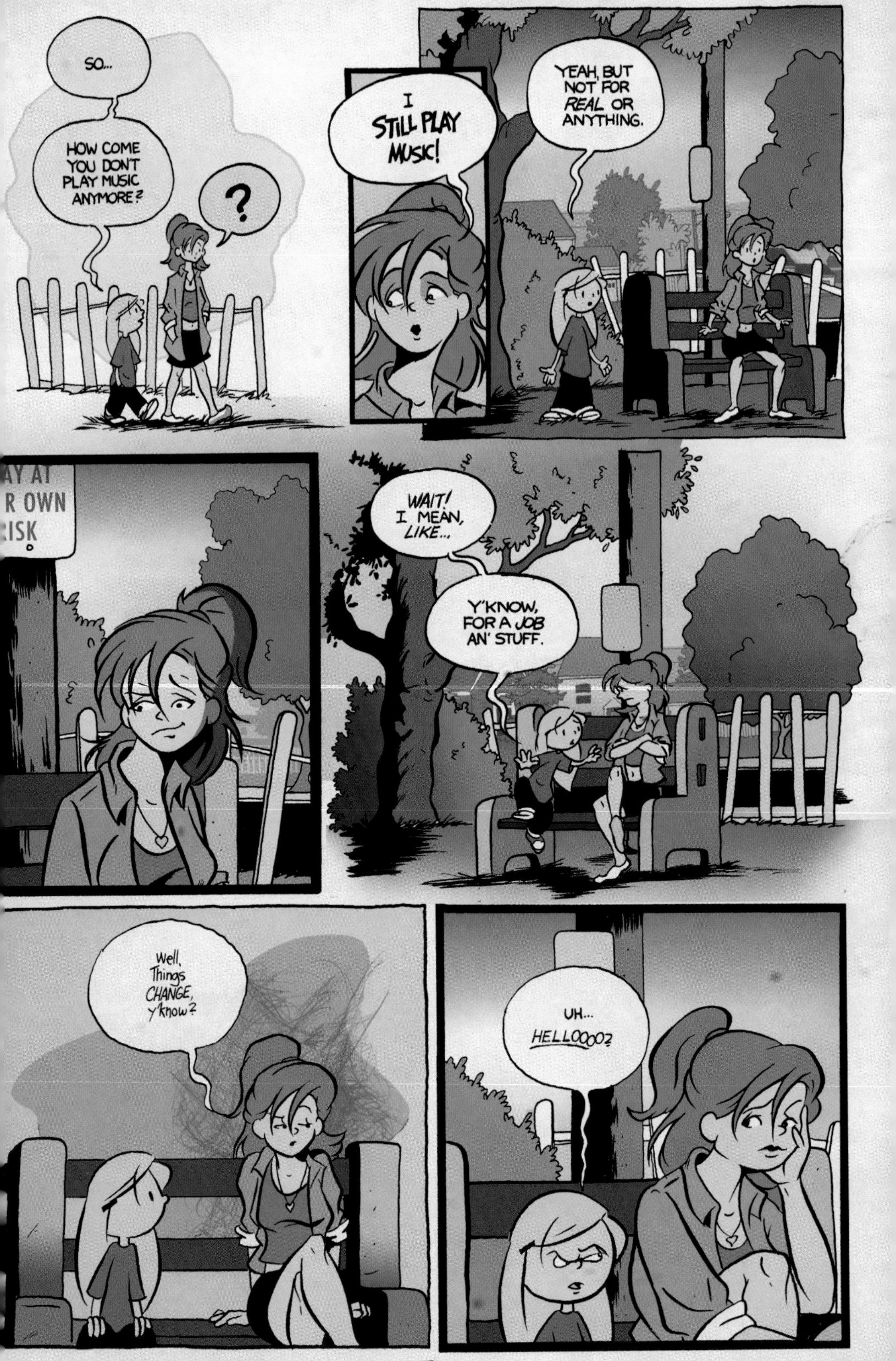
SO...
HOW COME YOU DON'T PLAY MUSIC ANYMORE?
?
I STILL PLAY MUSIC!
YEAH, BUT NOT FOR REAL OR ANYTHING.
AY AT R OWN ISK
WAIT! I MEAN, LIKE...
Y'KNOW, FOR A JOB AN' STUFF.
Well, Things CHANGE, y'know?
UH... HELLOOOO?

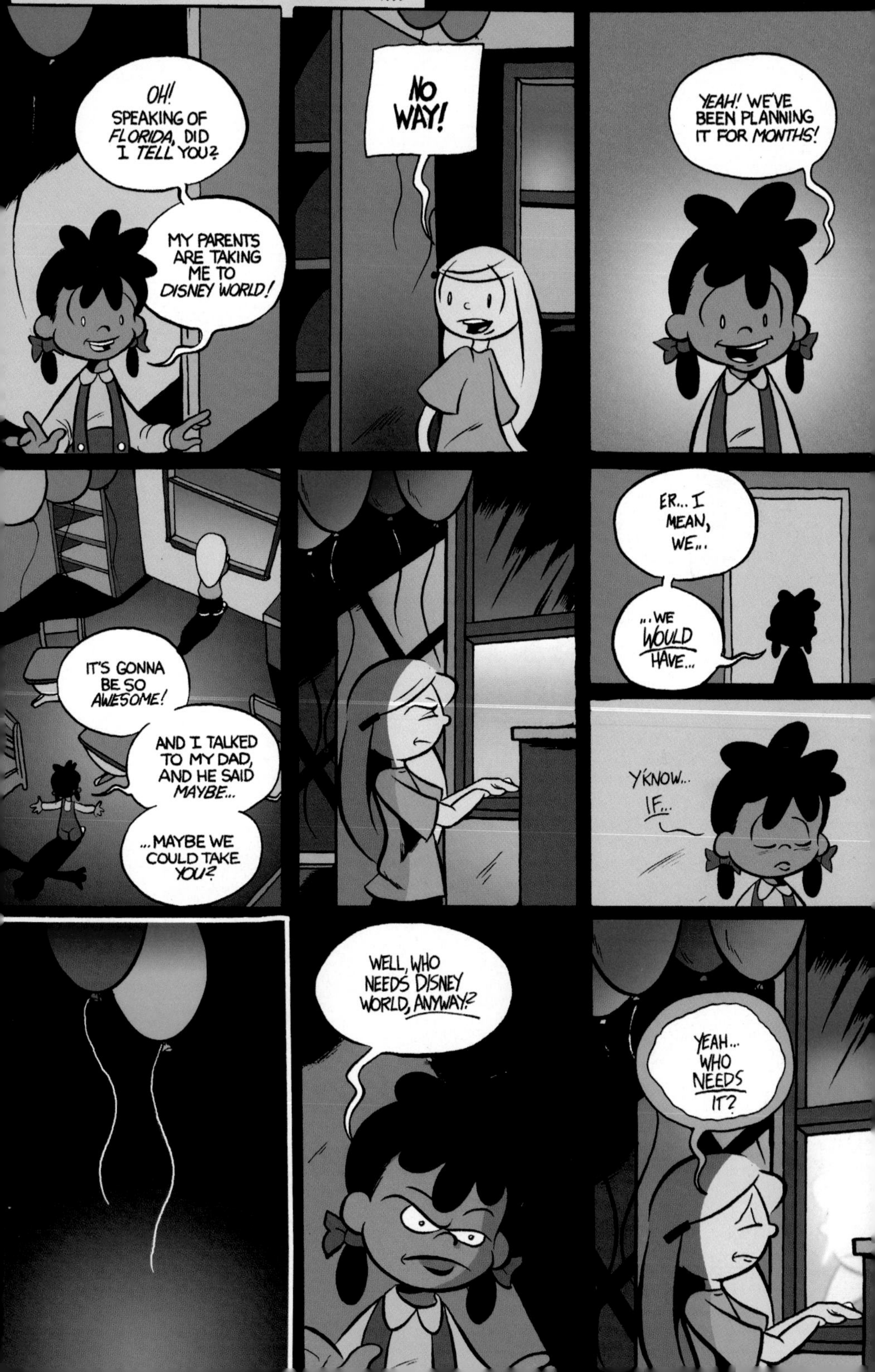

OH! SPEAKING OF FLORIDA, DID I TELL YOU?
MY PARENTS ARE TAKING ME TO DISNEY WORLD!
NO WAY!
YEAH! WE'VE BEEN PLANNING IT FOR MONTHS!
IT'S GONNA BE SO AWESOME!
AND I TALKED TO MY DAD, AND HE SAID MAYBE...
...MAYBE WE COULD TAKE YOU?
ER... I MEAN, WE...
...WE WOULD HAVE...
Y'KNOW... IF...
WELL, WHO NEEDS DISNEY WORLD, ANYWAY?
YEAH... WHO NEEDS IT?

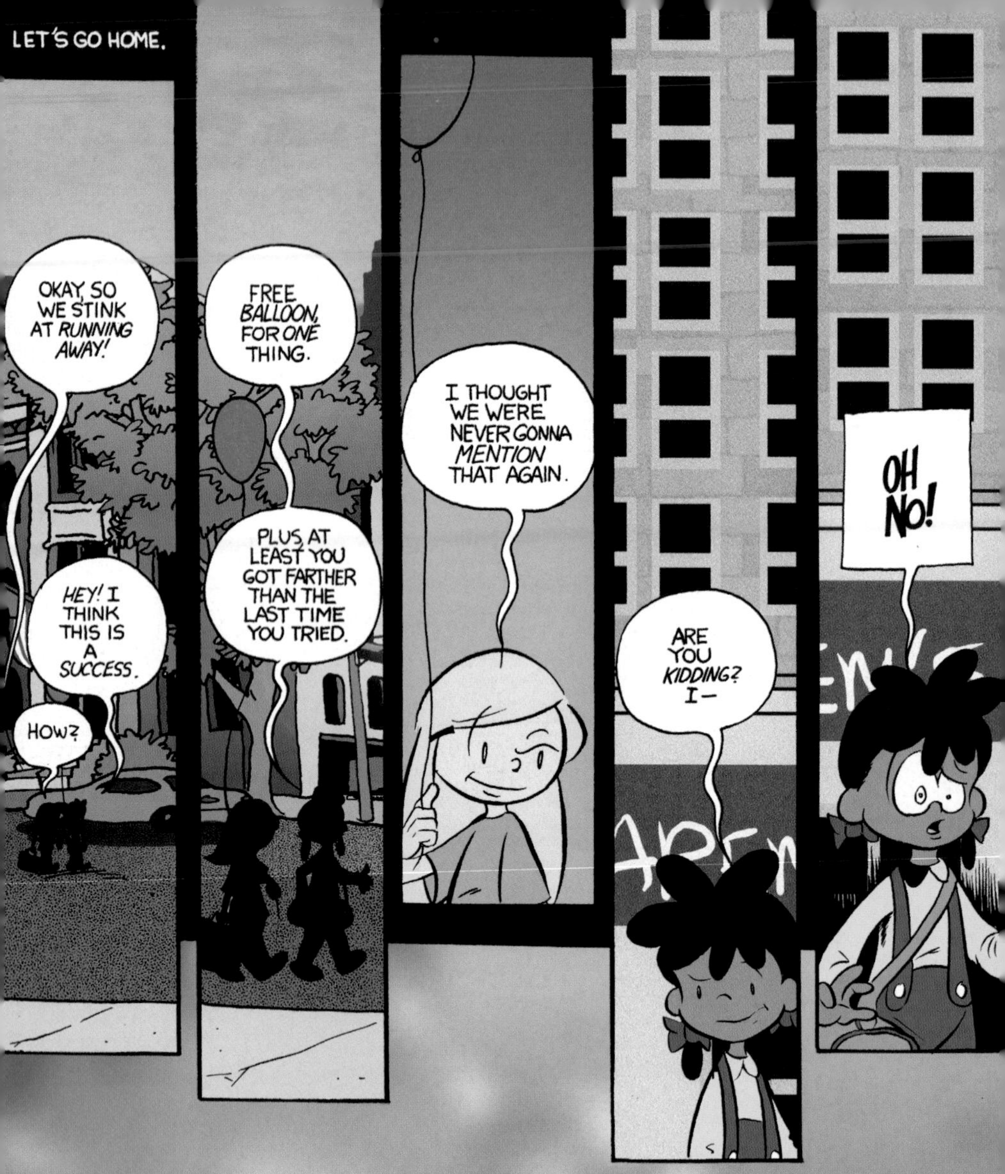
LET'S GO HOME.
OKAY, SO WE STINK AT *RUNNING AWAY!*
HEY! I THINK THIS IS A *SUCCESS*.
HOW?
FREE *BALLOON*, FOR *ONE* THING.
PLUS, AT LEAST YOU GOT FARTHER THAN THE LAST TIME YOU TRIED.
I THOUGHT WE WERE NEVER GONNA *MENTION* THAT AGAIN.
ARE YOU *KIDDING?* I—
OH NO!

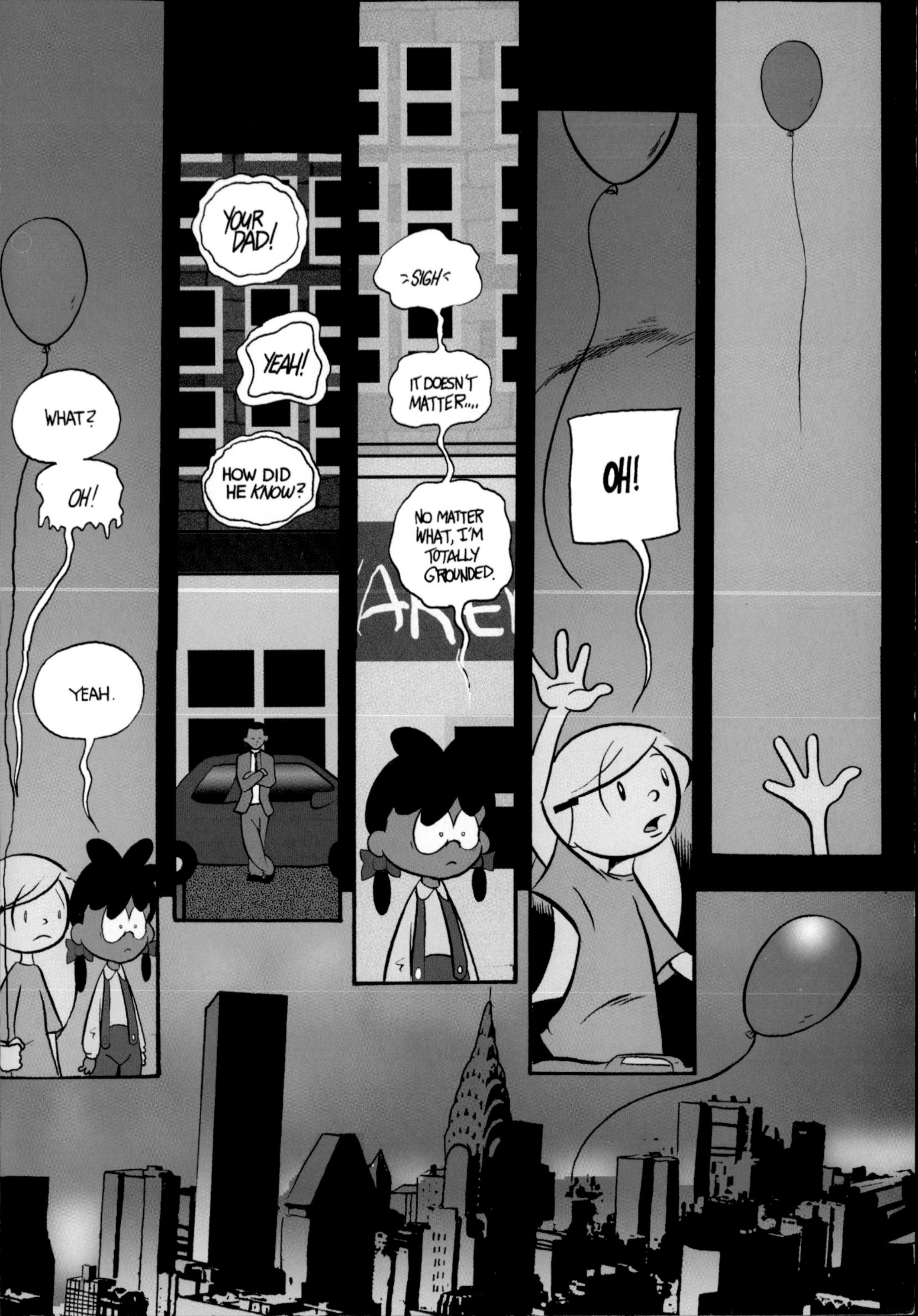
WHAT?
OH!
YEAH.
YOUR DAD!
YEAH!
HOW DID HE KNOW?
SIGH
IT DOESN'T MATTER....
NO MATTER WHAT, I'M TOTALLY GROUNDED.
OH!

69

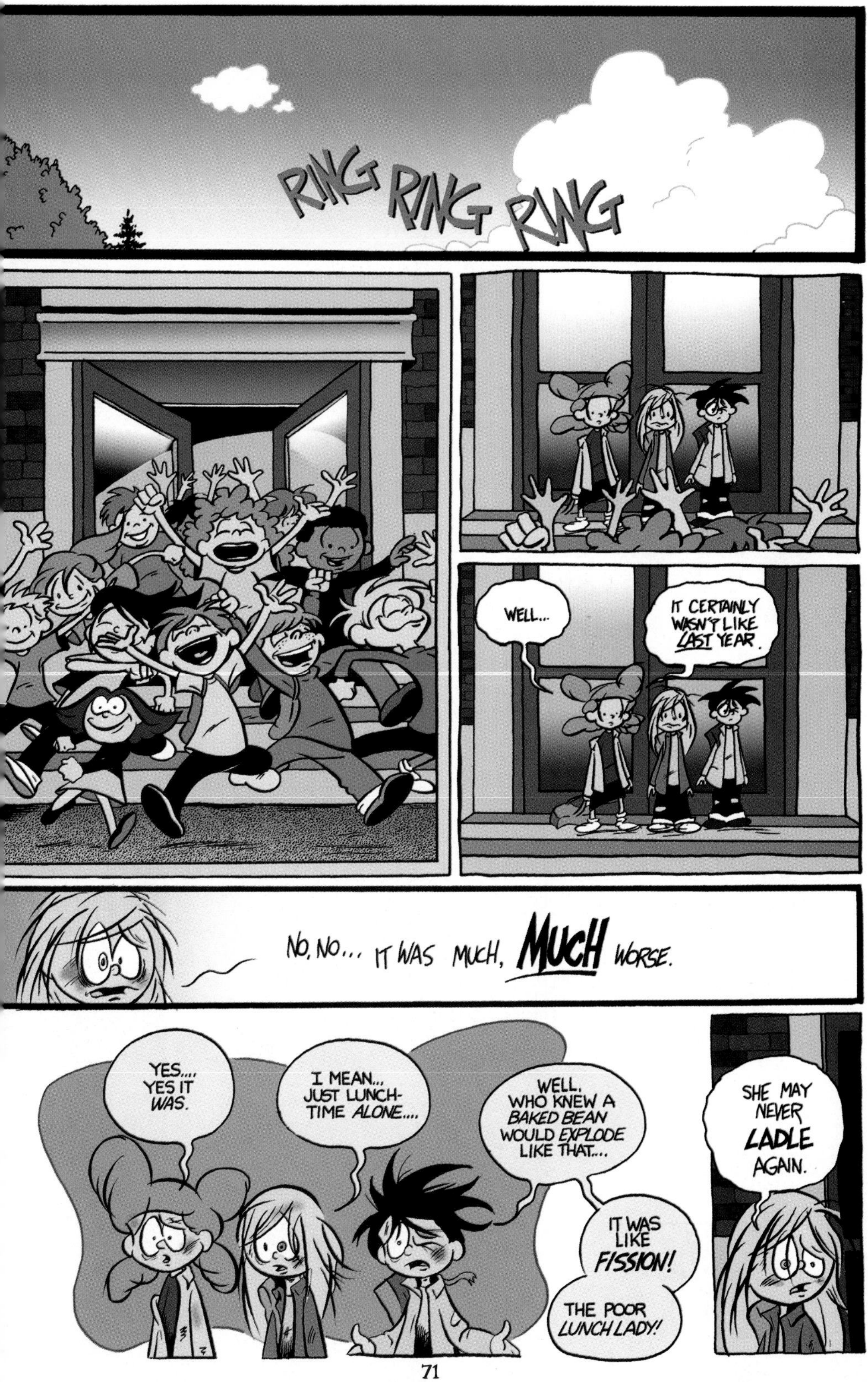
RING RING RING
WELL...
IT CERTAINLY WASN'T LIKE LAST YEAR.
NO, NO... IT WAS MUCH, MUCH WORSE.
YES.... YES IT WAS.
I MEAN... JUST LUNCH-TIME ALONE....
WELL, WHO KNEW A BAKED BEAN WOULD EXPLODE LIKE THAT....
IT WAS LIKE FISSION!
THE POOR LUNCH LADY!
SHE MAY NEVER LADLE AGAIN.

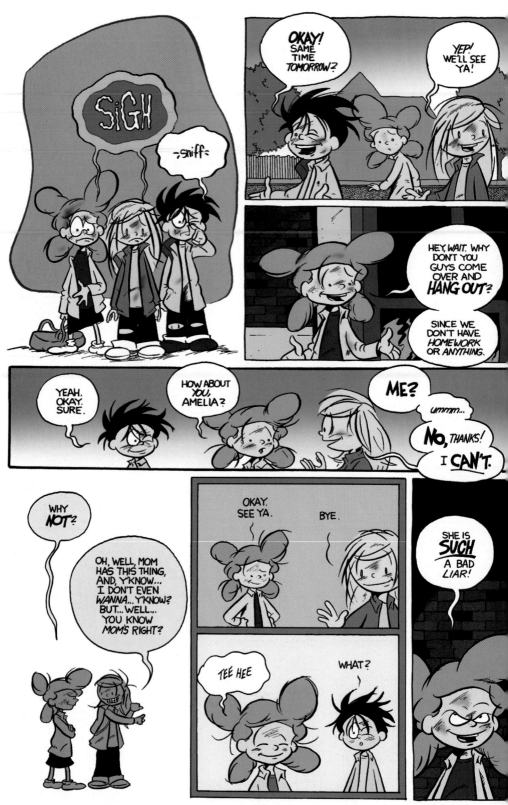

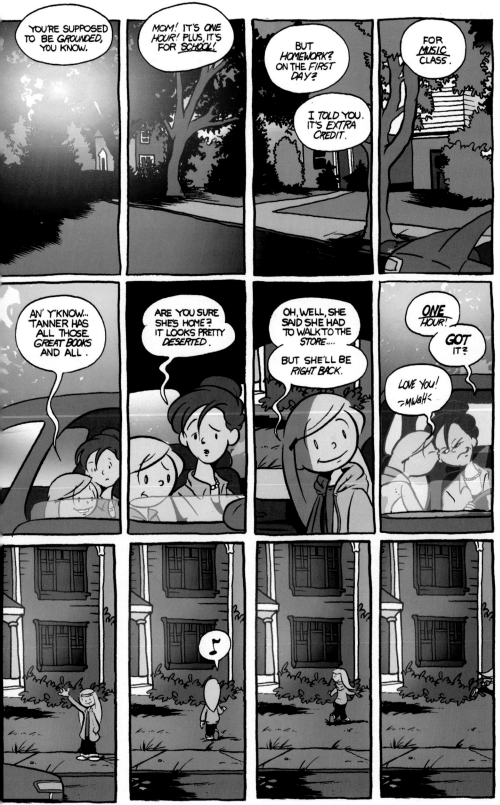

73

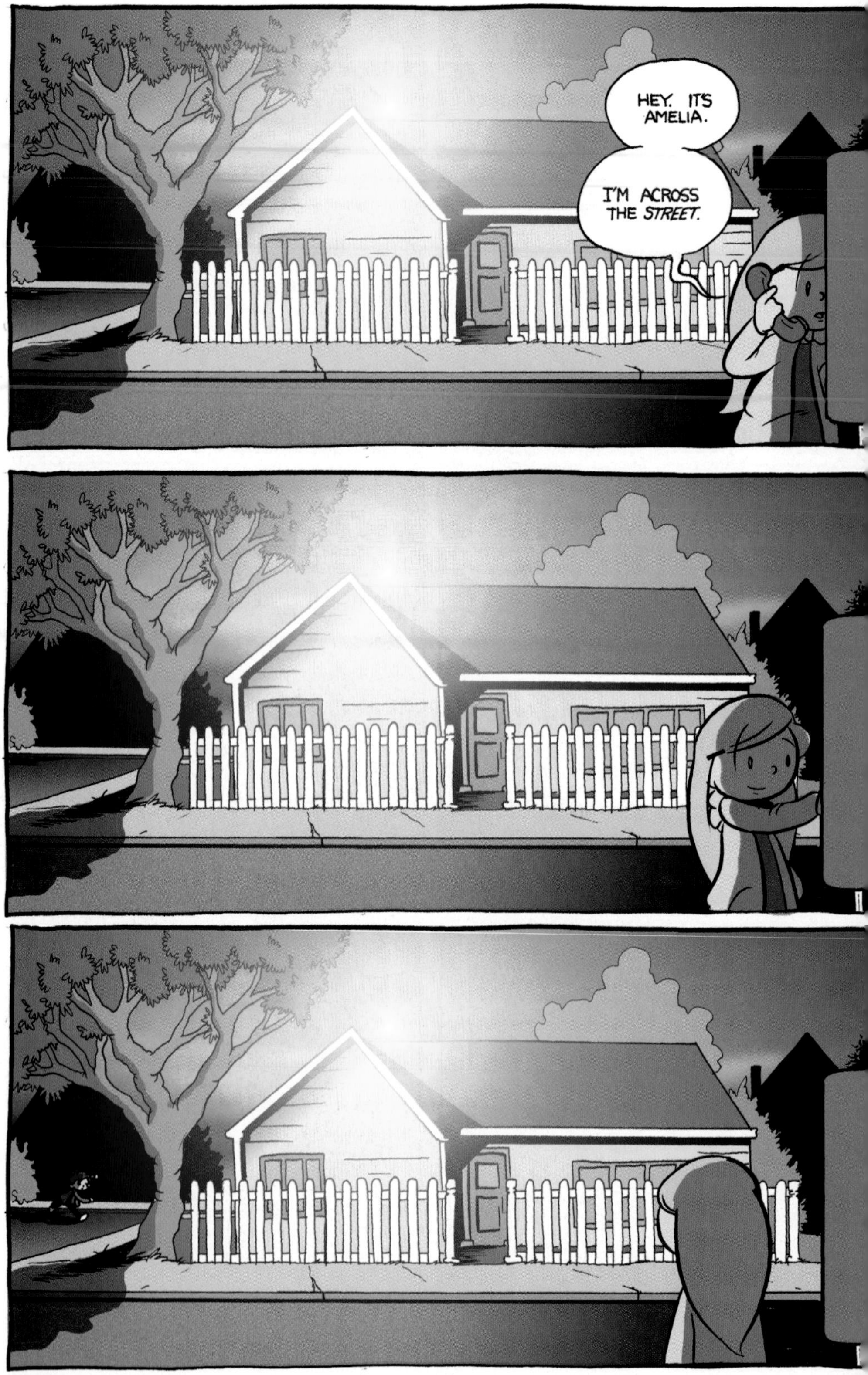
HEY. IT'S AMELIA.
I'M ACROSS THE *STREET*.

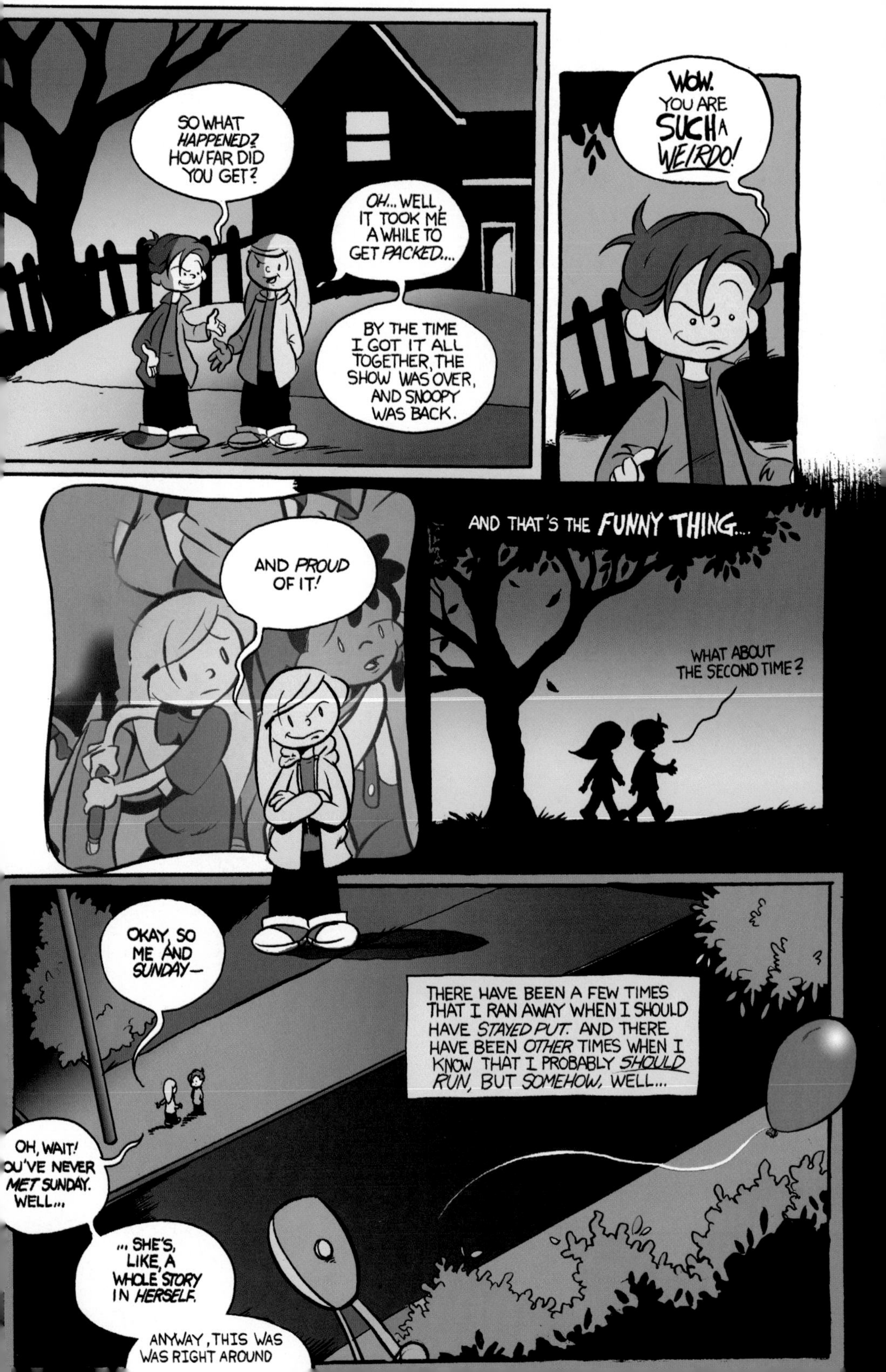
SO WHAT HAPPENED? HOW FAR DID YOU GET?
OH... WELL, IT TOOK ME A WHILE TO GET PACKED...
BY THE TIME I GOT IT ALL TOGETHER, THE SHOW WAS OVER, AND SNOOPY WAS BACK.
WOW. YOU ARE SUCH A WEIRDO!
AND PROUD OF IT!
AND THAT'S THE FUNNY THING...
WHAT ABOUT THE SECOND TIME?
OKAY, SO ME AND SUNDAY—
THERE HAVE BEEN A FEW TIMES THAT I RAN AWAY WHEN I SHOULD HAVE STAYED PUT. AND THERE HAVE BEEN OTHER TIMES WHEN I KNOW THAT I PROBABLY SHOULD RUN, BUT SOMEHOW, WELL...
OH, WAIT! OU'VE NEVER MET SUNDAY. WELL...
... SHE'S, LIKE, A WHOLE STORY IN HERSELF.
ANYWAY, THIS WAS WAS RIGHT AROUND

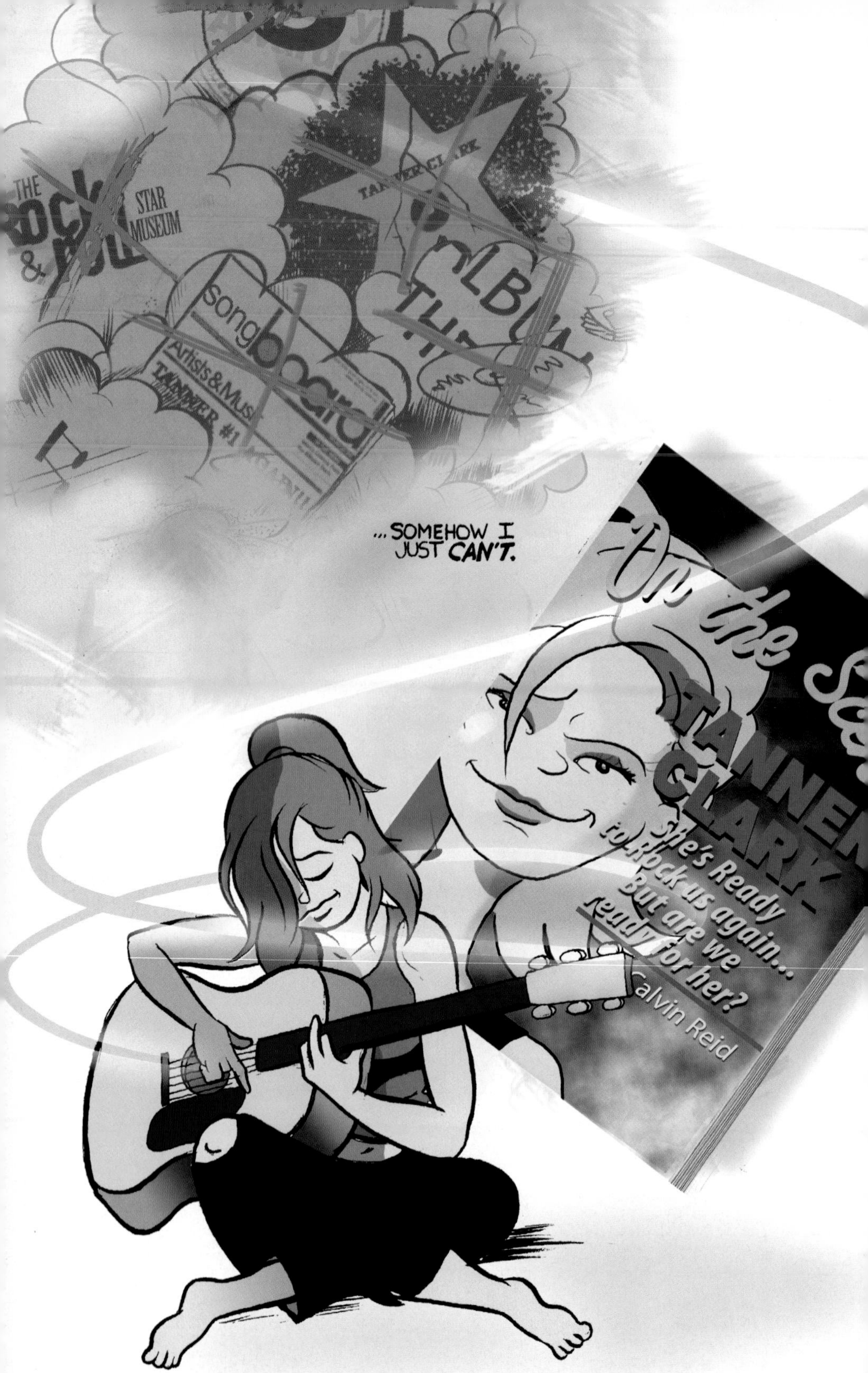
...SOMEHOW I JUST **CAN'T.**
STAR MUSEUM
TANNER CLARK
Artists&Music
TANNER #1
TANNER CLARK
She's Ready to Rock us again... But are we ready for her?
Calvin Reid

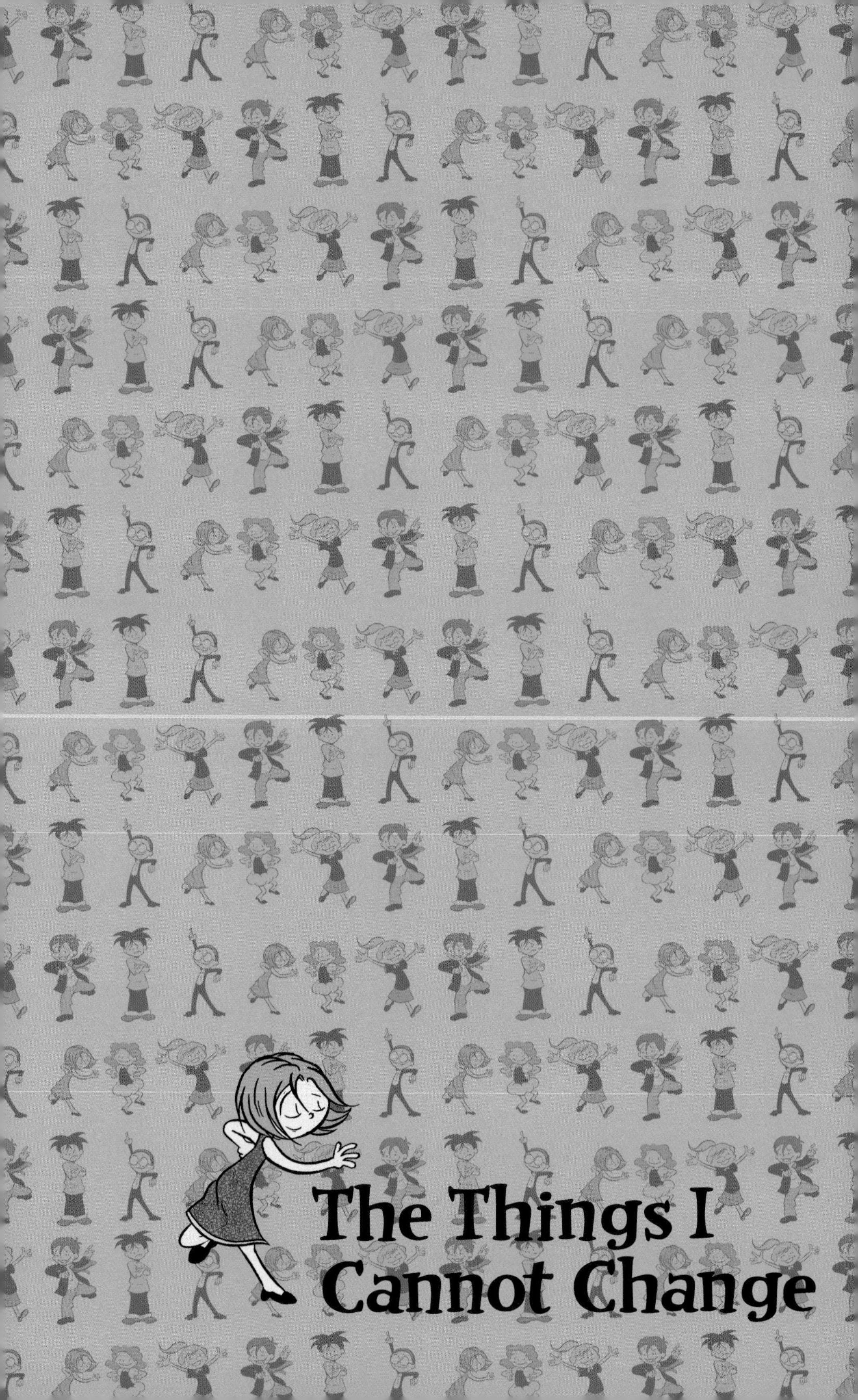

The Things I Cannot Change

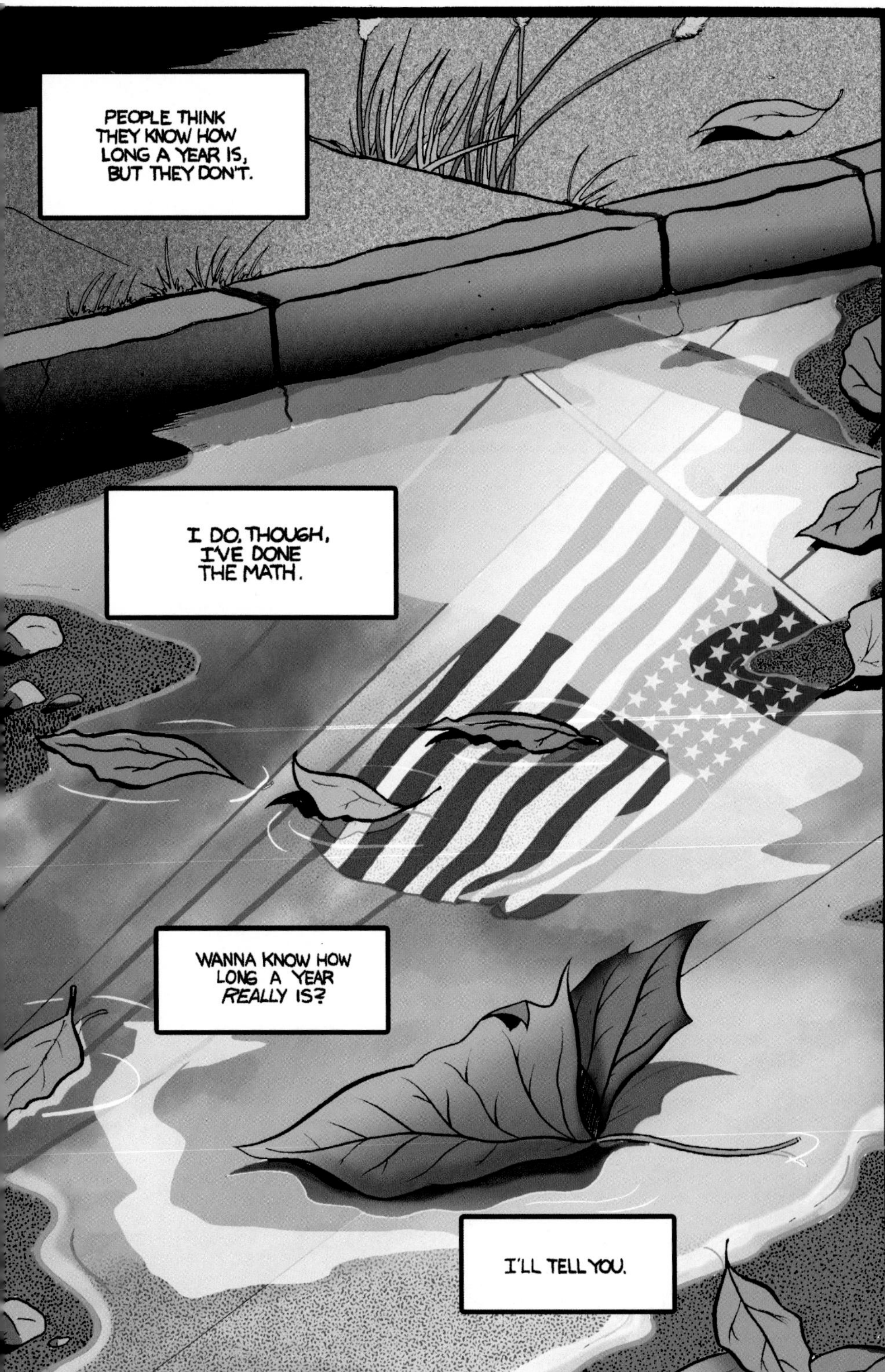
PEOPLE THINK THEY KNOW HOW LONG A YEAR IS, BUT THEY DON'T.
I DO, THOUGH. I'VE DONE THE MATH.
WANNA KNOW HOW LONG A YEAR *REALLY* IS?
I'LL TELL YOU.

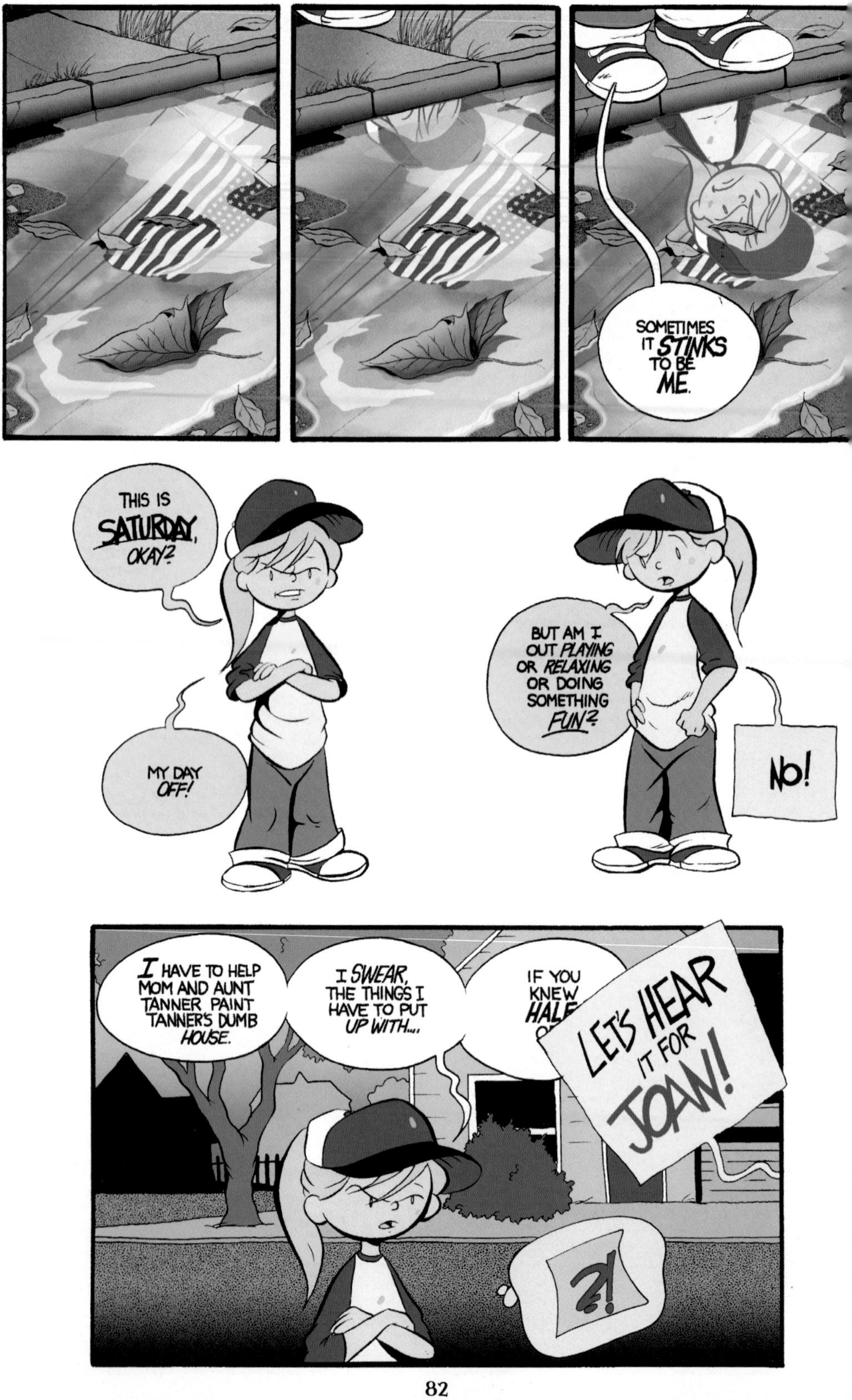

SOMETIMES IT STINKS TO BE ME.
THIS IS SATURDAY, OKAY?
MY DAY OFF!
BUT AM I OUT PLAYING OR RELAXING OR DOING SOMETHING FUN?
NO!
I HAVE TO HELP MOM AND AUNT TANNER PAINT TANNER'S DUMB HOUSE.
I SWEAR, THE THINGS I HAVE TO PUT UP WITH...
IF YOU KNEW HALF
LET'S HEAR IT FOR JOAN!
?!

83

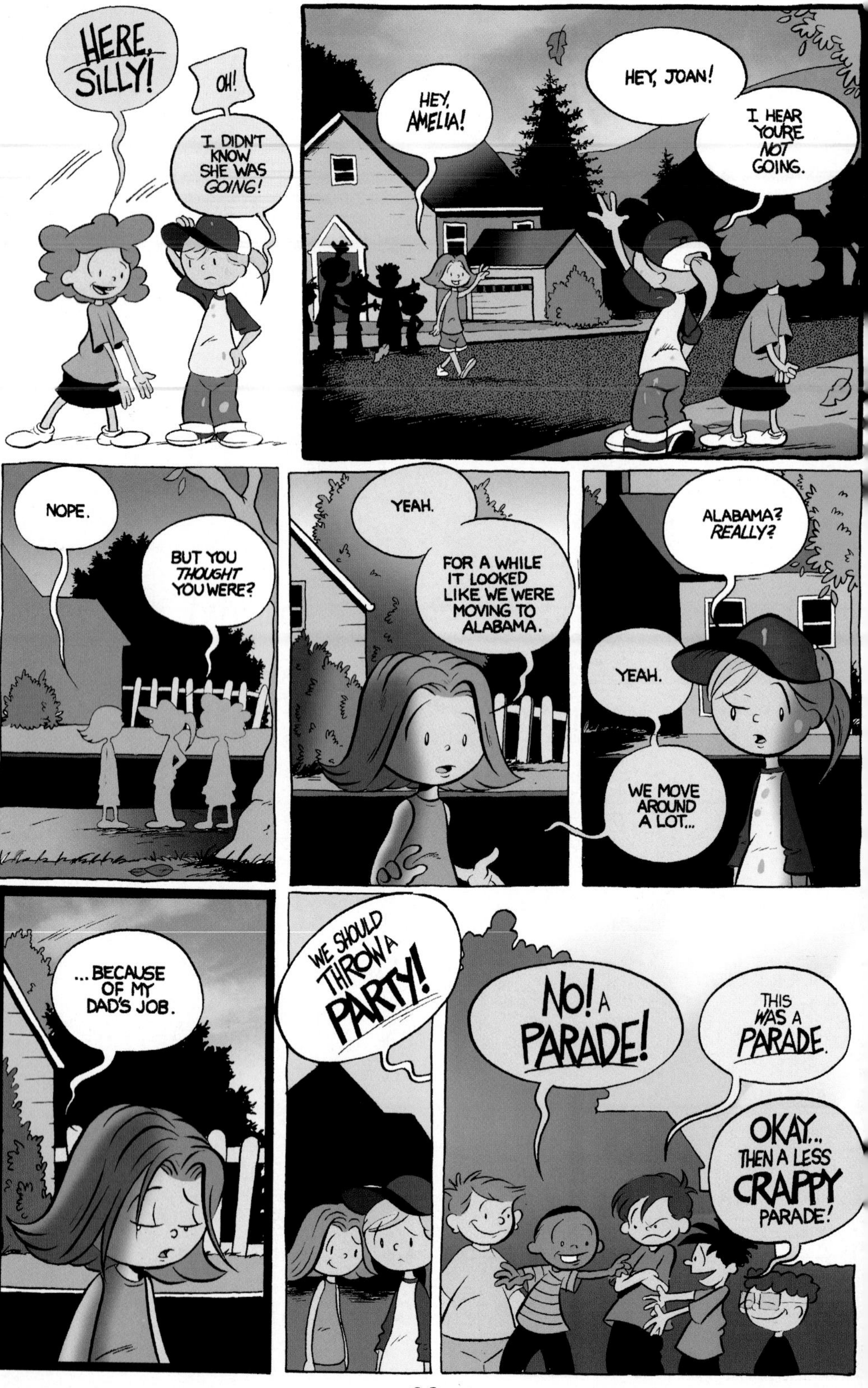
HERE, SILLY!
OH!
I DIDN'T KNOW SHE WAS GOING!
HEY, AMELIA!
HEY, JOAN!
I HEAR YOU'RE NOT GOING.
NOPE.
BUT YOU THOUGHT YOU WERE?
YEAH.
FOR A WHILE IT LOOKED LIKE WE WERE MOVING TO ALABAMA.
ALABAMA? REALLY?
YEAH.
WE MOVE AROUND A LOT...
...BECAUSE OF MY DAD'S JOB.
WE SHOULD THROW A PARTY!
NO! A PARADE!
THIS WAS A PARADE.
OKAY... THEN A LESS CRAPPY PARADE!

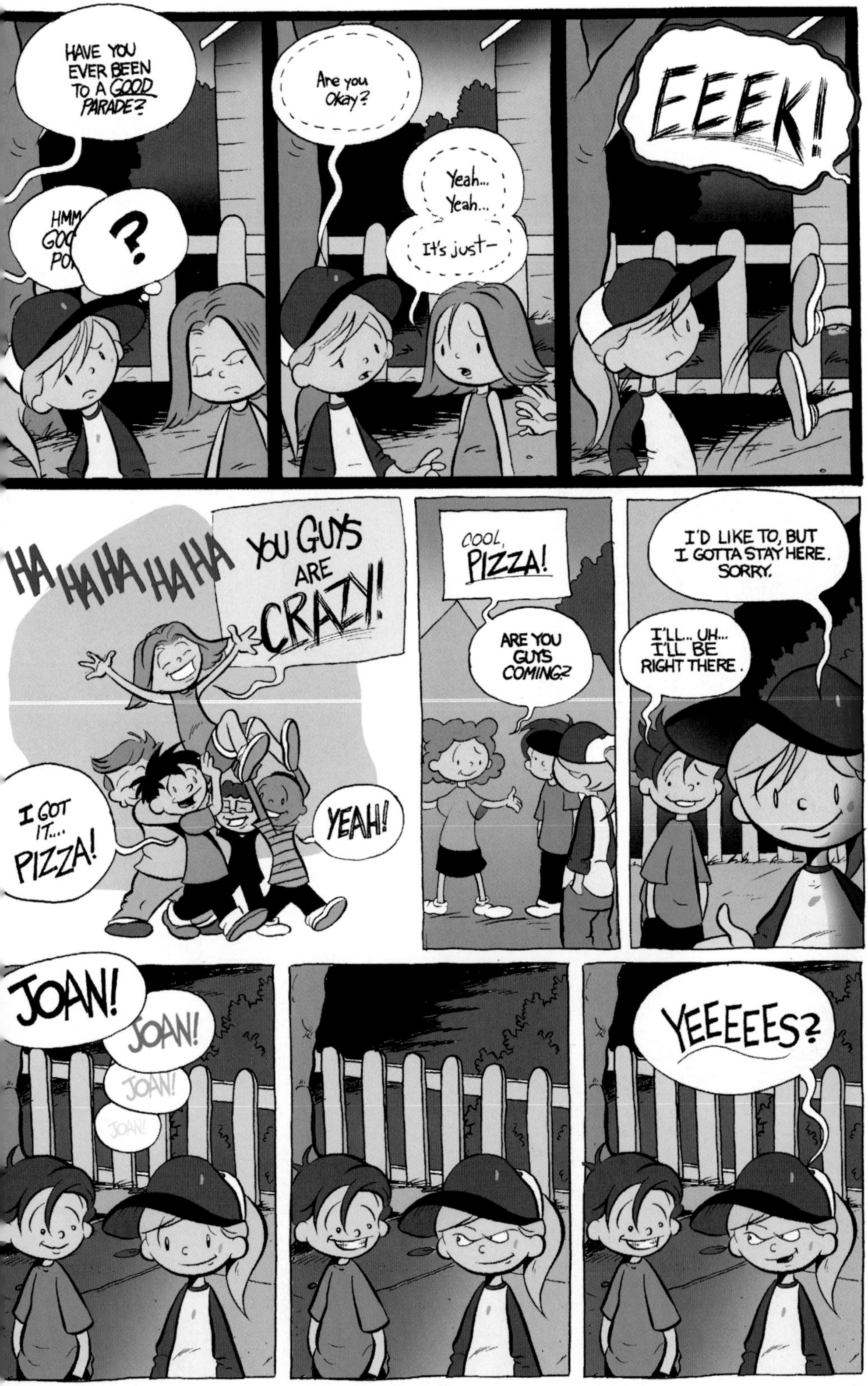
HAVE YOU EVER BEEN TO A GOOD PARADE?
HMM
?
Are you Okay?
Yeah... Yeah...
It's just—
EEEK!
HA HA HA HA HA HA
YOU GUYS ARE CRAZY!
I GOT IT.... PIZZA!
YEAH!
COOL, PIZZA!
ARE YOU GUYS COMING?
I'D LIKE TO, BUT I GOTTA STAY HERE. SORRY.
I'LL... UH... I'LL BE RIGHT THERE.
JOAN!
JOAN!
YEEEEES?

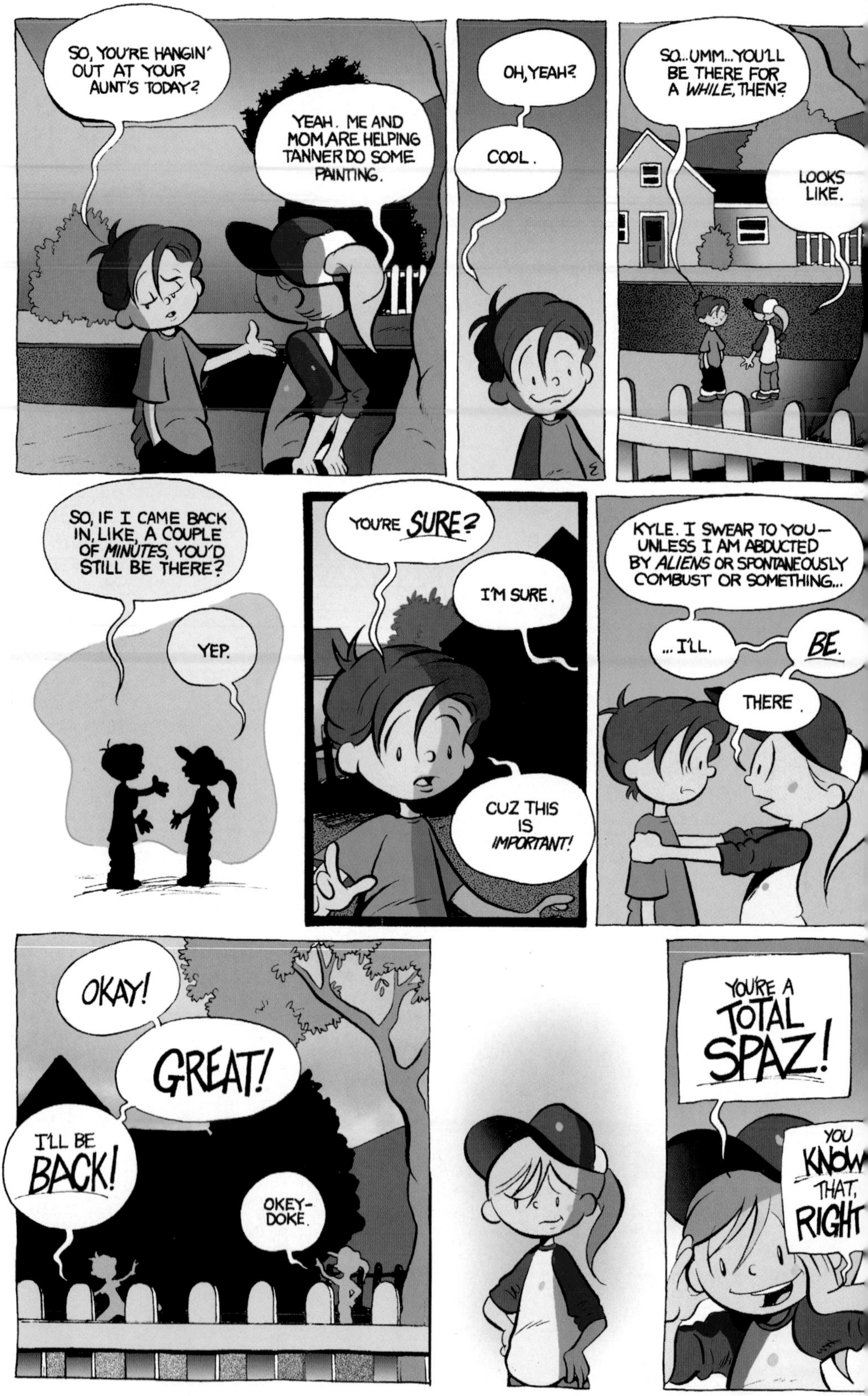
SO, YOU'RE HANGIN' OUT AT YOUR AUNT'S TODAY?
YEAH. ME AND MOM ARE HELPING TANNER DO SOME PAINTING.
OH, YEAH?
COOL.
SO...UMM...YOU'LL BE THERE FOR A WHILE, THEN?
LOOKS LIKE.
SO, IF I CAME BACK IN, LIKE, A COUPLE OF MINUTES, YOU'D STILL BE THERE?
YEP.
YOU'RE SURE?
I'M SURE.
CUZ THIS IS IMPORTANT!
KYLE. I SWEAR TO YOU— UNLESS I AM ABDUCTED BY ALIENS OR SPONTANEOUSLY COMBUST OR SOMETHING...
...I'LL.
BE.
THERE.
OKAY!
GREAT!
I'LL BE BACK!
OKEY-DOKE.
YOU'RE A TOTAL SPAZ!
YOU KNOW THAT, RIGHT

87

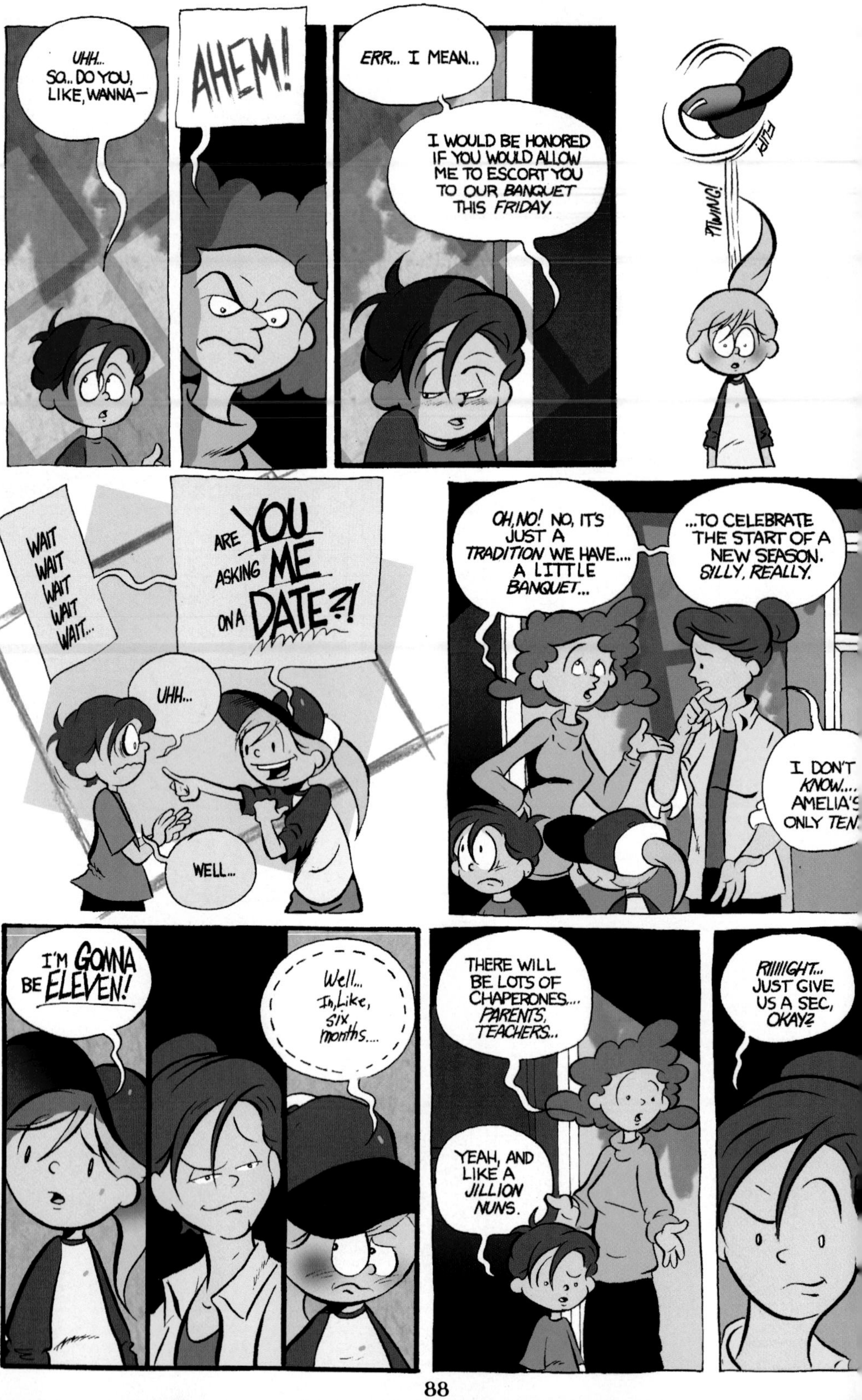
UHH... SO... DO YOU, LIKE, WANNA—
AHEM!
ERR... I MEAN...
I WOULD BE HONORED IF YOU WOULD ALLOW ME TO ESCORT YOU TO OUR BANQUET THIS FRIDAY.
FLIP
PTWING!
WAIT WAIT WAIT WAIT WAIT...
ARE YOU ASKING ME ON A DATE?!
UHH...
WELL...
OH, NO! NO, IT'S JUST A TRADITION WE HAVE.... A LITTLE BANQUET...
...TO CELEBRATE THE START OF A NEW SEASON. SILLY, REALLY.
I DON'T KNOW.... AMELIA'S ONLY TEN.
I'M GONNA BE ELEVEN!
Well... In, Like, six months....
THERE WILL BE LOTS OF CHAPERONES.... PARENTS, TEACHERS...
YEAH, AND LIKE A JILLION NUNS.
RIIIIGHT... JUST GIVE US A SEC, OKAY?

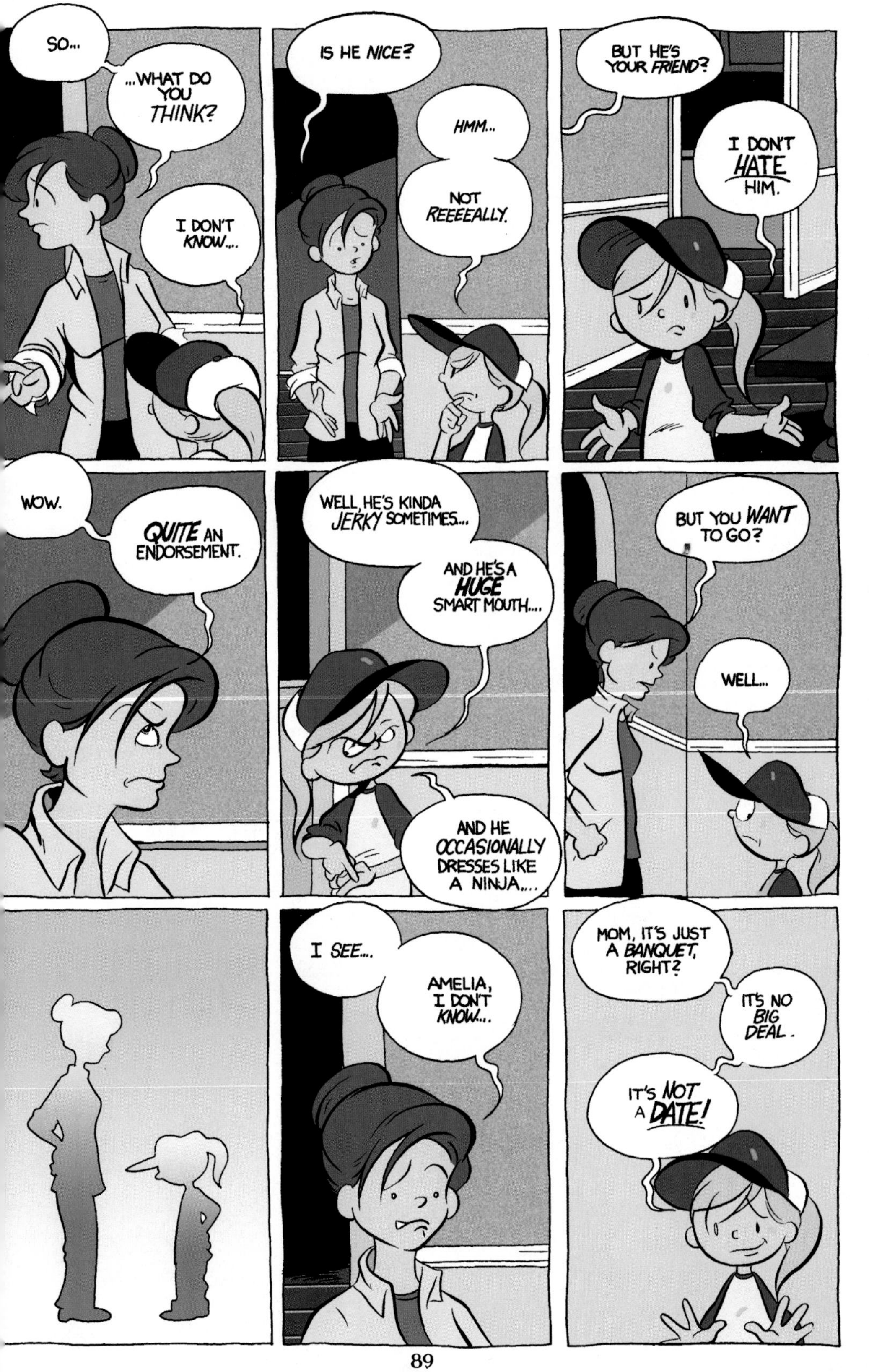
SO...
...WHAT DO YOU THINK?
I DON'T KNOW....
IS HE NICE?
HMM...
NOT REEEEALLY.
BUT HE'S YOUR FRIEND?
I DON'T HATE HIM.
WOW.
QUITE AN ENDORSEMENT.
WELL, HE'S KINDA JERKY SOMETIMES...
AND HE'S A HUGE SMART MOUTH....
AND HE OCCASIONALLY DRESSES LIKE A NINJA....
BUT YOU WANT TO GO?
WELL...
I SEE....
AMELIA, I DON'T KNOW...
MOM, IT'S JUST A BANQUET, RIGHT?
IT'S NO BIG DEAL.
IT'S NOT A DATE!

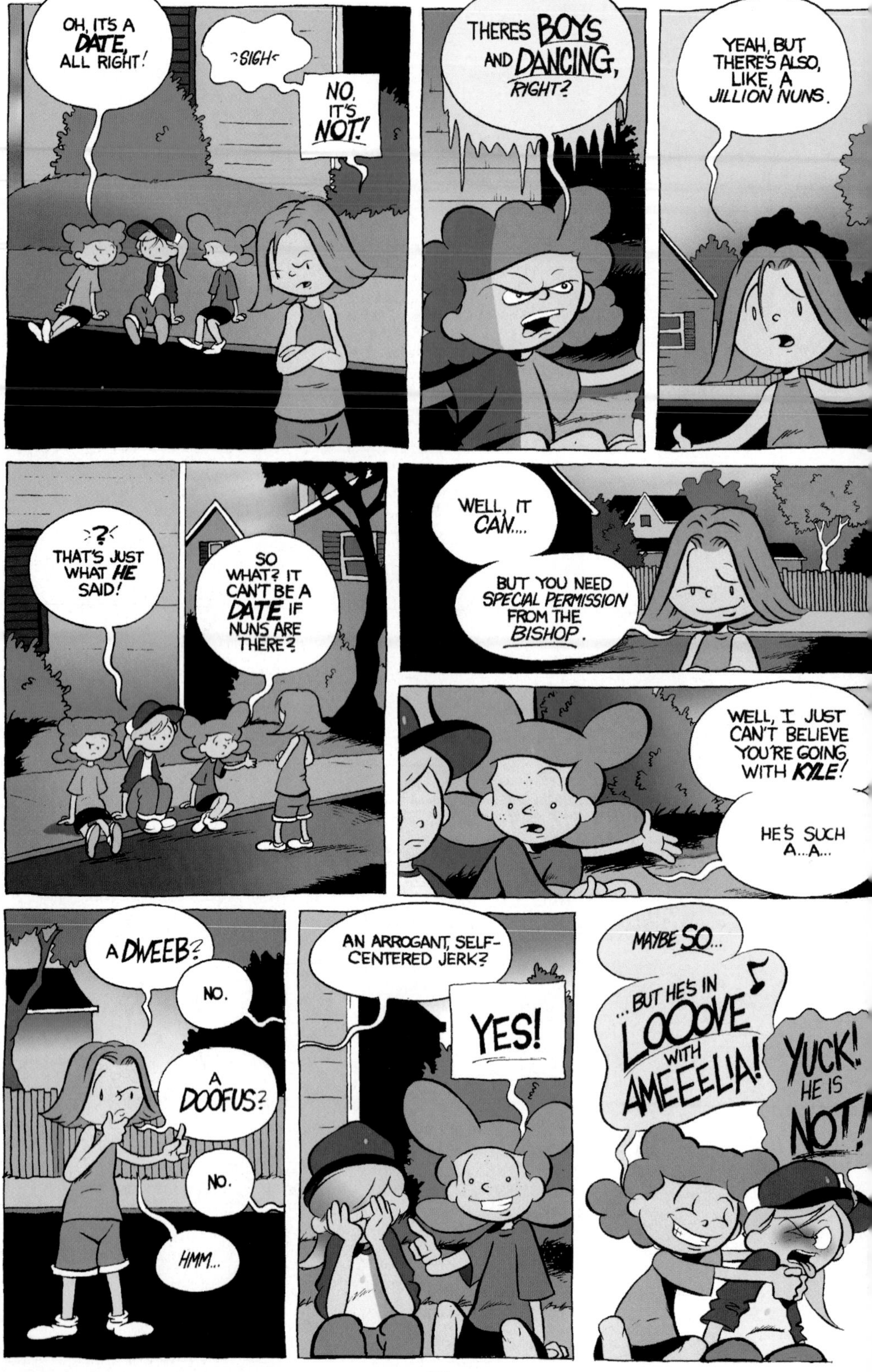

OH, IT'S A DATE, ALL RIGHT!
SIGH
NO, IT'S NOT!
THERE'S BOYS AND DANCING, RIGHT?
YEAH, BUT THERE'S ALSO, LIKE, A JILLION NUNS.
?
THAT'S JUST WHAT HE SAID!
SO WHAT? IT CAN'T BE A DATE IF NUNS ARE THERE?
WELL, IT CAN...
BUT YOU NEED SPECIAL PERMISSION FROM THE BISHOP.
WELL, I JUST CAN'T BELIEVE YOU'RE GOING WITH KYLE!
HE'S SUCH A...A...
A DWEEB?
NO.
A DOOFUS?
NO.
HMM...
AN ARROGANT, SELF-CENTERED JERK?
YES!
MAYBE SO...
...BUT HE'S IN LOOOVE WITH AMEEELIA!
YUCK! HE IS NOT!

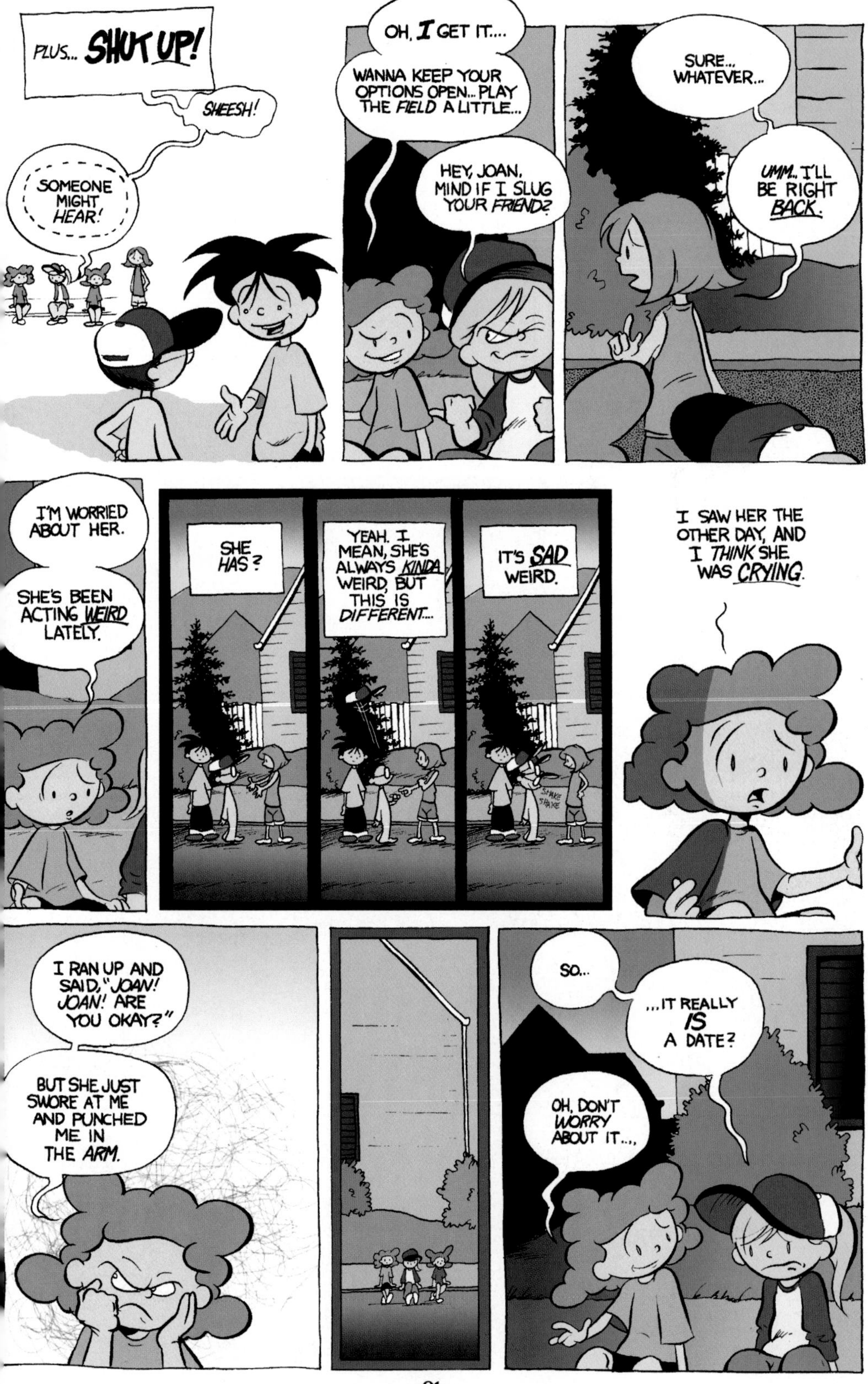
PLUS... SHUT UP!
SHEESH!
SOMEONE MIGHT HEAR!
OH, I GET IT....
WANNA KEEP YOUR OPTIONS OPEN... PLAY THE FIELD A LITTLE...
HEY, JOAN. MIND IF I SLUG YOUR FRIEND?
SURE... WHATEVER...
UMM.. I'LL BE RIGHT BACK.
I'M WORRIED ABOUT HER.
SHE'S BEEN ACTING WEIRD LATELY.
SHE HAS?
YEAH. I MEAN, SHE'S ALWAYS KINDA WEIRD, BUT THIS IS DIFFERENT....
IT'S SAD WEIRD.
I SAW HER THE OTHER DAY, AND I THINK SHE WAS CRYING.
I RAN UP AND SAID, "JOAN! JOAN! ARE YOU OKAY?"
BUT SHE JUST SWORE AT ME AND PUNCHED ME IN THE ARM.
SO...
...IT REALLY IS A DATE?
OH, DON'T WORRY ABOUT IT...,

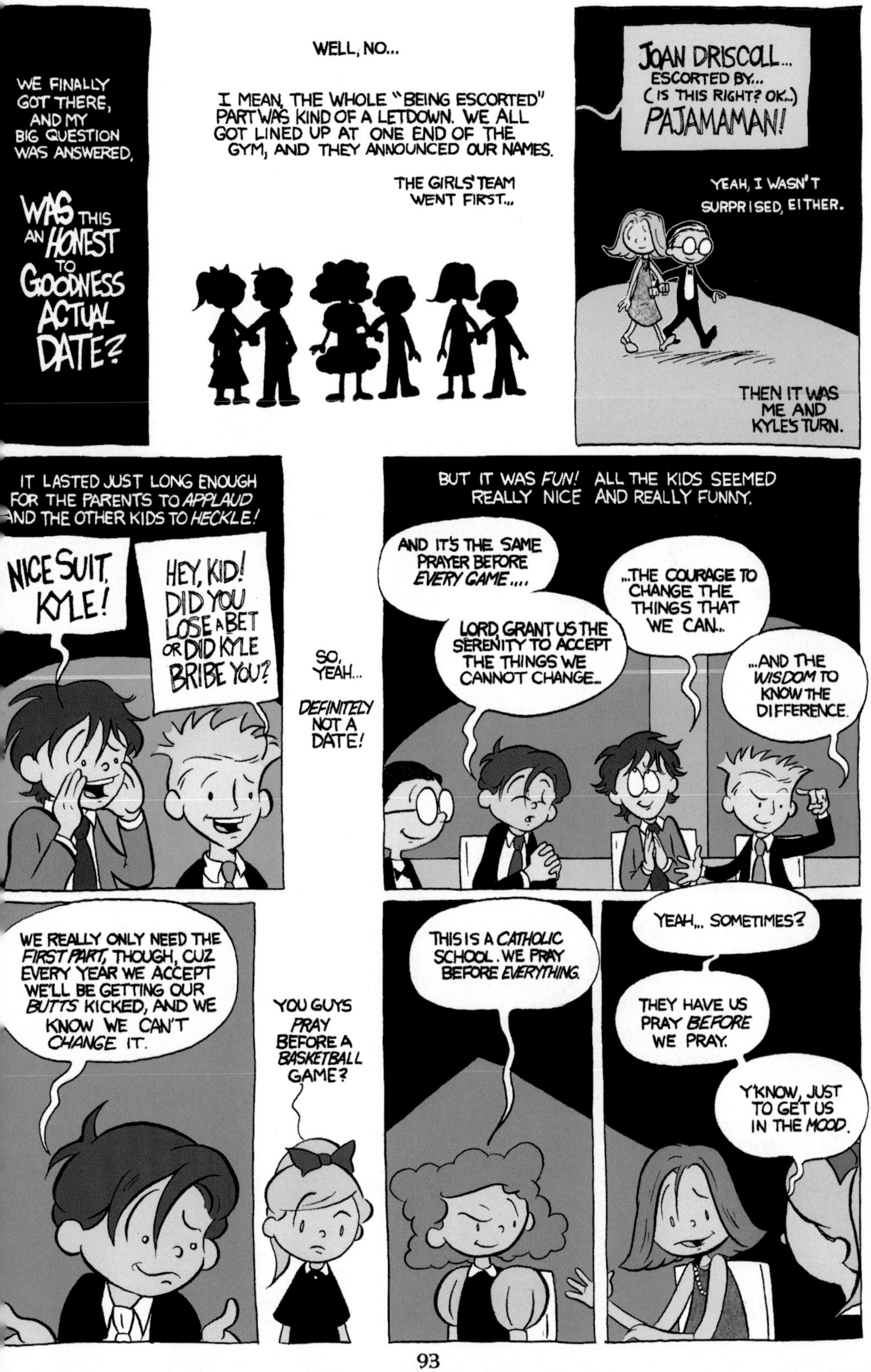

WE FINALLY GOT THERE, AND MY BIG QUESTION WAS ANSWERED.
WAS THIS AN HONEST TO GOODNESS ACTUAL DATE?
WELL, NO...
I MEAN, THE WHOLE "BEING ESCORTED" PART WAS KIND OF A LETDOWN. WE ALL GOT LINED UP AT ONE END OF THE GYM, AND THEY ANNOUNCED OUR NAMES.
THE GIRLS' TEAM WENT FIRST...
JOAN DRISCOLL... ESCORTED BY... (IS THIS RIGHT? OK..) PAJAMAMAN!
YEAH, I WASN'T SURPRISED, EITHER.
THEN IT WAS ME AND KYLE'S TURN.
IT LASTED JUST LONG ENOUGH FOR THE PARENTS TO APPLAUD AND THE OTHER KIDS TO HECKLE!
NICE SUIT, KYLE!
HEY, KID! DID YOU LOSE A BET OR DID KYLE BRIBE YOU?
SO, YEAH...
DEFINITELY NOT A DATE!
BUT IT WAS FUN! ALL THE KIDS SEEMED REALLY NICE AND REALLY FUNNY.
AND IT'S THE SAME PRAYER BEFORE EVERY GAME....
LORD GRANT US THE SERENITY TO ACCEPT THE THINGS WE CANNOT CHANGE..
...THE COURAGE TO CHANGE THE THINGS THAT WE CAN..
...AND THE WISDOM TO KNOW THE DIFFERENCE.
WE REALLY ONLY NEED THE FIRST PART, THOUGH, CUZ EVERY YEAR WE ACCEPT WE'LL BE GETTING OUR BUTTS KICKED, AND WE KNOW WE CAN'T CHANGE IT.
YOU GUYS PRAY BEFORE A BASKETBALL GAME?
THIS IS A CATHOLIC SCHOOL. WE PRAY BEFORE EVERYTHING.
YEAH... SOMETIMES?
THEY HAVE US PRAY BEFORE WE PRAY.
Y'KNOW, JUST TO GET US IN THE MOOD.

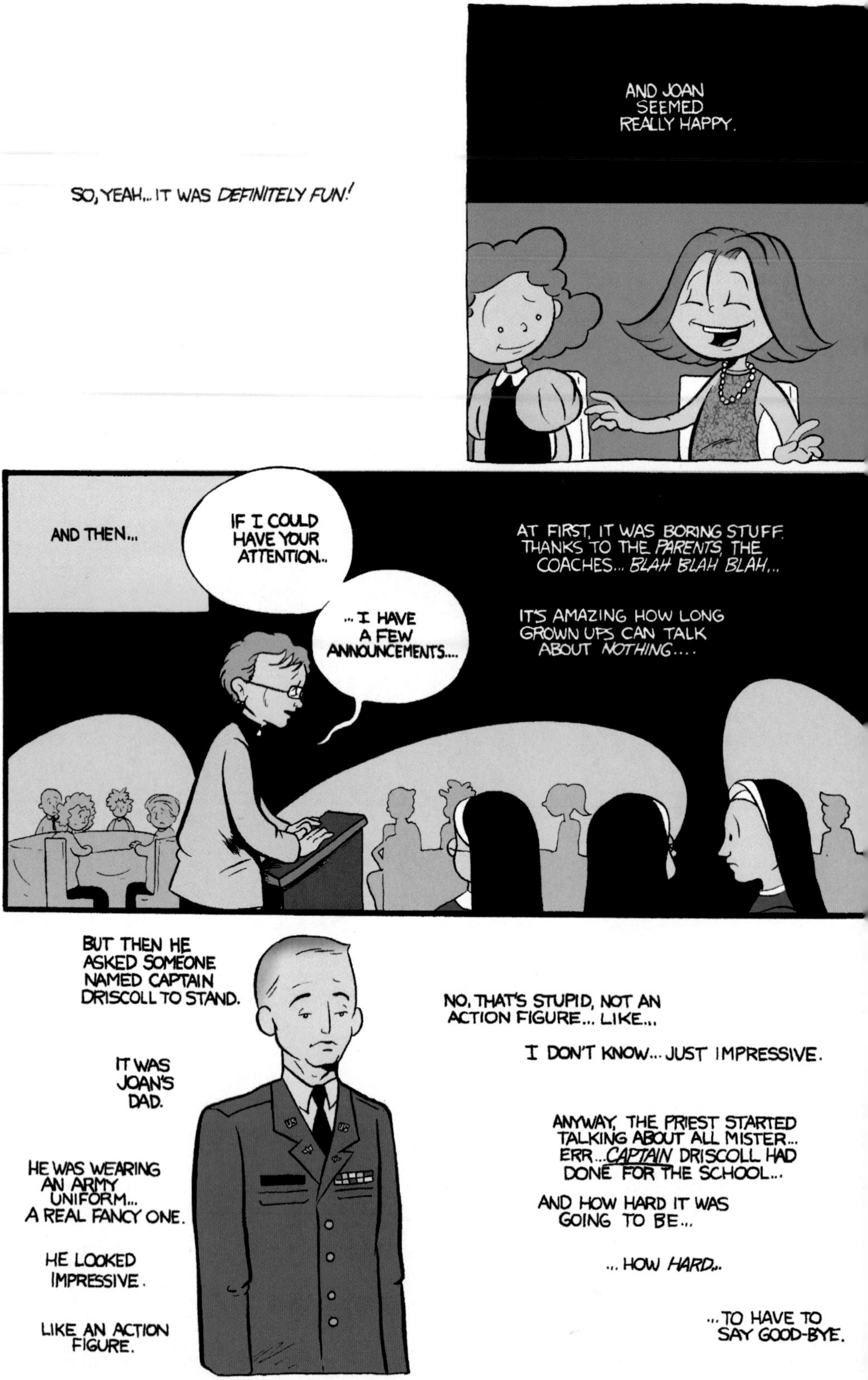
SO, YEAH... IT WAS DEFINITELY FUN!
AND JOAN SEEMED REALLY HAPPY.
AND THEN...
IF I COULD HAVE YOUR ATTENTION...
... I HAVE A FEW ANNOUNCEMENTS....
AT FIRST, IT WAS BORING STUFF. THANKS TO THE PARENTS, THE COACHES... BLAH BLAH BLAH...
IT'S AMAZING HOW LONG GROWN UPS CAN TALK ABOUT NOTHING....
BUT THEN HE ASKED SOMEONE NAMED CAPTAIN DRISCOLL TO STAND.
IT WAS JOAN'S DAD.
HE WAS WEARING AN ARMY UNIFORM... A REAL FANCY ONE.
HE LOOKED IMPRESSIVE.
LIKE AN ACTION FIGURE.
NO, THAT'S STUPID, NOT AN ACTION FIGURE... LIKE...
I DON'T KNOW... JUST IMPRESSIVE.
ANYWAY, THE PRIEST STARTED TALKING ABOUT ALL MISTER... ERR...CAPTAIN DRISCOLL HAD DONE FOR THE SCHOOL...
AND HOW HARD IT WAS GOING TO BE...
... HOW HARD...
... TO HAVE TO SAY GOOD-BYE.

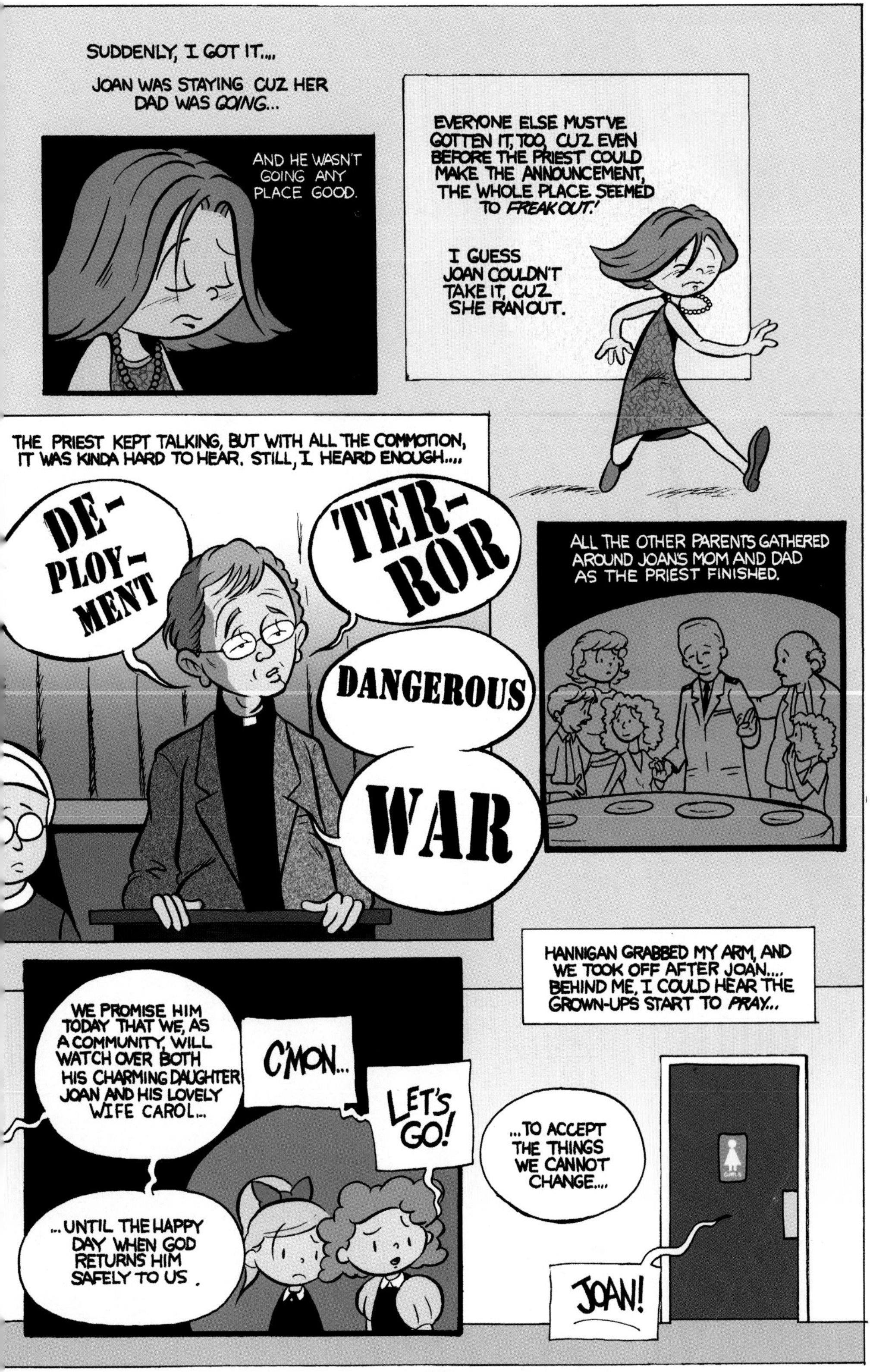
SUDDENLY, I GOT IT....
JOAN WAS STAYING CUZ HER DAD WAS GOING...
AND HE WASN'T GOING ANY PLACE GOOD.
EVERYONE ELSE MUST'VE GOTTEN IT, TOO, CUZ EVEN BEFORE THE PRIEST COULD MAKE THE ANNOUNCEMENT, THE WHOLE PLACE SEEMED TO FREAK OUT!
I GUESS JOAN COULDN'T TAKE IT, CUZ SHE RAN OUT.
THE PRIEST KEPT TALKING, BUT WITH ALL THE COMMOTION, IT WAS KINDA HARD TO HEAR. STILL, I HEARD ENOUGH....
DE-PLOY-MENT
TER-ROR
DANGEROUS
WAR
ALL THE OTHER PARENTS GATHERED AROUND JOAN'S MOM AND DAD AS THE PRIEST FINISHED.
WE PROMISE HIM TODAY THAT WE, AS A COMMUNITY, WILL WATCH OVER BOTH HIS CHARMING DAUGHTER JOAN AND HIS LOVELY WIFE CAROL...
C'MON...
LET'S GO!
...UNTIL THE HAPPY DAY WHEN GOD RETURNS HIM SAFELY TO US.
HANNIGAN GRABBED MY ARM, AND WE TOOK OFF AFTER JOAN.... BEHIND ME, I COULD HEAR THE GROWN-UPS START TO PRAY...
...TO ACCEPT THE THINGS WE CANNOT CHANGE....
JOAN!

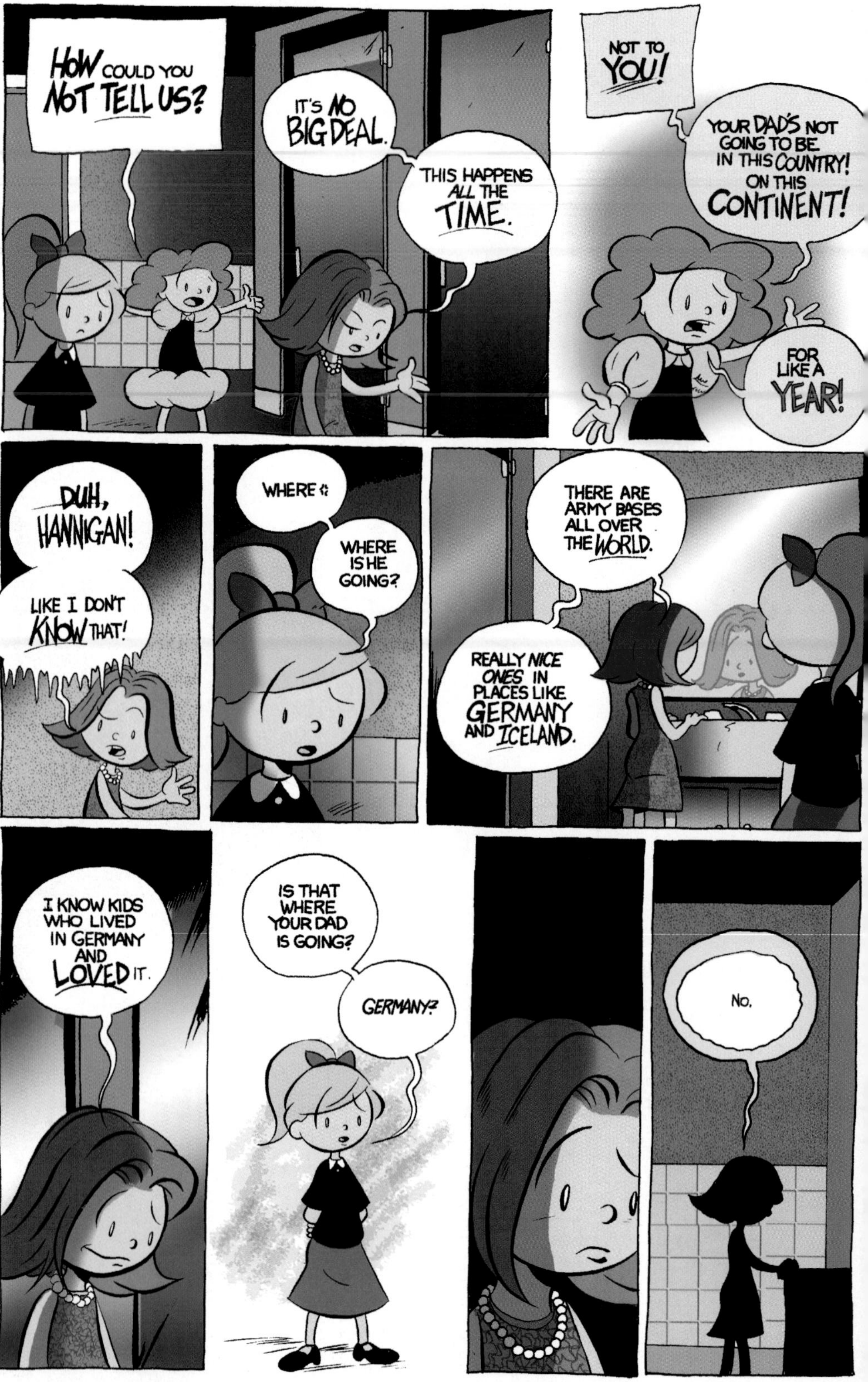
HOW COULD YOU NOT TELL US?
IT'S NO BIG DEAL.
THIS HAPPENS ALL THE TIME.
NOT TO YOU!
YOUR DAD'S NOT GOING TO BE IN THIS COUNTRY! ON THIS CONTINENT!
FOR LIKE A YEAR!
DUH, HANNIGAN!
LIKE I DON'T KNOW THAT!
WHERE…
WHERE IS HE GOING?
THERE ARE ARMY BASES ALL OVER THE WORLD.
REALLY NICE ONES IN PLACES LIKE GERMANY AND ICELAND.
I KNOW KIDS WHO LIVED IN GERMANY AND LOVED IT.
IS THAT WHERE YOUR DAD IS GOING?
GERMANY?
NO.

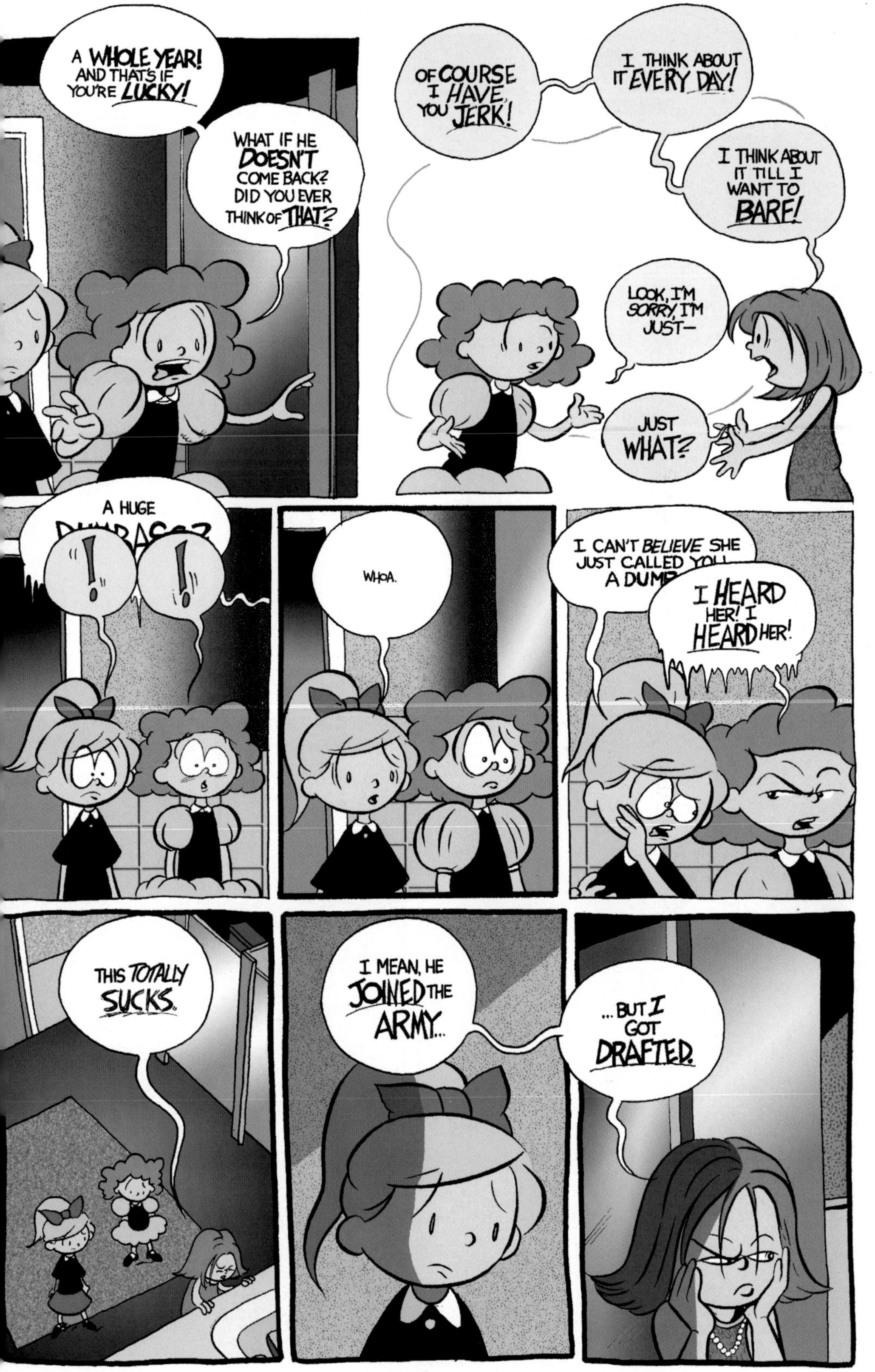
A WHOLE YEAR! AND THAT'S IF YOU'RE LUCKY!
WHAT IF HE DOESN'T COME BACK? DID YOU EVER THINK OF THAT?
OF COURSE I HAVE, YOU JERK!
I THINK ABOUT IT EVERY DAY!
I THINK ABOUT IT TILL I WANT TO BARF!
LOOK, I'M SORRY, I'M JUST—
JUST WHAT?
A HUGE
!
!
WHOA.
I CAN'T BELIEVE SHE JUST CALLED YOU A DUMB
I HEARD HER! I HEARD HER!
THIS TOTALLY SUCKS.
I MEAN, HE JOINED THE ARMY...
... BUT I GOT DRAFTED.

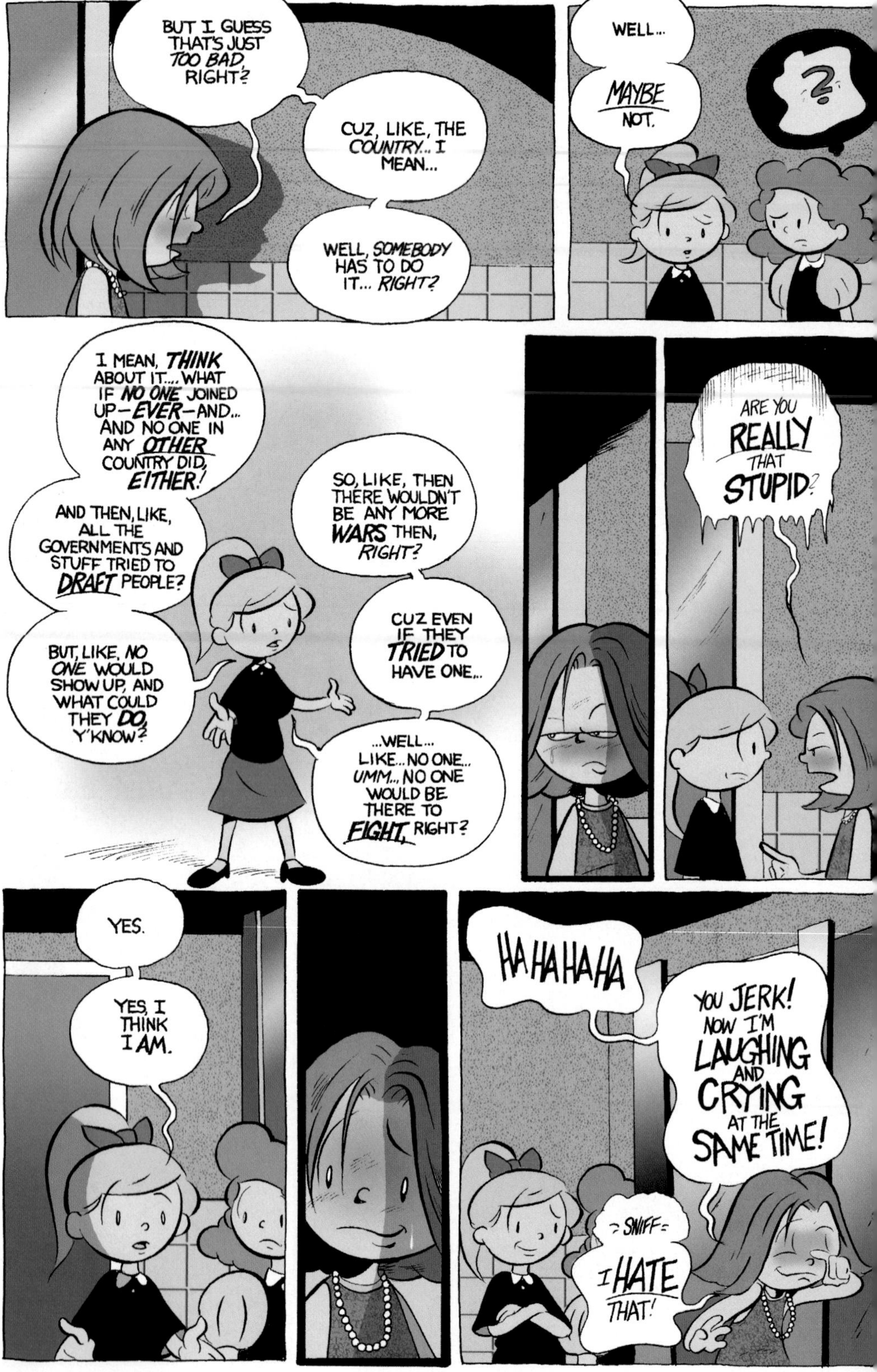

BUT I GUESS THAT'S JUST TOO BAD, RIGHT?
CUZ, LIKE, THE COUNTRY... I MEAN...
WELL, SOMEBODY HAS TO DO IT... RIGHT?
WELL...
MAYBE NOT.
?
I MEAN, THINK ABOUT IT.... WHAT IF NO ONE JOINED UP—EVER—AND... AND NO ONE IN ANY OTHER COUNTRY DID, EITHER!
AND THEN, LIKE, ALL THE GOVERNMENTS AND STUFF TRIED TO DRAFT PEOPLE?
BUT, LIKE, NO ONE WOULD SHOW UP, AND WHAT COULD THEY DO, Y'KNOW?
SO, LIKE, THEN THERE WOULDN'T BE ANY MORE WARS THEN, RIGHT?
CUZ EVEN IF THEY TRIED TO HAVE ONE...
...WELL... LIKE... NO ONE... UMM... NO ONE WOULD BE THERE TO FIGHT, RIGHT?
ARE YOU REALLY THAT STUPID?
YES.
YES, I THINK I AM.
HAHAHAHA
YOU JERK! NOW I'M LAUGHING AND CRYING AT THE SAME TIME!
SNIFF
I HATE THAT!

WOW, USUALLY I HAVE TO SING TO GET THAT *REACTION*.

PLEASE *DON'T*.

SO HOW... HOW HAVE YOU BEEN DEALING?

WELL...

I HAVE THIS FRIEND, T.J, AND HIS DAD JUST GOT BACK, SO WE'VE KINDA *TALKED* AN' STUFF...

...WHICH IS COOL.

CUZ, IT'S KINDA HARD TO TALK ABOUT, Y'KNOW? TO MAKE PEOPLE UNDERSTAND? CUZ, IT'S, LIKE, I'M *SAD* THAT HE'S *LEAVING*, BUT I'M *PROUD* THAT HE'S *GOING*, AND I'M *MAD* THAT THEY'RE *TAKING* HIM.

[K]NOW THAT DOESN'T MAKE [S]ENSE, BUT T.J UNDERSTOOD.

[PL]US, HE GAVE ME, *UMM*, TIPS?

[LI]KE, HE HAD HIS DAD READ [BO]OKS ONTO CD, SO HE COULD [LI]STEN TO THEM WHILE HIS [DA]D WAS GONE. MY DAD ALREADY [MA]DE A BUNCH FOR ME.

[T]J'S MOM ALSO HAD, LIKE, A LITTLE [PI]LLOW MADE WITH HIS DAD'S [PI]CTURE ON IT. T.J LOVED IT, BUT I'M NOT SURE....

I CAN SEE WHY IT WOULD BE GOOD, THOUGH. THE SCARIEST THING IS THINKING I MIGHT FORGET WHAT MY DAD LOOKS LIKE.

SEE... PEOPLE THINK THEY KNOW HOW LONG A YEAR IS, BUT THEY DON'T. I DO, THOUGH, I'VE DONE THE MATH.

ANYWAY, T.J ALSO SAID I SHOULD KEEP *BUSY*, SO I WOULDN'T THINK ABOUT IT SO MUCH....

AND THAT AT *NIGHT*, I SHOULD TRY TO FALL ASLEEP *RIGHT AWAY*...

...SO I DON'T LIE THERE *THINKING* ABOUT IT.

HE SAID IT'S *WORST* AT *NIGHT*.

OR IT WAS FOR *HIM*, ANYWAY.

THAT'S GONNA BE *HARD*, THOUGH... CUZ I'M *ALREADY* KIND OF AN...

ESOMIAC?

OR *WHATEVER* YOU CALL IT.

99

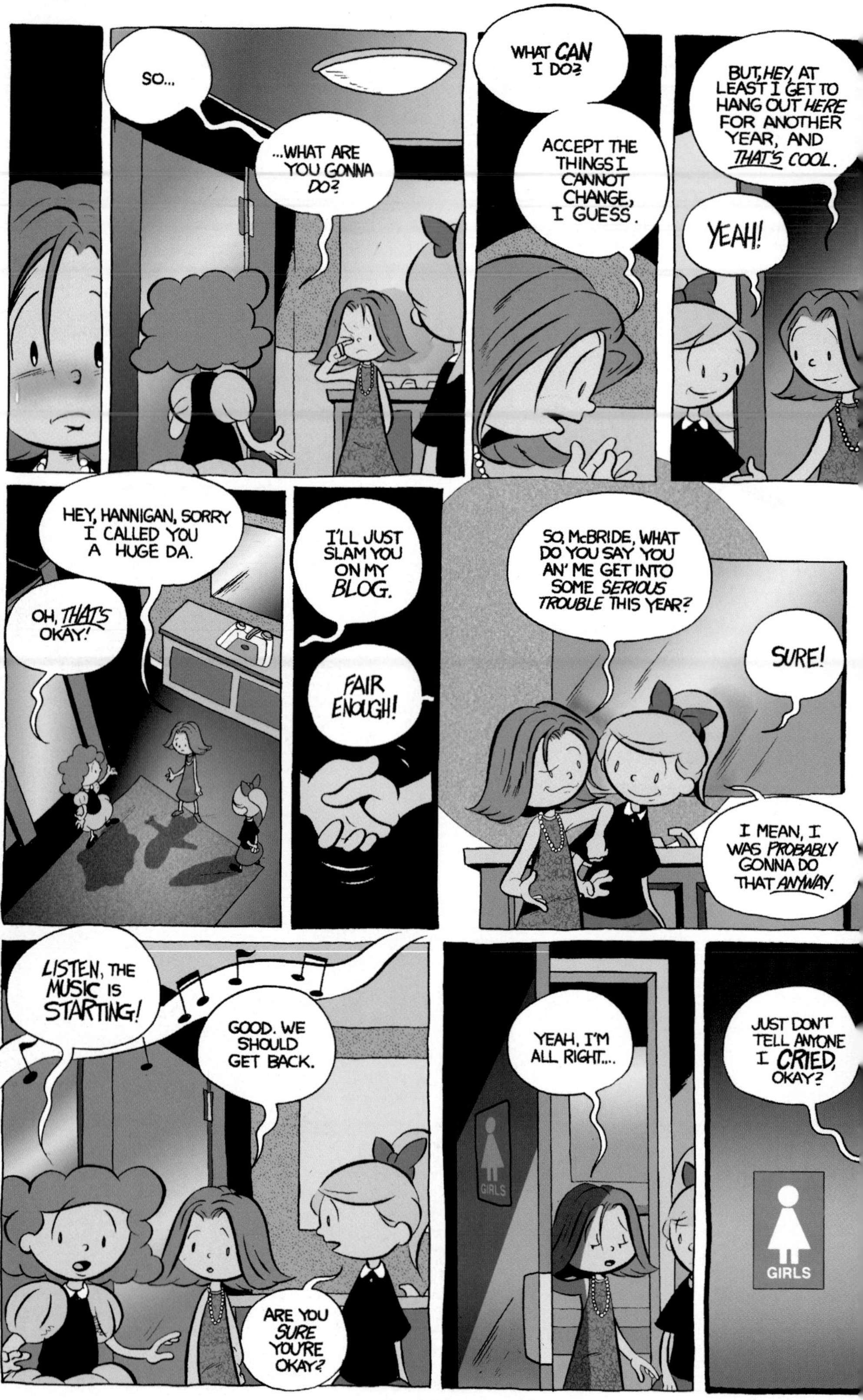
SO...
...WHAT ARE YOU GONNA DO?
WHAT CAN I DO?
ACCEPT THE THINGS I CANNOT CHANGE, I GUESS.
BUT, HEY, AT LEAST I GET TO HANG OUT HERE FOR ANOTHER YEAR, AND THAT'S COOL.
YEAH!
HEY, HANNIGAN, SORRY I CALLED YOU A HUGE DA.
OH, THAT'S OKAY!
I'LL JUST SLAM YOU ON MY BLOG.
FAIR ENOUGH!
SO, McBRIDE, WHAT DO YOU SAY YOU AN' ME GET INTO SOME SERIOUS TROUBLE THIS YEAR?
SURE!
I MEAN, I WAS PROBABLY GONNA DO THAT ANYWAY.
LISTEN, THE MUSIC IS STARTING!
GOOD. WE SHOULD GET BACK.
ARE YOU SURE YOU'RE OKAY?
YEAH, I'M ALL RIGHT...
GIRLS
JUST DON'T TELL ANYONE I CRIED, OKAY?
GIRLS

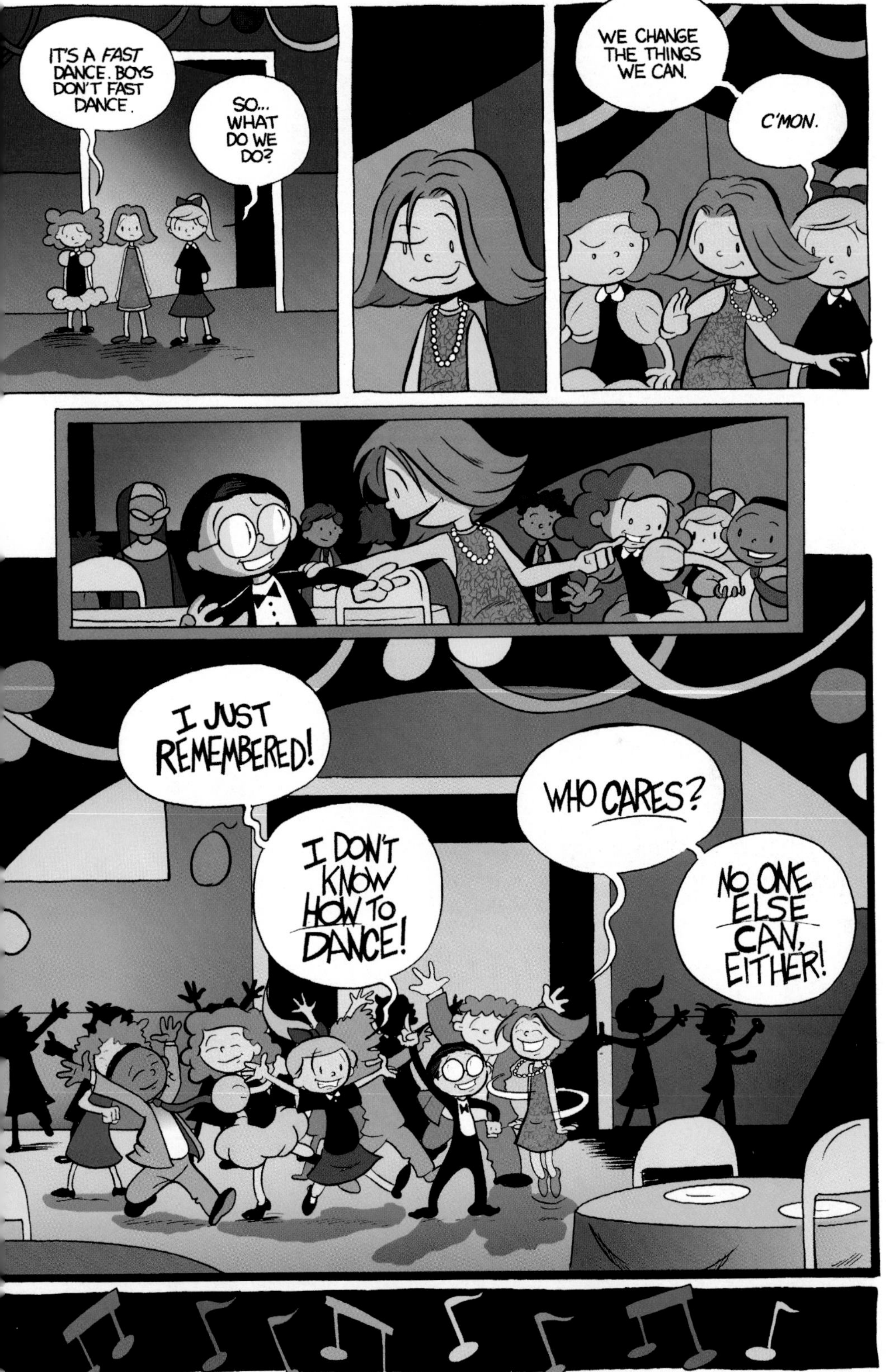
IT'S A FAST DANCE. BOYS DON'T FAST DANCE.
SO... WHAT DO WE DO?
WE CHANGE THE THINGS WE CAN.
C'MON.
I JUST REMEMBERED!
I DON'T KNOW HOW TO DANCE!
WHO CARES?
NO ONE ELSE CAN, EITHER!

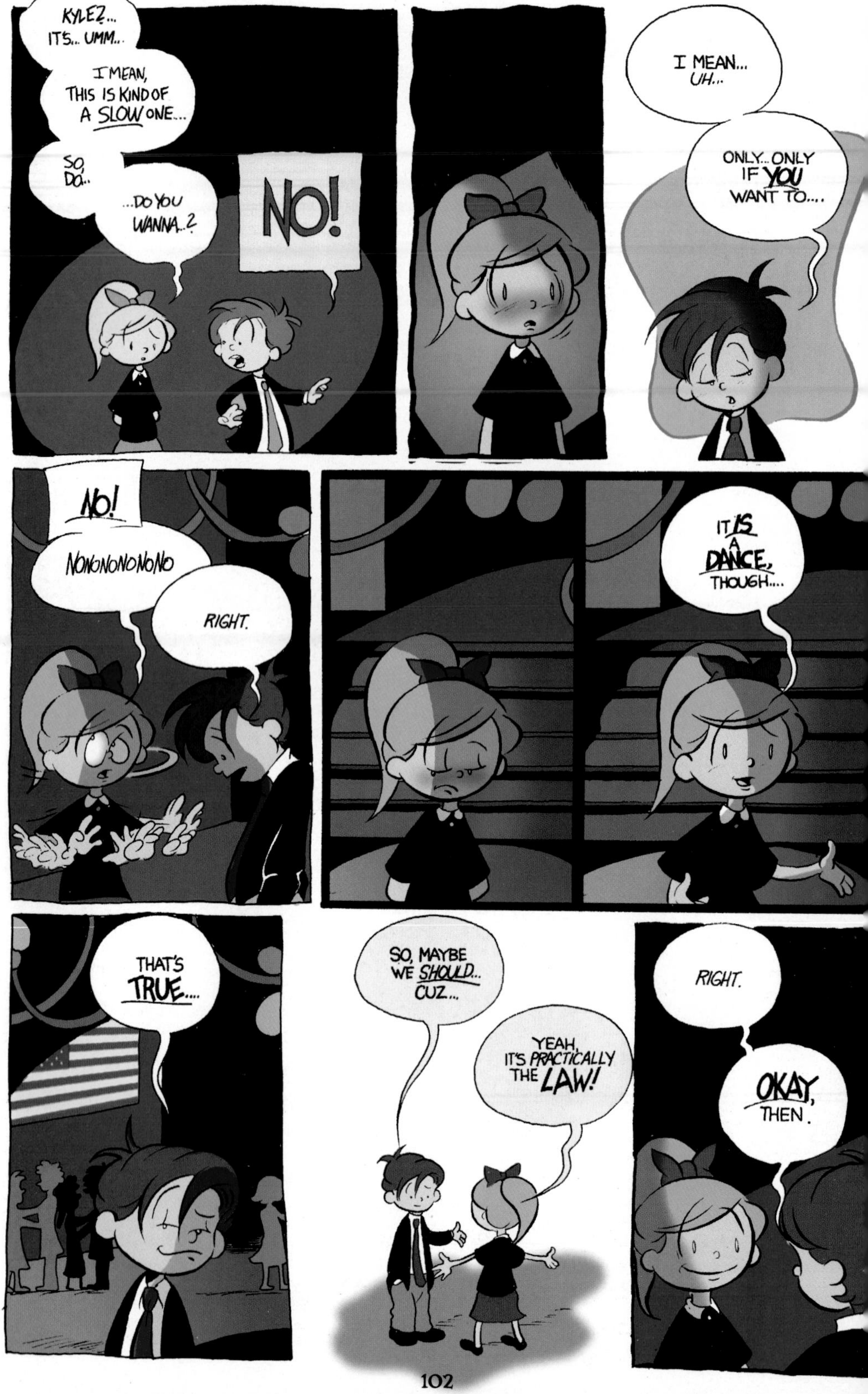
KYLE?...
IT'S... UMM...
I MEAN, THIS IS KIND OF A SLOW ONE...
SO, DO...
...DO YOU WANNA..?
NO!
I MEAN... UH...
ONLY... ONLY IF YOU WANT TO....
NO!
NONONONONONO
RIGHT.
IT IS A DANCE, THOUGH....
THAT'S TRUE....
SO, MAYBE WE SHOULD... CUZ...
YEAH, IT'S PRACTICALLY THE LAW!
RIGHT.
OKAY, THEN.

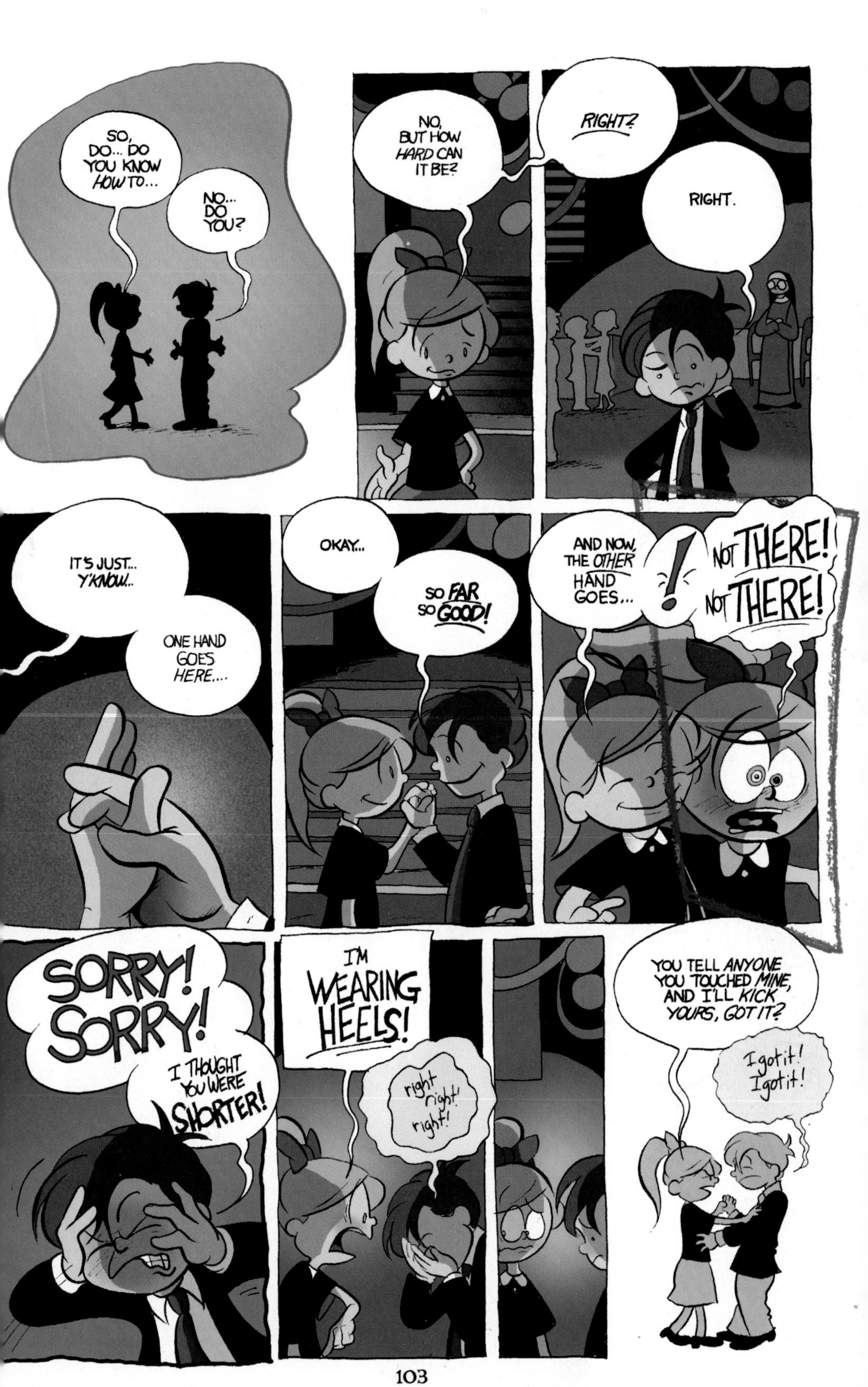
SO, DO... DO YOU KNOW HOW TO...
NO... DO YOU?
NO, BUT HOW HARD CAN IT BE?
RIGHT?
RIGHT.
IT'S JUST... Y'KNOW...
ONE HAND GOES HERE....
OKAY...
SO FAR SO GOOD!
AND NOW, THE OTHER HAND GOES...
!
NOT THERE! NOT THERE!
SORRY! SORRY!
I THOUGHT YOU WERE SHORTER!
I'M WEARING HEELS!
right right! right!
YOU TELL ANYONE YOU TOUCHED MINE, AND I'LL KICK YOURS, GOT IT?
I got it! I got it!

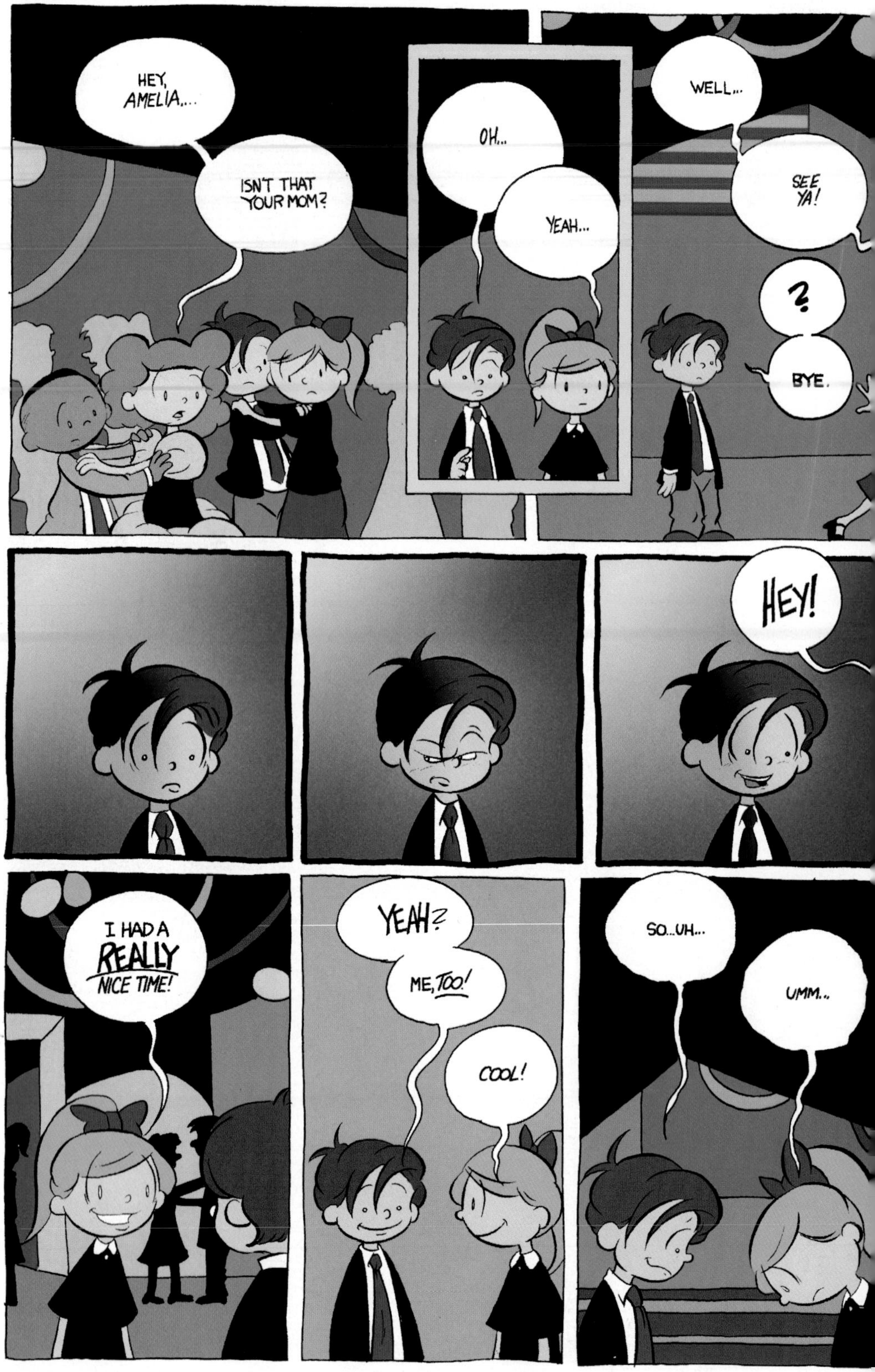
HEY, AMELIA,...
ISN'T THAT YOUR MOM?
OH...
YEAH...
WELL...
SEE YA!
?
BYE.
HEY!
I HAD A REALLY NICE TIME!
YEAH?
ME, TOO!
COOL!
SO...UH...
UMM...

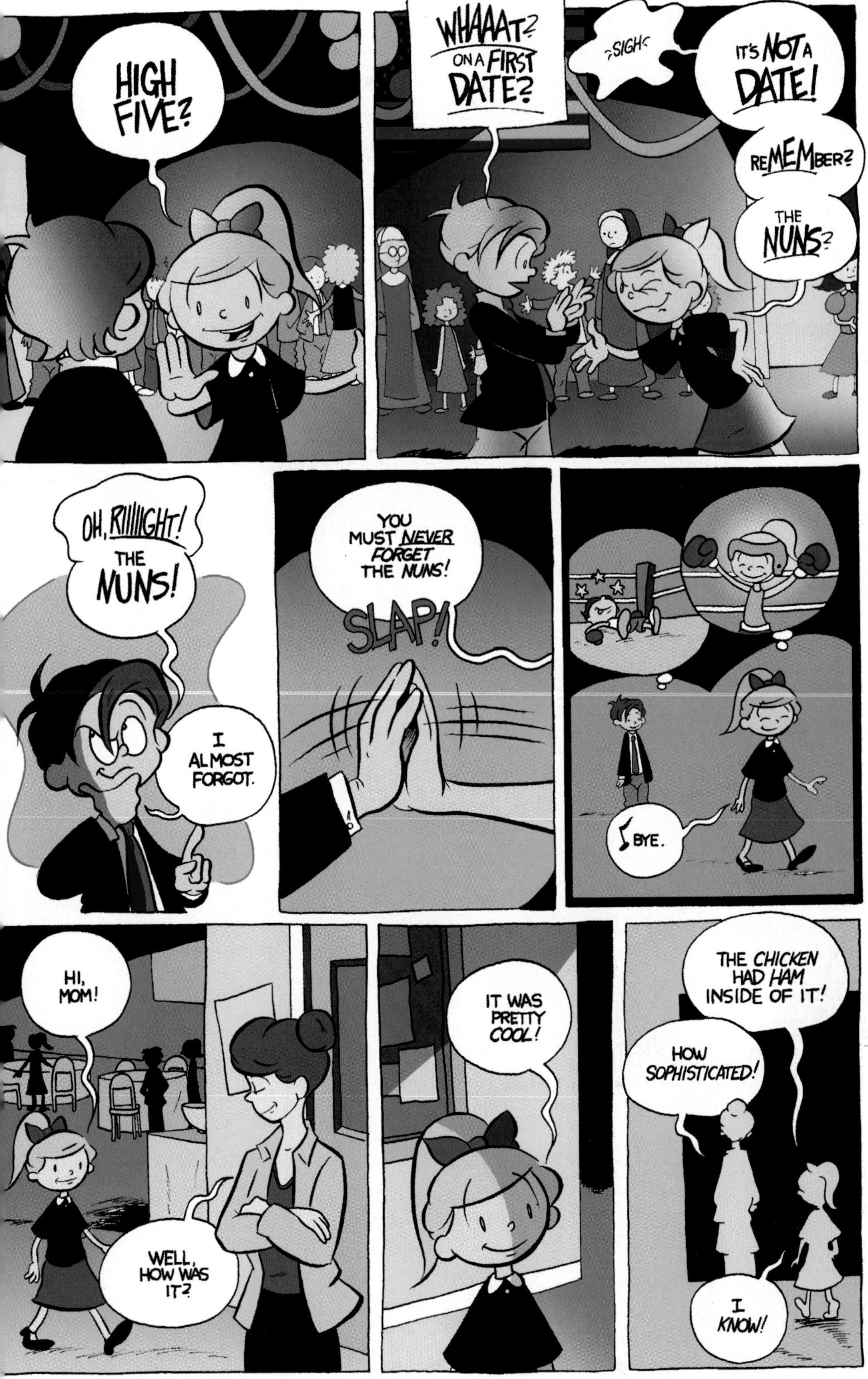
HIGH FIVE?
WHAAAT? ON A FIRST DATE?
SIGH
IT'S NOT A DATE!
REMEMBER?
THE NUNS?
OH, RIIIIGHT! THE NUNS!
I ALMOST FORGOT.
YOU MUST NEVER FORGET THE NUNS!
SLAP!
BYE.
HI, MOM!
WELL, HOW WAS IT?
IT WAS PRETTY COOL!
THE CHICKEN HAD HAM INSIDE OF IT!
HOW SOPHISTICATED!
I KNOW!

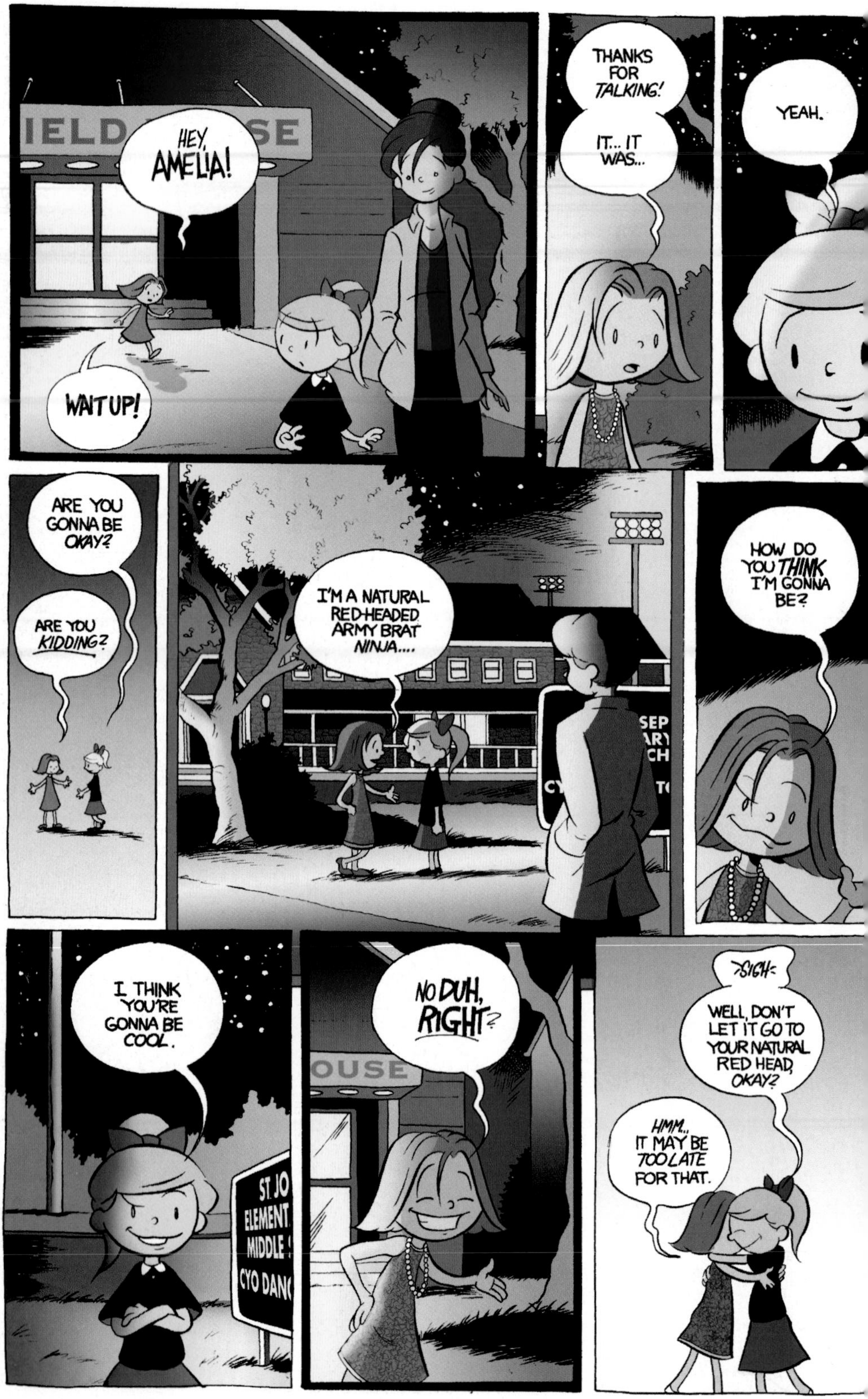
IELD
SE
HEY, AMELIA!
WAIT UP!
THANKS FOR TALKING!
IT... IT WAS...
YEAH.
ARE YOU GONNA BE OKAY?
ARE YOU KIDDING?
I'M A NATURAL RED-HEADED ARMY BRAT NINJA....
HOW DO YOU THINK I'M GONNA BE?
I THINK YOU'RE GONNA BE COOL.
ST. JO
ELEMENT
MIDDLE
CYO DANC
NO DUH, RIGHT?
OUSE
>SIGH<
WELL, DON'T LET IT GO TO YOUR NATURAL RED HEAD, OKAY?
HMM... IT MAY BE TOO LATE FOR THAT.

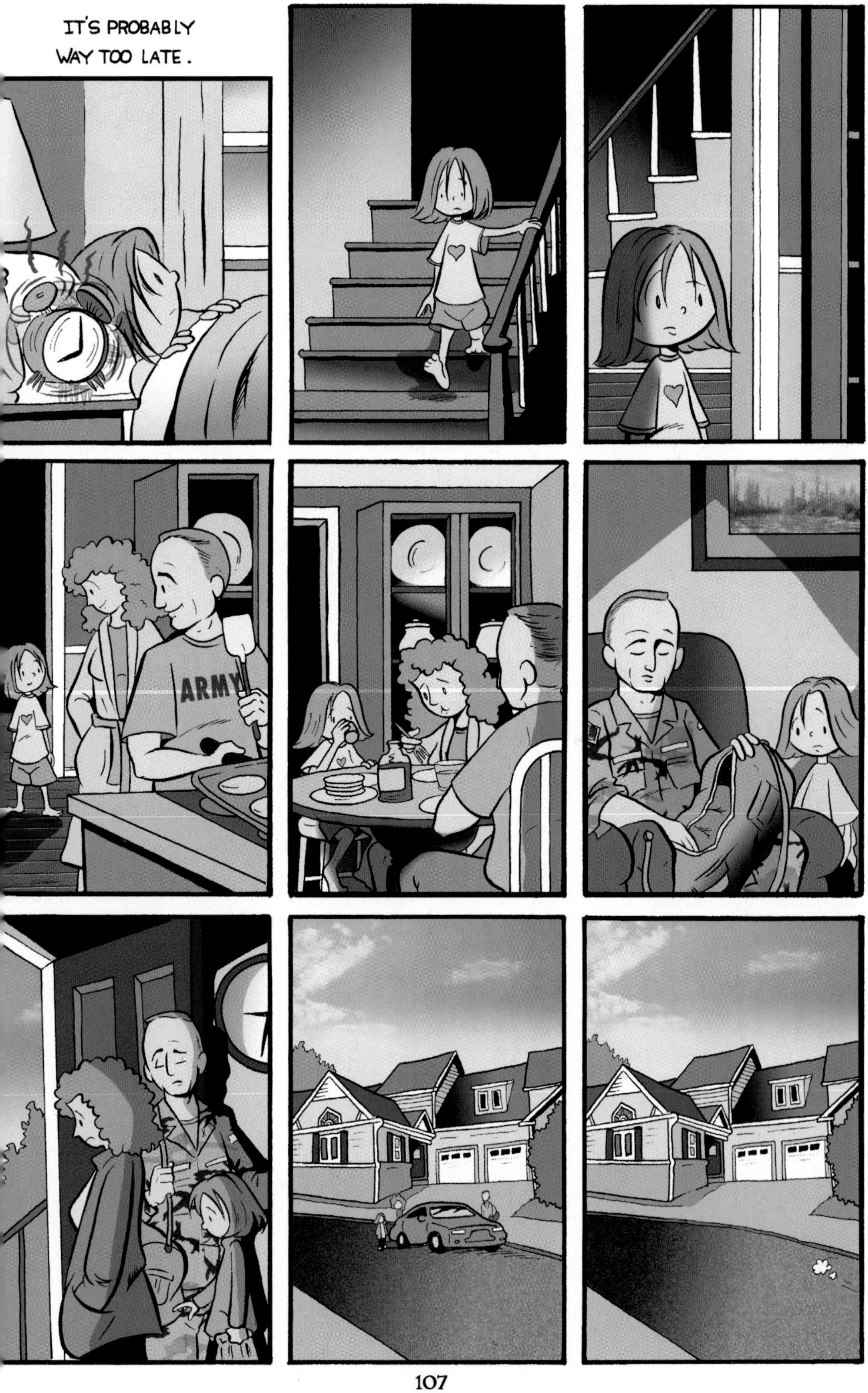
IT'S PROBABLY
WAY TOO LATE.
ARMY

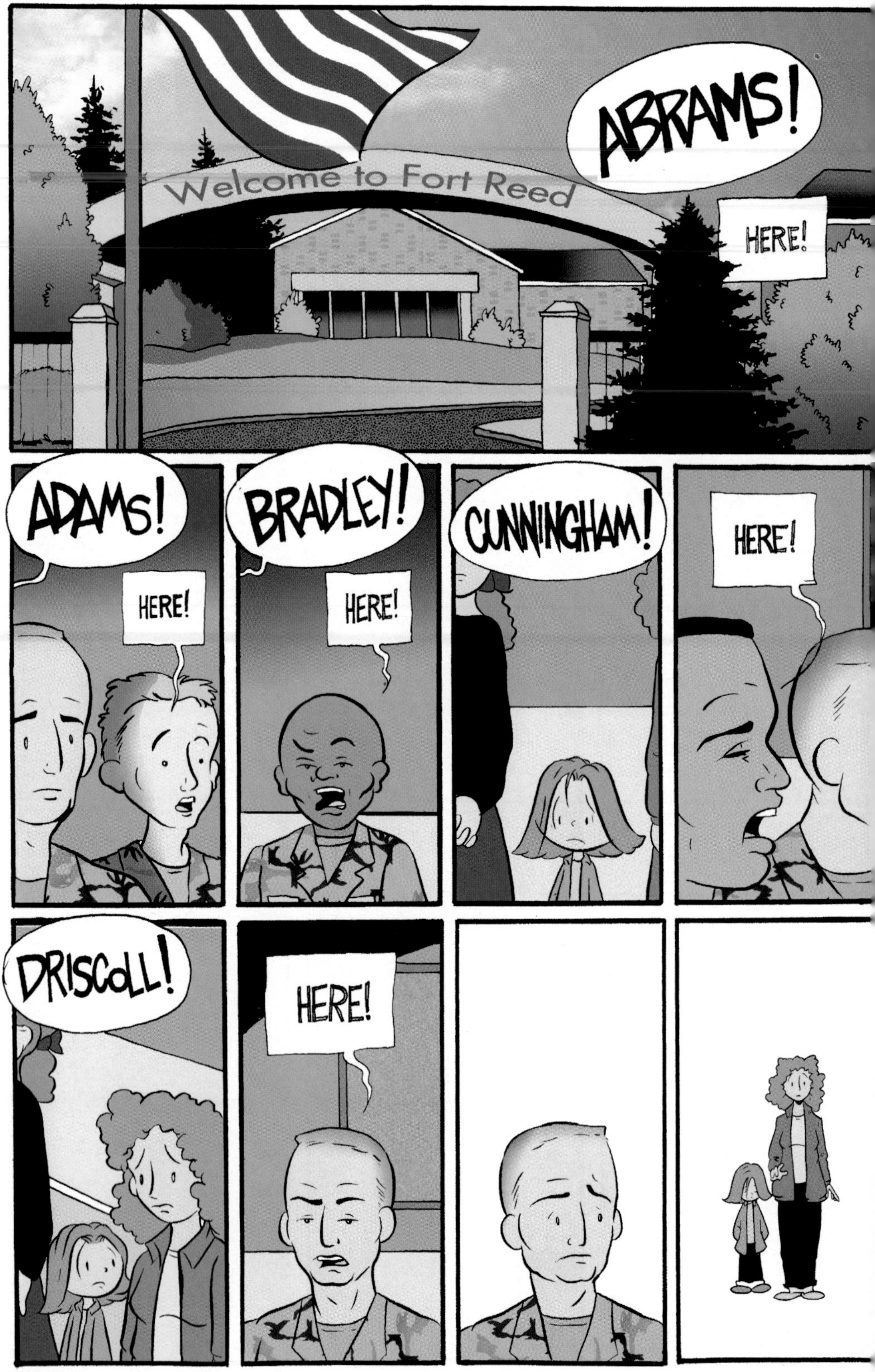
Welcome to Fort Reed
ABRAMS!
HERE!
ADAMS!
HERE!
BRADLEY!
HERE!
CUNNINGHAM!
HERE!
DRISCOLL!
HERE!

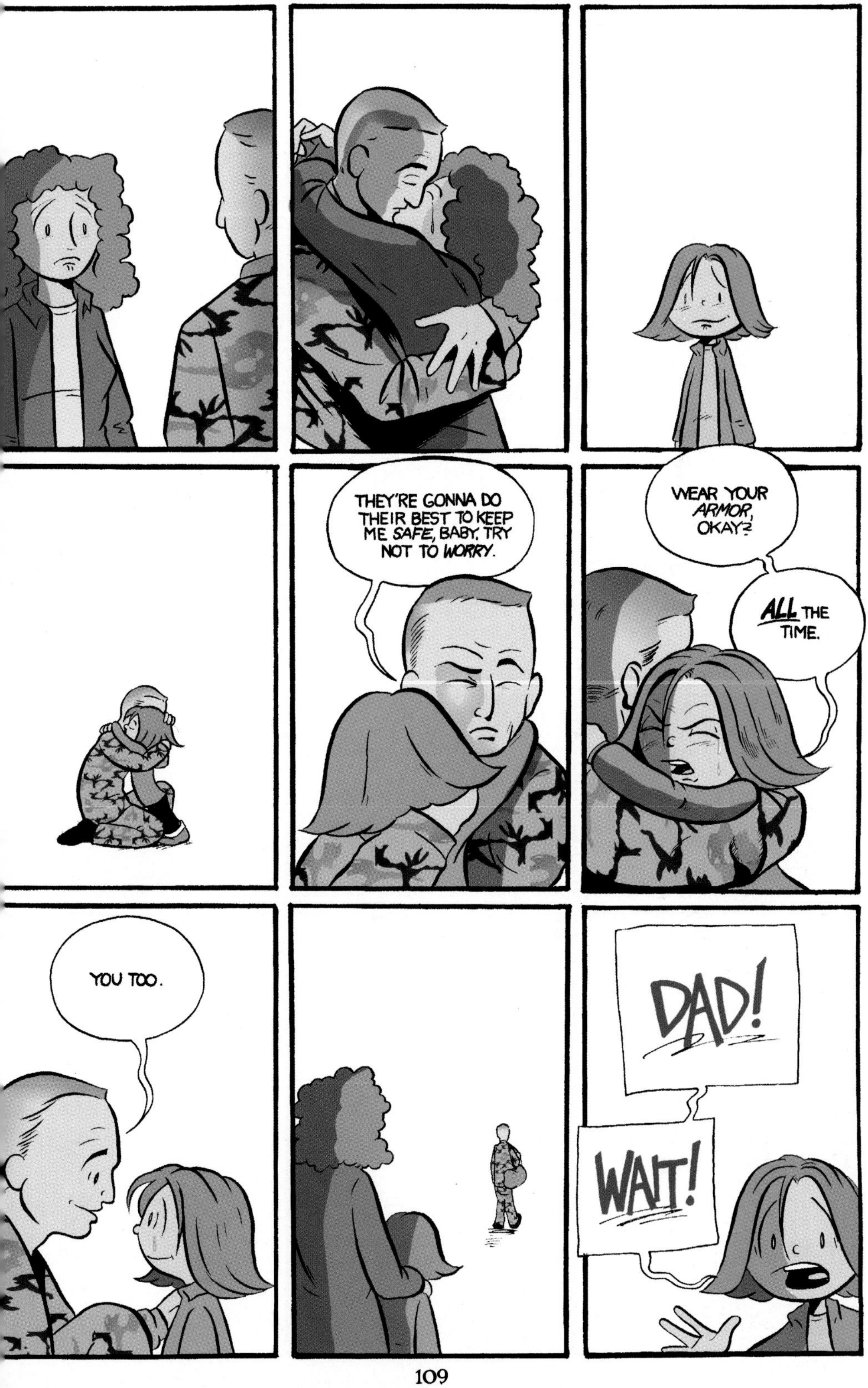
THEY'RE GONNA DO THEIR BEST TO KEEP ME SAFE, BABY. TRY NOT TO WORRY.
WEAR YOUR ARMOR, OKAY?
ALL THE TIME.
YOU TOO.
DAD!
WAIT!

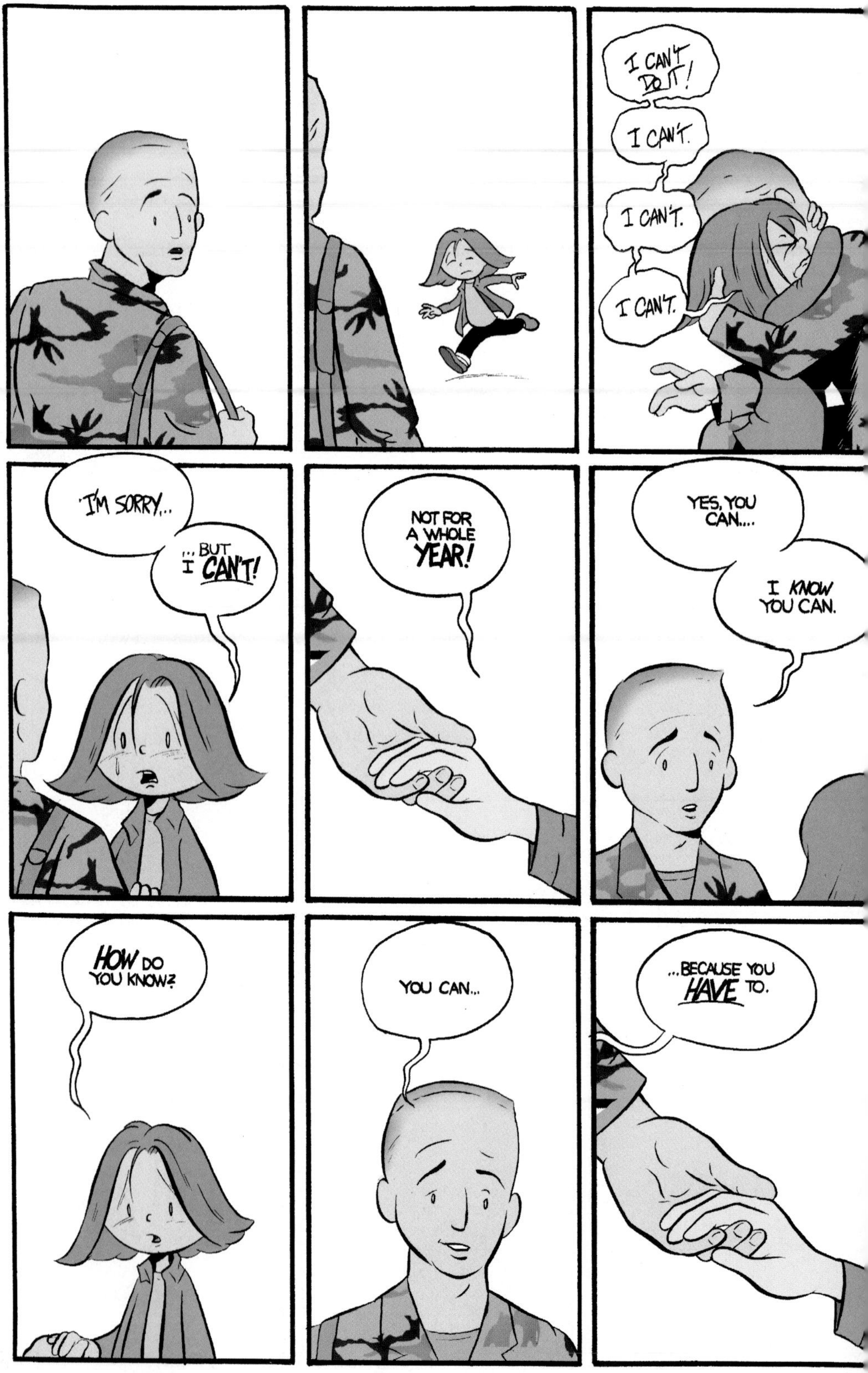
I CAN'T DO IT!
I CAN'T.
I CAN'T.
I CAN'T.
I'M SORRY...
...BUT I CAN'T!
NOT FOR A WHOLE YEAR!
YES, YOU CAN....
I KNOW YOU CAN.
HOW DO YOU KNOW?
YOU CAN...
...BECAUSE YOU HAVE TO.

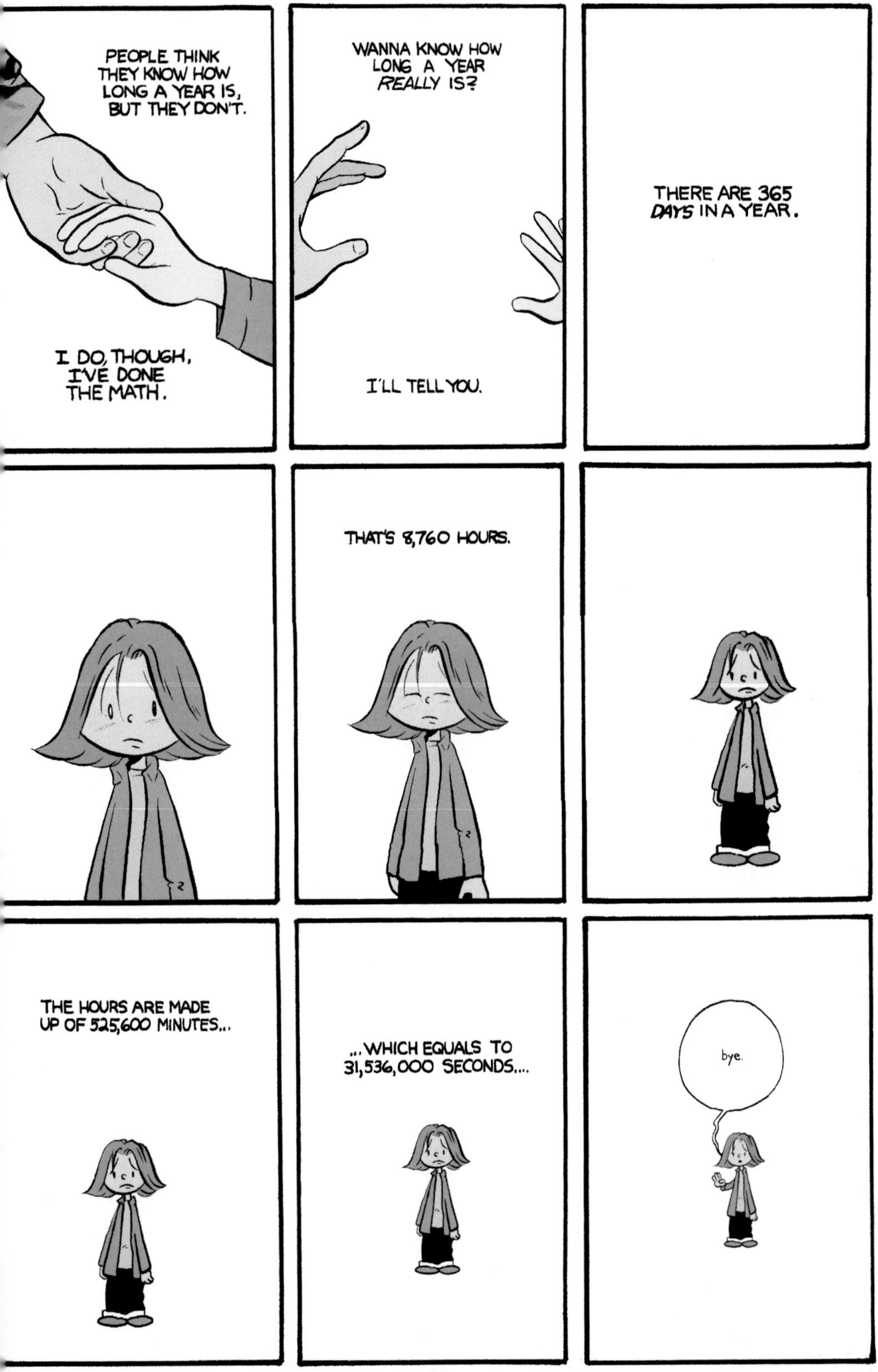
PEOPLE THINK THEY KNOW HOW LONG A YEAR IS, BUT THEY DON'T.
I DO, THOUGH, I'VE DONE THE MATH.
WANNA KNOW HOW LONG A YEAR *REALLY* IS?
I'LL TELL YOU.
THERE ARE 365 *DAYS* IN A YEAR.
THAT'S 8,760 HOURS.
THE HOURS ARE MADE UP OF 525,600 MINUTES...
...WHICH EQUALS TO 31,536,000 SECONDS....
bye.

ONE-ONE THOUSAND...

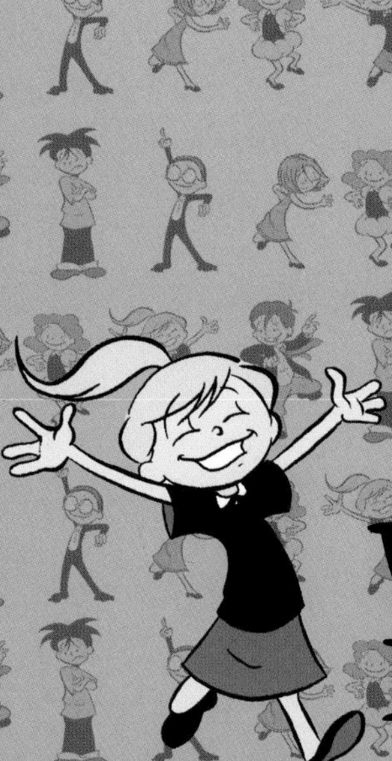

When the Past Is a Present

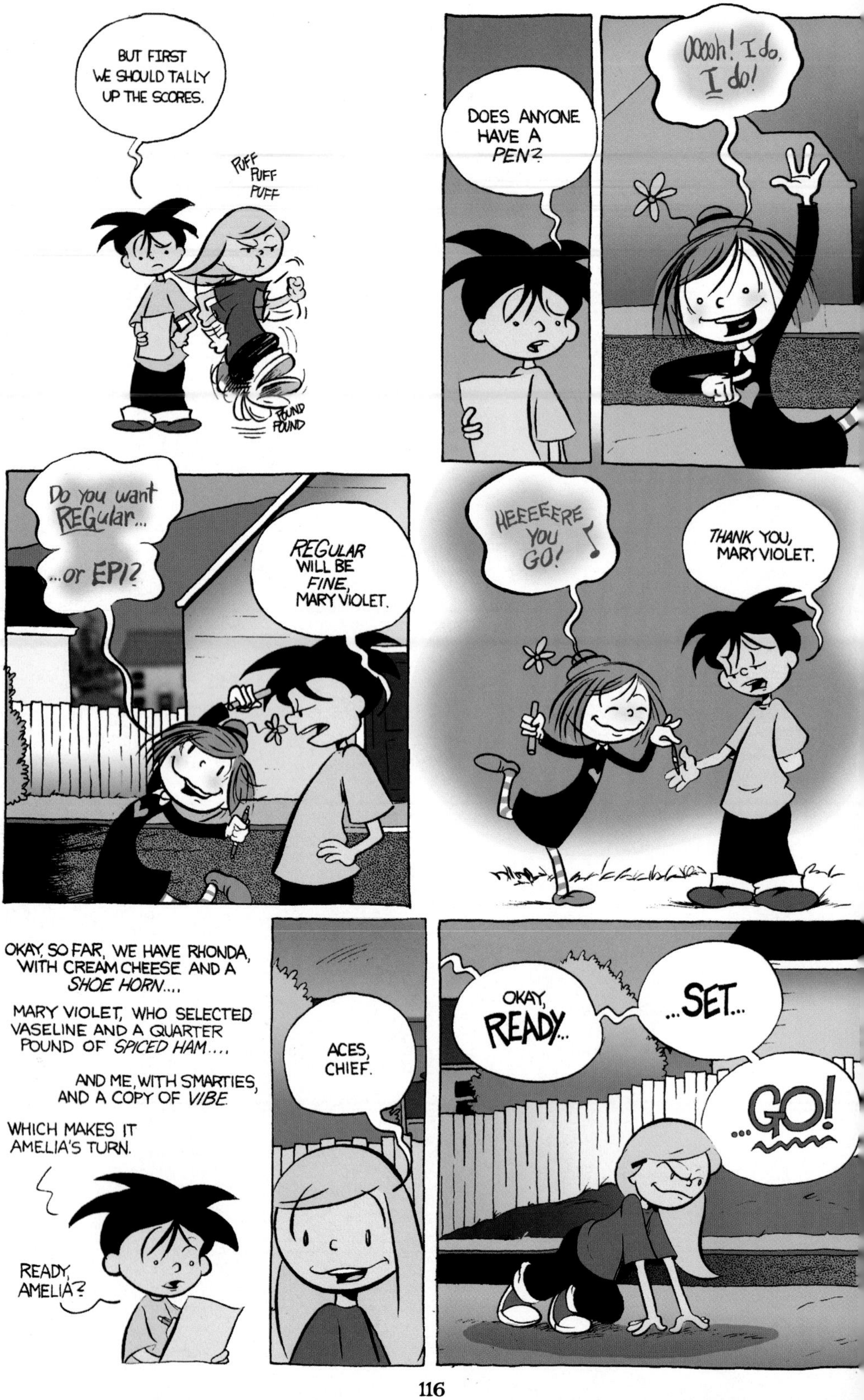
BUT FIRST WE SHOULD TALLY UP THE SCORES.
PUFF PUFF PUFF
POUND POUND
DOES ANYONE HAVE A PEN?
Ooooh! I do, I do!
Do you want REGular...
...or EPI?
REGULAR WILL BE FINE, MARY VIOLET.
HEEEEEERE YOU GO!
THANK YOU, MARY VIOLET.
OKAY, SO FAR, WE HAVE RHONDA, WITH CREAM CHEESE AND A SHOE HORN....
MARY VIOLET, WHO SELECTED VASELINE AND A QUARTER POUND OF SPICED HAM....
AND ME, WITH SMARTIES, AND A COPY OF VIBE.
WHICH MAKES IT AMELIA'S TURN.
READY, AMELIA?
ACES, CHIEF.
OKAY, READY...
...SET...
...GO!

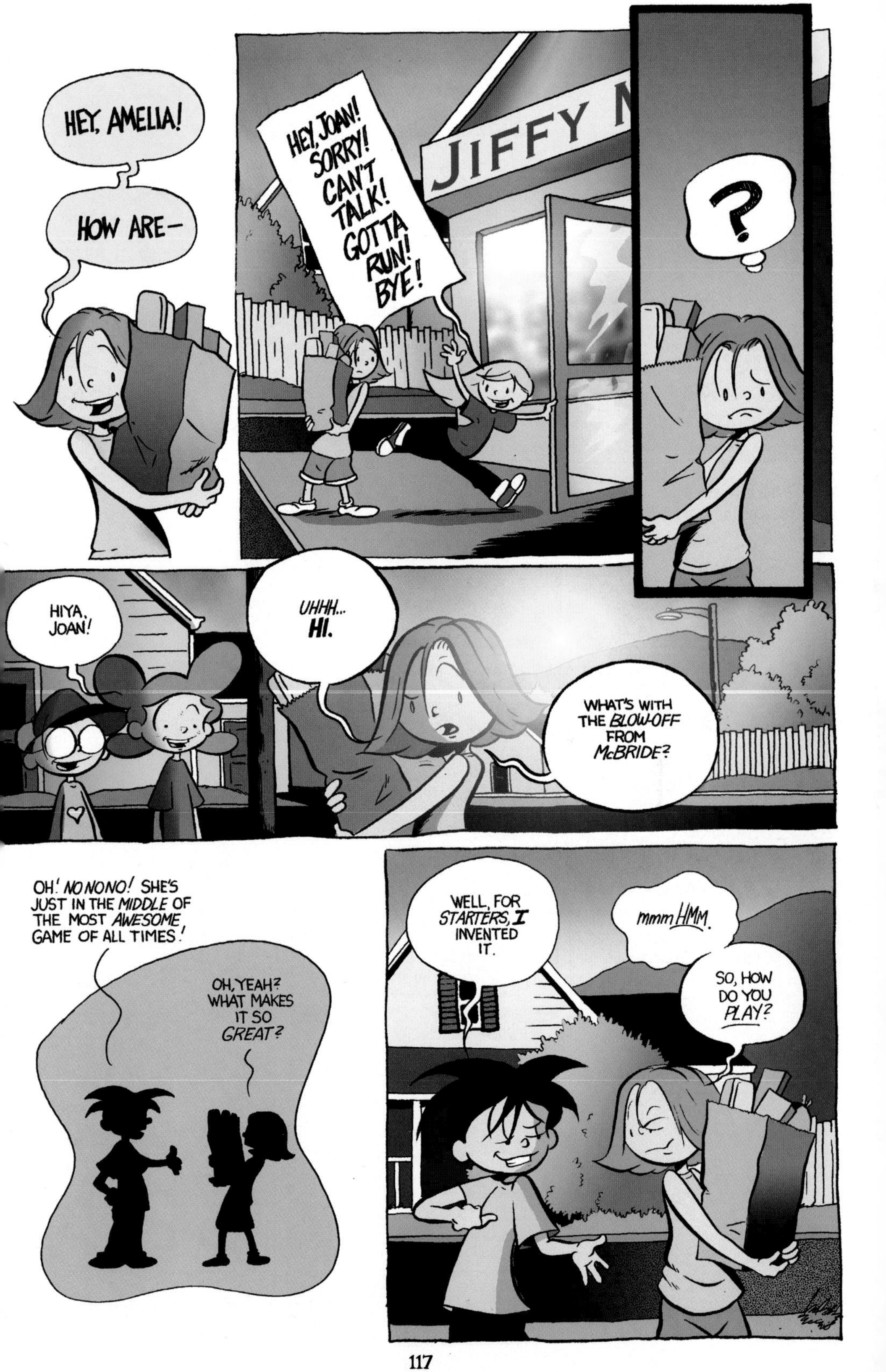
HEY, AMELIA!
HOW ARE—
HEY, JOAN! SORRY! CAN'T TALK! GOTTA RUN! BYE!
JIFFY M
?
HIYA, JOAN!
UHHH... HI.
WHAT'S WITH THE BLOW-OFF FROM McBRIDE?
OH! NONONO! SHE'S JUST IN THE MIDDLE OF THE MOST AWESOME GAME OF ALL TIMES!
OH, YEAH? WHAT MAKES IT SO GREAT?
WELL, FOR STARTERS, I INVENTED IT.
mmm HMM.
SO, HOW DO YOU PLAY?

Assemble the best athletes and brightest minds your town has to offer.

Failing that, just grab the usual group of knuckleheads you call friends.

Each player competes using only their wits, ingenuity...

... and anywhere from two to four US dollars.

(Which unfortunately eliminates SOME potential competitors immediately.)

The players then take turns barging into select convenience stores, racing frantically through the aisles, and choosing two completely unrelated items, such as:

LETTUCE and
GOLD BOND

or

POP ROCKS
and SPAM

or

BACTINE and a
NOTDOG.

Then, breathlessly and with panic in their eyes, the player races up to the clerk and shouts...

It's harmless, it's fun...

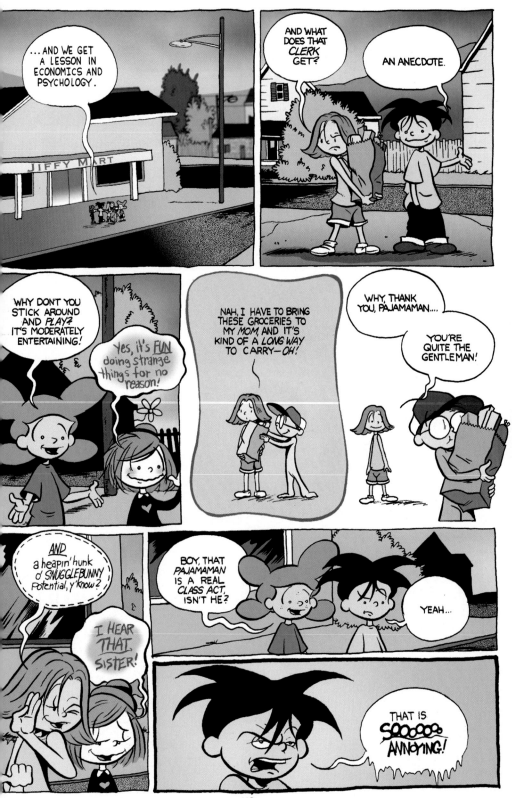

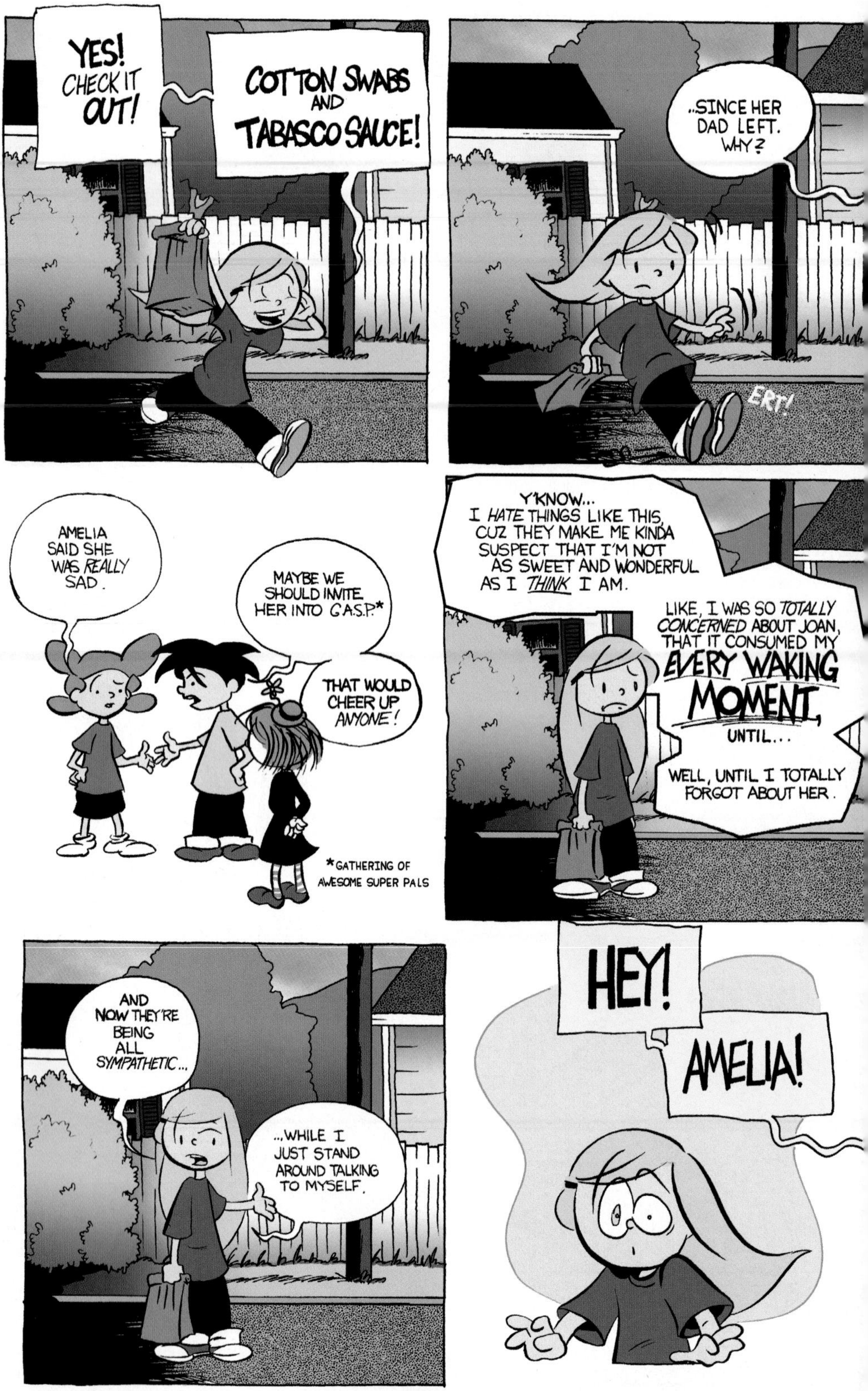
YES! CHECK IT OUT!
COTTON SWABS AND TABASCO SAUCE!
...SINCE HER DAD LEFT. WHY?
ERT!
AMELIA SAID SHE WAS REALLY SAD.
MAYBE WE SHOULD INVITE HER INTO G.A.S.P.*
THAT WOULD CHEER UP ANYONE!
*GATHERING OF AWESOME SUPER PALS
Y'KNOW... I HATE THINGS LIKE THIS, CUZ THEY MAKE ME KINDA SUSPECT THAT I'M NOT AS SWEET AND WONDERFUL AS I THINK I AM.
LIKE, I WAS SO TOTALLY CONCERNED ABOUT JOAN, THAT IT CONSUMED MY EVERY WAKING MOMENT, UNTIL...
WELL, UNTIL I TOTALLY FORGOT ABOUT HER.
AND NOW THEY'RE BEING ALL SYMPATHETIC...
...WHILE I JUST STAND AROUND TALKING TO MYSELF.
HEY!
AMELIA!

122

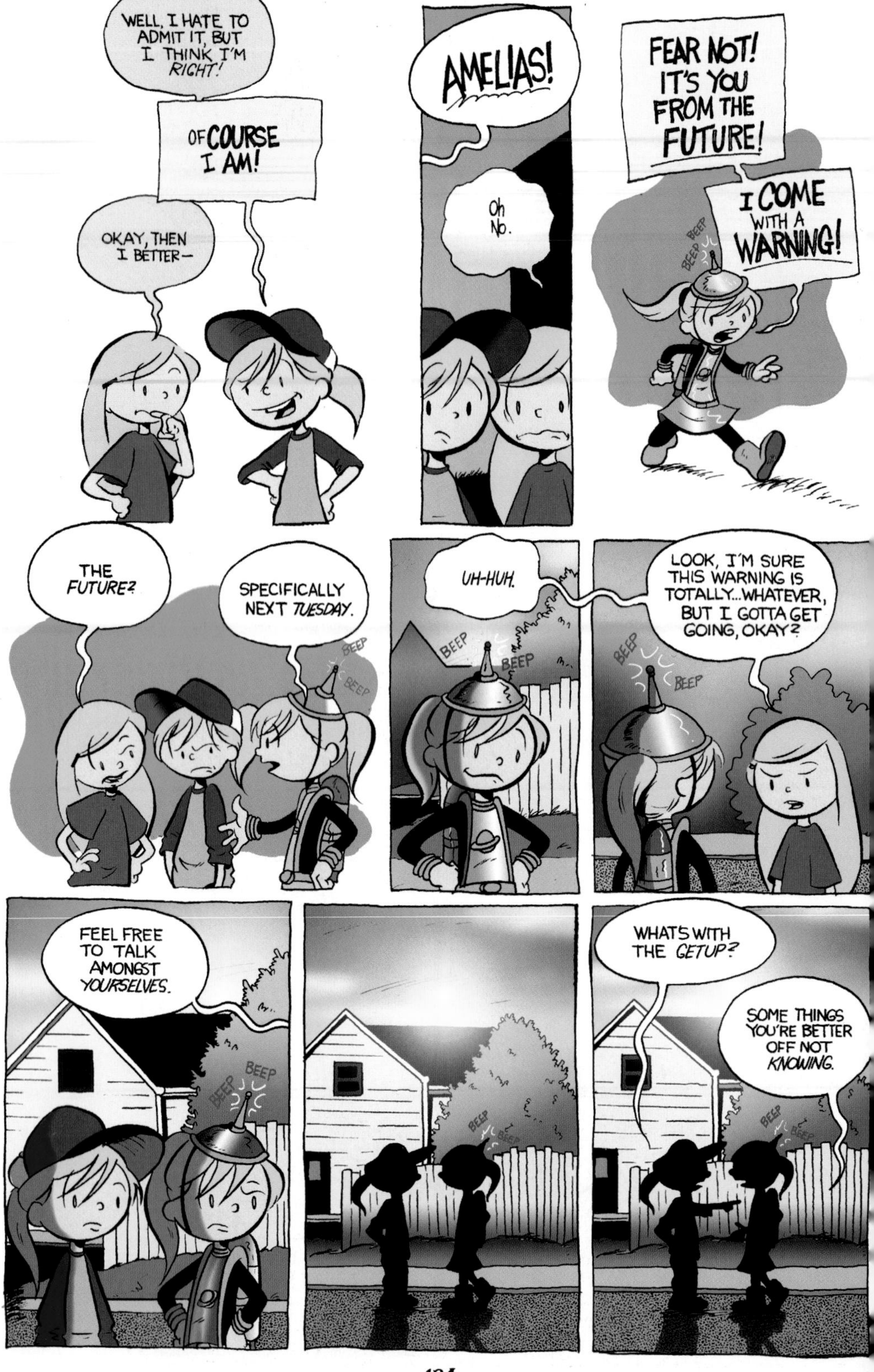
WELL, I HATE TO ADMIT IT, BUT I THINK I'M RIGHT!
OF COURSE I AM!
OKAY, THEN I BETTER—
AMELIAS!
Oh No.
FEAR NOT! IT'S YOU FROM THE FUTURE!
I COME WITH A WARNING!
BEEP BEEP
THE FUTURE?
SPECIFICALLY NEXT TUESDAY.
BEEP BEEP
UH-HUH.
BEEP BEEP
LOOK, I'M SURE THIS WARNING IS TOTALLY...WHATEVER, BUT I GOTTA GET GOING, OKAY?
BEEP BEEP
FEEL FREE TO TALK AMONGST YOURSELVES.
BEEP BEEP
BEEP BEEP
WHAT'S WITH THE GETUP?
SOME THINGS YOU'RE BETTER OFF NOT KNOWING.
BEEP BEEP

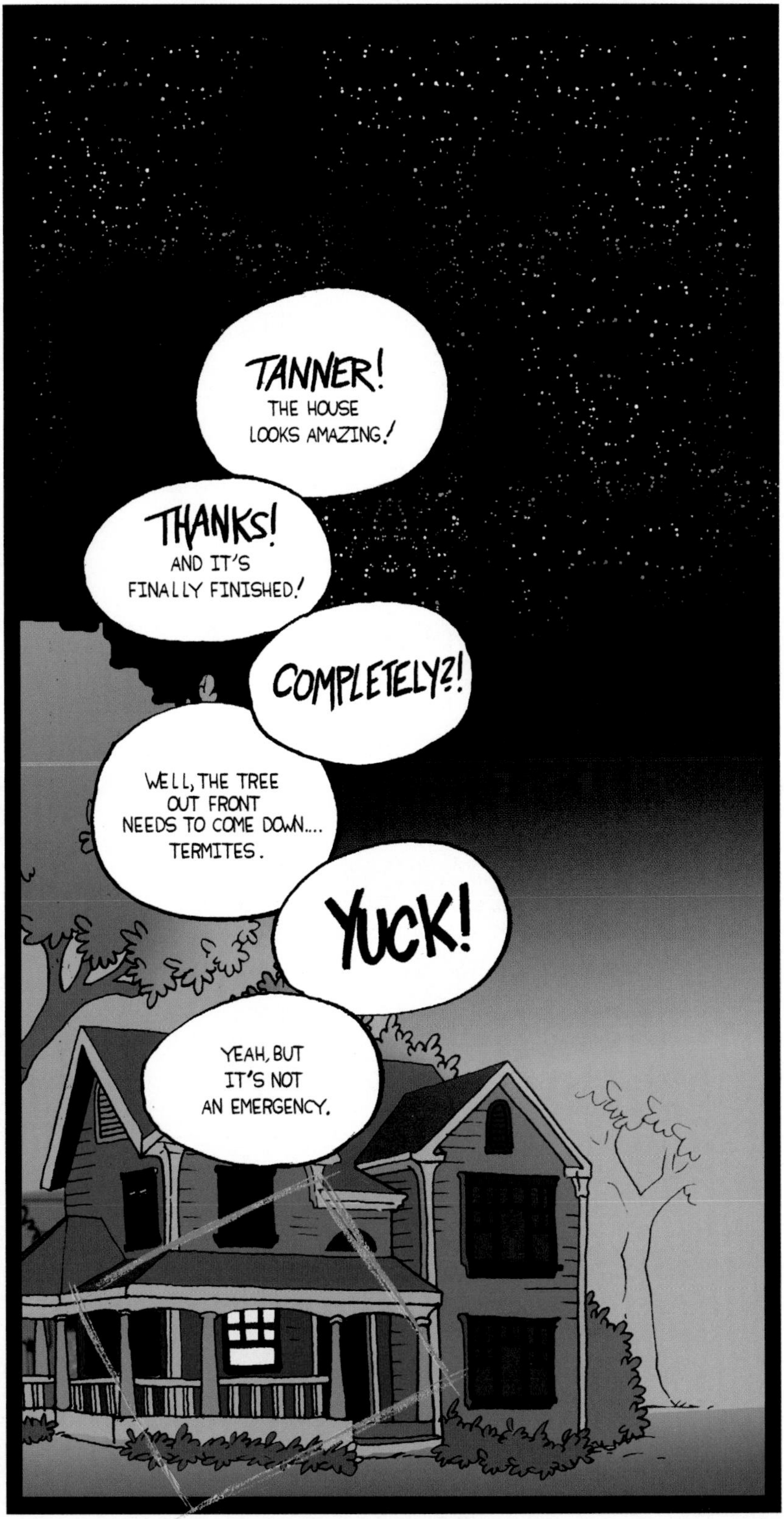
TANNER! THE HOUSE LOOKS AMAZING!
THANKS! AND IT'S FINALLY FINISHED!
COMPLETELY?!
WELL, THE TREE OUT FRONT NEEDS TO COME DOWN.... TERMITES.
YUCK!
YEAH, BUT IT'S NOT AN EMERGENCY.

ARTHUR T. FLETCHER ARRIVES IN USA

Joined by new bride Louise.

We don't know much about the Clark side of the family, and if you want to know about the Irish McBrides, you'll have to ask your dad.

But we know a lot about your grandmother's family, the Fletchers.

Arthur T. Fletcher grew up in England, the youngest child of George and Delores Fletcher. Now there were only two things Arthur wanted in the whole world: to marry his childhood sweetheart, Louise, and to move to America.

Unfortunately his entire family hated both Louise and the US, and made Arthur swear an oath that he would stay put and stay single (or at least marry someone more suitable).

So Arthur did what he believed was most sensible. He waited until everyone else in his family croaked and then did what he wanted.

So, as one century faded into the next, Arthur and Louise arrived in America.

FLETCHER'S FOLLIES

FLETCHER BUYS WIFE GIFT

Neighbors thrown into jealous rage.

Eventually the couple found themselves in Indiana, where a distant cousin of Louise owned a farm. Arthur was so happy to be in the land of his dreams and so grateful for the patience and devotion Louise had showed him that he bought her a present—a simple, delicate, and beautiful locket.

Louise kept the locket for the next thirty years until, on the day of her only son John's wedding, she passed it on to his bride Edna.

Now, Arthur had long since acquired his own farm, so John and Edna stayed on helping. By now, John and Edna had three children of their own: Jerome, Sarah, and Grace.

But try as he might, John just wasn't a farmer. So on the day of his tenth wedding anniversary, John Fletcher opened the Family Valley General Store. No one but Edna believed it would succeed. Even John himself doubted it.

But somehow, against unbelievable odds, it did. It thrived through depression and war.

It even outlived John himself. It's still there today.

Unfortunately, during all the chaos and commotion of building the store, Edna lost the locket. Even though she searched and searched, it never turned up.

One day, years after it was lost, Sarah found the locket in a field behind the store. She had no idea of the object's significance. It was weeks before she discovered that the little heart charm opened and she found a picture of her parents' wedding inside.

EXTRA DURING THE EXTRA

WAR!

Jerry enlisted in the Navy.

The oldest of the three children, Jerry, was just eighteen when he joined up. He got stationed on a destroyer, the USS *Gainard*. He never talked much about the war, but he would sometimes tell this one story....One night, while on patrol in the Pacific, the alarm sounded that another ship, the *Wadsworth*, had been hit and was on fire and sinking fast. The *Gainard* was called to rescue the crew and Jerry was one of the men hauling injured sailors off the *Wadsworth* to safety on the *Gainard*.

I don't know why the one incident stuck in Jerry's mind more than any other, but it was really the only war story he ever told.

Anyway, one Christmas your father and I had a big dinner with both sides of the family at our place in New York. When Jerry met your grandfather McBride and found out that he too was an ex-Navy man, he told his story. The look on your grandfather's face was pure amazement. He was one of the injured men that Jerry had pulled to safety. We couldn't believe that all those years after the fact, these two men were reconnected through us.

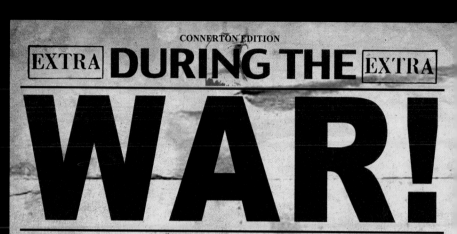

WE THOUGHT ABOUT JERRY WHEN WE WERE HAVING YOU, AMELIA.

SOMEHOW, IT SEEMED LIKE BECAUSE OF THAT EVENT, EVERYTHING THAT CAME LATER WASN'T JUST AN ACCIDENT...

IT'S NOT JUST ABOUT THE ADVENTURE, THOUGH...

BOOM!

WHAT WAS THAT?!

SNEAK ATTACK!

...IT WAS WHAT WAS MEANT TO BE.

137

138

139

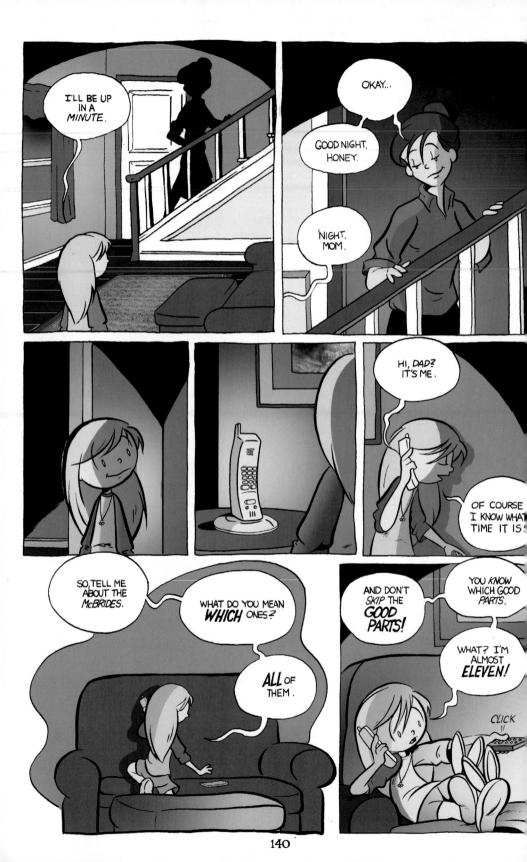

DAD AND I TALKED TILL THE
SUN CAME UP. MOSTLY, THOUGH,
WE TALKED ABOUT THE *YANKEES*,
WHICH IS *OKAY* CUZ THAT'S
HIS THING, AND IT WAS JUST
GOOD TO HEAR HIS *VOICE!*

IT'S FUNNY, BUT EVEN
THOUGH I'D BEEN UP ALL
NIGHT, I COULDN'T *SLEEP*
RIGHT AWAY. I WAS TRYING
TO REMEMBER ALL THE STORIES
I'D HEARD AND ALL OF
THE *PEOPLE*.

I WANTED TO MAKE SURE I
REMEMBERED THEM ALL, THAT
I DIDN'T *CONFUSE* ANYTHING.

AND I KNOW THIS IS WEIRD, BUT RIGHT
BEFORE I FELL ASLEEP, EVERYTHING
SEEMED–I DON'T KNOW–*DIFFERENT?*

LIKE, FOR JUST A SECOND THERE, IT WAS
LIKE EVERYTHING MADE *SENSE*, Y'KNOW?

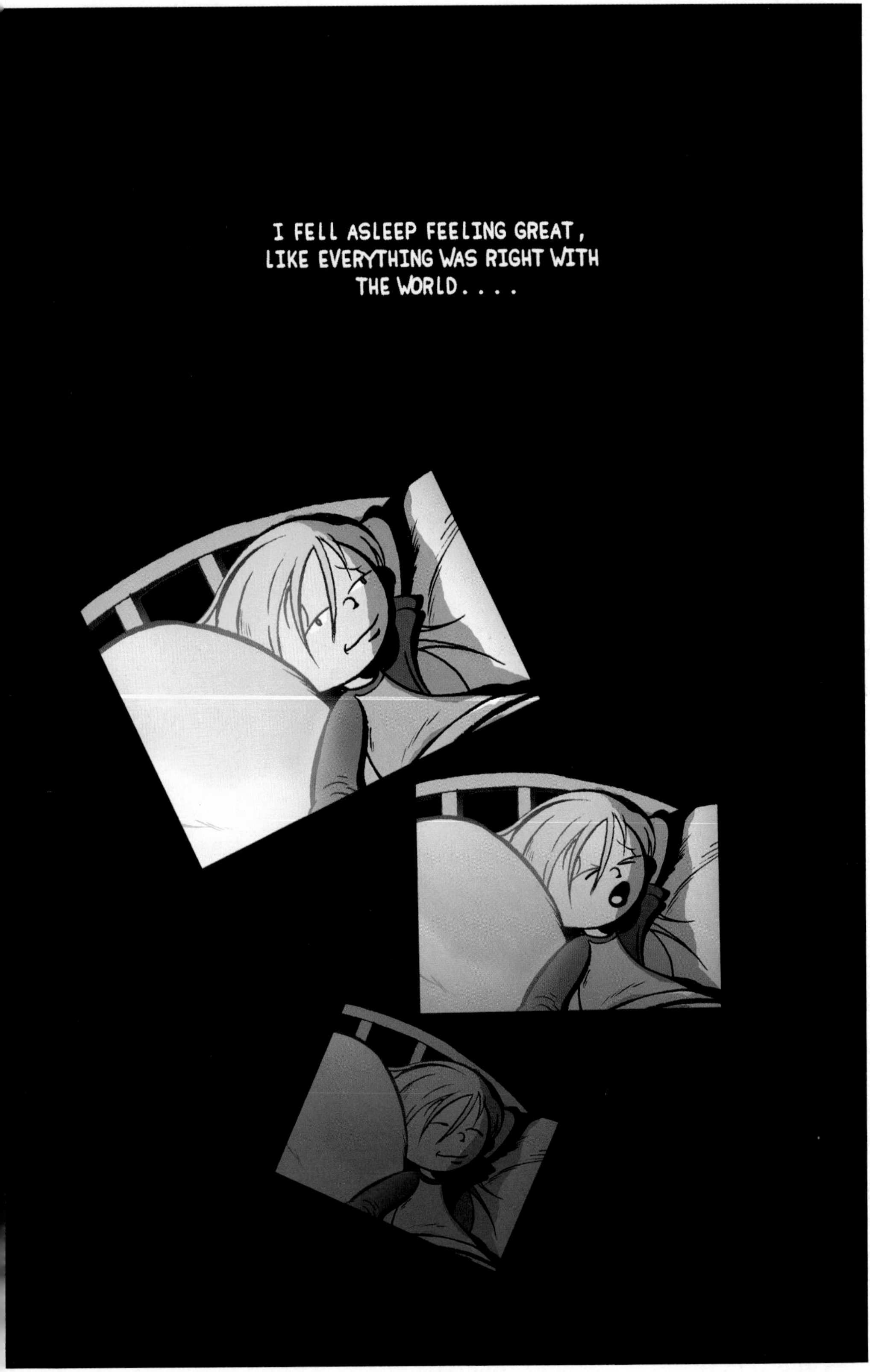
I FELL ASLEEP FEELING GREAT, LIKE EVERYTHING WAS RIGHT WITH THE WORLD....

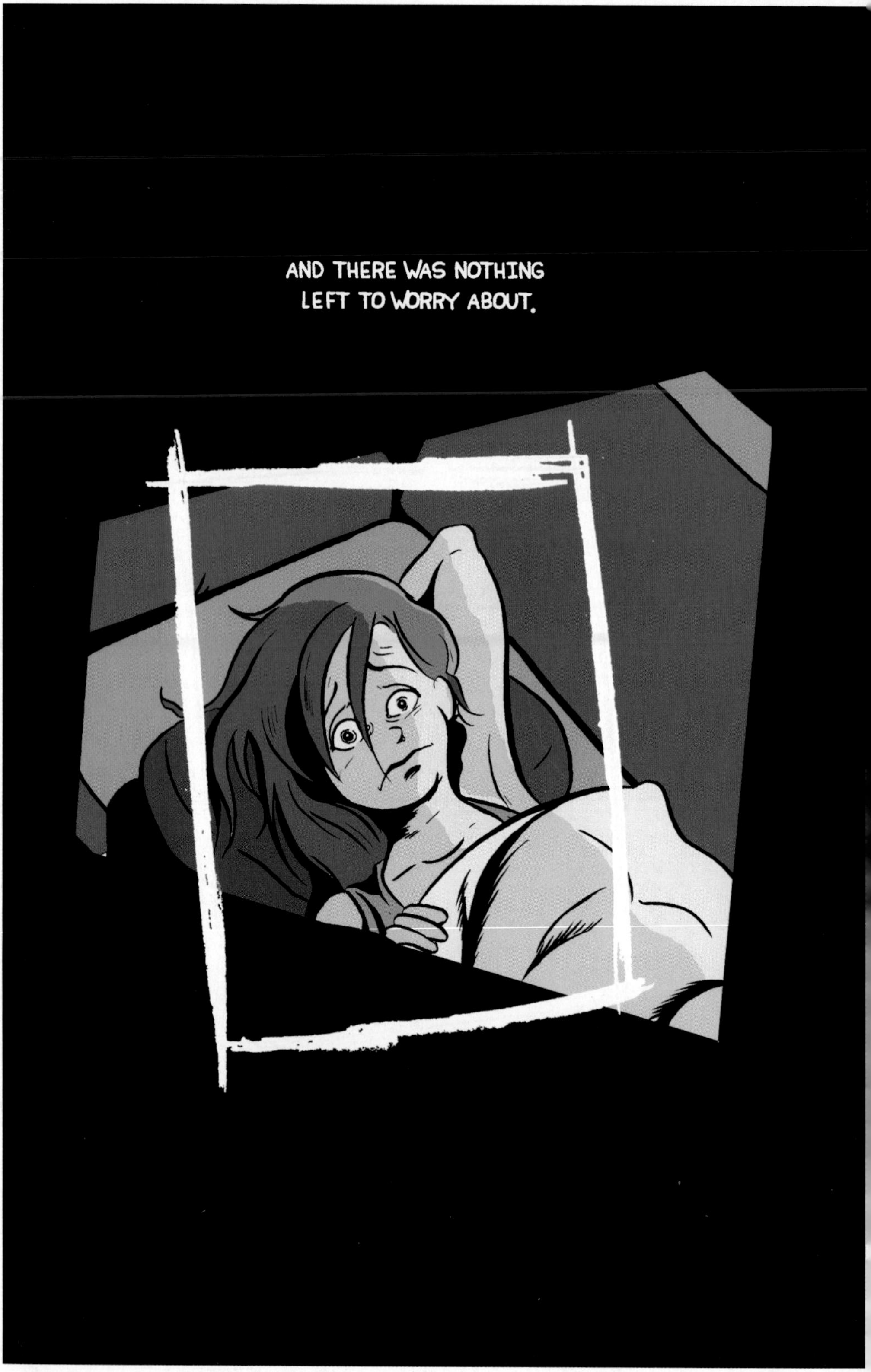
AND THERE WAS NOTHING LEFT TO WORRY ABOUT.

Hangin' Out

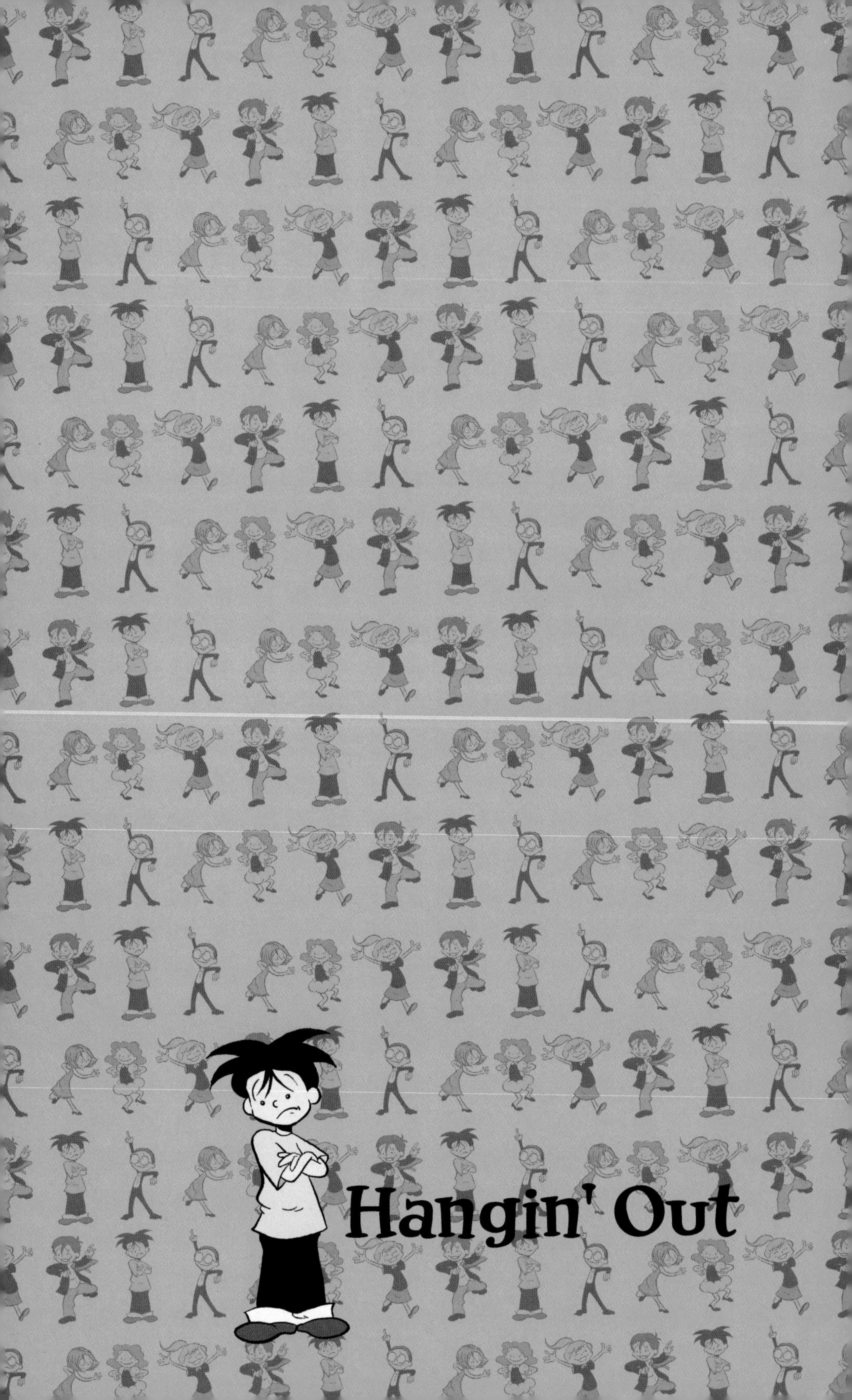

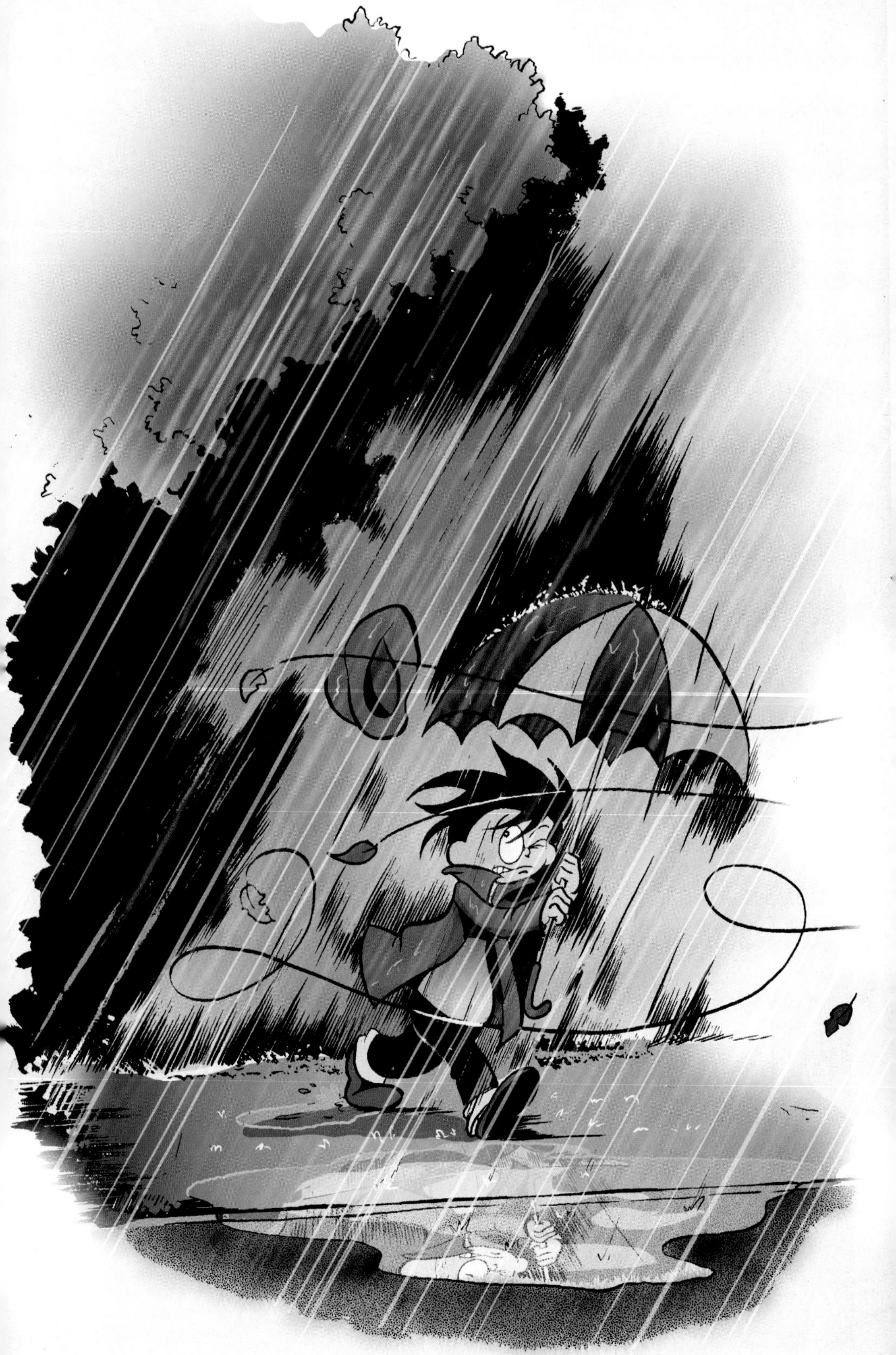

Hangin' Out

Hangtavious Outacus—More commonly known as "hanging out" is a twentieth-century American invention, in the vein of "bummin' around" or "chillin'." Although hanging out at first appears rather simple, in fact, its rules are myriad.

Hanging out cannot be done alone. That is called "moping" or "being a pariah," and neither one is particularly attractive (fig. 1).

Any group containing two to five people may engage in hanging out, so long as doing nothing is the primary activity. For example, "hanging out and talking" is acceptable while "hanging out and building shelters for Habitat for Humanity" is not. Snacks are not required, but are highly recommended (fig. 2).

There are strict restrictions on how many people may hang out and how often the hanging may occur. For example, more than five people is now a party, and while it may seem like you can hang out at a party, you can't because the music is too loud, and let's face it, there's no way you like more than five people anyway (fig. 3).

Here is where the slippery slope gets even slipperier.

More than five people who meet more than once a month is no longer a party but a club (fig. 4). This is fine, but you may be expected to pay dues or pretend to be interested in other people's boats and/or record collections. More than once a WEEK, and it becomes a cult. It is definitely advisable NOT to join a cult, but if you feel you must, remember that it is better to be the leader than the guy who collects the fingers (fig. 5).

158

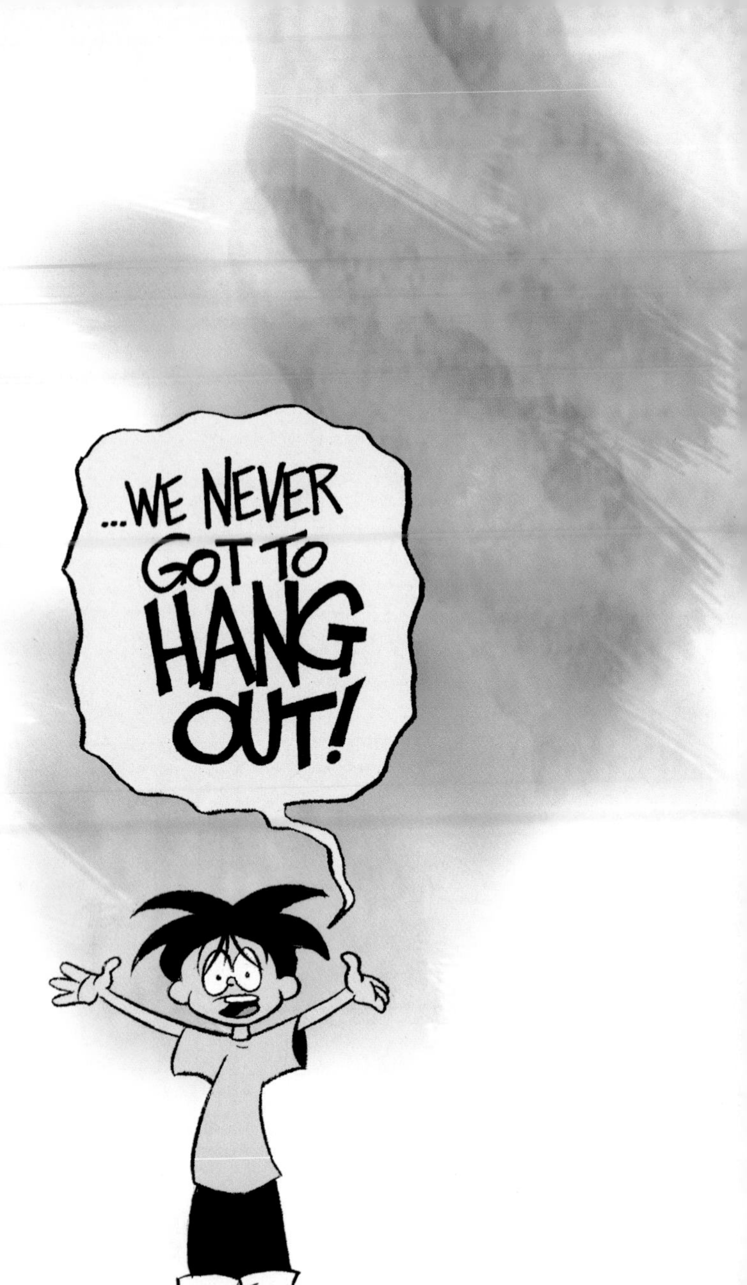
...WE NEVER GOT TO HANG OUT!

Turn the page for a sneak peek
of the brand-new Amelia Rules! book

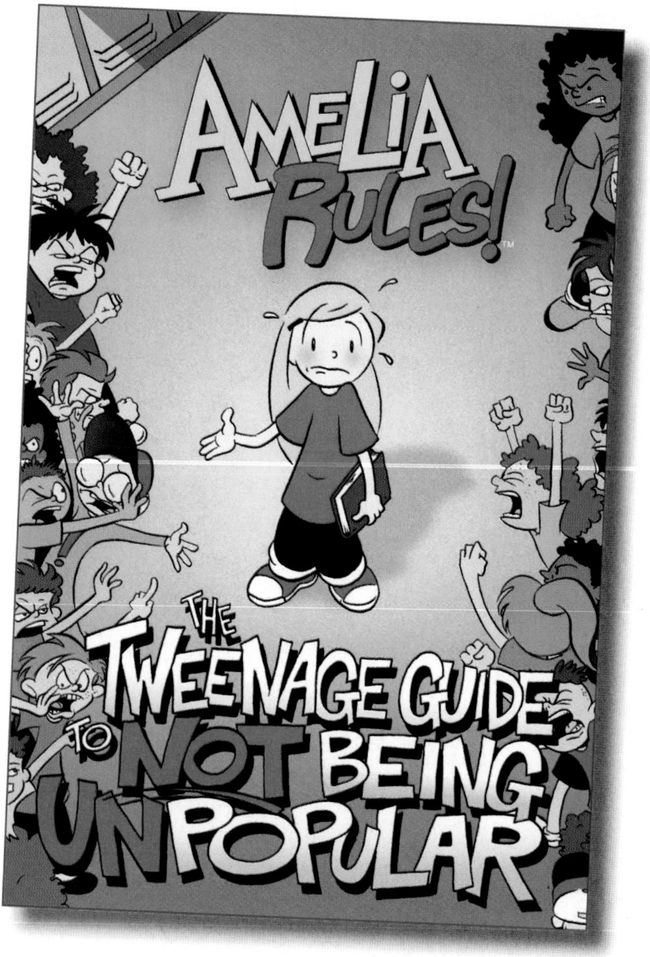
AMELIA RULES!
THE TWEENAGE GUIDE TO NOT BEING UNPOPULAR

Coming in April 2010!

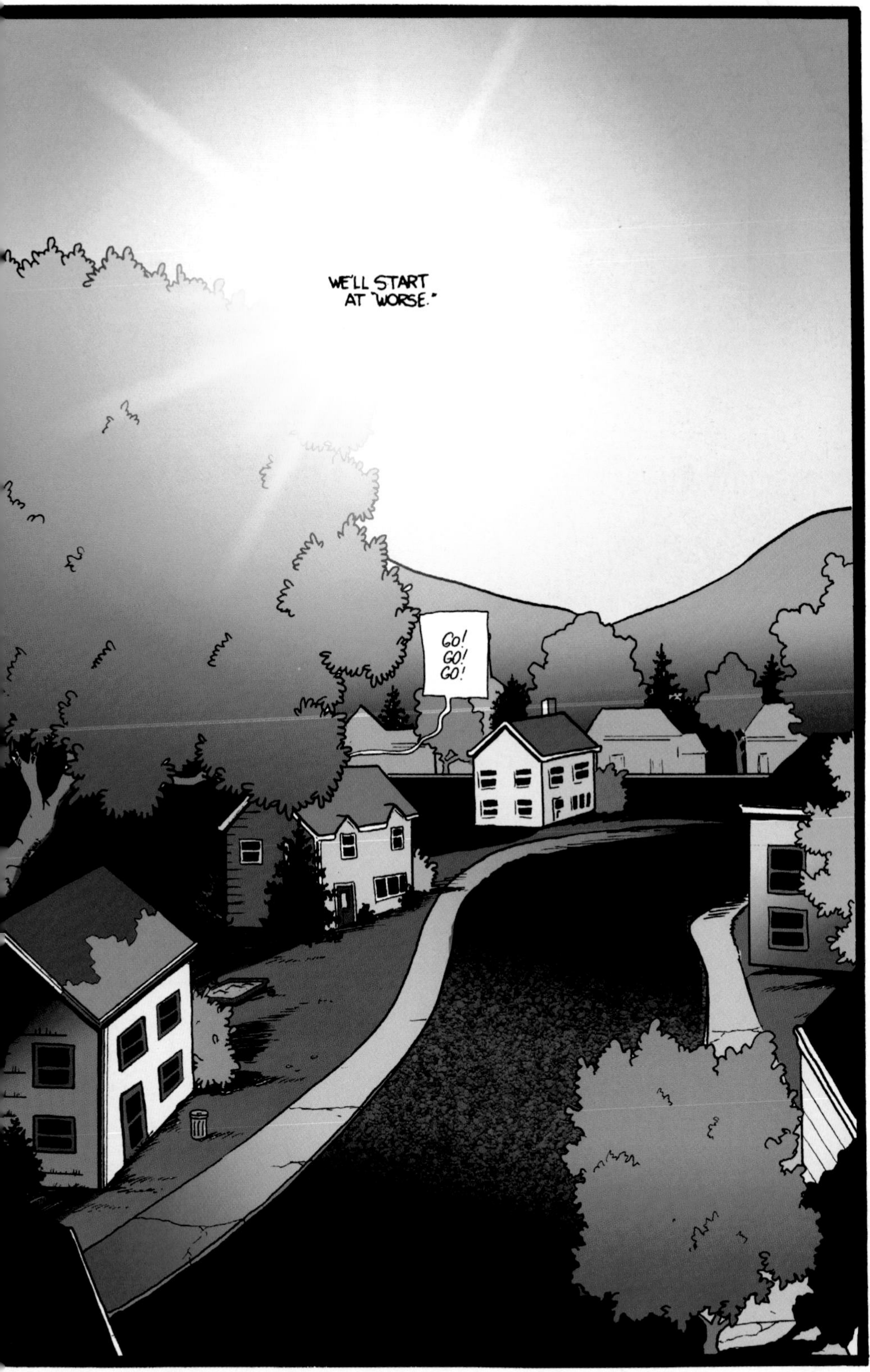
WE'LL START AT "WORSE."
GO! GO! GO!

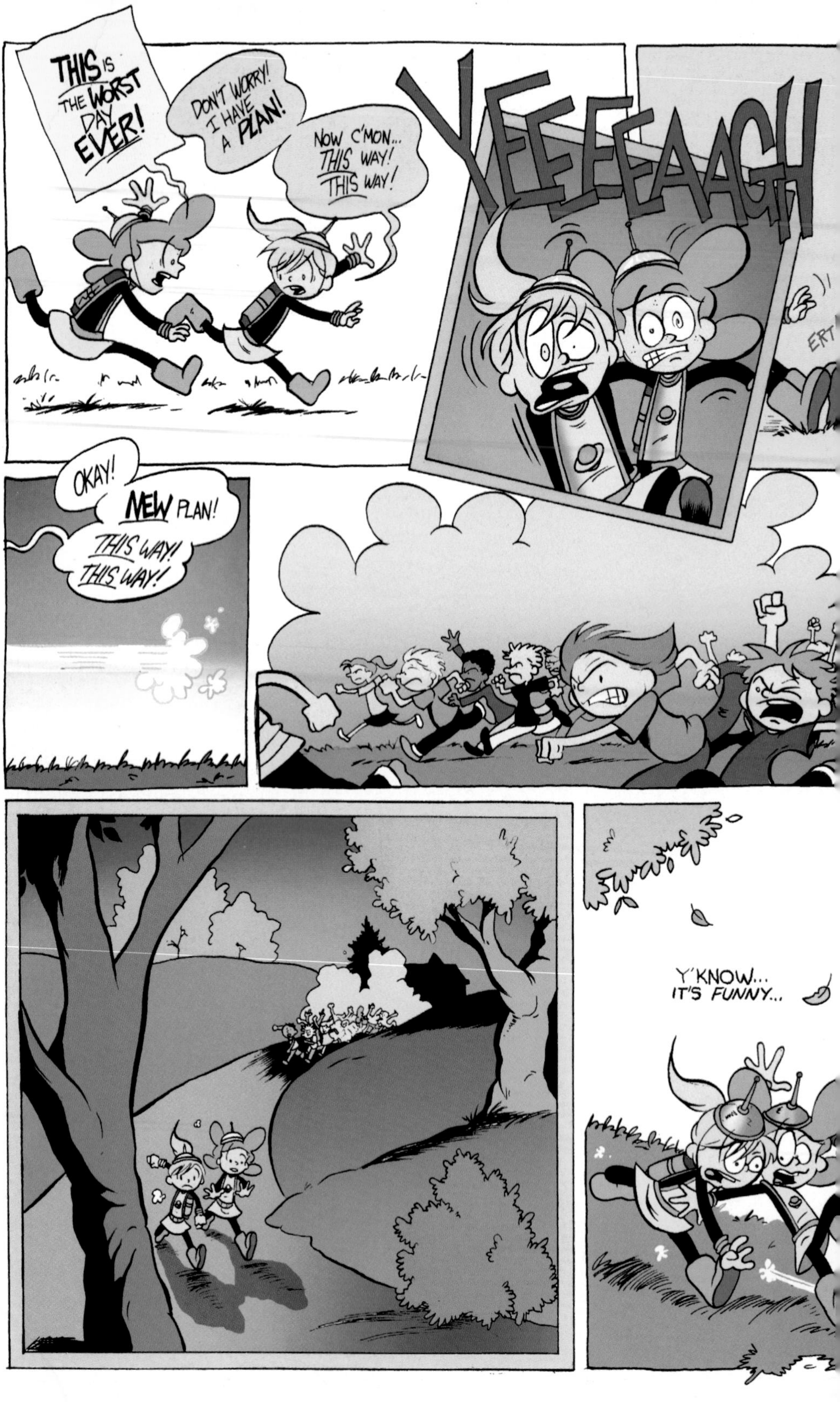
THIS IS THE WORST DAY EVER!
DON'T WORRY! I HAVE A PLAN!
NOW C'MON... THIS WAY! THIS WAY!
YEEEEEAAGH
ERT
OKAY! NEW PLAN! THIS WAY! THIS WAY!
Y'KNOW... IT'S FUNNY...